Inebolu

Kastamonu

• ANGORA

Polatli

Sivas

OLIA

ehir

Caesarea

National Boundaries — ·· — ·· —
Railways +++++++++

Konya

Marash

Adana

Tarsus

Aintab

Alexandretta

Aleppo

SYRIA

Latakia

CYPRUS

THE HOUSE OF WAR

BULGARIA

BLACK SEA

●Adrianople

GREECE

EASTERN
THRACE

R. Maritza

BOSPHORUS

Chatalja

CONSTANTINOPLE

Sea of
Marmara

Ismid

Gallipoli

●Chanak

Mudanya

●Brusa

R. Sakarya

AEGEAN SEA

●Ezine

Eskishet

Kütahya●

A N A   A

Dumlu Pinar ✄

Chios

Ushak●

Afyon K

Chesme

SMYRNA

Koja Tepe ✄

Cha

Aydin

R Menderes

Adalia

Rhodes

MEDITERRANEAN   SEA

0   50   100
|—|—|—|—|—|—| Mile

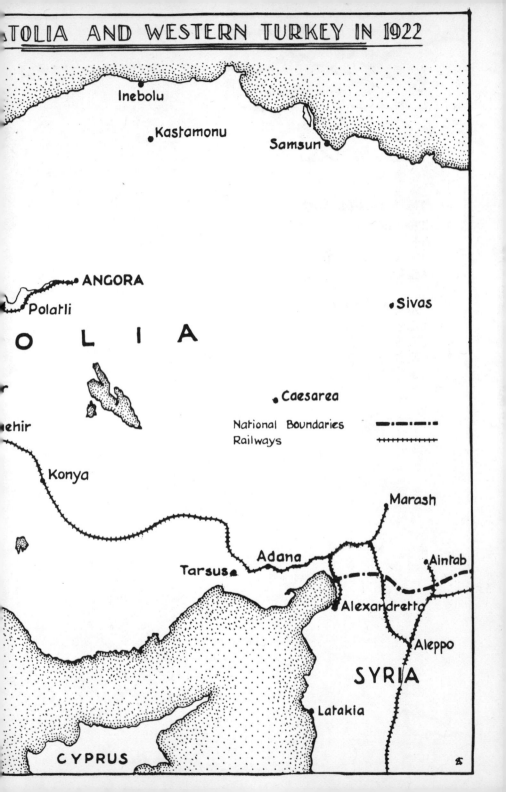

Inebolu

Kastamonu

Samsun

ANGORA

Polatli

Sivas

O L I A

╓ehir

Caesarea

National Boundaries ━ ∙ ━ ∙ ━ ∙ ━

Railways ┼┼┼┼┼┼┼┼┼

Konya

Marash

Adana

Tarsus

Aintab

Alexandretta

Aleppo

SYRIA

Latakia

CYPRUS

Catherine Gavin

THE HOUSE
OF WAR

WILLIAM MORROW AND COMPANY, INC.

NEW YORK 1970

To Meryem at Anit Kabir

AUTHOR'S FOREWORD

This novel is set in Turkey in 1922, at the close of the War of Independence, and the central situation turns on a fictitious episode in the life of the victor in that war, Mustafa Kemal.

Some of the characters existed in real life, and have their place in history. These include:

Mustafa Kemal Pasha, "The Gazi", at a later date Kemal Atatürk, founder of the Turkish Republic.

General Ismet, later President Ismet Inönü, and General Fevzi, commanders in the War of Independence.

Ali, a Turkish sergeant.

Rauf and Refet, two leaders of the Turkish Revolution.

Mehmed VI Vahed-ed-din, last Sultan of the House of Osman.

Fikriye and Latife, two young Turkish women.

General Tricoupis, a Greek commander in Anatolia.

A number of naval and military officers, government officials and newspapermen of the time are mentioned by name only. All the other characters are entirely fictitious, and any resemblance to any person living or dead is purely coincidental.

The Turkish cities known in 1922 as Angora, Constantinople and Smyrna are now named Ankara, Istanbul and Izmir. It was in those three cities that I prepared this book.

I

BARRETT STUMBLED AS HE went through the gates of
Chankaya, and as he regained his balance he could have
sworn the sentries smiled. They were two of Kemal's Laz
bodyguard, handpicked men from the mountain villages above
the Black Sea, superb in their black uniforms, and well accustomed
to standing watch while a Chankaya party roared its way to
dawn.

Barrett nodded to the sentries and went on down the new road,
picking his way with care. He was dizzy with fatigue but not
drunk, although the fumes of liquor were in his brain, mixed
with the fumes of Kemal's eloquence and Kemal's songs. The
songs had ended only when the Commander-in-Chief laid his
fair head on the piano keys and slept, but the poker session went
on two hours longer, and Barrett had held good cards up to the
end.

He was not quite the last guest to leave. Behind him, somewhere in the grounds of Chankaya, he could hear the voices of
Captain Hamdi and two other officers of the Turkish Nationalist
Army uplifted in argument with Kemal's secretary. They had
held their drink well, unlike the party of elderly Deputies farther
down the hill road, on their way back to Angora in a horse-drawn
carriage. The Deputies were still singing, and Barrett grinned as
the words of the Resistance song, droned out by four maudlin
voices, shattered the silence of the dawn.

> *"Let us march, friends!*
> *Let our voices be heard by the earth, by the sky,*
> *By the water—"*

Unconsciously Barrett fell into the cadence and kept it up even
after the sound of singing died away. Let us march, friends! He
was walking through the vineyards, where lamplight shone from
the windows of some of the new chalets hastily built to house
Kemal's staff officers. The lights were going out one by one in the

marvellous daybreak of a summer morning in Anatolia, a trans-
lucency of violet paling to the washed pink of sea-shells and
flecked by cirrus clouds. In those uplands the nights were cool,
even in late July, but already some warmth was rising from the
baked earth as Jeff Barrett turned off the Chankaya road and
entered a narrow lane. He stopped to light a cigarette, and although his mouth was parched with smoking he inhaled the
Roanoke gratefully. Standing on the quiet path he became aware
of the tranquil morning sounds, the muted chirp of birds and the
crowing of cocks in the little farmyards on the way to Angora;
and then of one sound, the insistent voice of war. He was listening to the hammers of the railway workshops in the town, where
scrap metal of every kind — ploughshares, pruning hooks and even
sections of railway line — was being forged into bayonets for the
Nationalist Army.

It was the summer of 1922, and in Europe the Great War had
been over for nearly four years. In Turkey, where the Ottoman
government had made the fatal mistake of fighting on the side of
Germany, the bitter aftermath of war had been prolonged. As
far back as 1915, Britain had made a secret offer to the Greek
government of large concessions in Turkey if Greece would join
in the war on the British side. At the Paris Peace Conference the
bill was presented by the Greek Prime Minister, Monsieur
Venizelos, who claimed the Aegean coast of Turkey and part of
the Anatolian hinterland as well as Thrace, and in May 1919, with
the enthusiastic support of David Lloyd George, the Greeks began
their invasion with the occupation of Smyrna.

Mustafa Kemal, whose guest Jeff Barrett had been through the
long summer night at Chankaya, was the Turkish commander of
genius who opposed the Greeks with all the resources that Anatolia
could then provide, and it was of his Nationalist Army and its
probable future that Barrett was thinking as he walked home,
treading with care on the carpet of pine needles and last year's
leaves. With any luck Evelyn would still be asleep, and he would
have an hour's grace before he had to tell her that he was going
back to Constantinople. But as soon as he came in sight of the
little wooden house he knew his luck was out. The front door
stood wide open, and Ayesha, their landlady, was vigorously
sweeping out the yard with a stout twig broom.

Barrett threw his half-smoked cigarette away. He tramped it

out carefully, for fire was a constant hazard at Angora, and Ayesha watched him with approval. She was pleased with her American tenants, both so high in the Gazi Mustafa Kemal's favour: the lady sometimes invited to join his morning rides, the gentleman a frequent guest at his famous Table at Chankaya. Ayesha did what she could to help the Barretts, keeping the yard neat, doing their washing and bargaining for their food, with milk in pewter jars and cooking charcoal, with the vendors who brought such things on donkey-back from the town. But she preferred to work out of doors, either in the pear orchard round the rammed-earth hut where she and her husband Ahmed lived while their house was rented, or among the apricots in the grove near the lane where the fruit was beginning to turn gold.

When Ahmed built the wooden house he also constructed a rough stone wall round the well which gave his property its greatest value in an arid land, and laid down a square of stone slabs before the door. It was this stone patio which Ayesha was sweeping, for the Americans liked to sit outside, and even to cook and eat some of their meals in the shade of the apricot trees.

She leaned on her broom and smiled when Barrett wished her good-morning in one of the few Turkish phrases he had picked up on two assignments in Turkey. Three years earlier she would have veiled her face from him with the long scarf of her headdress, but not now. Ayesha was a Moslem, but she was also an Anatolian matron, one of the heroic band who had hauled ammunition to the front from the moment Kemal had been forced by the Sultan into a civil war. She had carried on through the Greek invasion, a unit in the army of women who dragged the Turkish shells over mountain passes in wooden-wheeled carts or on their own aching shoulders, and it was her proud boast that she was a veteran of the Sakarya. Just one year earlier, when King Constantine and the Greeks were within fifty miles of Angora, Kemal had driven them back from the Sakarya River after a defensive battle lasting twenty-two days. "I was there!" said Ayesha; and now, sixty years old, fat but erect in her loose bright jacket and flowered trousers, she looked the American straight in the eyes and nodded as to a comrade. Jeff Barrett had been at the Sakarya too.

"Hallo, Jeff!" said his wife.

Evelyn Barrett stood in the doorway, wearing much the same smile as the sentry when Barrett stumbled at the Chankaya gates

—a smile sympathetic and critical at the same time. Her husband sat down unsteadily on the coping of the well. He had been married to Evelyn for four years and out of love with her for two, but he could appreciate how attractive she looked, with her bobbed fair hair clasped smoothly behind her ears and her white silk shirt immaculate. "Hallo there, Eve," he said. "Hope I din—didn't disturb you. Didn't realise it was this late."

"It's this early," she said, smiling. "Six o'clock!"

"Why're you up and around at this time of day?"

"I've got a riding date at seven," said Evelyn. "Come on in, Jeff. I've just made the coffee."

"What I need is about five hours' solid sleep," he said, as she stood back to let him pass. He went straight through the living-room to their bedroom. It was spartan in its simplicity. There were no bedsteads, but two mattresses laid on the floor were spread with clean linen and handwoven blankets, and between them stood a wooden stool holding a candlestick, a box of matches and a travelling alarm clock. Evelyn's mattress was neatly made up for the day. Against one wall stood a vast painted Turkish wardrobe, with suitcases stacked between the top and the ceiling. Jeff's head was aching. He went into the lean-to which served them as a washing place of the simplest sort, with a commode, a round zinc tub, and a deal table holding a tin basin and a china ewer. He splashed water into the basin and looked at his ruffianly reflection in the only sizeable mirror they possessed.

Jeff was a tall young man, with dark hair, regular features and sentimental dark eyes which made most women call him handsome. There were some traces of dissipation in his face, but what was more apparent was the look of irresolution, of some inability to come to terms with life, which hinted at a basic flaw of character. He had a normally heavy growth of beard, and to the overnight stubble on his upper lip and cheeks was added the disorder of a shirt with the collar-stud missing; his tie was loosened and pulled awry. He tore the tie off, plunged his face into the basin and splashed the water over his head. With his linen jacket over his arm he went back to the living-room, where Evelyn already had a coffee pot and a pan of milk bubbling over a spirit lamp.

She turned round as he began to fumble in his jacket pockets.

"My luck was in last night," said Jeff. "Look here!" His fumbling had produced a mass of Turkish lira notes, soiled and screwed together, which fluttered apart as Jeff flung them down on one of the hard divans which ran round three sides of the room.

"You play a swell game of poker, Jeff."

"So does the Gazi, mostly. This comes to about two hundred bucks and I sure can use it."

He took the large cup of coffee she held out and let her fill it to the brim with hot milk. They sat down side by side on the linen-covered divan, and Evelyn pulled up a low table which held a tray with a platter of unleavened *pide* bread and a bowl of *pekmes*, the wartime substitute for jam and sugar. "Do you want anything to eat?" she said.

"God, no!" But Jeff was feeling better. The coffee was clearing his head, and although he had hardly taken in what she said as he entered, he now realised that Evelyn was wearing whipcord breeches and high boots polished by herself to the glow of dark chestnuts.

"The riding date!" he said. "You're all dressed up and nowhere to go, honey. Your hero the Gazi passed out cold a couple hours ago—it took three of them to get him upstairs and into bed."

"It must have been quite a party!"

"It went on too long for most of us, was all."

"Poker all night, eh?"

"Not all night. No, it was the usual brawl. One hell of a lot to drink and dinner around midnight. The servants kept bringing the food in and the Gazi kept sending them away, and then when we finally ate he talked about his plans for a couple hours non-stop."

"In Turkish, of course?"

"Sure. Hamdi Bey translated for me, as and when he could."

"Ugh!"

"Why 'ugh'?"

"He's such a sly little man."

"Hamdi's all right. Well, then the Gazi gave us some music, you know, the beloved folk songs he learned at his mother's knee back in dear old Saloniki—"

He stopped. Evelyn's faintly smiling lips were set. Jeff knew she didn't like to hear him ribbing the Gazi, and this morning there was no sense in going out of his way to antagonise her.

"Any ladies present?" she asked, and filled his cup again.

"Strictly stag tonight. Poor little Fikriye was there at the start, trying to act hostess, chattering away and watching *him* out of the corner of her eye—"

"After all, she's his cousin, Jeff."

"And his mistress, don't forget."

"You don't know that for sure."

Jeff laughed. "Tell you the truth, I was kind of sorry for Fikriye last night. There she was in her fancy doodads, with a little dab of pink tulle, or something, on her head, and looking as sick as a dog under the powder. She didn't get to eat with us. She checked out around half past ten . . . Colonel Arif was there, and Riza Bey, in fact most of the military cabinet. Oh, and four hardshell Deputies from the back country, all set to act scandalised when they saw the liquor flowing. The Gazi had them eating out of his hand, and drinking with him too, before the *raki* finally knocked him out."

"But on the whole it was a soldiers' evening? Soldiers rather than politicians?"

"Yep."

"And no other foreign correspondents? Only you?"

"Only me."

"That was a big break for you, Jeff." Evelyn's tone was persuasive. "You said the Commander-in-Chief talked about his plans?"

"He talked for what seemed like forever about abolishing the Arabic script and reforming the language. It beats all get-out, the way he starts to lecture at the drop of a hat. If it's not education it's female emancipation, or the legal system — anything to stop him being asked questions about the war."

"Did *you* ask any questions?"

"I sure did, when the big story broke, but of course he clammed right up about that."

"What big story?"

Jeff grinned. He had been spinning it out, to tease her, but now he relented and explained: "The Greek government has issued a warning to the Allied Powers. They say they're sick of Turkish maltreatment of the Christian minorities, etcetera, and they're going to send two divisions from Anatolia into Eastern Thrace immediately."

"Good heavens!"

Evelyn sprang up and took two long strides across the room. It was sparsely furnished, with no pictures on the whitewashed walls: the only vivid colour was supplied by a dyed red Angora goatskin in the middle of the deal floor. Ahmed, their landlord, had knocked together a few shelves to hold the spirit lamp and some dishes, and about a hundred books, mostly Tauchnitz paperbacks bought in Constantinople. There were two wooden chairs and a heavy trestle table with Jeff's little typewriter at one end. The rest of the table space was occupied by an ordnance map of Asia Minor, on which pins with coloured heads represented the opposing forces of the War of Independence. Yellow pins marked the Greek Army, still far in advance of the line of demarcation laid down by the Treaty of Sèvres, while on the other side of the long Anatolian front green pins stood for the forces of Nationalist Turkey. The Neutral Zone created by the Allies, which extended from the Dardanelles to the Black Sea, with Constantinople as its centre, was marked by the colours of the Allied Occupation in red, white and blue.

Evelyn studied the map intently. Jeff watched her, utterly absorbed, a wing of ash-blond hair shaken loose from its clasp and her hand poised above the pins.

"Will they embark at Smyrna or Mudanya?" she asked.

"Don't know yet."

"I suppose the British will give their precious Greeks free passage across the Sea of Marmara."

He wanted to snap, "Aw, cut it out, Eve! Quit acting like Napoleon and be sensible!" But she had given him an opportunity to get to the point he had expected to reach much later in the morning, after he had slept. He said, lighting a cigarette:

"I'm not sure they will. You've only heard the half of it."

"What! Was there more?"

"Sure there was. Another despatch came in about one o'clock, while we were still sitting round the Table. The Greeks are not only going into Thrace, they're threatening to cross the Chatalja Lines into the Neutral Zone. King Constantine has announced his intention of occupying Constantinople."

"Is he crazy?"

"What do you think, Eve? Are the British, or even the French and the Italians, going to stand for that?" Jeff disliked having to ask his wife's opinion, but it flattered her, and he had to keep her pleased and happy if he meant to get away without a fuss. She

15

took the bait at once, of course, and launched into one of the reasoned political arguments to which Jeff only listened in an emergency. The sun had risen, and the white room was full of light. A breeze, which the cirrus clouds of daybreak had foretold, stirred in the fruit trees, and the moving leaves cast a dapple of light and shade over Evelyn's face. It wore the eager look which had fascinated Jeff Barrett when he first saw it across the city room of the New York *World*, and which had little power to move him now.

"Look, here's the thing," he interrupted. "The real story's obviously going to break in Constant. I figure I'd better get back over there as fast as I can travel."

"Back to Constantinople?"

"It makes sense, Eve. I can't miss out on a news break like this."

"But are you sure it's a real break? Maybe the Greeks are bluffing."

"They're not," Jeff said positively. "You know the British are thin on the ground along the Chatalja Lines. The Greeks will have the manpower to force a showdown within the next few days."

"It'll take you more than a few days to get to Constant. if you go the way we came, by the Black Sea and Inebolu."

"I know it. But if I could get down to the Zone, and take a train from Ismid?"

"Getting to Ismid, how? By buffalo cart?"

"The Gazi offered me a place in the Benz, last night."

"Kemal Pasha did? Is *he* leaving Angora?"

"He's sending Hamdi and three other guys down to the Nationalist outposts covering Ismid. We got talking about it before dinner, and the Gazi said, 'Jeff Bey!' (kidding, you know), 'you're always eager to get to the front, why don't you go along too?' They're leaving this afternoon, Eve. You must admit it's a swell chance! With any luck on the transportation, I could be in Constant. in thirty-six hours from now."

"I thought that old Benz was unserviceable."

"The French Mission's given him a new set of tyres."

"Well," said Evelyn, "this is unexpected. It seems just the other day we left Constantinople! I hadn't planned on staying alone out here," she added uncertainly. "How long would you be away?"

16

"A week—ten days—till the emergency's over." Jeff hesitated. "Want to come along?"

Evelyn appeared to be considering. "Four officers and you, and the driver. That's six passengers already," she said. "I don't believe that old Benz can carry seven, new tyres or no new tyres. I hardly think I want to try it, just to hang about in Constant. for a week."

"You could do some shopping, maybe?"

"In the Grande Rue de Pera? There's nothing there *I* want to buy."

It was delicately said, with the "I" barely emphasised, yet Barrett was alive to the inflection, and braced his weary nerves for a fight. But Evelyn turned back to the war map, looked from it to her husband, and said earnestly:

"Jeff, don't you think you ought to stay in Angora? The Greeks may very well put on an act in Eastern Thrace, but we all know the real showdown will be right here in Anatolia. Can you take a chance on missing it?"

"I'm not going to miss it," the young man said confidently. "This is the twenty-eighth—no, the twenty-ninth of July. Kemal won't try anything big until the end of September. If he tries anything at all."

"How do you mean, if he tries anything at all?"

"It's nearly a year since the Sakarya, Eve, and he's fought no major action in that time."

"Because of the terrible losses, you reported them yourself! It takes time to build up reserves for a new offensive—"

"Especially if you're playing Kemal's kind of politics. He's got his enemies in the Assembly—my God, it took him a lot of fast talking just a week ago today to get confirmed as Commander-in-Chief for the duration! If he'd been sure of beating the Greeks in combat you can bet he wouldn't have sent Yavuz to London last February, and Fethi Bey right now, to try to negotiate a peace conference."

"But the British have refused to talk to Fethi Bey."

Jeff shrugged. "A general's only as good as his last victory, and even the Sakarya wasn't a decisive victory. The British believe Kemal can't beat the Greeks, and chances are they're right. You want me to spell out why? First off, Kemal has got no air force worth the name. He had *one* aircraft at the time of the

17

Sakarya; how many has he now? He has one ace flyer, Captain Fazil, and a swell bunch of young pilots, but they can't fly packing cases! Second, he's got no navy, unless you count those two old gunboats he hijacked off the British in the Black Sea, which he can't get through the Bosphorus. He's got no tanks, and very little mechanisation; even his Supply Corps depends on bullock carts and camel trains. How the hell can he win a modern war with that?"

"With that plus an army fighting for its homeland," she said. "Think of all Kemal's achieved since the Sakarya! He's come to terms with the French and the Italians. They've withdrawn their troops from Turkey, and started selling arms to him instead."

"You think Kemal's a great guy, don't you?"

"I think he's a great man. And I think you'd be silly to go off to Chatalja now, when you could be on the Anatolian front with him."

Evelyn started piling up the breakfast dishes with a good deal of clatter, and Jeff caught roughly at her wrist.

"What the hell's got into you, Eve? Can't you see I'm only trying to do a good job? You know damn well what the *Clarion* wants is action pieces, big colour stuff like last year's fighting, and after that just plain old human interest. We've been short of that lately, so I've been playing up the Red menace, and how Kemal is paying for Italian guns with Bolshevik gold, and even so I hardly get a word into the paper. All this Angora political dope and in-fighting is just so much junk to Donnelly and the Commodore. And if they start taking spot news off the wire services I'm finished, don't you understand that? They'll haul me out of Turkey, and maybe send me to be Halliday's number two in Vienna—if I'm lucky—or else to Greenbaum in the Paris bureau. And how long d'you think I'd last with two hatchet men like Greenbaum and Halliday?"

Evelyn was silent. She knew that what he had just said was true enough. She also knew Jeff's deep, abiding fear of losing his status as a foreign correspondent, and finding himself demoted to the sports desk at the Chicago *Clarion*. He was a fine combat reporter who saw a battle as a baseball game; his political judgment was almost nil.

"If the Greeks really move on Constant. and you're there,"

she began, "what happens if the Nationalists mount a new attack in Anatolia? Who's going to cover that story for the *Clarion*?"

"I figured you'd backstop me, Eve, you've done it plenty times before."

"At the front?"

"Hell no, not at the front, but you could write up the Angora communiqués, and keep Donnelly happy while I'm on my way back. We'd still be doing a better job than the Hearst boys, they sit on their duffs in Paris and fake their Turkish stories from the French and English clips."

Frowning: "What are you going to say to Red Donnelly right now? He doesn't like his correspondents to move without orders, you know that."

"He'll like it all right when he hears about the emergency, and reads the uncensored stuff I'll get away by train to Paris! I'll cable Chicago just before we leave this afternoon, and if anything comes in after I've gone you can reach me at the Pera Palace. Come on, Eve baby, you can go through the motions well enough! You might even get some stuff into the paper again, like that think-piece on Mussolini they ran way back last spring."

"Under your by-line, remember?"

"All in the family," said Jeff easily. "You didn't care, did you?"

"Oh, but that's not the problem, Jeff! It's just this hunch I have, that the big show *must* start soon."

"Well," said Barrett, "why don't you find out? You've been seeing quite a lot of the great man lately. Doesn't he consult you on his battle plans when you're out riding?"

"Don't be a fool, Jeff." He saw the angry colour come into her pale face. He said, "What do you two talk about, when you gabble French together? Love? Romance?"

"You can't talk much when you're galloping."

"But don't you ever stop and admire the view?"

"Yes, there *is* a place with a wonderful view of Angora, and if we stop there he tells me about the great city he means to build here some day, and the University, and the Opera House—he's very keen about the Opera House. Or sometimes he just talks about himself."

"That's the Gazi's favourite topic."

"I wish you wouldn't call Kemal Pasha by that ugly name."

"Gazi? It's only a Turkish military rank: Conqueror; and he won it fair and square, at the Sakarya."

"It also means Destroyer of Christians, that's what's so ugly."

"What do you call him, Eve? *Pasha'm*, my Pasha, like all his other female adorers, or *Monsieur le maréchal*, or what?"

"I call him Excellency. He likes that." Evelyn stole a glance at her wrist watch.

"I'll bet," said Barrett with a grin. "*Excellence!* D'you know what that reminds me of? That fool book all the gals were raving about, back home last fall. *The Sheik*, wasn't it, by E. M. Dell?"

"E. M. Hull."

"Anyhow, the one about this Arab sheik who kidnapped an English girl and fell in love with her. Remember how they used to rave on? *'Diane, obey me!' 'Ahmed! Monseigneur!'* I can just hear you and the Gazi. 'Madame Evelyn . . !' *'Excellence!'*"

"Very funny," said Evelyn. "But Kemal Pasha's not an Arab sheik."

"He's the next thing to it."

"What, and born in Macedonia?"

"He's an Oriental all right when it comes to women. Did I tell you what he said last time I ate at Chankaya? Not last night, the time before. Some guy asked him what he thought the most important quality in a woman. Kemal told him in one word. 'Availability!' he said."

"Probably most men would say the same."

Her retort exasperated Jeff. "Just watch your step there, Eve," he said. "You'd better cut out the morning rides while I'm away. I don't want half Angora saying Jeff Barrett's wife's— available."

Evelyn gave him a disdainful look. "You'd better watch your own step at the Pera Palace, Jeff. Especially at the tea dances."

"What does that mean?"

"It means you needn't think you're fooling me with your great news-break in Constant. You're going back because you want to see that girl from the scent shop in the Rue de Pera."

"Rosette Mavros?"

"Oh, come on now, not Rosette. She's only the front girl, or should I say the madam? No, I mean Leila, of course. Your sweet little Greek friend who was so thrilled when she saw you come in to the tearoom at the Palace, and then nearly fainted

20

when she realised you'd brought your wife along this time. All terribly emotional, and very touching, I suppose. But it certainly showed me how you spent your time in Constant."

"My God," said Jeff Barrett, "you sure know how to pick on a guy. Whenever you see I'm feeling kind of punk you start jabbing and jabbing . . . okay, so I used to go to Rosette's place with the boys for a drink and a game of poker. Leila was just a little kid last year . . ."

"She seems quite grown up now."

"You don't really believe I was cheating on you with Leila Mavros, Eve?"

"It wouldn't be the first time, would it?"

"All right," said Jeff grimly. "If you get the name you can have the game, remember that, will you?"

"I'll remember," said Evelyn. "I only wonder what sort of sense you think we're making, going on like this."

"Going on like *what*?" said Jeff. "I swear it, I don't believe you know what you're saying, and I'm a damn sight too tired to care. Aw, skip it, Eve! I've got a hell of a trip ahead of me today."

"But it isn't possible to *talk* to you any more," the girl said, and her calm face was tense now, her shoulders taut under the white silk shirt. "You slide out of everything! You're always sleepy, or going on a trip, or playing poker; you don't even listen to what I have to say!"

"Sure I listen to you!" Jeff got up and tried unsuccessfully to take her in his arms. "Don't let's fight, honey bunny! Don't you think you've a pretty nice life, batting around with me and seeing all those crazy places? You liked it in Paris and Rome, didn't you? I know we haven't much of a place to live in right now, but it's better than the dumps they call hotels, and it's only till the end of September, after all, unless the big hawk lights—"

"Oh, Jeff." Evelyn was tall enough to lay her forehead, in a moment of weakness, against his shoulder. "It doesn't really matter how we live, or where we go. We're all wrong for one another, and we always have been; don't you feel it too?"

He did feel it, he would not admit it, he kissed her unconvincingly and whispered, "Just give me one more chance, sweetie! I won't go anywhere near the Mavros girls if you ask me nicely!"

But Evelyn pulled away from him. "Listen!" she said, "I

hear horses. It's the orderly from Chankaya, on the stroke of seven o'clock!" She looked out of the window. "Good heavens, Jeff! Kemal Pasha has come himself, today!"

The man whose personality had dominated the whole of their conversation was dismounting at the gate and throwing his reins to an orderly in a black uniform. He started across the patio as Evelyn pulled the door wide open. Mustafa Kemal Pasha, Gazi, Field-Marshal, Commander-in-Chief, and President of the Grand National Assembly of a Turkey fighting for its independence, looked almost too slim and youthful to bear the weight of such impressive titles. He was a man just above medium height, dressed in a hacking jacket and breeches, and unconventionally his head was bare for the morning ride. His hair, like his clipped moustache, was astonishingly fair, his eyes a pale steel blue. His blond good looks were emphasised by the presence, two paces behind him, of his crony Colonel Arif. Arif, too, was a fair Turk, but his hair had dulled with the years, and his bloodshot eyes revealed the excesses of the past night as plainly as Jeff Barrett's face.

Kemal, closely shaved, looked no more tired than a man with his crushing load of responsibility had a right to be. His face, thin and with high cheekbones, was as pale as if the light of his fierce intelligence shone through the smooth unwrinkled skin. As he came up to the door, walking gracefully over the stone flags, he seemed to be supercharged with the vitality which communicated itself to everyone he met. The long night of drinking, singing, gambling and talking, which had exhausted Jeff Barrett, had passed over Kemal Pasha as if it had never been.

"Good morning, madame," he said. "Good morning, Mr. Barrett! I'm sorry to intrude on you so early, but I want to explain a slight change in the plans for Ismid."

"We're honoured, Excellency," said Evelyn. "Won't you come in? Good morning, Colonel Arif. I'm afraid I'm not quite ready yet, do please excuse me."

"I'm glad to see you dressed for riding, madame," said Kemal pleasantly. "I was afraid you might have decided to go to Constantinople with Mr. Barrett, and be busy with your preparations."

"Oh, no, I'm going to stay here," said Evelyn. She was aware of a glint in the blue eyes which noted every expression, and every detail of the living-room from the used breakfast cups to the

22

grimy lira notes strewn on the divan. "I mustn't keep you waiting —I'll get my coat," she said. She went quickly to the bedroom. As she opened the wardrobe she heard the men beginning to talk in English, Kemal's deep voice slower than usual as he selected the words. She put on the small felt hat and skirted coat which as a concession to Turkish feelings she wore on those morning rides. Very few people ever saw the Gazi and his party when they were out on the steppe, but as the officers' wives who lived near Chankaya were quite ready to be shocked at the sight of a woman riding astride, Evelyn felt in honour bound to spare them a view of her breeches.

Jeff had not asked the visitors to sit down. He was looking sulky; taken aback, she guessed, by Kemal's brisk appearance, and repeating rather stupidly the new arrangements for the departure of the staff car to Ismid.

"They're planning to leave at noon, Eve, I'll have some copy to type up before then," he flung at her, and she at once offered to stay at home and do the typing.

"No, no, go ahead and enjoy your ride, you can type up all I've got there in an hour," he said, and put his arm round her shoulders. "She's a great gal," he told the Turkish officers, "she's going to do my job for me while I'm away."

"I think you should sleep for a while, Mr. Barrett," said Kemal. "I'm afraid we can't guarantee you a comfortable drive to the coast, and you look tired."

"I'm very glad to have a place in the car, sir, thanks again," said Jeff. "You go along, Eve, and don't worry about me. I *am* going to nap till about nine."

"You don't care to accompany us?" grinned Colonel Arif.

"Only as far as the gate," said Jeff, who was no horseman. He walked beside Evelyn to the lane where the horses were waiting, and watched while Kemal himself helped his wife into the saddle. She looked well on horseback, with her coat hanging in graceful folds to her boot tops, and her gloved hands firm on the reins.

"Do you want a whip, madame?" Colonel Arif offered his crop.

"I'm afraid it might scare her . . . Be back soon, Jeff!" But Evelyn hardly glanced at him as she said it; she was patting her mare's neck.

"Have fun," Jeff said laconically. He sketched a salute to the

Commander-in-Chief, still bitterly conscious of his own un-kempt condition, and turned back to the house without waiting to see them start. He heard the creak of leathers and the jingle of stirrup irons as he slammed the door and flung himself down to count his poker winnings. The voices died away beneath the trees. From far down the lane he heard Evelyn's gay excited laugh.

2

THE PARTITION OF TURKEY and the occupation of
Constantinople by the Allied Powers had been accepted by
the Sultan Mehmed VI and his government, who saw no
other course open to them but to submit. When the standard of a
nationalist revolt was raised by General Mustafa Kemal, the victor
of Gallipoli, he was thus in conflict with the Ottoman government as well as with the Allies, and against their combined
strength he could only muster the scanty forces of Anatolia. In
that bleak province, half of whose young manhood had died in the
Great War, he and the few friends who joined him found that
weapons, ammunition, food, shelter and clothing were all in short
supply, but here and there they were able to lay hands on some of
the imperial treasures. At Eskishehir, before that ancient city fell
to the Greek invaders in 1921, they seized the famous stud where
horses had been bred for the Sultans for over a hundred years. It
was two of these magnificent creatures which the Commander-in-
Chief and Colonel Arif were riding now.

Evelyn had a quieter mount. She rode behind the men as they
went past the gates of Chankaya and made for the steppe, but
out on the open turf Kemal waited for her to draw alongside, and
at once she urged her horse to a gallop. On the first of the
morning rides—there had been only three so far—she had felt
uncomfortable in the heavy Anatolian saddle, but now she had
confidence in the beautiful mare and in the watchfulness of
Kemal Pasha. They rode east together into the sun.

Presently Evelyn checked her pace, and called out, "Go on a-
head! Don't wait for me!" She dropped back to a trot, the soldier
falling in behind her, while the two officers raced on like boys at
play in the great burst of speed and exuberance which was
Kemal's relief from strain. Evelyn rode along slowly in the fresh
breeze blowing out of Asia, bringing with it the scent of aromatic
herbs and grasses and short springing turf. She felt as if she were
riding on the roof of the world. One thousand miles to the east

25

lay the frontiers of Persia and Russia, and to the west, barred by the Greek armies, lay the way to the seas of antiquity, the Aegean and the Mediterranean. Here between east and west lay nothing but the Anatolian plateau, four thousand feet above the sea, the mountains rising range upon range in sombre folds of ochreous brown and umbered green, with a drift of cloud shadows barring their peaks with sun and shade. It was a fitting stage for the great struggle for liberty going on day by day in this, the heartland of the Turkish nation.

The majesty of the steppe and the sense of her own freedom drew out of Evelyn's heart some of the bitterness left in it by the scene with Jeff. But her pulses were beating faster than usual, for one of the results of Jeff's attack had been to make her for the first time self-conscious with Kemal Pasha. In her nature there was a strong vein of hero-worship, and ever since reading Jeff's despatches from the Turkish front in 1921 she had made a hero of the undefeated commander, the leader of a people struggling to regain their national identity. When they first met, Kemal was for Evelyn Barrett a myth much more than a man. She had never been a flirt, and in spite of his reputation with women he had not flirted with her; their brief talks on horseback had given her only intellectual pleasure. But now, with Jeff's foolish words burning in her recollection, Evelyn saw the Commander-in-Chief in a new light, and felt a physical thrill, quite strange to her, when the rider on the imperial black horse came racing back towards her. Kemal was laughing. His keen face was alight with so much gay assurance that no one, seeing him in this perfect setting, could suppose that the man was in fact an outlaw, condemned to death by the Sultan, a rebel with a price upon his head.

"One more gallop, and then back to Chankaya!" he said. Evelyn touched her horse's sides with her heels and followed him headlong until the last burst of speed was over, and they cantered down to the poplars which protected the Gazi's house from the east winds of the steppe. This was the point at which on their previous rides Evelyn had said goodbye, and with the orderly for escort had trotted home.

Today, where the bridle path ran through a plantation of young firs, Kemal laid a gloved hand on her rein.

"Come and have coffee at my house, madame," he said. "There's a favour I want you to do me, if you will."

"But Jeff's expecting me at home."

"He's sound asleep. And I need your help. Please come!"

"But your appointments, Excellency? Won't your first visitors be there by now?"

"I'm free today until ten o'clock, when I've got to meet the Cabinet at Angora. I don't want to talk to anyone but you till then, Madame Evelyn."

The flattery, the soft pronunciation of her name, which in French he made to sound like "Yve-leen", were all the encouragement Jeff Barrett's wife required. She said gently, "If you wish, then," and with Colonel Arif smiling to himself they rode along to the broad terrace before the door of Chankaya.

The place, built by a Levantine merchant with a taste for solitude, had not been in Kemal's possession very long. Chankaya was twenty minutes' drive by automobile from the centre of the town, and that fact alone ensured some privacy when the private cars in Angora could be counted on the fingers of two hands. Kemal bought it when life became impossible in the house near the railway station where he was importuned, questioned, serenaded and interviewed by day and night. Now he lived near trees and running water, both of which he loved, in a plain square house of the local stone, built on two floors, with bay windows at one end under an ugly, conical, slated turret. A meanly proportioned wooden porch, painted the colour of ox-blood to match the window frames and with a small balcony above, further disfigured the exterior. Chankaya from the outside was less attractive than its owner thought, but was redeemed by its magnificent situation on the hillside with the high steppe beyond.

The morning hours of that day might have been kept free of appointments, but half a dozen people were at Kemal's stirrup before Colonel Arif could help Evelyn to dismount. His secretary, Hayati Bey, came hurrying out of the house with a sheaf of telegrams, followed by a servant lamenting over the shards of a broken vase. Two aides-de-camp came smartly to attention, the grooms ran up to take the horses, and a motor cyclist from Angora carrying a bag with the latest European periodicals and reviews jostled a messenger from the telegraph office. The noise they made was considerable. Kemal turned apologetically to his guest.

"Madame, will you excuse me for five minutes?" He took the

27

fountain pen Hayati offered and began to sign the telegrams rapidly. "Tell them to bring coffee to the study for the Hanim Efendi and myself," he threw at the man with the broken vase, and then to Eve again, "I'm sorry, but the messenger is waiting."

"*Je vous en prie, Excellence.*" Evelyn moved away to admire the view from the terrace. The prospect, which from the steppe had been majestic, assumed a dimension of humanity from Chankaya, for Evelyn could see the ancient citadel of Angora and the red roofs of the town spilt down the hillside like blown poppies, beyond the treeless empty acres where Kemal planned to build his splendid city. She had seen the view from Chankaya once before. Within a week of their arrival at Angora the Barretts had been invited to a reception there, when Evelyn met Kemal for the first time. It was not a particularly successful party, for Kemal's mother had been present, a handsome, domineering old lady who refused on the grounds of infirmity to get out of the low phaeton which brought her from her own house, and who appeared to be criticising everybody and everything as she sat sipping sherbet near the front door of Chankaya. The young Turkish women, already disturbed by Kemal's orders to appear unveiled, had been absolutely quelled by the blue eyes of his mother: conversation died away, and the reception collapsed under an excess of constraint.

There was still, in the sunshine of a working day, a feeling of constraint about Chankaya. The porch through which Kemal ushered Evelyn was overfull of wood carvings, and darkened rather than lit by small leaded windows. The hall, which held a little ornamental fountain, awkwardly combined the functions of a living-room and an anteroom to Kemal's study, with a red leather sofa for visitors awaiting an interview. The room of the famous Table, still being cleaned up after the all-night party, reeked of spirits and tobacco like the London pubs Evelyn had visited with Jeff.

"The coffee is ready, my Pasha," said a submissive voice. "I saw to it myself."

A very pretty Turkish girl of about Eve's age was standing in an open doorway to the right of the hall. She was small, with eyes so brown as to be almost black beneath black brows which met, in the approved style of Turkish beauty, almost above her pretty

28

nose. She wore a blue dress and little blue velvet slippers which made no sound.

"H'm, Fikriye, thank you," said Kemal. "You remember Mrs. Barrett? Madame Evelyn, I think you've met my cousin Fikriye?"

"I had the pleasure of meeting Fikriye Hanim at your reception, Excellency." Evelyn held out her hand to the Turkish girl. The little fingers she touched were hot and moist.

"I hope Mr. Barrett is well this morning, madame?" Fikriye's voice was sweet and hoarse, her French indifferent.

"Thank you, very well."

"Take the Hanim Efendi's coat," barked Kemal to a hovering servant. Evelyn gave the man her hat and gloves as well, and rubbed her hands with her handkerchief. Though the guest had been on horseback Fikriye made no offer of hot water, but led the way determinedly into a formal drawing-room. Kemal's fair bristling eyebrows drew together when he saw a coffee tray set for three on a marquetry table, but he made no comment as he pulled out one of three green velvet chairs for Evelyn except, "I ordered coffee in the study."

"You will be more comfortable in the salon, my Pasha," said Fikriye. She began to fill the tiny coffee cups in their filigree holders.

"What are those cats doing here?" her Pasha asked, as two beautiful white animals jumped off the velvet sofa and came up to the table. Evelyn tactfully bent down to stroke them.

"They're lovely," she said. "Your pets, Fikriye Hanim?"

"This is my precious boy from Lake Van," murmured Fikriye, petting the cat with amber eyes and auburn markings, "and this is my sweet fellow from Angora." The fluffy Angora cat, with one blue eye and one green, looked consideringly at Evelyn.

"Which does His Excellency prefer?" she asked, and Kemal smiled. "Pious Moslems obey the Prophet's injunction to cherish all cats," he said. "Personally I prefer dogs."

"Pasha has a beautiful English dog," said Fikriye.

"Yes, but I don't allow him in the drawing room."

On the gilt-enamelled tray there were, as well as the coffee service, three pots of rose-petal jam, three glasses of water and a plate of sugar cakes. "Is this what you like, madame?" said

Kemal abruptly. "Do you care for sweet stuff? Don't you eat eggs and bacon in the morning?" Fikriye's eyes grew larger than ever at the idea of cooking bacon in a Moslem kitchen.

"I've had some breakfast already, thank you. And I'm very fond of Turkish coffee." Evelyn ate a spoonful of the rose jam for good manners. It was roses all the way at Chankaya, for Fikriye wore a strong scent made from rose attar, and there was a vase of the real flowers on a console table. "What beautiful roses! How did you manage to grow them here?" she asked, and her tact in changing the subject was rewarded when her host used the difficulty of keeping the bushes watered as the theme of one of the lectures which bored Jeff so much—this time on irrigation and his plans for building dams and a barrage near Angora. Fikriye watched the Pasha. Something in her intent look made Evelyn uneasy. Kemal had said that *she* was the only person he wanted to talk to before he met his Cabinet. Had this possessive cousin the right to be present every time a guest entered his house? A little pang of jealousy added itself to the new disturbance in her heart. But the awkward scene was quickly over, for Turkish coffee had the merit of being drunk quickly, and as soon as the tiny cups were empty for the second time Kemal rose to his feet.

"Have you visited my mother this morning, cousin?"

"Not yet, Pasha'm. There was so much to do at home."

"Go and see if she needs anything, and ask if I may kiss her hand on my way back from Angora."

"Yes, Pasha'm." The hurt brown eyes were veiled as Fikriye bowed to the guest in farewell. When she left the room, followed by her cats, Kemal turned to Evelyn. "Let's have our talk out of doors," he said. "I'd like to show you the gardens, such as they are."

It was a relief to get out of the salon, where the scent of red roses fought with the lingering tavern smell of the dining-room, and pass through a décor of wall-hung tiger skins, polar bear skin rugs and massive oil paintings, out at the front door held open by two iron doorstops in the shape of lions, into the fresh air. Side by side, Kemal and Evelyn crossed the gravelled sweep to the retaining wall above the terraced gardens where unpruned pear trees heavy with fruit were almost choked by wild lilac past its blossoming season. Kemal, pointing out the rivulets of water which had been diverted to the cultivated patches of the garden, had to break off to check the frantic greeting of a brown retriever.

"Good boy! Master's busy! Back to the kennels!" It was the same sort of dismissal, indulgent but firm, as he had given Fikriye.

"Your house is—" Evelyn couldn't truthfully say "beautiful", she changed it to "beautifully situated, Excellency".

"It suits me well enough. The rooms need something done to them, although I'm sure I don't know what. I've lived in camps or barracks all my life, I'm not supposed to know about interior decoration! I thought I could leave arranging a house to the women-folk, but when a man has *two* sick women on his hands—"

"Your mother—Zübeyde Hanim—isn't any better, then?"

"She isn't well at all. And stubborn as a mule, of course! She insists on living in her own house, in the old-fashioned style, but she needs nursing now, and that's a problem . . . we go down this way . . ."

The Van cat, on paws as silent as Fikriye's velvet slippers, followed them down a flight of steps into a flagged patio, where a spring bubbled from the rock wall into a basin, the water spilling over to feed a small ornamental pool. Tiny streams trickled out of the pool through cracks between the flagstones, towards flower borders in which many-coloured carnations, some un-staked and collapsing from their own weight, struggled for space with a fine crop of weeds.

"My cousin takes care of this little garden," said Kemal. "I wish she were well enough to look after it better."

"You don't mean Fikriye Hanim is the other sick woman on your hands?"

"I'm afraid so."

"But she looks so well and pretty this morning!"

"She's been in poor health for some time now. The doctor thinks her lungs may be affected, and *I* don't think she ever really recovered from the terrible journey to Constantinople in 1912, after the Greeks captured Saloniki. Fikriye was only fifteen then, living in my mother's care, and she wasn't as robust as some of the other—refugees."

"Where were you then, Excellency?"

"I'd been fighting the Italians in Tripoli."

They sat down on two of the small stone benches by the pool, and Evelyn said,

"You mean your mother was a refugee too?"

"And my sister. But my mother was a strong woman then, and she never lost her fighting spirit. Do you know that even now, ten years later, she says she'll never wear a new dress until the day I free my birthplace from the Greeks? That's an obstinate old lady's delusion—one has to humour it. But poor little Fikriye's health was shattered. I hoped when she married and went to live in Egypt, the climate there would do her good—"

"Oh, she's *married*? I didn't know that."

"They were divorced some time ago—before the Revolution."

"Divorce is easy in a Moslem country, isn't it?"

"For a man, yes. Cigarette?"

Kemal produced a gold cigarette case and slapped his pockets ruefully. "No matches!" Evelyn laughed, "I've got some." She reached into her hip pocket for a flat silver matchbox. The man watched the smooth muscled movement intently. Evelyn caught his bold look. She was not experienced enough to understand the subtle pleasure which the sight of a girl in breeches, shirt and boots gave to the Macedonian, or to realise that he was enough of an Oriental to have a streak of ambivalence in his nature. Kemal enjoyed the submission of women like Fikriye, but Evelyn Barrett's small breasts and broad shoulders, narrow thighs and square hands were irresistibly attractive to a man ready to be charmed by a woman's heart in the body of a boy.

He struck a light for her cigarette. "What are you looking so thoughtful about?" he said across the flame.

"I was wondering if you were planning to do what your mother wants."

"What she—?"

"Recapture Saloniki from the Greeks."

"Oh, that! My mother's not a strategist, I'm afraid. And I shall never carry the war across the Aegean Sea."

"I'm very glad."

"How much do you know about the Turkish Revolution, Madame Evelyn?"

"As much as I could find out by reading, ever since the battle of the Sakarya. Enough to wonder—when you asked me today— what somebody like me could possibly do to help someone like you."

"It occurred to me when we were riding, after you told

32

me you weren't going to Constantinople with your husband."

"Jeff didn't exactly insist that I should go."

"I thought it mightn't be too uncomfortable for you in my car."

"The car," said Evelyn. "You know, that did surprise me, your offering Jeff a seat in the Benz, when transportation's such a problem here."

"Jeff Bey's an old acquaintance. I was glad to be able to do him a kindness."

"Did Jeff ask for this particular kindness?"

"No, I offered it. Did *that* surprise you?"

"I figured that if you did him *such* a favour, you might expect a favour in return."

"Such as?"

"Perhaps to carry a message or a letter to Constantinople, or bring some information back."

"Did he say so?"

"Jeff wouldn't tell me a thing like that even if I asked him, and I didn't ask him."

"So you keep secrets from each other, you two pleasant, smiling Americans?"

"Sometimes."

"How long have you been married?"

"Four years."

"The marriage was arranged by your parents?"

"Good heavens, no!" said Evelyn. "Our parents haven't even met!"

"Not *met*?"

"Jeff's father and mother live in Winnetka, Illinois, and mine in San Francisco. Jeff took me to visit his parents when he joined the Chicago *Clarion*, but he's been abroad too much to plan on a trip to California."

"But then where were you married?"

"In New York, at City Hall. Jeff had enlisted, and was expecting to be shipped overseas, so we hurried up the wedding."

"I never knew Barrett served in France," said the Commander-in-Chief.

"He didn't," said Evelyn. "He never got nearer France than Plattsburg." And that, she thought, explains so much of Jeff's frustrations: I wonder if this man, who has commanded armies, could ever understand?

"I've still a lot to learn about Western customs," said Kemal. "In Turkey the parents have much to say in the arrangement of a marriage." He took a string of coral prayer beads from his pocket and looped it thoughtfully round his left wrist. "So you were married in New York. Was that where you met?"

"Yes. I went east to college, and after I was graduated I got a job on a paper called the *World*, where Jeff was on the sports desk."

"Your parents allowed you to go so far away to college, when you were a mere schoolgirl?"

"I was seventeen then," said Evelyn. "Twenty-one the month before we married. But this can't possibly interest you!"

"Yes it does," insisted Kemal. "I know so little about life in America; this is fascinating! Tell me about your father and mother and your home."

Evelyn laughed. She was rather amused by the soldierly interrogation. "There isn't much to tell. My father's a banker; in fact he's the president of the Pioneer Merchants Bank of California, and he was born and raised in San Francisco, like myself."

"You didn't learn to ride like that in San Francisco."

"My father owns a small ranch in Nevada, where my brother and I used to spend our holidays. The cowboys taught us to ride, and I'm afraid it shows!"

"You're not an only child, then. I was going to say, your mother must miss her daughter very much."

"She did at first, I think, but she gets on very well with my brother's wife, and adores her grandchildren. And then her religions take up a lot of her time."

"Religions, plural?"

"Plural. My mother goes in for different faiths—like Christian Science, and Vedanta, and Zen Buddhism—at least I think it was Zen Buddhism, last time she wrote—"

"But surely yours is a Christian family?"

"I hope so."

Kemal clicked the red beads mechanically, and studied Evelyn Barrett. She was facing him across the pool, where the Van cat was walking round the stone rim and eyeing the goldfish. One booted leg was crossed over the other, and Evelyn's hands

34

were clasped round her knee. Her expression was very serious. But her eyes, which her ash-blond hair and fair complexion suggested should be grey and instead were brown, had a sparkle in them which made Kemal Pasha wonder if the unthinkable had happened and he was being delicately mocked. He said,

"So you and Barrett were married before the armistice. Why have you no children?"

Evelyn's gaze shifted to the cat, which was testing the water with its paw. "Just look at that creature," she said. "Is he going in swimming?"

"Van cats are supposed to be good swimmers," said Kemal. His perception, at times almost feminine, told him he had blundered. "I'm sorry," he said. "An American friend wouldn't have asked you such a question, I suppose?"

"That would depend on the degree of friendship, Excellency."

"Forgive me," the man said again. "I'm so accustomed to think of my young officers and their wives as members of my family that I ask them anything I like and when I like; it's a bad habit. I hope you and I will become better friends, madame. I'm glad you prefer Angora to the fleshpots of Constantinople. But what do you find to do all day?"

"Oh, there's plenty to do!" the girl said readily. "For one thing, I help out at the American Near East Relief depot. They're very short of supplies, but when any packages arrive I help to distribute them in the truck—that's to say when there's any gasoline."

Kemal pulled at his moustache. He had his own views on the work done by the Relief Mission, believing many of the Americans engaged in it to be spies for the oil companies, looking over the oilfields in Mesopotamia and Mosul; but, in all fairness, he knew this could not apply to the two elderly ladies who ran the depot in Angora. He said,

"Can you drive the truck, too?"

"Oh yes. But they have an Armenian driver; he goes with me to unload the cartons."

"You go about the countryside with an Armenian driver! No wonder you're not afraid to spend a few nights alone in your little house."

"I shan't really be alone, Ahmed and Ayesha live only a few hundred yards away."

35

"I know Ahmed and his wife. She used to carry shells to the men at the front."

"Their twin sons were killed at Gallipoli," said Evelyn. "Ayesha says she went to the front in memory of them."

"Some day I'll raise a statue to the women like Ayesha," said Kemal. "When the last victory is won."

"There won't be long to wait now," said Evelyn with conviction. Kemal's blue glance was sharp. "What makes you think so?" he said.

"Because I believe you'll attack as soon as the Greek defence is weakened—when they ship fifty thousand men out to Eastern Thrace."

"It's not as simple as all that. A good deal depends on *which* divisions General Hajianestis decides to transfer from Anatolia. He's half-mad, as it happens, and he may well be mad enough to transfer regiments loyal to the Crown. If he leaves disaffected regiments on this front, so much the better. Men who've spent a year in what they think of as a wilderness won't be too eager to defend their positions, and the officers are sick to death of King Constantine and his Great Idea."

"I'm afraid I don't know what that is."

"The Great Idea is that King Constantine should enter Constantinople in triumph, and rule there like the Emperor Constantine who was defeated by the Sultan Mehmed II, the Conqueror. After that the whole of Asia Minor is to be part of the new Greek Empire. Of course King Constantine, who's half Russian and half Danish, and has a German wife, didn't dream up these Byzantine splendours without considerable assistance. The man at the bottom of all our troubles is in exile for the time being, but it was he who inspired the Great Idea—I mean the Cretan, Venizelos."

Evelyn shivered. She had been carried away, as so many were carried away, by the sheer force and conviction of this man: she heard murder in the hiss of "Venizelos".

Kemal saw the shiver and wondered at himself. For a few minutes he had been talking to this American girl as if she were one of his junior officers, and not a woman to be cajoled into serving his complex purposes. He smiled and said,

"Of course you're right, the victory mustn't be delayed much longer. I wish it could have been won by diplomacy, but that appears to be impossible. Venizelos is in Switzerland and out of office, but his crony Lloyd George is still behind the Greeks, and Lord Curzon declines even to receive my envoy, Fethi Bey."

"That's what I said to Jeff," said Evelyn unguardedly.

"Ah! Barrett thinks I won't give battle, does he?"

"Well—"

"He's not the only one. But you know better?"

"I know you can't—can't make Turkey whole again until you've driven out the Greeks. You can't build a new Angora, or the dams and barrages, and the schools, and the Opera House you want, or anything, until you win!"

"If you realise that," said Kemal, "then it may be very fortunate for us that you'll be taking Barrett's place while he's away."

"Oh, but wait!" said Evelyn. She sat forward, tense, with her hands suddenly gripping the stone seat. "You don't suppose I can possibly do Jeff's job for him, do you?"

"But he said himself—"

"He was only joking, Excellency! Jeff's a very experienced journalist, and I'm not! I wasn't much more than a copy-girl when we were married! I can type up his stories, and answer the office queries, and I do some background research, but that's about all, it really is!"

"But if you *had* to write a what do you call it, a story, you could do it, couldn't you?"

"I could try."

"How would you manage about the language? Barrett knows half a dozen words of Turkish, and that's all."

"I can talk to Ayesha about the house things, now, and to Abdul, a little bit. Only Abdul always wants to practise his English on me."

"Which Abdul is that?"

"Abdul the son of Riad. He's Jeff's stringer—he reads the Turkish press for him. He's a reporter on one of the Angora papers."

"Ah," said Kemal, "we're not short of reporters in Angora. Perhaps it's a blessing that we *are* short of newsprint. Will this man be any real help to you, while you're alone?"

"I think so."

"Then, *chère madame*, the favour I have to ask of you is just what I ask of all the foreign correspondents: when you're in a position to do so, please write the truth about the Greeks."

"About how they marched into Anatolia, though the treaty only gave them Smyrna, three years ago? Or about the Great Idea, which is something new?"

"About the devastation and misery they've brought to Turkey," said the leader of the Turkish Revolution.

Evelyn considered. Kemal was lighting another cigarette, and she had time to choose her words. In this man's presence, under those steel-blue eyes, she felt that her brain was pinned by a searchlight, and knew she must speak with care. Then Kemal, too, leaned forward in his seat, and the coral beads jingled faintly on the edge of the stone.

"May I tell you something, Excellency?" she began. "Last year my husband wrote some very fine stories about the battle of the Sakarya—"

"I know, I read them all."

"But not the complete stories! I've seen the carbons, and I know that every word Jeff filed from the battlefield that seemed to criticise the Greeks was cut before it appeared in the *Clarion*. Right up to the end, when it had to be admitted the Greeks turned and fled. And anything he wrote from Constantinople that didn't favour the Greeks was edited out too."

"But why, if it was the truth?"

"It was contrary to *Clarion* policy."

"Is there a press censorship in America?"

"Not in the way you mean, no. The publisher of the *Clarion* personally decided to support the Greeks last year. And that's saying something, because he happens to be violently anti-British—anti any British, anywhere."

"But this year he sent your husband back to Turkey?"

"Just in case another big story breaks."

"It'll break all right."

"You've got to remember," said Evelyn gently, "you're up against a whole century of prejudice. Ever since the British got excited about the Greek War of Independence, they've thought of Greeks as heroes, like Hector and Achilles—"

"While we're what their Lord Bryce called us—'the unspeakable Turk'."

"I wouldn't know about Lord Bryce," said Evelyn, "but I

know you can't buck Lord Byron. He's the one who put it into immortal poetry:

> '*The isles of Greece, the isles of Greece,*
> *Where burning Sappho loved and sung,*
> *Where grew the arts of war and peace,*
> *Where Delos rose and Phoebus sprung*'

That's it, you see. That's what all the Philhellenes are crazy for. The arts of war and peace. Greece, the birthplace of democracy—"

"And Sappho, too," said Kemal drily. "Some day I may show you the Greeks at closer quarters. Intent on their civilising mission. As they civilised Smyrna three years ago, bayoneting the Turkish garrison after they surrendered, raping and murdering civilians, encouraged by a Christian Archbishop, until the streets ran red with blood—"

"Oh, don't!" said Evelyn.

"I'm sorry." Kemal came swiftly round the pool to sit beside her. "I'm afraid I've lived too long in the House of War to suit my language to a lady."

"What is the House of War?"

"I meant it literally in this case. As I told you, I've been a soldier all my life. When I was sixteen, I ran away from military training school to volunteer for the army when the Greeks attacked us on the island of Crete. That time I was caught and sent back to Monastir. But almost from the day I graduated from Harbiye, the Staff College, Turkey has been at war. First internally, after the Young Turk *coup d'état*. Then the Italians invaded Tripoli, Tripoli was Turkish then. Next came the two disastrous Balkan Wars. Then the Great War, when we made the fatal mistake of fighting on the side of Germany. And the aftermath, *this* war—the war I'm waging to set Turkey free."

"And that's what you meant by living in the House of War?"

"I said, in the literal sense. 'The House of War' is a figure of speech, madame. Pious Moslems believe that the world is divided into two races of men: the followers of the Prophet, who live in the House of Islam, and the infidels, condemned to live for ever in the House of War."

It occurred to Evelyn Barrett that twice in half an hour Kemal had used the expression "pious Moslems" in a tone which suggested he gave little for their piety, but since to say so would have been as tactless as his question about her childless marriage, she replied instead:

"But Excellency, you're a Moslem, and yet you don't say you live in the House of Islam?"

Kemal shrugged. "My devout mother brought me up a Moslem, certainly. But I believe in toleration of all creeds, and some day I hope Turkey will throw off the shackles of Islam."

Evelyn's eyes were mischievous. "In the meantime you carry your prayer beads, I see."

Kemal looked annoyed. He pulled the *tesbih* off his wrist and laid it on the warm stone between them. "It's a silly bazaar habit," he said briefly. "I started it the other day because I'm trying to cut down on smoking."

"Not with much success, so far?"

"You're too observant, Madame Evelyn."

Evelyn picked up the beads and admired their intricate carving. "What a pretty colour," she said. "I've a silk dress just the same shade that I bought in the Grand Bazaar at Constantinople."

"Then take the beads!" Kemal exclaimed. "If they match your dress, you could wear them as a necklace, couldn't you?"

"Oh, I couldn't accept— "

"Of course you could. You must have a gift to remind you of your visit to Chankaya! And this tesbih is long enough to go round your neck." He shook it out at full length, and the Van cat, which had been half asleep, came up and tried to paw the dangling finial.

"Yes, it is quite long. How many beads are there?"

"This one has ninety-nine. Three times thirty-three, for the Names of the Divine Attributes of God."

"And the hundredth Name?"

"The Hundredth Name is the Final Name, which is Un-nameable.'

The Commander-in-Chief gathered the beads together and closed Evelyn's hands over the clustered coral.

"When you wear them, will you remember what we talked about today?"

"I'll remember," said Evelyn. "And if I ever get a chance to write the truth . . . you have my promise . . . that I will."

"I'm very grateful. Will you ride with me again soon? And may I, even in your husband's absence, be permitted to call upon you at your home?"

Softly: "Oh, but I hope you will."

3

WHEN THE TRAIN WHICH had crawled along the shore of the Sea of Marmara reached the Asiatic terminal at Haydar Pasha, Jeff Barrett hired a caïque to row him across the water to Constantinople. While the other passengers were still shouting for porters to drag their army packs and valises aboard the Galata ferry, Jeff was halfway over to Stamboul, the caïque threading its way among the Allied ships at anchor, with a wet breeze blowing down the Golden Horn.

Nearly sixty hours had passed, instead of the hoped-for thirty-six, since Jeff left Angora. In the first twenty miles the venerable Benz developed engine trouble, and Jeff, who was an excellent mechanic, had to go to the rescue of the soldier-driver. Twenty miles further on it became clear that the new tyres presented by the French Mission were not proof against the flints and stones of the mountain track, and there were so many halts for changing and patching that Jeff felt a new admiration for Kemal's feat in crossing Anatolia in the Benz three years earlier, when its tyres were stuffed with rags. Darkness fell. The headlamps then gave trouble, and the party was glad to bivouac in a village inn, where the only food available was eggs fried in oil and the thin yogurt drink called *ayran*. Jeff and the four Turkish officers shared an upstairs room, while the driver slept in the stable below with a team of camel drivers and their beasts.

Of course they reached the Neutral Zone next morning after the one train of the day had left for Constantinople. Jeff spent the night under canvas with his benefactors, having seen so many signs of a big build-up in the Nationalist forces along the perimeter that he reckoned Kemal must now have three divisions covering the Ismid area. For the first time since his confident words to Evelyn, he wondered if he was wise to be leaving Anatolia.

Once he passed the checkpoint the correspondent of the Chicago *Clarion* was at the mercy of the British, who examined his passport

42

and press card with an arrogance developed through four years of Occupation, and sent him off to the station to argue with a harassed RTO about his right to a seat in what was now virtually a troop train. He walked through the streets of the uninviting little town and called at the British headquarters, where a few bored young officers could tell him nothing about the situation in the area threatened by the new Greek move. Their chief interest seemed to be the possibility of boxing horses down the Bagdad Railway for the Anatolian Hunt, which pursued foxes, jackals and even wolves down the Ismid peninsula on two days out of every seven.

But now the British and the boredom were behind him, and in a light summer rain Constantinople lay on her seven hills beneath grey skies, with all the mosques and palaces repeating other shades and harmonies of grey. It was not the Arabian Nights city Jeff had naïvely pictured before his first assignment in Turkey; the rose gardens had been built over long ago, and the noise of traffic had drowned the bulbuls' song. But where the narrow thrust of the minarets pierced the outline of the softly rounded domes Stamboul from Seraglio Point to the Phanar retained even in defeat and decay its ancient, sensuous appeal. Jeff Barrett was not susceptible to beautiful townscapes, but as the caïque approached the landing-stage at Eminönü he found himself saying to the uncomprehending boatmen:

"That sure is one lovely sight!"

He found a lounger on the quay to carry his suitcase and typewriter, and hurried on to the European railway terminal. Sirkeci, the station built in the old quarter of the vinegar makers, was a Turkish Gothic nightmare, castellated, crenellated and painted in shades of mauve and pistachio green, with a swarm of cats and beggars haunting the entrance steps. Jeff ran through the small but crowded concourse to the bookstall. There it was possible to buy the London *Times* and the Paris edition of the New York *Herald*, but these were four days old, and Jeff's immediate concern was with the little English-language paper called *The Orient News*, which gave local information and carried the agency lines. He scanned the day's news hurriedly. The Greek reinforcements had arrived in Thrace, but their main columns were proceeding towards Adrianople, the ancient city they had already captured from the Turks. Only a token force had turned aside to confront the Allies west of Constantinople, along the Chatalja Lines.

Jeff read the news with a feeling of relief. He wasn't too late for the big show after all, nor did he have to add a line to the feature copy which Evelyn had typed up for him while he shaved and packed in the little wooden house. He now had an opportunity of sending it straight to the *Clarion*'s Paris office without the irritating and time-consuming process of going through three Allied censorships, and with the lounger and the luggage still at his heels he made for the main departure platform.

Not the least of his worries during the delays on the road had been that he would arrive at Constantinople on the wrong day for the Orient Express, now leaving Turkey only twice a week on its long run to the European capitals. But he had hit it right. The train was standing without an engine at platform one, and the attendants were making up the berths in the *wagon-lits* and setting out the pale-blue crockery in the restaurant cars. The *chef de train*, found counting various currencies in his little compartment, at once accepted the thick manila envelope Jeff had carried from Angora.

"You're not travelling with us, Monsieur Barrett?"

"No such luck."

"Some day soon you will go back to Paris." He looked at the address on the envelope. "Monsieur Irving Greenbaum, Chicago *Clarion*, Place de l'Opéra"—*c'est parfait*. I'll post it for you as soon as we get in."

"Thanks a lot." A very substantial tip changed hands. "Any trouble on the run these days?"

"We came in two hours late last night, but we go out on time, of course. *Messieurs les Grecs* seem to be in an excitable mood, and there may be delays at the border, but we don't expect real trouble."

"That's fine, Monsieur Pierre. Take care of yourself, and thanks a lot."

"*A votre service, monsieur.*"

So that was that, and Jeff Barrett had fooled the censors, not for the first time. He was whistling as the man carrying his luggage found him a ramshackle taxi, and he was hurried away over the Galata Bridge. It was, as it had been for years, the nerve-centre of the city. A British sergeant, armed with a fly whisk, was coping efficiently with the flow of tramcars, taxis, cabs, fish trucks, a string of jibbing donkeys, and men carrying everything from vegetable crates to wardrobes on their backs. A bunch of singing sailors in the summer whites of the U.S. Navy were inviting the attentions of Admiral Bristol's Shore Patrols, while French soldiers in horizon blue jostled Italians in theatrically plumed headgear. The only Turkish uniforms to be seen in the occupied city were those of the Ottoman police, and there were few women in the crowd. They slipped along the pavements like faceless shadows, tied up lumpily in the black *charshafs* which covered them from the head to the heels, and Barrett thought, as he encountered one woman's frightened eyes above the thick veil, of Ayesha working among her fruit trees at Angora, and her frank and fearless stare.

The taxi crossed the bridge into the Galata quarter, where the shabby streets were lined with banks and commercial buildings, nearly all representing capital and management which, under the Capitulations signed by earlier Sultans, had passed into the hands of foreign powers. This had been, almost from the earliest days of the House of Osman, the quarter of the Franks — English, French, Italians, Germans, as well as of Greeks, Jews, Armenians and all the others in that melting-pot of races called Levantine, who lived free of Turkish jurisdiction, exempt from Turkish taxes and customs dues, citizens of their own states inside the Ottoman Empire. Another British NCO was directing a camel convoy past that relic of an earlier Occupation, the Galata Tower, and at the top of a steep hill crowds of Turkish office workers were streaming out of the Tunnel Underground. The taxi rattled on over uneven cobbles to the door of the Pera Palace Hotel.

The Pera Palace, famous for more than thirty years as the best hotel in the Near East, stood not far from the United States Consulate in the Petits Champs, and a short walk away from the palace which housed the British Ambassador, who was also the British High Commissioner in Occupied Turkey. Since the war the Pera quarter had begun to go downhill, and some of the hotel guests complained of the noise of the Fatih–Harbiye tram in front and the nearness of a Turkish cemetery in the rear. But the Pera Palace had kept its style, in spite of four hectic years of requisitioning by Allied Control, and hard usage by the army of foreign newspapermen who had passed through the hotel like locusts. Jeff Barrett had lived there on his own both before and after the battle of the Sakarya. The porter who took his belongings greeted him with a smile, the doorman saluted and said "Welcome, Mister Barrett", while he chased away the beggars and the bootblacks who mobbed the new arrival at the entrance to the hotel. There seemed to be more of them than there used to be.

"Hallo, Mr. Bechara, any messages for me?" Jeff asked the young reception clerk.

"One telegram, sir, it came this morning."

Jeff tore the envelope open, noted the despatch time, Angora Sunday afternoon, and the Constantinople censor's stamp.

"Cable received exclarion quote okay but get frontward regards donnelly unquote best evelyn"

Get frontward, how d'you like that? Where the hell did Donnelly think he was going? Or—an uneasier thought—where did Donnelly think the front *was*? In Thrace or in Anatolia? Jeff stood cursing inwardly, folding the flimsy paper into four, into eight, while Mr. Bechara turned the register towards him, and the assistant manager, a discreet Swiss from Zürich, came out of his little office behind the desk.

"Welcome back, Mr. Barrett, it's nice to have you with us again."

"Nice to be back, Mr. Braun. Got a good single with bath for me?"

"Mrs. Barrett isn't with you?"

"Not this time, no."

"I'm afraid I can't give you a single with a private bathroom, Mr. Barrett, we're very full up. How about a nice double on the second floor—203, Mr. Rafferty's old room?"

"I know 203," grinned Jeff. "We had some pretty good bull sessions there. Sure, that'll do fine."

They stood between potted palms, waiting for the lift as it creaked down through its central ironwork shaft. The sound of a dance tune and the tinkle of tea cups floated out into the lobby. "What's new?" asked Jeff automatically, and Albert Braun laughed.

"What's new is what brings you here, I imagine," he said. "I've been expecting you for the last couple of days."

"All the other guys here already, eh?"

"I don't think you've missed much. There's a deadlock at Chatalja," said Braun as the lift moved slowly upwards. "General Harington sent the Greeks a stiff warning about crossing into the Zone."

"So I gathered. Is it worth while going out there tonight?"

"I shouldn't think so. Most of your colleagues are coming back here for dinner, and I can arrange to have a car for you first thing tomorrow morning, if you like."

"Hey," said Jeff, as the porter carrying his luggage ran ahead to open the door of room 203, "somebody's got a story, anyway!" The sound of typing came from further along the corridor.

"That's the new man from the London *Times*. I understand he's writing a special article on Venetian Trade with Constantinople in the Seventeenth Century."

"Good old *Times*," grinned Jeff. Mr. Braun ushered him into a large room with a high ceiling, french-grey wall paper and much white enamel paint. A wide brass bed, with frilled pillows and a crimson silk spread complemented a suite of heavy dark mahogany in the style of 1900. The porter opened the wooden shutters and the balcony doors. The rain had stopped, and sunset light suffused the grey clouds over the Golden Horn.

"This is swell," said Jeff. "You've had it all done over since Pat Rafferty was here."

"We had to," said Braun in his non-committal way. "Can I have anything sent up, Mr. Barrett, or may I offer you a drink downstairs?"

"Just give me time to change," said Jeff. "I'll be down in twenty minutes. It'll have to be a quick drink, though; I'm going out right away." As soon as he was alone he unpacked, laying out clean underwear and a dark blue suit. Albert Braun was a valuable news source, and—for a consideration—had done the *Clarion* several good turns in the past. Meanwhile there was the comfort of a quick shave and a bath in a real bathroom with white porcelain fittings and six towels of assorted sizes on the heated rails. As the hot water gushed out of the tap Jeff thought of Evelyn, patiently heating water from the well on the outdoor brazier, and reminded himself that he had given her a fair chance to come on to Constantinople.

When he was dressed he walked down the two flights of stairs, enjoying the hum of the Pera Palace as it quickened its tempo for

47

the evening hours. The staircase was made of white marble, with a thick red carpet, and on each landing and half-landing white enamelled wooden tubs, as large as miniature balconies, held potted palms, hydrangeas and maidenhair ferns. Electric chandeliers were reflected in the mirrored walls. From the wide landing on the first floor Jeff was able to look down into the vast hall, decorated in a western version of the Turkish style, with a carved and fretworked balcony, and set with tea tables for one of the Pera Palace's famous *thés dansants*. A string orchestra was playing *"J'en ai marre"*. He remembered Rosette Mavros sitting there with Leila, showing her off to the Allied officers, on the unlucky afternoon when he'd walked in with Eve.

Now only half a dozen couples were revolving on the floor, with as many more looking on from tables laden with tea trays, iced coffee, sherbets and aperitifs. There were no Allied uniforms to be seen; most of the men were Levantines, although three wore the fez; the women were Levantine or Greek without exception, in tight black satin dresses and smart hats trimmed with osprey plumes or tiny veils. He could smell the scent of chypre and jasmine mounting heavily through the warm air.

Before joining Braun in his office Jeff took a quick look at the ground floor bar. The big room was almost deserted, the barman reading the *Journal d'Orient* behind the bar, but Jeff was reassured to see the correspondent of the London *Daily Mail* at a table for two in one of the window bays, holding forth to a young man with a round ingenuous face adorned by a toothbrush moustache. Things couldn't be all that bad out at Chatalja if the *Mail* man was in town! He said as much to Braun when they were alone in the office, with a bottle of rye on the assistant manager's desk.

"Who's the kid with him, hanging on his lips?"

"A new man, here for a Toronto paper, but he doesn't know the ropes yet, and tries to pick the old hands' brains."

"Canadian?"

"American. Straight or mineral water, Mr. Barrett?"

"Straight, thanks. Say, you're not doing much of a trade in the tearoom!"

"It's the season. Most of our Turkish regulars are at their *yalis* on the Bosphorus."

"And what about my old Russian pals? Vava Vorosilov and his gang? I asked about them last time, remember?"

"You did indeed. We've traced Prince Ivan for you; he's driving a phaeton for hire at Prinkipo."

"Good God! So the diamonds finally ran out, did they?"

"I never really believed in the Vorosilov diamonds."

"Nor did I," said Jeff. "Say, changing the subject, Al, what do you know about a Britisher called Gilbert Elliott?"

"Mr. Elliott—he stayed here with his wife and daughter last April, before they found a flat. He's a charming man, about sixty I should think; he speaks Turkish very well."

"That old?"

"Yes, he's a very senior official. Seconded from the Foreign Office as economics adviser to the High Commissioner; they're trying to work out an agreement on the Capitulations."

"Still at that, are they?"

"Yes, and this time the talks are likely to succeed. If you're interested, you might try to see Monsieur Trakas, who checked in this morning. They say he's the only man on the Ottoman side who can negotiate an agreement likely to please the Allies *and* the Sultan's Government."

"Trakas. Greek?"

"Yes. He was a big entrepreneur here for many years, but now he lives in retirement near Smyrna—at Bornova, I believe."

"But if the British make a deal with Kemal, the first thing *he'll* ask for is the *end* of the Capitulations."

"And if they don't make a deal with him pretty quickly, there'll be bad trouble in the capital."

"Things were quiet enough a month ago," said Jeff.

"Is it only a month since you were here? It seems longer. The Kemalist . . . underground, I suppose you'd call it, has been greatly strengthened in the past four weeks. A lot of Nationalist officers have been infiltrated, wearing civilian clothes of course, and they contact the resistance groups inside the city, risking summary execution to spread propaganda for their chief. Result: Kemal now has key men everywhere, from the Red Crescent administration to the Imperial Ottoman Bank."

"How about the Pera Palace?"

"We're strictly neutral," said the Swiss with his discreet smile. "But they don't stop at political propaganda. In the last month half a dozen of Kemal's opponents have been kidnapped—from their homes, from their offices, one from a night club.

49

They're said to have been smuggled across the Bosphorus into Anatolia. It's known that one of them was to be put on trial at Inebolu, but was lynched by the mob before the court could sit. What has happened to the other God only knows."

"Can you give me the name of this man you say was lynched at Inebolu?"

"Excuse me, Mr. Braun!"

The assistant manager turned with irritation to Mr. Bechara, who had burst into the room without knocking. The reception clerk, correct in his morning coat and striped trousers, looked distracted, and sweat was breaking out on his olive-skinned face. "What is it, Mr. Bechara?" snapped Albert Braun.

The young man glanced at Jeff. "Could I have a word with you in private, Mr. Braun? About—about Monsieur Trakas?"

"Speak up, Mr. Bechara, *please!* Has anything happened to Mr. Trakas?"

"He's been murdered."

*   *   *

There was something discreet and controlled, Jeff noted, in the Swiss hotel man's way of hurrying to the scene of a crime. True, Mr. Braun ran up the stairs three at a time, with Jeff and Bechara at his heels, but he walked across the broad first-floor landing quietly, with a pleasant greeting for two hotel guests chatting in velvet armchairs, and even knocked formally at a door immediately opened to him by an agitated French valet. The chambermaid, also French, was crying in a corner of the small lobby, with her frilled apron hiding her face. The valet explained that they had come in together to straighten the rooms and prepare the bedroom for the night—"at our usual time, monsieur"—and there, in the salon, they found this—this terrible thing.

"Quiet, please," said Albert Braun. He opened the door to the salon, which in their terror the servants had closed behind them. The french windows were open, and between one window and a disordered writing desk lay the body of a stout old man with white hair, wearing a frock coat and patent leather boots. He had been shot twice, in the stomach and through the neck. The Oriental rug beneath him was soaked with blood.

"Yes," said Mr. Braun. "Mr. Bechara, will you be good enough

—observing the greatest possible discretion—to go back to my office and telephone for the police? Antoine and Isabelle, stay in the lobby until they arrive." The servants nodded; they had no desire to come inside the room of death.

"Two shots, *two*," said Mr. Braun, looking down at the shattered body. "Is it possible nobody heard them?"

"Whoever did it used a silencer." Jeff stooped to touch one of the dead man's hands. "Still warm," he said, "it can't have happened long ago."

"The first thing the police will ask is if he had any visitors this afternoon."

"Or if someone just dropped by, using the balcony door." Jeff went out on the balcony. Monsieur Trakas's much grander suite was almost immediately below his own bedroom, with the same dramatic view over the Golden Horn to the Sultaniye and Fethiye mosques, now silhouetted against a flaming sunset. The balconies were exactly the same on the first floor as above, with very low railings, a wooden bar on top of the ironwork, dividing one apartment from the other.

"Even a little guy could step across here," he said.

"Come and look at this," said Mr. Braun quietly. He had remained by the dead body, and had seen, half-hidden by the skirts of the frock-coat, a shining object on the Oriental rug. It was a silver Turkish coin, the top of a slender silver paper-knife, dabbled to the hilt with blood.

"From the desk," said Mr. Braun. "There's one in every suite. I've often thought they were dangerous; they're as sharp as daggers."

"He used it as a dagger, all right. He got in one blow in self-defence. But when?"

"Between the two shots, possibly. The killer closed in for the second—"

"And got himself ripped up somewhere, by the look of it. Anyway it's a clue for the police," said Jeff.

"The police will go through this hotel with a fine tooth comb, and find twenty clues in every bedroom, but not the murderer. *Herr Gott!* It had to happen on my night off duty! Not," said Mr. Braun, recollecting himself, "that I'm not very sorry it happened at all. Monsieur Trakas was a good man. I shouldn't have thought he had an enemy in the world."

"You said he was very wealthy. Maybe it was a thief—"

"It doesn't seem like theft, does it?" They both looked round the handsome room, in which nothing had been disturbed but the old man working at the writing desk, and their eyes met. The thought of Kemal's agents was in both their minds.

"A Greek . . ." said Jeff. He kept his eyes averted from the body on the floor. The blood was still seeping from neck and belly into the Oriental rug. He had seen death in battle a hundred times, and murder in Chicago more than once, but it had not shocked him like this killing of an old man in the civilised setting of the Pera Palace, while the complex life of a great hotel went on. "They must have been dancing to '*J'en ai marre*' when the old chap swiped out with his paper-knife." Jeff spoke his thoughts aloud. "What was his first name?"

"Hercules."

"Did he have a middle name?"

"Oh, for God's sake, Mr. Barrett!'

"*La police, monsieur*," said Antoine at the door.

An Ottoman police lieutenant, booted and spurred, came storming in. A doctor, at his back, was no less emotional; the two policemen, their escort, seemed prepared to arrest everybody on the spot. Antoine and Isabelle, obvious suspects as foreigners and "finders of the body", were in fact arrested in the first three minutes, and taken out protesting; the lieutenant then turned his attention to Jeff. He was quite a young man, with the thin dark moustache made popular by Enver Pasha in the days of the Young Turks, and he was almost visibly trembling with excitement as he began his interrogation.

Jeff produced his passport and press card. Thomas Jefferson Barrett, born 1894, at Winnetka, Illinois, Civil state, married. Profession, newspaperman.

"Your paper, monsieur?"

"Chicago *Clarion*. It's on my card."

But the policeman was still studying Jeff's passport, while the doctor knelt beside the body on the floor.

"You entered Turkey on the tenth of June. Coming from where?"

"From Rome."

"But you were in this country for some time last year."

"That's right."

"Mr. Barrett is an old and valued guest of this hotel," put in Mr. Braun.

"You have been living at the Pera Palace, since the tenth of June?"

"No, sir. I left at the beginning of July, and I only checked in about half an hour before this—horrible murder happened."

"And where have you been living in the meantime?"

"At Angora."

"Aha!" The police lieutenant bristled with suspicion. "Have you been in touch with the man calling himself Mustafa Kemal?"

"Only in the execution of my duties."

"Your duties, sir! I've a good mind to take you along to the station immediately—"

"Lieutenant," said the Swiss, "may I remind you that you have absolutely no authority to detain an American citizen? What explanation could you possibly give to your superiors?"

"I shall explain, sir," the lieutenant was almost stammering in his excitement, "that in my view, my professional view, the murder of Monsieur Trakas is—is—*another Kemalist outrage!*"

*　　　*　　　*

Jeff Barrett got out of the room at last. He got out before any steps were taken to remove the body, which was what mattered, because the moment the murder was known every newsman in town would be on to a story right up the *Clarion*'s alley. He stopped at the reception desk, where Mr. Bechara's place had been taken by another man, twirled the register towards him, memorised a name, and shouted to a taxi-driver who had just set down his fare. It was no distance at all to the Eastern Telegraph Office, but there was no time to lose, and thank God when he got inside the place there were plenty of cable forms, too often in short supply. Standing at the high wooden counter, using his fountain pen in preference to the official pencil, he wrote swiftly in block capitals:

"31722 exbarrett constantinople begins hercules spiridion trakas comma sultans troubleshooter in capitulations probe comma shot dead tonite in perapalace hotel—"

When he had finished he looked over the telegraph clerks for a familiar face. Everything was breaking his way now; he recognised one of the men who was always willing to help a hardworking

53

newsman to get past the Allied censors. The lira notes were handed over with the cable sheets, there was a nod and a smile, and Barrett was out on the Grande Rue de Pera, wiping his face and hands with his clean handkerchief. He figured that ought to hold Red Donnelly for a few hours.

It was highly likely that he had a clear world beat.

He was nearly opposite the Galata Saray, the famous school for Turkish boys of aristocratic family, and thus not very far from the scent shop in which a year ago Leila Mavros had been helping her aunt Rosette. Jeff shook his head involuntarily. He was not going in that direction, no sir! .. or at least not yet; the first thing was to get to this man Elliott, who had taken on a new importance in Jeff's mind by his association with the murdered Greek. He walked off down the way he had come, past the sentries at the gates of the British Embassy, into the Rue des Petits Champs.

New arrivals from Paris, aware of the Pera quarter's imitation of all things Parisian, sometimes smiled at the name of this street, and compared it with a still more famous street in France. Old "Constant." hands knew the name had been curtailed in the course of years, for it had once been the Rue des Petits Champs des Morts, to commemorate the old Turkish cemetery which ran down to the gardens of the Pera Palace. The cemetery was closed now, but a little old wooden theatre on its very edge was still functioning, and just opposite was the apartment building Jeff was looking for. It was one of a row of tall houses, among them two hotels where life was lived at a less breakneck pace than in the Pera Palace. He checked the right number, and went up the steps: there was actually a *loge*, as in Paris, and a realistically French concierge glaring out of the inner window. Jeff asked for "Mr. Elliott's apartment". The woman was in honour bound to correct him. "*Monsieur* Jeelbair *Elliott?*" she snarled. "*Deuxième étage!*" A ten-watt electric light briefly illuminated a shallow, carpeted staircase and one substantial oak door on each landing. Jeff rang a noisy bell at the second, and almost at once heard a girl's voice shouting "I'll get it! I'll get it, Halide!" The door was pulled open in a grand gesture of welcome.

"Oh! I thought—"

"I beg your pardon," said Jeff Barrett. "Uh—is Mr. Gilbert Elliott at home?"

54

"Is he expecting you, please?" The girl who had rushed to the door looked round uncertainly at the Turkish maid hovering in the hall.

"I've an urgent message for Mr. Elliott. I was asked to deliver it to him personally."

"Oh!" said the girl, still doubtfully. "You'd better come in, then." She led the way to an impersonally furnished drawing-room with the high painted ceiling typical of old Pera, and fine rugs on the parquet floor. By the light of silk-shaded electric lamps Jeff saw that the tall girl was wearing a pale blue evening dress. "I'm Jean Elliott," she said. "Are you from the American Consulate?"

"No, I'm not, Miss Elliott. My name's Barrett, correspondent of the Chicago *Clarion*."

"I'm awfully sorry, but Daddy doesn't see any journalists, unless they ask for an interview through the High Commissioner's office."

"Please don't worry," Jeff said reassuringly. "I'm not about to bother your father. I just came to deliver a message. I'd appreciate it very much if you'd let me wait."

Jean Elliott seemed to have made up her mind about him. "It's quite all right," she said. "Daddy'll be home any minute, in fact he's usually home by now. He must have been detained at the Embassy. Will you have a glass of sherry, while you're waiting?"

"Thanks a lot." Jeff wondered if Daddy was still at the office because someone had phoned in the news of the Trakas murder. He watched Jean Elliott selecting glasses and bottles from the drinks tray at the far end of the room, and wondered how old she was. Not very old, he imagined; there was a good deal of puppy fat to be got rid of still. But she was dressed too old for her age: the evening dresses of 1922 were not kind to big clumsy girls, and the lace panels floating from the low waist of her taffeta frock made her look bigger than she was. She had long narrow feet, he saw, as she came towards him carrying a brimming glass, in grey satin shoes with crystal buckles, and big pink ringless hands with well-buffed nails. Her only ornament was a long string of pearl beads. Her hair, a lively shade of red, was coiled low on the nape of her neck and precariously controlled by a large tortoiseshell comb.

Jeff stood up. "Can't I pour some sherry for you too?"

"Oh no, I'll wait, thank you. I'm—expecting somebody."

So much her rush to the front door had told him. They faced each other in armchairs across the empty marble fireplace.

"I thought all the Embassy ladies spent the summer at Therapia," he said.

"We were there until last week, and then everybody came back because of the Emergency," said Jean Elliott. "It was rather horrid having to come back to town."

"You like Therapia better, eh?"

"It's a topping place. I played tennis all day long. But my mother wasn't aw'fly fit, while we were there."

"I'm sorry. Pera isn't the brightest place in the world, in summer."

"Oh, there's plenty of fun in Constantinople," the girl said gaily. "Do you know it well?"

"Pretty well. And you?"

"Mummy and I only came out here last April. But Daddy was *en poste* years ago, he speaks Turkish most aw'fly well. Do you?"

"I'm no good at languages, but my wife has picked up quite a bit since she's been in Angora."

"Oh, is Mrs. Barrett in Angora? That must be simply ripping, I should think . . . do smoke if you want to, *please.*"

There were Players, far too mild for Jeff's taste, in a silver box on the table by his chair. There was also, underneath the lamp, a slightly faded photograph of a young man in the uniform of the Royal Navy, signed in a schoolboy hand: "All my love, mummy darling— Ron.'

The sound of men's voices was heard in the hall, and Jean started up clumsily, her round face all one blush, as an elderly man carrying a bulging briefcase ushered a new guest into the room.

"Well, Jean," he said cheerfully, "I met Mr. Munro on the doorstep, and here he is. Er"— to Jeff— "good-evening?"

"Oh, hallo, Daddy. Hallo, Archie," said Jean shyly. "This is Mr. Barrett, a journalist from Chicago, he's been waiting to see you, Dad."

"Indeed," said Mr. Elliott frostily. He was a small man in whose hair the Scots red had long ago faded to pepper and salt.

His blue eyes had faded too, but they were not without a calm authority. Jeff was sure he hadn't heard about Trakas.

"I'm not here for my paper, sir," he said. "I've brought you a message from Angora. From an old friend."

Mr. Elliott's eyebrows rose. "That sounds most interesting," he said. "Have you met Mr. Munro?"

The two young men shook hands. Munro's dark good looks were in their way not unlike Jeff Barrett's; when he spoke it was obvious that he was a Highland Scot, and although he wore a dinner-jacket and black tie it was equally obvious that he was a naval officer. There was no mistaking the Service manner or the Service craze for punctuality. He declined the drink Mr. Elliott offered, glanced at his wrist watch, said the cab was waiting, and they were due at Tokatlian's at eight precisely.

"Run along then, dear," said Mr. Elliott to his daughter. "Is mummy feeling better now? Does she know who your chaperone will be?"

"Mrs. Windsor—it's Julia Windsor's birthday party."

"Oh yes, of course. That'll be fun, won't it?" Jean nodded enthusiastically. Archie Munro laid a taffeta cloak round her shoulders, and she picked up her white gloves and Dorothy bag from a side table. "Mummy was sound asleep last time I peeped in," she said.

"I won't disturb her, then. But she'll be wanting you, Jean, so don't be late. Mr. Munro, you'll bring her back before eleven, won't you?"

"Half past ten, sir, I'm sorry to say: we're at four hours for steam."

"So I mustn't detain you now. There!" as the girl kissed him, "have a pleasant evening, both of you." When the front door shut he turned to Barrett. "Miss Windsor and her friends must have had an anxious afternoon. It was reported that some of the battle-ships would leave harbour to defend the Neutral Zone."

"I figured Mr. Munro was a naval officer." said Jeff.

"He's a Lieutenant in the *Iron Duke*, the flagship." Mr. Elliott looked at Jeff's empty glass. "This is my time of day for a whisky and soda, Mr. Barrett, wouldn't you prefer that to sherry?"

"I would indeed, sir."

Mr. Elliott poured the drinks, and settling down in the

armchair where Jean had sat, took a pipe from his pocket and began the methodical process of scraping, packing, tamping, lighting and sucking which, as Jeff knew from a score of interviews, was any British official's first line of defence. He produced his own cigarettes as his host said,

"Which American newspaper do you represent, Mr. Barrett?"

"The Chicago *Clarion*."

"Ah! Not exactly a pro-British publication!"

"I guess not."

"Mr. Weintraub, your proprietor—ah, publisher do you call him?—must be a remarkable man. Why is he known as the Commodore?"

"As the story goes, he was a deckhand on a Lake Erie scow in his younger days."

"And went on to become a newspaper magnate. Remarkable! Well, Mr. Barrett, I hope you'll be sending home less lurid accounts of life in Turkey than some of your colleagues. You've arrived to cover the latest Greek adventure, I suppose?"

"Things seem to have calmed down tonight, on the Chatalja Lines."

"That was the last report when I left the Embassy. General Harington has been very tactful, very firm; I believe the danger has been greatly exaggerated in the city. People remember 1912, when the Bulgarians were at Chatalja, and the sound of their guns was heard in Constantinople. That has increased the present tension, beyond a doubt."

"Was your last—uh—tour of duty here in 1912?" Jeff asked.

"Bless me, no, it was over thirty years ago. I was a young man when I first came out to Constantinople. A very unimportant young man in the chancery, working hard for a qualification in the language and enjoying every minute of it. Those were wonderful days, Mr. Barrett. People talk about the crimes of the bad old Sultan Abdul Hamid—they called him Abdul the Damned—but Constantinople was a wonderful place for a young Englishman . . ."

Jeff allowed the Englishman to ramble on. All old people did it; and Jeff at twenty-eight had no interest in ancient history. He was taken aback when Mr. Elliott interrupted his gentle reminiscences, and said in a different tone:

"Now give me the message from Angora. Who sent you here?"

"It was the Gazi Mustafa Kemal, sir, the Commander-in-Chief."

"Kemal Pasha!" Mr. Elliott laid aside his pipe. "What on earth can Kemal have to say to me?"

"His exact words were, 'Watch out for the whip!' "

4

"WATCH OUT FOR THE WHIP!" Mr. Elliott repeated in amazement. "What an extraordinary — Have you any idea what he meant?"

"None whatever. It was two, well I guess three nights ago, at a party at Chankaya, when he took me aside and gave me your name and address, and asked me to give you that message, in those words. That was all!"

"Speaking in English?"

"He always speaks English to me."

"Even so," said Mr. Elliott, " 'Watch out!' — that's almost a slang expression, and Kemal's English was never idiomatic — quite the reverse."

"You've often talked to him, I guess?"

"Eh? No, not very often. I met him once or twice just after the war."

"Any idea who or what the whip could be?"

"Who or what?" Mr. Elliott's eyelids flickered, falling for an instant over his faded eyes, and in that instant Jeff said to himself "He's on to it! Whatever it is, he's on to it!" He said,

"Your daughter said you'd only been here since last April."

"With my family. I was here alone on a special mission just after the armistice. That was when I met Kemal Pasha, when we were both living at the Pera Palace. It's really," said Mr. Elliott, starting the business with the pipe again, "a very personal story. I'd no idea he remembered me."

Jeff realised that they had reached the point when in any interview an ill-timed question could check the flow of confidence. He said persuasively,

"The Gazi not only remembers you, he's obviously taken the trouble to find out where you're living now."

"Exactly. That's always been his strength, of course — he takes more trouble than his adversaries. When I met him in 1918 he was an out-of-work general, looking for a job. He asked me to recommend him to Allied Control for a local governorship in Anatolia. What was in his favour with the Commissioners was that he was known to have opposed Enver Pasha, and the German alliance too, but even so his record was a little too strong to make him acceptable. The Turks called him the Saviour of Gallipoli, and so no doubt he was, from their point of view. He beat us every time we challenged him. He beat the Russians at Kars, he even fought a magnificent rearguard action at Aleppo while the Sultan was fumbling with an armistice. So the British turned him down when he asked for a job in the winter of 1918."

"And that's all you know about him? He remembered, after four years, that you put in a good word for him?"

Mr. Elliott hesitated. "That's a matter of public record. What I'm going to tell you now is absolutely personal, and on no account for publication. I have your word for that?"

"Of course."

"I did see Kemal Pasha twice again, after he left the Pera Palace and rented a house in Shishli. You know the locality, about a mile north of the War College? It had rather an odd reputation in those days—still has, I believe—and Kemal's house was a queer sort of place, rather like a Swiss chalet, with a gimcrack balcony and fretwork roof. There were a lot of rooms, hardly furnished at all, and I had a feeling that a lot of plotting and planning for the future was going on behind the scenes."

"So it was."

"As we discovered when Kemal slipped through our fingers next May, and was off to start the Revolution in Anatolia."

"I reckon *you* didn't go to Shishli as a conspirator, Mr. Elliott."

"I went to get news of my son," the older man said gravely. "That's his photograph on the table by your side." He cleared his throat. "Ronald was our only boy. He was taken prisoner at the Dardanelles in March '15. We had one letter through the Red Crescent, saying how well the Turks were treating him in hospital at Chankaya. But then fighting began at Gallipoli, and Ronald was taken far inland on a brutal march to a place called Afyon Karahisar—you've heard of it?"

"Sure. They used to call it the Turkish Verdun, but it's been in Greek hands for over a year."

"Yes. Well, we heard nothing more of Ronald from that time forward. Nobody, none of the British officers who survived

Afyon, no one in Whitehall, could give us any information about our boy. His mother kept on hoping and believing that he was alive. I saw the suspense was killing her, so when I had a chance to go to Constantinople as adviser to the Economic Commission I snatched at it. In fact," said Mr. Elliott apologetically, "I moved heaven and earth to get the job."

"And Kemal helped you find out what happened?"

"He went to no end of trouble to have the Turkish records searched. He discovered that our boy died on the march, and was buried with three others by the roadside, not far from the town of Kütahya. Not a Christian burial, I fear, and the grave was left unmarked. But at least when I returned to London I could put my wife out of her misery—we knew the truth at last."

"It was a hell of a note for her, sir."

"Yes," said Mr. Elliott steadily, "it was a hell of a note for all of us."

Jeff set down his empty glass. It was tough all right, he was sorry for the old boy, but what about 'the whip'? What about Trakas? He moved the conversation away from Ronald Elliott's death by saying,

"You're doing the same sort of job now, aren't you, with the Economic Commission? Working on the Capitulations problem?"

"I didn't know that was a matter of interest to the American press," said Mr. Elliott dryly. He seemed to be regretting his moment of expansiveness.

"I heard of it today in connection with Mr. Trakas."

Still more dryly: "Did Monsieur Trakas give you an interview?"

"I see I'll have to break some bad news to you, Mr. Elliott. Mr. Trakas was shot and killed in his room at the Pera Palace this afternoon."

*　　　*　　　*

Jeff Barrett walked away down the Rue des Petits Champs with his hands in his trouser pockets and his shoulders hunched. On the same pavement, but going in the opposite direction, Mr. Elliott was hurrying up the hill towards the British Embassy. It had been the fastest brush-off anyone had given Barrett for years, and he almost grinned to think of the way that little Limey guy had gone into action. After the first furious "Why the devil didn't you tell me sooner?" there had been a fire of questions of the how-when-where variety (yes, and *who*?) and all Jeff could get out of the diplomat was a testy "Whoever committed the murder will be morally responsible for sabotaging the Capitulations settlement!" before he found himself on the way downstairs.

Five minutes' walk away the Pera Palace rose like a cliff out of the waves of traffic, with all its windows lighted, and Jeff could picture what was going on behind some of those drawn curtains as the correspondents returning from an abortive sortie to Chatalja caught up with the story of the Trakas murder. He could also picture himself as part of the scene, sitting on somebody's bed with a drink in his hand and his jacket and tie off, while the heat of the room and the noise of the discussion mounted. On the long road from Angora he had looked forward to being with a bunch of regular fellows again, trading tall stories and bawdy talk, but his inner restlessness drove him away from the hotel. He turned up an alley leading to Pera Street.

At once he was inside another world. Every lane linking the principal streets in Pera, those streets where Europeans were above the law, was a little Turkish poem, a series of Arabian Nights adventures, and Jeff remembered that Evelyn had liked those narrow alleys, roofed with hanging vines and creepers, better than anything in Constantinople. She never seemed to tire of wandering there, exchanging smiles—and soon, greetings—with the merchants sitting cross-legged by their wares. Dark shops selling brass and copper *nargiles,* sacks of millet and peas, trays of Smyrna dates and raisins, bread strewn with poppy seeds and crescent rolls—Eve had thought there was a story in them all. Not, as he told her, a story she could ever write for Donnelly.

Jeff walked up the middle of the alley and saw only the dirt between the broken stones.

He emerged on the lower stretch of the Grande Rue de Pera, near the great building which had once housed the Imperial Russian Embassy. It was locked and dark, and had been so since 1914; the new Russians were at Angora, representing the first of all the Powers to recognise Kemal as the ruler of the new Turkey. "Kemal and his Bolos!" Jeff had once heard the British Ambassador using very undiplomatic language about "that brigand" and his Bolshevik friends. He wondered again about the meaning of the message he had carried from Angora.

There was a small Turkish restaurant opposite the vacant Embassy where Jeff had eaten once or twice, and reasonably well. He turned in there now, and found it full of men in the red fez and black frock coat of minor officialdom. Jeff ordered a *döner kebab* and a glass of raki. When it came it was *yeni raki*, new and crude, tasting sharp even when he diluted the colourless spirit with mineral water. The aniseed taste dominated the flavours of the white cheese and cold chick peas which accompanied the drink, and brought a sudden memory of the Table at Chankaya, and Kemal pouring raki into his glass with a slender, steady hand. How that guy could put the stuff away! Jeff signalled to the waiter to fill his own glass again. The döner kebab was served.

He had thought he was hungry, for he had eaten nothing since before the train left Ismid, restaurant cars being things of the past, but after a few mouthfuls he pushed the shallow dish away. The thin grilled slices of lamb were excellent, the yogurt fresh, but the red tomato sauce spread over all was horribly reminiscent of an old man's blood slowly soaking into an Oriental rug, and Jeff's appetite was gone. He ate some of the pide bread and ordered coffee. The raki had started a train of thought he was disposed to encourage: the recollection of Kemal and Evelyn riding down the lane between the poplars, halting their horses on the steppe to talk. Of course "that brigand" was excited by her: he, Jeff, had seen it from the word go, but for all his successes with women her husband was prepared to bet he wouldn't get to first base with Evelyn Barrett. She wasn't interested in sex. Only in politics and military history and all that junk.

To increase his resentment of her, Jeff took Evelyn's telegram out and read it again. 'Regards Donnelly' and 'Best Evelyn' — there was nothing to choose between the two signatures in warmth. It wouldn't have killed her, surely, to put "Love, Evelyn"? Even if a cold fish like Eve didn't understand what was meant by love.

He had known she was a cold fish before he began to date her, of course. Her nickname in the city room had been The Icicle, and that in itself was a challenge to his masculinity; she was beautiful and very smart, a college graduate, and where others had failed Jeff Barrett was sure he could make The Icicle melt. He remembered punching a guy in the men's room at Bleeck's for saying, admittedly before their engagement was announced, that he bet the Icicle would be a lousy lay. I owe that guy an apology, thought the man who had married her.

So now he was paying his bill, and getting out of the restaurant, and it was the moment of choice. He didn't have to go to Rosette's, and if Eve had "asked him nicely", as he wanted, he wouldn't have gone near the damned place. He just happened to be strolling in that direction.

At that hour, early in the night, the Grande Rue de Pera was a promenade for young men. The luxury shops, closed for business but still lighted, were a prime excuse for loitering and staring; the boy prostitutes lingered in the doorways, with sloe-eyed glances right and left into the darkness of the alleys. Jeff Barrett did not loiter, he walked on, dodging the tramcars, but he was solicited three times before he came abreast of the Galata Saray. He passed Tokatlian's restaurant, and thought of Miss Windsor's birthday party, and that great mare of a Jean Elliott waltzing with that stuffed-shirt naval officer to violins played by Russian refugees. A chaperone, and home to mummy at half past ten! "It's a queer world!" he said aloud, and with that he was where he had intended to be, ever since he started down the hill from Chankaya.

The scent-shop was not far from Tokatlian's on the one side, from the Cercle d'Orient on the other, in the most fashionable part of the Grande Rue de Pera on the way to Taksim Square. The name flowed across the plate glass window in white enamel lettering

Parfums　　ROSETTE　　*Colifichets*

easily legible although the shop front was in darkness, so that the scent bottles, boxes of powder and rouge, diamanté combs and beaten silver bracelets were hidden from view. But there was a light in the flat immediately above, and Jeff, releasing his held breath in a long sigh, turned down the narrow street which ran beside the shop to Rosette's private door. He had never been sure where, in that old warren of dwellings, the tenants of the upper apartments entered, but he did know that there was also a staircase which led from the back of the shop to Rosette's flat, and that it suited some of her clients very well to use two entrances and exits.

Jeff knocked at the street door several times before there was an answer. Then he heard the well-remembered creak of the carpetless staircase, and knew that she would come close to the door 'and look out through the judas. "Open up, Rosie," he said cheerfully, "it's me—Jeff Barrett."

"Jeff! You naughty boy! Are you alone?"

"Sure."

He heard the chain being taken off, and the door was opened. Jeff was enfolded in two lean powerful arms, sleeved in some sequinned fabric which scratched his cheek, and in the cloud of scent and perfumed powder which normally surrounded Rosette Mavros. They kissed each other by the light of the little oil lamp above the door.

"I am so happy to see you, bad boy, but why didn't you telephone, or send a messenger?"

"No time, Rosie, I just got here. Don't tell me you're not pleased to see me?"

"Pleased? I'm delighted, Jeff, of course, only tonight I 'ave a guest—"

"Am I butting in on something? Aren't you going to invite me upstairs?"

The woman made up her mind. "I think 'e won't stay very long. He has an important engagement, I know that. Yes, come up, *mon petit* Jeff, 'ere you are at home, no?"

She went before him up the creaking stair, with her neat haunches swaying in the black satin dress which was almost a uniform for the women of Pera. In the brighter light on the landing he saw that the sequins on her sleeves were copper-coloured, almost the same shade as the copper dye she used on her hair, and her black eyes were as shrewd as ever.

"A French officer," she said in a stage whisper, "just returned from Paris. Ver' clever man! You'll see!"

She ushered Jeff into a stuffy little salon, crowded with the inevitable sofa, velvet armchairs and round table. There was no sign of Leila, whom Jeff had so often seen curled up on the sofa like a kitten, singing to her guitar. There was only the French officer, rising to a great height, and accepting the introduction of Jeff with glum condescension.

"*Le commandant* Cravache!" said Rosette Mavros. "Monsieur Barrett, a famous American newspaper correspondent, just returned from Angora."

"From Angora," said Major Cravache heavily. His rather dull

66

eyes, hooded by heavy lids, showed a spark of interest. "Did you make a long stay there, monsieur?"

"Just a month, this trip, but I was there for quite a while last year."

"Monsieur Barrett reported the battle of the Sakarya for 'is American readers," said Rosette.

A twist of Cravache's small pouting mouth showed what he thought of the American press. The mouth, under a clipped dark moustache, seemed oddly out of proportion to the rest of his features, which were arranged in a series of ellipses, the pouches beneath the eyes symmetric with the rings of flesh which marked the beginnings of a double chin. He held his small head awkwardly on his long neck, like a camel.

"Well, how are you, Rosette, and how's Leila?" said Jeff.

"Leila? She's very well, and prettier than ever. *N'est ce pas, mon commandant?*"

Cravache flapped one limp hand as if despising prettiness.

"Isn't she going to join us?" persisted Jeff.

"She isn't here, *mon cher*, she 'ad to go out this evening. She'll be sorry to 'ave missed you."

"What time do you expect her home?"

"You must 'ave a glass of brandy, Jeff." Rosette was talking to Barrett, but she looked at the Frenchman, and moved her red head imperceptibly towards the door.

"Thanks, Rosette. What's your opinion on the situation at Chatalja, major?"

"The British will not fight. The Lion roars, but has no spirit left for biting." Major Cravache was not drinking brandy; he had a half-empty glass of beer in his hand, and it struck Jeff that without the uniform and the Great War ribbons, Cravache would look like any coarse-featured French shopkeeper pontificating at a corner table of a smalltown Café du Commerce.

"I think the British have a lot of guts," he said.

"I fought with them in Syria, monsieur, and I know better."

The pouting mouth snapped as if to end all future argument. Cravache stood up and reached for his gloves and képi, which he had laid on top of his riding crop. He was not wearing the insignia of a cavalry regiment, but many Allied officers carried a whip or a fly-whisk in the streets of Constantinople. It was a symbol

67

of the Occupation much disliked by the Turkish population.

"I'll show you to the door, *mon commandant.*" Rosette was on her feet at once. The two men nodded at each other without more words. Jeff, left to himself, looked round the familiar room. The scent of perfume was strong enough to drown the odour of a half-smoked cigar, and Jeff deduced that Rosette and the old man who worked in her basement had been brewing up a new batch of her celebrated violet hair wash. The smell never quite came out of the heavy velvet drapes. Behind the sofa was a collection of photographs, arranged with some art on the red flock wallpaper, and ranging from the *cartes de visite* of the previous century to the snapshots of the Nineteen Twenties; according to Rosette nearly all the subjects were members of her family. She was popularly supposed to be a Jewess, but she undoubtedly had Christian relatives in Smyrna, of whom the girl Leila was one. Rosette Mavros claimed to have cousins in Beirut who were Maronite Christians, relatives in Athens who were Greek Orthodox, and kinsmen in Alexandria who professed the Coptic faith. From this melting-pot of city and creed Rosette had emerged a true Levantine, as complete a product of Pera as any trader in human flesh since the Galata Tower was built.

One unexpected picture was a cabinet photograph of the deposed Sultan Abdul Hamid II, called Abdul the Damned. There was a legend in the Grande Rue that as a beautiful red-haired girl of twenty Rosette had been seen by the Sultan on one of his rare visits to the Sweet Waters of Asia, and after a stay in one of his pleasure kiosks at Yildiz had returned to Pera with the wherewithal to set herself up in the scent shop. This story, after the war, she would neither confirm nor deny, but the picture of the tyrant with his haunted black eyes and huge hooked nose still held the place of honour in the middle of Rosette's portrait gallery.

Jeff Barrett heard the murmur of French on the landing, and subconsciously waited for the sound of feet going downstairs. He heard nothing but the sound of a door opening and closing, he was by no means certain it was the door on the street. If it was, Rosette and her visitor must have gone down the creaking stair like mice. The silence began to get on Jeff's nerves. He remembered the crop in the Frenchman's hand; the fellow was all keyed up, he was beating it against his boot when he nodded goodbye to

68

Jeff. The American remembered the horses moving off down the lane on Saturday morning, and Colonel Arif offering his riding whip to Evelyn with the words, *"Voulez-vous une cravache, madame?"* Rosette, with a heightened colour, returned to the room.

"One of your regulars, Rosie?"

"Cravache? Oh no! 'E is very serious, him."

"That's a funny sort of moniker he's got. Is it some sort of a *nom de guerre*? I thought Cravache was the French word for a whip."

"Yes, *une cravache* is a whip, *mon cher*, but it is 'is family name. Per'aps it's a northern name; 'e is Lilleois, I believe."

"He may be a clever guy, but he sure has it in for the British. Say, why did you shut me up when I asked about Leila? Is Cravache interested in her?"

"In a chit of a girl like Leila? Of course not!"

"Why not? Is he queer?"

"Naughty boy! 'E simply isn't sexy, 'e is too interested in *la politique*. In Paris, they say, 'e is ver' close to Monsieur Franklin-Bouillon, who 'elped to make that treaty with Kemal."

"Say, what's become of good old Boiling Frankie, has he turned up again?"

"Naughty boy!" said Rosette automatically, "you picked up that silly name from the British. Monsieur Franklin-Bouillon is in Paris; Cravache is 'is—how shall I say—unofficial representative here."

"Well, for a French publicist turned Deputy, old Frankie sure is going up in the world if he needs a representative. What about Cravache himself? Is he going into politics too?"

"'E means some day to be the President of the French Republic," said Rosette solemnly.

"Oh balls," said Jeff. ". . . Look here, Rosie, you still haven't told me why you didn't answer when I asked you what time Leila would be home."

"She won't be home till two o'clock, *mon cher*. She's got a job now, singing in cabaret."

"What cabaret, for God's sake?"

Rosette again evaded his question. "Come now, you knew she was 'oping to appear in public. It was you who praised 'er singing so highly last year, wasn't it?"

"I never thought you'd let her work in cabaret."

Rosette shrugged. "What can I do? When 'er poor old grand-mother begged me to take Leila away from Smyrna, when the troubles broke out three years ago, I let 'er come here to help in the shop and make 'erself useful. But trade is bad, Jeff, is ver' ver' bad in Pera. Nobody knows if that bandit in Angora will give up 'is fight, or if 'e comes down from the mountains to destroy us all. I can't afford to keep a *jeune fille* eating 'er head off and singing to 'er guitar. So I allowed 'er to ask for a chance to sing at the Palais Kristal."

Jeff was not listening. He had heard Rosette's complaints before. His ear had caught another sound: a man's tread, deliberately softened, coming along the corridor which led to the bedrooms, crossing the landing, going down the creaking stair. Realising that the woman had stopped, and was waiting for him to speak, he caught at her last words, and said,

"The Kristal! So that's where she is right now?"

"*Attendez voir!* She got an audience—no, how do you call it, an audition at the Kristal. It was no damn good. Napoo, as the Tommies say. I warned 'er before we started—because, *bien entendu*, I went with 'er, me, to show those people they had Rosette Mavros to reckon with if they made Leila bad proposals —yes, I warned 'er to sing something *très connu*, something created in Paris, by Spinelli, by Mistinguett. Paris is what they want in Pera, Paris is the stuff to give the troops—*n'est ce pas*, Jeff?"

"She knew a whole slew of French songs," said Jeff.

"But this silly little Leila insisted to sing them first a Turkish song, an old style *gazel*, like she used to sing to you and Rafferty; and then, though I made the signs to her, imitating Mistinguett, she next sang 'Maid of Athens' and then burst into tears. I tell you, Jeff, *mon vieux copain*, if I had tears left to shed *I* should have shed them, me, to see the faces of *ces messieurs* of the Palais Kristal. The musical director said, ver' nicely, that 'Maid of Athens' is a song for a man, and the manager said 'You will 'ear from us'. That was the last of it, of course, as I told 'er it would be, as soon as I got 'er home."

"But you just said she *was* singing in cabaret!"

"Yes, but not at the Kristal."

"Where then?"

Rosette refilled the glasses. With a slightly defiant air she said, "In the chorus at the Petits Champs."

"You let her go to *that* dump?"

"It was 'er own wish, *mon cher*. And I don't know how Leila's career can conern *you*."

"Do you expect her to have a *career* at the Petits Champs?"

"It is a start in show business, after all. What 'appens now is up to Leila. She can work 'ard, and earn good money, or she can let 'erself be ruined, and die on straw as her mother did in Athens eighteen years ago. Leila, at least, 'as a good home to come back to every night."

"A *good* home, Rosie?"

The powdered face hardened viciously. "Now don' get fresh with me, my friend. I tell you frankly, I'm not too pleased with you. I remember when your friend Rafferty first brought you 'ere when you both came out of Anatolia. You 'ad been in combat and you wanted women. I got two pretty girls for you, you 'ad a nice party, *une belle partouze*, eh? You came back for more, of course. Then Rafferty was recalled and you came alone, but not for my call girls, oh no! To talk to *me*, and ask questions about this one and that one, men who have used my rooms as you used them; you say you never print what I tell you, but who knows? I admit you 'ere, to my own salon, and what 'appens? You turn poor little Leila's head. You make 'er think she is a great singer, a cabaret queen. You spoil 'er for selling in my shop or pleasing the ladies who come here privately. Then you go away. That, she can bear. She knew you were not 'ere to stay. But you come back to Constant., and this time you bring your wife."

"You both knew I was married, Rosie."

"*Yes*, and you told me Madame Barrett does not understand you. You know something, Jeff? I think that lady, with the proud face, I think she understand you very well. She despised me and Leila at the Pera Palace, that I saw, but I think she despise you too, Jeff, and maybe she is right."

"Oh cut it out," said Jeff. "Eve did not either despise you! She was shy when she came to Constant., and when Evelyn's shy she acts stiff—"

"You don't 'ave to explain. Leila was hurt, much hurt, because she 'ave this *béguin* for you, but now she makes new friends at the cabaret, and she forget you soon. I tell 'er not to be a fool, I tell 'er when *I* was young I knew 'ow to make my *marché*—"

Her black eyes moved to the dead Sultan's photograph.

71

"You? You'd sell her to the highest bidder, and take your cut on the deal!"

"Are you prepared to join in the bidding, Jeff?"

Jeff Barrett uncoiled his long limbs from the armchair. "I'll be on my way, Rosette. See you around some time." He opened the door, and the woman followed him to the landing without a word. All was silent in the scented flat. Jeff said casually,

"Not doing any business here tonight? Been in trouble with the MPs at last?"

"I spit upon the Military Police," said Rosette Mavros. "I gave up my Army customers six months ago. Only ladies come to meet their *chères amies* here now, *mon petit*. So much quieter and more discreet than men!"

"*Women* use this as a house of call—with other women?"

"Ah, now *monsieur l'américain* is really shocked! You don' know your Constant., Jeff. The 'abits of the harem will take a long time to die!"

* * *

The night was airless and tainted as Jeff Barrett returned down the Rue des Petits Champs to the cabaret behind the theatre on the verge of the old graveyard. It was late enough for all the concierges in that ambiguous neighbourhood to have set out their dustbins for the morning collection, and even at the door of the Cabaret des Petits Champs there was a line of the tall iron bins, brimming with the refuse of the night before. The ragpickers of Pera, who came out of their cellars as the evening wore on, made raids on the dustbins while the doorman's back was turned, and carried their loot into the shadow of the cypress trees lining the cemetery walls. Some of the filthy bundles of trash, from which even the ragpickers could extract nothing of value, were actually smouldering as Jeff went by. A cigarette butt, a lit match thrown away might start a combustion of stained cloths and tarnished tinsel which would burn for hours, unheeded, between the broken paving stones.

Although Rosette Mavros called the Petits Champs a start in show business, for most of the European artistes it was the abysmal end. The programme on an average night was composed of rejects from the music-halls and night clubs of Bucharest and

Sofia, with a sprinkling of blonde English and German dancers whose best days were over before the Great War, but who kept the war alive by a series of noisy rows in the dressing-rooms heard and enjoyed by the bored audience. The turns alternated with dancing, and the little floor was crowded with American sailors and their girls as the *maître d'hôtel* led Jeff to a table in the centre of the room. The curtains of the stage were drawn and the footlights extinguished.

"Good show tonight?" he asked the man, who with a snap of the fingers had already brought a waiter hurrying with the bottle of sweet champagne and the two glasses which were standard equipment for every table at the Petits Champs.

"First-class show, yes *sir*! Top of the bill, Mam'selle Zizi, favourite of the Folies Bergère! You care to see the supper menu, sir?"

"Not yet," said Jeff. "What time do your singing girls come on?"

"In about a quarter of an hour, sir, they present their first *tour de chant*. American hits which you are certain to enjoy!"

"Right. But don't open the champagne until I tell you."

"Monsieur is expecting a guest?"

"Possibly," said Jeff. "Right now I want a cup of coffee— filter, not your Turkish stuff."

"*Un bon filtre, parfaitement, monsieur.*"

A decent cup of coffee might settle his stomach. The nausea which he had felt when he saw the murdered man in the hotel room had returned, made worse by the assortment of drinks he had had since his arrival in the city. Rye, sherry, Scotch, raki, cheap brandy; he hadn't had a lot of any one, but they seemed to have mixed badly in his stomach and to be spinning in a head wearied by the long sequence of events since he woke in the Nationalist camp outside Ismid. The coffee was brought quickly, and was good; Jeff sat sipping it and wondering if he might be smart to let himself be clipped for once. He only had to lay down the money for the wine and get out; get back to the Pera Palace and catch a good night's sleep before the early start to the Chatalja Lines. He didn't *have* to stay and speak to Leila. Better let the kid forget him— Rosette was dead right there.

But then Jeff thought of Rosette's house of call, closed now to soldiers and foreign correspondents but open to lesbians, and poor little Leila moving between that house, where she was expected to "please the ladies"—God! and this rotten cabaret, where she would get her commission on the wine if she pleased the gentlemen. Pet Leila, singing "Maid of Athens" at the Kristal because it had been his own little name for her, and bursting into tears at her pathetic audition! Was he really responsible for so much unhappiness? And the basic sentimentality of Jeff Barrett's nature, which his wife was not capable of understanding, told him to stay still, to see poor little Leila once again—just one more time.

His thoughts shifted to Major Charles Cravache. All his instinct for a story—which, though it sometimes played him false, was good—told him that there was something wildly improbable in a politically ambitious Frenchman's dropping in for a quiet glass of beer with a woman like Rosette Mavros. Jeff was pretty sure that Cravache had a girl, or more probably a boy, in one of those sleazy bedrooms down the hall. He had gone back there to leave a present, or make another date, before the stair creaked and he left the house. It might be interesting to know more about Major Cravache and his background.

But at that moment the lights went up on the stage, the curtains parted, and the pony line pranced out kicking high and squealing, the singing girls behind them beginning the "Wild Rose" number from—as promised—an American hit show called *Sally*.

> "She's jussa—wile rose,
> Notta prim—and mil' rose!"

The singers were got up in a travesty of harem dress, with trousers of transparent golden gauze and bodices edged with gilt coins which swayed above their bare midriffs. They were heavily made up with kohl and mascara, their eyelashes beaded "in threes", their faces half covered by tinsel veils. Jeff could not distinguish Leila from the others. Then her voice came through to him, pure and warm, as he had often heard it:

> "Some passion flower,
> This is her hour—"

and there she was, the second from the left, by far the youngest and also the prettiest of those painted girls. It was with irrational anger that he saw her, when the next number started, seized in the

74

arms of one of the muscular girl dancers. Across the stage the girls were pairing off, dancers with singers, into a wild foxtrot of hugging and writhing which made Jeff remember Rosette's comment on the habits of the harem. The Turks in the audience gasped and sighed as the veils were flung off and the legs jerked under the transparent gauze. And all the girls, entwined, were singing

"I'm the Sheik—of A-rabee
Your love—belongs to me-ee!"

Jeff saw his own taunt to Evelyn acted out with vile suggestiveness by the cabaret girls of Pera. The Arab chieftain and the English lady! *"Diane, obey me!"* *"Ahmed! Monseigneur!"* *"Madame Evelyn!"* *"Excellence!"*

It was the last thing he needed to push him over the edge. As soon as the number ended Jeff scribbled a few words on his card and gave it to the hovering waiter. "For Mademoiselle Mavros," he said curtly. "I expect she'll be joining me. I want a better table, not quite so public, and bring a bottle of decent champagne instead of this rotgut."

"Monsieur would prefer one of the alcoves by the trellis?"

"Yes."

"This way, please."

The way to the trellis lay between the tables. The place was filling up now, and one large party of men wearing the red fez politely moved their chairs back a few inches to let the American pass. One looked up and met Jeff's eyes: it was Hamdi Bey.

Jeff Barrett had the wits, as the Turkish officer's black eyes stared up at him without a trace of recognition, to pass on without moving a muscle of his face. He sat down in the alcove, which was formed by lattices woven with dirty artifical flowers, and moved his chair to get a better view of Captain Hamdi and his friends. He had not been mistaken, it *was* Kemal's aide-de-camp, from whom he had parted—Hamdi in the Nationalist *kalpak* and khaki—outside Ismid nearly eighteen hours before. "He must have come up on the same train with me," he thought. "How the hell did he get through the British check-point? And what's his business in Constantinople?" The three men with Hamdi were all strangers to him. One had his right arm in a sling. Jeff remembered all that Braun had said in his little office, while the body of Trakas lay in a pool of blood upstairs, about the

Nationalist officers who were infiltrating Constantinople, kidnapping their opponents into silence and to death. He remembered that somewhere in this city, where such dark forces were abroad tonight, there was a man with a knife wound—in his murderous right arm perhaps—dealt by an old man in desperate defence of his life.

"This is the best champagne in our cellar, monsieur," said the waiter, arriving at his side. "And the lady is coming."

"What is it? Veuve Clicquot '18? Yes, that'll do. And can't you bring some roses, or real flowers of some kind? It smells like the devil up here against the open trellis."

"It's the smouldering rags outside, sir, the *chiffoniers* come round stealing from the bins, and the doorkeeper throws water over the trash . . . I'm sorry, sir. I'll bring red roses, instantly."

But Leila came before the roses, making her way between the tables with her dark head high, and responding only with nervous smiles to the men who invited her to sit down and have a drink. Her stage costume was covered by a long light cloak of violet silk. Under the stage make-up her face was as fresh as a nectarine, her brow, nose, lips and chin as beautifully modelled as a face on an old Greek coin.

She came up to the alcove timidly, looking for Jeff through the shadows and the candlelight. Then he stood up, and when she saw he was alone Leila Mavros almost ran towards him with her hands outstretched.

"Oh Jeff, you are coming back!"

He took her hands, and swung her round, so that his tall body was between her and the floor of the cabaret, a fourth wall to the tawdry alcove.

"Yes, Leila, I've come back."

"Did the lady . . ?"

"No," he said. "No. I'm all alone."

"Oh-h!" He felt Leila's small body relax against him, and he stooped down to kiss her, gathering her close in his arms, while he felt her ready tears upon his cheek.

"And you are coming here—just to see me?"

"Yes, baby," said Jeff Barrett, "only for you." His mouth was in her hair, on her lips, on her neck: the freshness of her skin and the scent on her soft hands dominated the smell of burning from the Little Fields of the Dead.

76

5

THE ANGORA PRESS REPORTED the Trakas murder very
briefly, adding that suspicion now rested on a man employed
in the kitchens of the Pera Palace, the only member of the
staff not present and accounted for in the police check. This news
item aroused no comment, for Angora had lived on wilder
sensations for nearly three years, ever since the night in December
1919 when, after his seven months' trek across Anatolia, Kemal
had been escorted into the little mountain town by bands of the
local men and even women, dancing in the starlight, clashing
cymbals and singing to celebrate the coming of the Revolution.
Before that great night, Angora had lived through two thousand
years of recorded history. The Hittites, the Galatians, the Byzantine Greeks and the Ottoman Turks had successively made a
battleground of the Angora plateau, and the citizens, barricaded
in their citadel, had become inured through the centuries to
murder and starvation.

Before the coming of Kemal, however, the centre of activity in
Angora had shifted from the citadel high on its rock to the marshy
valley below, so far celebrated for nothing but malaria. In that
valley, in the days of Sultan Abdul Hamid II, the German
engineers who built the *Bagdadbahn* had marked out the terminal
of a spur line from the railway's junction at Eskishehir, and a
telegraph office—always an important part of the Sultan's
espionage network—was built beside it. The Young Turks, officially known as the Committee of Union and Progress, and to
their enemies as those damned *komitajis,* added a few more
modern buildings after they swept Abdul Hamid from his throne.
This was the new hub of Angora, which in the week after Jeff's
departure Evelyn Barrett visited every day.

It was a long walk in the hot August mornings, but she
was always able to hire one of the gaily painted, horse-drawn
carts called arabas to drive her back to Kavaklidere, as the slope
where the vines and poplars grew was beginning to be called. And

Evelyn went willingly, for she was very anxious to visit the telegraph office early each day so as to keep in close touch with
Chicago. But after the message relayed to Jeff no further instructions or queries arrived from Mr. Donnelly, although from Jeff
himself one telegram was received on the second of August. It
read:

> Going press camp chatalja but still contactable perapalace stop
> please ask monseigneur for bioperse commandant charles
> cravache attached french high commission love jeff

Evelyn stood in the dusty yard outside the telegraph office and
wondered what the English-speaking clerk had made of that.
Monseigneur, of course, was the silly nickname from *The Sheik*
which Jeff had pinned on Kemal Pasha; she had no idea how
Kemal himself would react to a request for "biographical and
personal" information about an officer in the French Army.
Meantime it was impossible to ask him, for Kemal had left the
city and was far away at Akshekir, the forward headquarters of his
Western Army. He had gone there to see an Army football
match, an engagement which aroused some criticism in the
National Assembly, where the Deputies were thirsting after blood.

So Evelyn was told by Abdul the son of Riad, Jeff's stringer,
an excitable elderly Turk who had learned English at the famous
Robert College in Constantinople and now worked for an Angora
paper. He translated the newspapers well, although he had an
annoying habit of tacking some wild speculation of his own
on to the information he put into English, and also of shouting
"There you are!" in a patronising way, after he had finished an
explanation for the ignorant Americans. Evelyn found Abdul
chiefly useful in buying her something to eat at noon from
the shanty which served as the station buffet. It was only
pide bread and cheese, but with Abdul as messenger she could at
least eat it in the fresh air. All the eating places in Angora were
terribly crowded, like the few hotels where not only the rooms,
shared by ten or twelve men, were numbered, but even each
separate step of the wooden stairs, one sleeper allocated to
every step. Evelyn's only luxury in that first week of August
was luncheon at the home of the Swiss manager of the
Osmanli Bank. His wife, a lively lady from Lugano, knew
how to make the very best of the extra food supplies which

sometimes arrived from the Bank's head office in Constantinople.

There was not much to do at the Relief Mission depot, but Evelyn decided to go there on Saturday afternoon, when Jeff had been away from Angora for a week. There had been great doings at the station that day, when everybody from the offices and even from the workshops turned out to see a new detachment of troops entraining for the front. They arrived in army lorries, tall Circassians and Kurds, some of the former as blond as the Commander-in-Chief himself, some of the latter belonging to the tribes which had risen against his authority in the early days of the Revolution. It had been the worst moment of his fight for independence, when his enemies faced him on all fronts, the Sultan's government and the Allies in Constantinople, the French in the south, the Greeks in the west, and the rebellious tribesmen in the east. He had lived through it: the rebels became auxiliaries and, finally, disciplined troops, an integral part of the Nationalist Army. Let us march, friends! Evelyn, in her yellow cotton dress and wide-brimmed white hat, stood well back in the station yard and watched sympathetically as the crowd joined in the singing. It was a valiant departure, considering that Eskishehir Junction was in the hands of the Greeks, and that probably the train could carry the new troops no further than Polatli.

The battered Ford truck was in its usual place in the yard of the Relief Mission depot, but there was no sign of George, the Armenian driver, who was generally found squatting beside his vehicle, an object of respect to the small boys of the neighbourhood. But when Evelyn knocked, the door was opened by George himself, freshly shaved, and wearing a houseman's white linen jacket above his shabby trousers and cloth slippers.

"Why, George, how smart you look!" smiled Evelyn, and then, looking beyond him into the livingroom, "Oh, dear, you're having a party!"

"We didn't expect you today, Evie, and that's a fact, but I'm real glad you stopped by," said Miss Mabel Livermore, coming forward hospitably. "We just got word this morning that our dear old pupil, Madame Emine, would be free to visit us this afternoon. I just said to Lily, didn't I, Lily, what a treat it would be for Evie Barrett to meet her—"

"Oh, but I'm not going to stay!" Evelyn quickly reassured the two flustered old ladies. "I know how much Madame Emine's visits mean to you, you'll want to have her all to yourselves. She was your star pupil, wasn't she?"

"She was the brightest girl who was ever graduated from the American College," said Miss Lily solemnly, "and just as lovely as she was smart. Do you remember what a beautiful bride she was, Mabel?"

"Do I not!" sighed the elder sister. "Lily and I were among the lady guests at Emine's wedding, Evie. Now that would be a nice experience for you to share—a Turkish wedding."

"I know she's a widow now," said Evelyn, "Has she any children?"

"No, that's what's so sad. She and Fuad Bey were only married a year before he was killed."

Evelyn nodded sympathetically. She had often heard the two old ladies, superannuated teachers from the American Women's College in Constantinople, speak of the legendary Emine, who had made a daring escape from the capital dressed as a gipsy, to put part of her considerable fortune at the disposal of the Revolution.

"She lives out at Chubuk, doesn't she?"

"Yes. It's a mite too far to walk every day—oh, not as far as you walk, Evie, but you're young—and she's given up her saddle horse. She hasn't quite so many irons in the fire now, since she quarrelled with You-Know-Who."

"But she was never one of his ladies, dearie, you mustn't think that," said Miss Lily impulsively, and Evelyn caught the slightest shake of Miss Mabel's fluffy white head.

"I'm not even going to sit down," she said firmly. "I know you don't like to open the depot on Sundays, so I just thought I'd find out if any supplies came in today that George and I could deliver on Monday."

"Nothing came in today but a letter from the Fisters at Konya, asking for any surplus we could give them. Surplus! When we've only got a few cans of powdered milk left from the last consignment."

"I believe you're lonely, dearie, out in that wild place all by yourself, you're so eager to be at work," said Miss Lily shrewdly. "When is hubby coming home?"

"I really don't know, they've set up a press camp at Chatalja now, so—" She broke off as George, with a very deep bow, announced:

"The Hanim Efendi!"

The lady who came in had certainly once been beautiful. The outlines of her heart-shaped face were a little blurred and heavy now, and there were fine lines at the corners of her large black eyes, but her figure was still as slender as a girl's. Madame Emine wore a walking dress of pale grey, the top almost concealed by the folds of a black silk headdress caught by a pearl brooch beneath her chin. She greeted the Mission ladies as dear friends, and held out her hand to Evelyn.

"I'm delighted to meet you at last, Mrs. Barrett. I've been hearing so much about you lately, from Colonel Arif and others."

"I believe my husband had the pleasure of meeting you last year, Emine Hanim," said Evelyn. Jeff had in fact described the lady as the biggest goddamned bore in Anatolia, bar none.

"Yes, we met several times after the Sakarya," said Emine with a smile so sour under the sweetness that Evelyn's own mouth contracted slightly, as if she had bitten into a persimmon fruit.

"Evie's husband's at the Chatalja Lines right now," said Miss Mabel. "We depend on her for all the latest news."

"I haven't any real news from Chatalja," said Evelyn, "but in Angora today I saw a magnificent body of men, mostly Kurds and Circassians, entraining for some point up the line—Polatli, I believe."

"*More* troops from the mountains," said Emine with a sigh. "Kemal is fortunate in finding so many men to die for him."

"Here comes George with the tea-pot," said Evelyn. "I really must be going now."

"Come and have tea with *me* some day, and tell me about America," said Emine graciously. "I have so many dear friends there."

"Thank you, I'd like that." Evelyn said her goodbyes and made her escape from the awkward little encounter. She was not anxious to know the Turkish lady better: that persimmons smile, the burning eyes, and the intensity Madame Emine gave to the simplest remark warned the girl that here was a neurotic personality rather than a pleasant friend. But the sight of Miss Mabel's dainty tea-table, on which the great treat of a fruit cake had the place of honour, stayed with Evelyn as a reminder that she herself was both hungry and thirsty. On the way back to the

81

station she went into the public garden opposite the National Assembly to buy a drink of ayran.

It was a dusty little garden, laid out on a roughly levelled plateau at the top of a slope, and not improved by the existence, at the foot of the slope, of a large park for army lorries. There were some scrub trees, none of which had yet grown to their full height, some public benches, and stances for one or two vendors of sweets and soft drinks. Evelyn went up smiling to the woman who sold ayran; she was a fat, jolly person rather like Ayesha, who was always willing to help her American customer to practise her Turkish. The little cart from which she sold ayran and sherbet was a delight to see; the beverages ran out of taps shaped like lions' heads, and on the front panel, of brightly polished brass, there was an outline of the Crescent and the Star.

The Crescent and the Star on the national flag floated from the roof of the National Assembly. Evelyn sipped the ayran, which tasted rather like buttermilk, and looked across the wide dusty road at the Assembly building. It always looked so curious standing there on its own, with nothing but fields and the wide steppe beyond; she had never been inside, and it was hard to realise that inside that incongruous building the destiny of a nation was being forged. The place was an architectural insult to the splendid landscape of Anatolia. Erected by the Young Turks in their brief heyday, it was built of the local stone with a red tiled roof and fussy bay windows, like an English parish hall or an outsize golf club-house. The horses which several Deputies rode to the daily sessions were tethered to the rails, as in a Western movie; today, still an object of wonder to some of the bystanders, there were also two open touring cars.

Evelyn, as interested in the unusual sight as the Turkish women peering over their veils or the heads of the swaddled infants in their arms, did not identify either of the cars for a moment. Then she said aloud, "Why, that's the Benz!" and handing back the drinking cup impulsively started to cross the road. It was certainly the old Benz in which Jeff had left for Angora, the new tyres now covered with patches, and even while she looked at it, wondering where the passengers were, and where Jeff was, Captain Hamdi came running down the steps of the Assembly.

"Mrs. Barrett! This is a pleasant surprise! Can I give you a lift on your way home? Or aren't you ready to go home yet?"

"Perfectly. I was on my way to the station to pick up an araba."

"Then do let me take you, I was just—here's my driver—just going to Chankaya, so it's the easiest thing in the world to drop you off."

"How marvellous," said Evelyn, getting into the car. "I always drive back, but the araba horses take a long time on the road, poor little beasts."

"Chankaya," said Captain Hamdi to the soldier-driver. He showed Evelyn a sealed packet in his hand. "I had to collect some papers from the Gazi's office," he explained. "He's at Akshehir headquarters, and his secretary wants some information in a hurry."

"Captain Hamdi, when did you come back from Ismid?"

"This morning, madame."

"Did you bring my husband with you? Is he at our house now?"

Captain Hamdi looked at her. He was not a favourite with Evelyn Barrett, who found his manner supercilious and over-confident, but now there was nothing but surprise in his look.

"He didn't plan to come back with our party," he said. "Didn't you know that?"

To her annoyance Evelyn found herself stammering. "N-no, I —I don't quite know what I thought," she confessed. "He went away in such a hurry, and I was typing for him up to the last moment, we didn't discuss . . . somehow I thought he meant to come as he went, with you. Then when I saw the car—"

"Hasn't he been in touch with you at all?" said Hamdi Bey, amused. "You must scold your wandering boy for that when you get him back, Mrs. Barrett."

"Certainly he's been in touch with me by telegram," said Evelyn coldly. "He's probably still at the press camp at Chatalja."

"He's not at Chatalja all the time," said Hamdi, and now his smile was as supercilious as Evelyn remembered. "I saw him last Monday evening in a Constantinople restaurant."

"You were in Constantinople— But how?"

"Oh, we come and go pretty much as we please now, getting ready for the great day."

"So did you and Jeff have dinner together? Was it at the Pera Palace?"

"It was not," said Hamdi. "And it wasn't really a restaurant, it was a night club. The Petits Champs, do you know it? No, your husband wouldn't take *you* there. But he seemed to be enjoying himself very much with that pretty little girl from the scent shop in the Rue de Pera. She's singing at the night club now."

*　　　*　　　*

At ten o'clock that night Evelyn Barrett was sitting in the patio of her little house among the fruit trees, where a cool breeze was bringing some quiet to her spirit. She had tried to keep busy from the moment Captain Hamdi, smiling, had bowed over her hand at the corner of the lane, first in helping Ahmed and Ayesha in their nightly struggle to round up a dozen skinny fowls and shut them into the hen-roost, and then in taking as refreshing a tepid bath as was possible in the zinc tub. She washed the dust of the Angora roads out of her hair, so that golden lights appeared in the straight ash-blond bob which now fell uncut to the firm line of her jaw. She put on the coral red dress of fine Brusa silk which she had bought in the Grand Bazaar at Constantinople, and the gilt bazaar slippers with the turned-up toes. Instead of lighting the charcoal brazier in the patio, used for cooking meals outdoors, she ate some cold food and made some coffee over the spirit lamp. Then she sat down at the deal table to write a letter to her parents.

"Dearest Dad and Mother, Angora really is the most incredible place—"

It was no good. As one stilted paragraph followed another, San Francisco became the incredible place, lost in a mirage at the other side of the world, and only Angora was real. The lamp beside her on the table, for which she was careful to use only the one rationed measure of petroleum each evening, grew hot and smoky in the little room. At last Evelyn put the unfinished letter in her writing case, took two of Ayesha's embroidered cushions from the hard divan and laid them on the stone door step. She sat there, leaning against the doorpost with only the moon for company, thinking of Jeff and "that little Levantine" at the cabaret and listening to the clink of hammers in the distant army workshops. The sound filled the night silence so completely that Evelyn failed to hear the quiet footsteps on the dead leaves in the lane. She was startled when a big brown retriever ran into the yard and stood wagging his tail beside her.

"Dog! Where did *you* come from?" But then Evelyn realised that the dog's master must be near, and rising in one lithe movement she looked beneath the moonlit boughs to the already open gate, where Kemal waited with his hand on the top bar.

"*On peut entrer, madame?*" he said.

"*Soyez le bienvenu, Excellence*—you are welcome!" She held out her hand to him, and Kemal crossed the patio quickly and kissed it. "Have you missed me?" he said.

"I missed our morning rides."

"I've been at Akshekir HQ for the past few days."

"Watching a football match, they said."

The moon was nearly at its full, and in its clear light the loose bright hair, the flowing kaftan and the gilt slippers seemed to have transformed the horsewoman of the steppe. "You're lovely tonight," Kemal told her. "And dressed like a Turkish girl, too!"

"I don't look like a Turkish girl, surely?"

"My mother was fairer than you are, when she was young," Kemal said quickly. "But why were you sitting on the ground, *à la Turque*? I don't like to see that."

"It's more comfortable than the divan. And talking about looks, I think *you* look like an English country gentleman this evening."

Kemal grinned. "My quarrel with the British doesn't extend to my London tailor." He was wearing a brown tweed suit and brown brogue shoes, and with the brown retriever at his side there was something of the country squire about him, which suited the quiet orchards and the scent of fruit. Evelyn drew a long breath. Kemal was back, and loneliness and bitterness melted away in the warmth of his presence. "Will you come indoors, *Excellence*?" she said, "or shall we sit outside? There *are* chairs—"

His answer was to pick up the cushions from the doorstep and lay them on the broad coping of the well.

"Let's sit here," he said, and obediently she sat down beside him, while the dog, at a word, lay down near the charcoal *mangal* and crossed his paws.

"When did you come back from Akshehir?" the girl enquired.

"This morning, just before noon. I was chained to my desk until dinner-time, and then I had to go to see my mother."

"How *is* Zübeyde Hanim?"

"Much as usual."

"Captain Hamdi drove me back from the town this afternoon. He didn't happen to say that you'd come back."

"He didn't know it himself, then. I hadn't time to listen to his Ismid report until eight o'clock." He took out his cigarettes and offered them to Evelyn. "Hamdi told me you and he had a talk."

"I was so interested to hear he'd been in Constantinople. Will you have some brandy, or a glass of raki?"

"Don't tell me you've been breaking the law and buying raki! My Cabinet, like President Harding's, is strong on Prohibition."

"I'm not a connoisseur, but according to Jeff it's the same raki you all drink up at Chankaya," said Evelyn lightly, and stood up. "I'll get the glasses."

Kemal watched the shimmer of coral silk pass from the patio into the lamp-lit livingroom and felt somewhat baffled by Evelyn's reserve. Experienced in all the techniques of seduction, he had planned to follow on from Hamdi's talk with Evelyn, every word of which had been reported to him by the young man, with a discreet reference to Jeff's Constantinople amusements which would show his own sympathy with a beautiful, neglected wife and a marriage heading for disaster. In short order, he had expected, she would be weeping on his shoulder, and then lying in his arms, an easy conquest for the Conqueror in that secluded house among the vines. But she had refused his lead, and offered him instead a glass of raki, in itself a comment on his notorious fondness for the spirit. He waited without moving, as he knew so well how to wait, for Evelyn's next words.

They surprised him. She came back with a tray holding a glass jug, tumblers, a bottle of French brandy and another of raki, and with Kemal's help drew a measure of the pure well water, which misted the sides of the jug. Then she said, resuming the conversation:

"Jeff is having such an interesting time in Constantinople!"

"You've heard from him, then?"

"Of course. Actually . . . oh! will you help yourself to water, or shall I pour?"

"Thank you." Kemal had meant to ask for brandy. But the aniseed scent from the uncorked bottle, the habit of raki, were too strong for him. He took the jug, and poured just enough water to turn the strong grape spirit milky.

"No raki for you, Evelyn?"

"It tastes like cough medicine to me. I'll have a *fine à l'eau.*"

"You were saying 'actually' — "

"Actually Jeff sent a telegram asking me to ask you a question. Did you know?"

"My child, I'm not as thorough as our late lamented Sultan Abdul Hamid, whose spies brought him a copy of every telegram dispatched every day in the Ottoman Empire! What was this important question?"

"Jeff wants to know more about an officer attached to the French High Commission. Commandant Charles Cravache."

Kemal threw back his head and laughed. He had a hearty laugh, and at the sound his dog lifted its head from its forepaws and watched its master.

"Well done, Jeff Bey!" he said. "That puzzle didn't take long to solve."

"Puzzle?"

"You remember in the garden at Chankaya, you said there must be something I wanted Barrett to do for me in Constantinople? You were quite right, of course. I asked him to take a message to a certain English diplomat, warning him against a dangerous intriguer. Barrett has obviously found out that Major Cravache is the man I meant."

"This Cravache is a dangerous man?"

"*Le Commandant Cravache, quel sale monsieur!*" said Kemal. "He would steal, murder, betray any cause or any human being who trusted him, to forward the career of Charles Cravache. He hates the British because *they* trusted him, and then found him out for a coward and a cheat, and he hates *me* because I once bested him—I suppose that's what your—what Barrett wanted to find out?"

"Can you tell me more?" asked Evelyn uneasily. "Jeff doesn't handle personality stories much, and when he does he likes a lot of background."

"There are only two chapters of an ugly story I need tell you. I first ran across Cravache when I was serving in Syria; long before the Great War, we were both young officers then. He was posing as a tourist, but I discovered that he had been seconded from the French Army to prepare the way for French infiltration of what was then a Turkish province. When he went into the desert to stir up trouble among the Druses I had him arrested and run out of the country."

Automatically Kemal reached out for the raki bottle.

"Cravache and I were never in the same area again until just before the armistice in 1918," he went on. "At that time I was commanding the Seventh Army in Syria, and he was a liaison officer with the British, attached to General Allenby's staff. Allenby was moving very fast, and although he had two to one superiority—our Seventh was literally a skeleton army by that time—he had no use for dead wood on his staff. Every officer was thrown into combat. Now Cravache was great on theory, he'd written one manual on Tactics, and another on Strategy, heaven help us! But when it came to the pinch he led a company of Tommies into one of our ambushes and then ran off and left them to it. The British came up in support and our men retreated, but the whole thing had been seen and understood by the relief force, and Cravache was sent back for Allenby to deal with."

"What happened then?"

"On the way, he and his escort were taken prisoner by one of my corps commanders, General Ismet. You've never met Ismet Pasha? Ismet had to take his own men and the prisoners across the Jordan waist deep in water, with the horses swimming alongside. He had about thirty British prisoners already, plus Cravache and his escort, and he asked them to give their parole not to attempt an escape on such a dangerous crossing. They all gave it, standing on the river bank."

"And Cravache broke his, I suppose?"

"Exactly. I remember the prisoners coming in to my HQ at Nablus, looking like drowned rats of course, but all raging at the 'filthy Frog' who'd taken French leave in mid-stream. He got clean away and made his way back to the Druse rebels he already knew. I heard of him later in Damascus, dancing attendance on the Emir Feisal, but he kept out of Turkey until a short time ago. I'm pretty well sure that his appearance in Constantinople means trouble for the British."

Evelyn was thoughtful. She had watched Kemal intently as he talked, less interested in the story of Cravache than in his telling of it. His intense power of communication had shown her, as clearly as the moonlit garden where they sat, the background of his stories, shifting from the Syrian desert of years ago to the flooding Jordan and the British prisoners, honourable though captive, stumbling to the headquarters of a Turkish army in retreat. Kemal never raised his voice, and its deep, deliberate tones were all the more impressive when he occasionally halted to find the exact word in French; he had long ago learned never to use the gesticulations of the bazaars. It was a little masterpiece of narrative, utterly convincing to the girl who listened.

"Now I know about Cravache," she said at last. "What I don't understand is this: you've come to terms with the French, and you think of the British as your enemies. Yet you send an English diplomat a message warning him against one particular Frenchman who could do the British harm. Why did you trouble?"

"Perhaps because that Englishman tried to do me a good turn once, when I was down on my luck. Or perhaps because the British, whatever sort of governments they elect, always fight clean."

"I've heard it said that the British, even at Gallipoli, respected the Turkish soldiers."

"I think they did. 'Johnny Turk' was what they called 'Mehmedjik', which is our own name for the Turkish soldier."

"And did your men call the British 'Tommy Atkins?' "

"No, we called the Englishmen 'Johnny Kikirik,' because they were always laughing."

"I like that better than 'Dough-boys'," said Evelyn.

"Though now I've read Lloyd George's latest piece of nonsense," said Kemal, who had been following his own train of thought, "I feel less inclined to be generous with my warnings!"

"What's Lloyd George been saying now?"

"Didn't the Anatolian Agency have it, before you left Angora? No, there would hardly have been time," said Kemal. "He made a speech in the House of Commons last night, praising the Greeks for their great advance across Turkey, and saying the British people couldn't allow this war to go on indefinitely . . . I suppose he thought the fourth of August was the right day for what amounts to a declaration of war on *us*."

"Meaning the British would intervene? Would send their own troops into Anatolia?"

"That's what the Greeks hope he means. Our forward pickets reported wild enthusiasm all along the Greek lines this afternoon. They've been waving flags and flowers, and cheering Lloyd George, and singing 'The Son of the Eagle' in honour of King Constantine. We've heard of dances being got up in some of the towns, to celebrate."

"And you intend to interrupt the ball?"

"Eventually."

"I knew it!" Instinctively Evelyn raised her hand to her lips. The long sleeve of the silk kaftan fell back, and round her slender forearm Kemal saw twisted, in a triple strand, his own red coral tesbih.

"You're wearing the beads!"

She tried to steady her voice, to say in her cool way, "They make a pretty bracelet", but the words refused to come. And then Kemal's arms were round her, and his lean hard cheek was pressed against her own.

She turned her mouth away from his. All the false frigidity of her body, chilled through four years of an inharmonious marriage, was melting at his touch. But Evelyn's impulse to recoil was very strong: it was expressed in the one word "Don't!"

"You mustn't refuse me, Evelyn," Kemal said with his lips in her hair. "You've guessed, you *know*, we haven't long to be together."

She pulled away and tried to see his face. "How long?"

Kemal's eyes narrowed. Then he smiled, "No," he said, "not even for you, my beautiful and clever Evelyn, will I say 'how long'. Remember what I told you about living in the House of War? One of the first rules to observe—if you want to keep on living—is strict security."

"I shouldn't have asked."

In her arms he could feel her shaking, as if her heartbeats were driving her body very fast, and, releasing her, Kemal said, "You're getting cold now, sitting above the well. Let's go indoors."

Passively, she went before him into the lighted living-room. When he had been there in the morning, the little place had not struck Kemal in the same way as it did now. It was not exactly comfortless, and Kemal's mother was living by her own choice in a small house furnished in the same simple Turkish style. But the Commander-in-Chief had seen Paris, Berlin, Vienna; he realised that this room with the hard divans and the deal floor, where two cushions laid on the doorstep made the most comfortable seat, was a bleak setting for the rich merchant banker's daughter from San Francisco.

He looked about him. The door leading to the bedroom was

closed. The petrol lamp flickered on the work table, illuminating a plan the Commander-in-Chief knew by heart, and could have drawn blindfold.

"Why, you've got a war map here," he said.

"Don't look at it. I'm sure it's full of errors—and you'll laugh."

"I'm not laughing."

Kemal studied the map of Asia Minor, where the Turkish pins confronted the Greek on the high plateaus of Anatolia. There was some amusement in his face, but much more interest; once he seemed to be about to move a pin, but shook his head. And Evelyn Barrett watched from the shadows, studying the planes of that strange face, with its harsh planes softened by the lamplight, and the hollows beneath the high cheekbones telling their own tale of fatigue.

"Did you prepare this map? Or did Barrett?" he asked in his abrupt way.

"It's meant to be a reference map for Jeff, but I set it up."

"It's amazingly well done." Kemal took up a book lying beside the map. "*Clausewitz on War*," he said. "Have *you* read this?"

"I read it in college. I've been reading it again."

Kemal turned to the flyleaf and read the name written there. " 'Evelyn Anderson'. Was that your name before you married?"

"Yes. My father's name is John Anderson, but *his* father spelled it A-n-d-e-r-s-s-e-n."

"Danish?"

"Norwegian. He was a sailor from Bergen who signed off in San Francisco about—oh, I don't know, about sixty years ago."

Kemal looked at the book again. "Clausewitz. That takes me back to the classrooms at Harbiye, before Harbiye became a British HQ. Tell me, do you understand what he's writing about?"

"Some of it. Only he makes war sound like a game of chess."

· "Sometimes it's more like a game of poker." He laid the book down on the table. "Why are you so interested in the art of war?"

"Because if I were a man I would have been a soldier."

"A soldier, and brave?"

"I hope, brave."

Kemal stared at her. If Evelyn had indulged in that military fantasy on one of their morning rides, when she was astride a horse, in boots and breeches, the boy-girl who had first stirred his easily-aroused desire, there would have been nothing incongruous in the confession to a man whose whole life had been built upon the Turkish Army. But the contrast between the words and the graceful girl before him with her loosened hair, beguiling in silk and with his corals round her arm, was too much for Kemal's gravity. He began to laugh. Then he swept Evelyn into his clasp and kissed her.

This time she was unable to reject him. His body, which she now realised was as hard and powerful as a tiger's, enfolded hers completely; the feel of his thin lips under the clipped moustache was so utterly strange that Evelyn grew limp under the kisses she was as yet powerless to return. Only when she realised that he was drawing her gently towards the bedroom door did she resist him, and spoke again the one word "Don't!"

"Don't what?"

"Don't diminish yourself."

He stared at her, utterly confounded, and Evelyn whispered, "Please go now. I've had all I can stand."

"Evelyn, let me stay!"

She crossed her arms over her breast as if to still her heart, and said, "I'm all alone here. How about you? Are you going back to your—cousin at Chankaya?"

Kemal shook his head. "Fikriye is living with my mother now. She'll stay there until we can arrange for her medical care in Europe."

"I—see."

"There is no other woman in my house tonight," the man said violently. "There will be nothing but the memory of you."

6

THE MAN IN WHOSE hands lay the future of Turkey strode home through the vineyards with mixed emotions blunting his usually incisive mind. It was rare for Kemal to walk alone at night, and the scent of the firs, the poplars and the fruit trees was a refreshment; he was surprised to find that it was almost equally refreshing to have been rebuffed. The list of his sexual triumphs stretched back to his fifteenth year, and few if any refusals had ever come his way. Women, even in the Saloniki days, had thrown themselves at the handsome blond cadet, as later, with still more abandon, at the Saviour of Gallipoli. There had been some denials, of course, but only denials which implied the ultimate surrender of a partner who knew the game as well as he did himself. "Oh no, no, no, my husband would kill me if he ever found out!" — that was the sort of protest, meant to be overborne at the next rendezvous, which Kemal understood. But Evelyn Barrett had not withdrawn behind her husband's honour, or even her own. "Don't diminish *yourself!*" It was Kemal alone whom she had thought of in that strange appeal.

Was he then for her, as for so many of his countrymen, a man on a pedestal? He knew she admired him. He had seen it in her eyes, in her attention to everything he said on their morning rides. But a man was not diminished, surely, by trying to possess a woman? A married woman, sophisticated, travelled, clever? Kemal had never had an American mistress. At the first sight of Evelyn Barrett he had thought that with her this new experience would be his. He knew her husband to be a hard-drinking, cheerful amoralist, hard-living and careless like many of his kind. Jeff's wife, when he brought her to Angora, was to Kemal's perceptive eyes a surprising choice, better bred and far more intelligent than the man, but given the freedom of their roving lives no more likely than Jeff Barrett to respect conventional morality. He had thought, once Jeff had been got out of the way, that the victory would be easy. Philosophically, as he turned in at the gates of

93

Chankaya with his dog at his heels and acknowledged the salutes of the Lazes on duty, the Commander-in-Chief admitted that his shock tactics had failed. He meant to have her—Evelyn's gentle rebuff had only increased Kemal's utter determination to succeed—but he saw now that success would not be won in a night, nor perhaps in several nights. And he admired Evelyn Barrett all the more for that.

The inside of his house was hot and airless, and as usual Hayati Bey was hovering in the anteroom with a manila folder in his hand.

"Despatches?" snapped Kemal.

"Two from Akshehir, Pasha'm. And one from Kars, extremely interesting."

Kemal held out his hand for the folder. "I'll ring when I want you," he said curtly, and went alone into the study. He was still, against his will, under the spell of the night hour and the girl. Do not diminish yourself! The study was as hot as the rest of the house. He threw the window open. The lights in the little chalets were shining down the hill as far as the poplar valley. He wondered if Evelyn's rooms were in darkness now, and Evelyn in bed, perhaps regretting her dismissal of himself? Kemal sat down, took a key from a thin chain round his waist, and unlocked a shallow drawer in his big desk. A single map of the western front was pinned to the bottom, professionally drawn by himself to illustrate his future battle plan. He studied it with a slight smile. As far as the positions of the two armies went, Evelyn's map was very nearly right. Unconsciously, with the fingers of his left hand, he counted forward on his desk top: twenty-one days.

Kemal locked the map drawer and checked the security of its key on his chain. Then he pulled the despatch folder towards him. The telegram from Kars was on the top. He read it with his blond eyebrows raised and something like a grin on his lean face. Then he rang for his secretary and forgot Evelyn Barrett and the world of womankind.

*   *   *

Very early next morning, so early that Ayesha was still noisily busy in the patio, a trooper rode down from Chankaya with a letter in his pouch. Evelyn, half dressed, pulled on her yellow

94

cotton frock when Ayesha called her out to receive it, and read Kemal's first letter standing at the gate.

"*Chère madame*", the letter began, in the schoolboy scrawl to which Kemal's exquisite Arabic script deteriorated when he wrote in a western language, "I had hoped to invite you to ride with me this morning. But I have arranged several interviews, and must remain at Chankaya. If you will do me the honour of joining my guests at luncheon, a car will be waiting for you on the highway at half past twelve o'clock. With my respectful homage—K."

Evelyn knew enough Turkish now to tell the messenger, while Ayesha beamed approval, "Please say yes, and thank you, to the Gazi for me." The man saluted and rode off. Evelyn had the whole morning in hand, more than time enough to walk into Angora and telegraph to Jeff.

It was more than he deserved, of course, but the habit of helping him died hard, and she didn't like the sound of the Cravache story, it was out of his line entirely. Still she telegraphed:

"Subject your enquiry active syria prewar etaccused cowardice broken parole while liaising allenby september 1918 stop suggest you upcheck British HQ stop when you returning query evelyn"

She came back at once by araba, bathed, and dressed very carefully for Kemal's luncheon party. She darkened her fair eyebrows slightly, reddened her lips and buffed her fingernails with pink powder before putting on a dress of emerald green charmeuse and a small hat with Mercury wings of matching green feathers fitting closely over her ears. It kept Evelyn's hair tidy in the fresh breeze which had risen that morning, as she walked down the lane too narrow for an automobile to where Kemal's own car waited on the Angora road. She was driven in solitary state up the hill and through the gates of Chankaya.

On this occasion the green salon where Fikriye had attempted to preside was empty, and a manservant led Evelyn upstairs to Kemal's little library, from which she could hear the sound of voices. He was there, wearing a plain khaki uniform without insignia or the ribbons of the many decorations he had won in the Sultan's wars, and after kissing Evelyn's hand he ceremoniously presented two other gentlemen, both in civilian clothes. One, broad and burly, was Rauf Bey, the Prime Minister; the other, short and dapper with a neat waxed moustache, was Refet, who until recently had been the Minister of Defence. Both had been closely associated with Kemal since the beginning of the Revolution.

Their greeting was very courteous, but stilted, as if the two Ministers hardly knew what to make of an American girl at Chankaya. Glasses of dry sherry were handed by the manservant (the raki bottle was conspicuous by its absence) and the four stood chatting awkwardly while Evelyn stole a few sidelong glances at the library shelves. The books had been arranged with compulsive neatness by their owner. Those whose titles she could read were all in French, and seemed to deal chiefly with the campaigns of Napoleon. Then the last guests arrived, having walked up the hill from their chalet: they were Captain Riza, one of Kemal's aides-de-camp, and his pretty young wife Feride. Together they had made a dangerous escape from Constantinople two years earlier, and this adventure seemed to have made Feride one of the least shy of Kemal's youthful entourage. Her laughing chatter helped to break the ice, and her impulsive "But where's Fikriye Hanim?" was covered by the announcement that luncheon was served. They went downstairs to the diningroom.

Kemal placed Captain Riza's wife at his left hand and Evelyn at his right. She was fascinated at finding herself at the famous Table, in the room which according to Angora gossip was the scene of nameless orgies, and which today was fresh and airy, with flowers on the side tables and on top of Kemal's piano. In the corner bay, beside the window, four saddle-bag chairs were arranged round a table on which cigars and cigarettes had been placed in readiness for what would presumably be a masculine conference. The rest of the furniture was of the same sort, heavy leather, heavy woods in the Teutonic style which Kemal seemed to favour, with presentation china in glass-fronted cabinets and various trophies on the walls.

"Have you heard the news about Enver Pasha, Mrs. Barrett?" asked Kemal as he shook out his table napkin.

"I heard in Angora this morning that he was dead," said Evelyn. "No more than that."

"A telegram came in from Kars last night," said Kemal. "We checked the facts at once, and they seem to be quite accurate."

"They are accurate," said Rauf. "Enver died leading a revolt against his Russian friends, at Douchembe in Turkestan, not far from the Afghan frontier."

"It's something, I suppose, that he was killed in action," Rauf commented. "A better fate than Javid's last month, or Talaat's a year ago."

Kemal nodded. "Two assassinations, and one death in a border raid, and that's the end of the leaders of the Young Turks. . . . All over, within fourteen years of the great Macedonian revolt. God, but I was jealous of Enver then! God, how I grew to hate his guts!"

"Why?" asked Evelyn.

"Why? Because after Enver and his friends threw the Sultan out they called in foreigners to reorganise the country. A German army mission, a British naval mission, French bankers at the Treasury and Italians in command of the Gendarmerie, as if we native-born Turkish citizens were powerless to rule ourselves! This is one of the first principles of our Revolution, madame; the salvation of the new Turkey must come from within!" There was a dutiful murmur of assent.

"Enver Pasha became the Emir of Bukhara, didn't he?" asked Evelyn.

"Much good the title did him! He bolted from Turkey after the armistice and went over to the Russians; it was from them he held the emirate. Enver was never very stable," said Kemal with his savage grin, "so he didn't get on with his new friends for long. And he was never any good in action. He thought riding into battle with the Koran at his breast made up for having no idea how to handle troops . . . I imagine the battle of Douchembe, if you can call it a battle, was a walkover for the Bolsheviks."

"You warned him how it would all end," said Refet, coming in on cue.

"Every time he condescended to receive me at the Ministry of War. And I like to remember that somewhere in the Seraskerkapisi archives there must still be the memorandum I wrote him in July '14, when the world war was imminent, warning him to keep out of an alliance with Germany. He was too vain to listen to advice from a mere lieutenant-colonel, of course. He packed me off to Rodosto—out of the way."

There was a general laugh. "Enver lived like a prince while the Young Turks were in power," said Rauf. "Do you remember his palace, gentlemen, and the army of servants, and the sumptuous meals? And when Enver married, the bride had to be a princess, nothing less would do—"

"The princess did him more harm with the common people than anything else," said Kemal.

"You must take care to marry a commoner, Pasha'm," said Feride slyly. "But when, oh when, shall we share in the festivities of *your* wedding?"

"Now, Feride!" said her young husband, blushing for her; but Kemal only laughed and quoted a favourite proverb, "To be a bachelor is to be a Sultan!"

There was nothing princely about the luncheon served at Chankaya. It conformed to the strict austerity standards of Angora, and was of two courses only: a dish of chicken in the Circassian style, with a nut sauce, and a rice pudding slightly flavoured with saffron. Bowls of fruit were then placed on the table, and Evelyn began to talk about the fruits of California, beautiful in appearance but tasteless (so she tactfully said) by comparison with the less outwardly tempting fruits of Anatolia.

"Then you must have one of our ugly sweet pears!" said Kemal in high good humour. He refilled her wine glass deftly with a light Bordeaux which had not travelled well, and began to ask questions about the wine industry in California. Evelyn observed that the Turkish girl had only pretended to sip the wine, in spite of an encouraging nod from her husband.

Rauf and Refet had drunk wine. Their difficulty was in making conversation with the two girls. They were Turkish gentlemen of distinguished backgrounds, and men of the world who had travelled beyond their country's frontiers, but it was still not easy for them to accept women on their own level or take a woman's questions seriously. Evelyn Barrett, whose perceptions were becoming so quick and tender where Kemal was concerned, understood that his luncheon party had a double purpose: it was an attempt at entertaining in the western style, and at the same time an assurance to herself that she was not a woman to whom he went in darkness and stealth, but one whom he was proud to place beside his closest friends. She admired his own self-control, for not once had he launched into the lengthy monologues which Jeff and other Americans found so tedious. Even his self-satisfaction at the warning given to Enver Pasha had been curbed, and now, over the coffee which was served at table, he was devoting himself to the two young women, encouraging Feride to talk about a memorable visit to Italy with her parents as a child of twelve, before the outbreak of the Great War.

"I was far too young to appreciate it." Feride's large black eyes were soft with the recollection of the Florentine spring. "I want to go back some day with Riza, and show him the Uffizi and the Pitti Palace, and Fiesole—"

"When the Gazi can spare me," Captain Riza said hastily.

"My child, I shall certainly spare you, one of these days," said Kemal. ". . . Mrs. Barrett was in Italy, not very long ago."

"I knew that lovely dress had to come from Rome or Paris," said Feride. Wearing a home-made circlet of plaited silk as the headdress which replaced the veil, she had been looking enviously at the emerald feathers which just revealed Evelyn's pearl earrings.

"From Rome, as a matter of fact," smiled Evelyn. "My husband had a long assignment in Italy earlier this year."

"Was that at the time of the Genoa Conference?" asked Refet.

"He did cover the conference, but we went there first for the February elections, just before the Fascists took over the government of Fiume."

"How serious was that?" asked Rauf Bey curiously. "We always understood that most of the Fiume trouble was caused by d'Annunzio."

"Benito Mussolini is much cleverer and much more dangerous than d'Annunzio," said Eve. "He really knows how to sway the people. And he won't stop at a local *coup d'état* like Fiume. Remember, only last May he and his Blackshirts chased out the communist city council of Bologna, and they're moving into all the big cities so fast that the whole of Italy may become Fascist soon."

"And what will be the effect on the monarchy? Will Mussolini risk proclaiming a Republic?" asked Refet. He was taking Evelyn seriously now, and she answered calmly, "In my opinion—for what it's worth—he'll settle for being Prime Minister under a puppet king."

The Turkish Ministers looked at one another, and Kemal said lightly, "So much for Victor Emmanuel III!"

Evelyn glanced at Madame Feride. She was uncertain whether

according to protocol, on an occasion so formal, she or the lady who was present with her husband should make the move to leave. But after all it was rather like lunching in an army mess, for as soon as the coffee cups were removed the Commander-in-Chief stood up, thanked his guests for their good company, and escorted the ladies to the door, where his car was waiting.

"My chauffeur will take you home, Feride Hanim, and then take Mrs. Barrett to her private road," he said pleasantly, and in the same tone spoke the beautiful Turkish words which speed the parting guest. "Go smiling!" said Kemal Pasha to them both. To Evelyn his lips hardly moved in the word "Tonight!"

*   *   *

It was nearer eleven than ten o'clock that night before Evelyn heard a car stopping on the Angora road, and soon afterwards Kemal's knock on her closed door.

"*On peut entrer, madame?*"

"*Soyez le bienvenu, Excellence.*" It was their question and answer of the night before, unvaried by a word.

"You are gracious, Evelyn."

"Come and sit down."

Kemal looked more tired than Evelyn had yet seen him, his features sharpened by fatigue and his deep voice hoarse. She knew better than to ask where he had been, but his uniform was so dusty that she knew he had driven a long way from the city since the early afternoon. She fetched the raki and the brandy, while Kemal used a tumbler to pour himself a long drink of the pure water from Ahmed's well. He laid his fair head back on one of the cushions propped against the window ledge, and closed his eyes. Evelyn looked at the regulation army kalpak, which he had taken off when he came in; the thick brown astrakhan made it a heavy head-covering for August weather. She waited while the intense vitality which never failed him for long seemed visibly to flow back into his pale face. At last he opened his blue eyes and smiled.

"It's peaceful here with you," he said, "I'm glad you're still wearing that pretty dress."

Evelyn glanced down at the green charmeuse. "It was so much cooler this afternoon, I didn't trouble to change."

Kemal touched the thin green fold above her knee. "The colour of Islam," he said. "Did you know that?"

"Green? I suppose I did know it, but I didn't think of it when I wore this dress today. Green happens to be my favourite colour."

"It suits you so well . . . May I smoke indoors?"

"Of course."

"You like Turkish tobacco, don't you?"

"Very much."

The smoke from two cigarettes rose companionably in the lamplit room. Kemal said, "You greatly impressed my friends Rauf and Refet!"

"Really? I didn't think they liked me at all. I found them very difficult to talk to."

"They aren't accustomed to ladies who can talk intelligently about politics." Kemal laughed suddenly. "It was what you said about Mussolini that took Rauf aback."

"What in particular about Mussolini?"

"That he would become the Prime Minister of a puppet king." Then, seeing her puzzled look, Kemal explained. "You see, my dear Evelyn, that is the future our excellent Rauf has in mind for me."

"*You* to be Prime Minister under the Sultan who outlawed you? But surely you would never—"

"*Never*. But poor Rauf still believes that somehow, some day, after the Son of the Eagle has flapped off back to Athens, we can come to a compromise that will keep the House of Osman on the throne. Even though nobody could possibly be more of a puppet ruler than the present Sultan, Mehmed VI, known as Vahed-ed-Din, he's still the Caliph of Islam, and thus a sacred figure."

Kemal's mouth twisted as it did when he spoke of "pious Moslems", and Evelyn said quickly, "People will never compare you to Mussolini, *Excellence*! To Garibaldi, perhaps, but not to Mussolini!"

"Could you be persuaded to call me by my name, Evelyn? Not the name my father whispered in my ear when I was born, but just Kemal?"

Smiling: "I thought Kemal did mean 'excellence'."

"It means Perfection," said the owner of the name with a grin. "My schoolmaster gave it to me because I was always top in arithmetic!"

He linked his hand in Evelyn's. The green dress had elbow

sleeves, and Kemal gently caressed the inside of her arm before linking their fingers again and contemplating their clasped hands. The contrast between them was fascinating: the soldier's hand narrow, with the long supple fingers of an artist or a musician, the girl's as square and capable as a boy's. Kemal moved his head lazily on the cushion and brought his face closer to Evelyn's.

"Beautiful eyes!" he said softly. "You have such beautiful brown eyes, Evelyn!"

"How can you say so, you who live in a land where nearly every girl has such huge dark eyes!"

"Yes, they are lovely," said the connoisseur. "Huge black eyes without much expression in the ordinary way. Yours change as one watches you; I thought sometimes at luncheon they were sparkling with mischief . . . why are they sad tonight?"

"Perhaps because I was worrying, before you came."

"About what?"

"It was what you said at lunch about two leaders of the Young Turks being murdered—you did say their names—"

"Talaat and Javid. I won't say they both deserved it, but Talaat sealed his own doom when he ordered the massacre of the Armenians in March '15; it was an Armenian boy who killed him in Berlin."

"But *you've* never done such a thing!"

"Not deliberately. The guerillas got out of hand at Marash in Cilicia two years ago, and went for the Armenians, but that was before I had a disciplined Army of Independence."

"I was thinking about assassination, not massacre."

Kemal touched the pistol holster at his belt. "I'm my own policeman," he said significantly.

"Have you had to use that, in your own defence?"

"Oh, several times. Enver's ruffians tried to dispose of me more than once in the old days, and there was one very near thing during the trouble with the Kurds. After that the Lazes were recruited to be my bodyguard."

"But you haven't a bodyguard tonight," Evelyn whispered. Instinctively Kemal looked behind him, through the dark window pane, at the moonlit orchard.

"There are two of them waiting in the car," he said. "No one will be allowed to pass."

"I kept thinking about the lane and the darkness under the

trees . . . if anything happened to you when you were coming to me—" But Kemal stopped her with his mouth on hers.

It was a long kiss, warm and tender, and deliberately unlike the greedy embrace in which he had tried to master her the night before. Once again, with inward triumph, Kemal felt Evelyn relaxing, consenting, in his arms. But this time he did not risk a rebuff. He printed a line of light kisses from Evelyn's lips to the warm hollow of her throat, and took her hands again.

"You mustn't worry your lovely head about me," he said. "Assassination is a risk that any Chief of State must run, and I've more enemies than most! But don't you know that I'm believed to bear a charmed life?"

"Who believes that?"

" 'Mehmedjik' does!' Ask any man in the Army of Independence—any man in any of my old commands, they'll all tell you the Gazi can't be touched by shot or shell."

"But do *you* believe it?" she persisted.

"No, of course I don't, "said Kemal. "I've had fantastic luck, that's all. I'm a lucky general, which Napoleon thought was important, and it's excellent for 'Mehmedjik's' morale, which is what really counts."

"So in all those years in the House of War, as you call it, you've never once been wounded?"

"Oh, there've been several narrow shaves. My watch was smashed by a bullet on the morning we started to drive the enemy from Sari Bair in August '15. Later on a British airman machine-gunned my staff car, and at the very end, at Aleppo, the Arab rebels flung grenades at me from the roof-tops while I was directing the evacuation in the street below. Once again, no harm done!"

Smiling: "Didn't I hear about a broken rib, on the eve of the Sakarya?"

"Well!" Kemal smiled too. "Any man who's fool enough to light a cigarette while mounting his horse is pushing his luck too far."

"It it luck or is it *kismet*?"

"Don't use that word!" Kemal sat up abruptly, and his face was grimmer than Evelyn had ever seen it. "It's part, it's a big part, of all I'm up against. Kismet, fate, no use struggling against your destiny: that cursed fatalism is at the bottom of all the apathy and corruption of Ottoman Turkey. Passive acceptance of the worst—it's like Islam, which means a total submission to God's will."

"Are you an atheist, Kemal?"

"No," he said. "I'm not a religious man, but I believe in the One God, your God as well as mine, who is above us all. Only remember, the Turks in their religion are living in the seventh century; in their civilisation, in the seventeenth; and there is no one, literally no one, but me to lead them into the twentieth . . . And now I must go," he concluded, "you beguile me into talking too much, Evelyn. We'll meet tomorrow, won't we, at Captain Riza's evening party?"

Evelyn rose to her feet as he got up. The force of Kemal's personality, of his passionate dedication to his task, had once again broken over her like a great wave. She felt it almost frivolous to say, "His wife invited me, on the drive back from Chankaya."

"Good for her."

"And when I got home I found a dinner invitation from the Russian Ambassador. Kemal! You arranged for both those invitations, didn't you?"

"Of course I did. I told you last night, we haven't got much time. I want to be with you, whenever and wherever I can."

"Oh, Kemal!" said Evelyn, and her brown eyes were full of trouble, "what is happening to us two?"

"*This!*" he said, and caught her to him, and kissed her fiercely, and was gone.

*   *   *

There now began for Evelyn Barrett a time intolerably fleeting, time suspended, time revolving round the man she saw for some part of every day and thought of for most of her waking hours. Each morning she awoke expecting to hear that Jeff was on his way back to Angora; every evening when Kemal left her she searched his face for some betrayal that this was the last time they would be together before he left to lead the army into action. But the solitary letter which arrived from Jeff, complaining bitterly of conditions at the press camp on the Chatalja Lines, made no mention of his return, and all along the Anatolian front the guns were silent. The Greeks, it was reported, were weary of the long stalemate. The optimism fanned by Lloyd George's reckless speech into a belief that the British would soon be fighting by their side had dwindled into apathy. Women were brought up from Smyrna and public dances were organised in the capured Turkish towns to improve the morale of the Greek troops.

There was no public dancing at Angora, where any social gathering of men and women was still frowned on by conservative Moslems, but Evelyn waltzed with Kemal at the Russian Embassy, where a pianist and a balalaika player were brought in after dinner to play for a little impromptu dance. Kemal was in high spirits that night, deferred to by the representatives of the Soviets, who always gave him the honours due to a Chief of State, and apparently as happy as a boy with the American girl in his arms. Evelyn made the discovery of his natural sense of rhythm, just as the night before she had discovered his cultivated love of music when he sat down at Madame Feride's piano and played a Bach prelude.

She found herself invited to all the entertainments given by the foreign envoys in Angora. The Russians, the Azerbaijanis, the representatives of Afghanistan and of all the Soviet satellites emerging from the Great War, the special Moslem mission from India, the group of French "observers" in civilian clothes—all of official Angora now made a point of asking Mrs. Barrett to their receptions, and there Evelyn had an immediate success. On similar occasions in Europe she had been deliberately self-effacing. She knew that Jeff resented her interest in politics, because it was based on a far more solid grounding than his own; his sense of inferiority drove him to halt his wife's conversation with any distinguished person with some deflating or humorous remark. It had been so at the Paris Peace Conference, it had been so in Rome and Genoa; by the time they were together in Turkey Evelyn had learned to avoid the limelight whenever she could and let Jeff bask in it instead. But now there was no need to be retiring, nor indeed any possibility of it, with the Gazi always by her side. Kemal heard her discussing the League of Nations, the quarrel between Britain and France over reparations and the Ruhr, and the poetry of Gabriele d'Annunzio with men who obviously felt that Mrs. Barrett brought an air of the great world into their claustrophobic existence in Angora. He saw his boy-girl of the steppe in a series of beautiful dresses, tactful and charming to everyone she met, able to speak three foreign languages, and in his mind Evelyn took on a new dimension, for which he had not yet found a name.

Of course "the Gazi's latest" was a topic for discussion wherever the ladies of Angora met. It was a welcome break in the long hot summer and the feminine boredom which had followed the battles and emotions of 1921. At the Red Crescent work parties, where wives who had accompanied their husbands from Constantinople looked down on the Angora girls as hopeless provincials, and the Angora girls despised the newcomers as useless dolls who had never shared in the great task of carrying weapons and ammunition to the front, both sides united in giggling comment on the Gazi's latest conquest.

"He's mad about her," confided Feride, whose husband Captain Riza would have been furious if he had heard her gossiping about the Commander-in-Chief. "The night they were at our house he played the piano *at* her, if you know what I mean, and hardly had eyes for anybody else—"

"I wonder what Fikriye thinks of it—" put in another woman, and a chorus of voices said "Hush!" It was not prudent to mention the former favourite, ailing and sad, and now tyrannised over in the house of Kemal's mother. Fikriye had as completely disappeared from Angora society as if, like some harem transgressor of the past, she had been tied up in a sack and thrown into the Bosphorus.

"If we were all at Topkapi Saray in the bad old days," suggested a girl, "I suppose we'd be saying Madame Evelyn was 'gözde', in the Sultan's eye, wouldn't we?"

"She's a great deal more than gözde if you ask me," said the indiscreet Feride. "The silken curtain has already dropped over *that* divan, I'm sure!"

"Poor girl, I'm rather sorry for her. We all know what *he* is, and how long his fancies last—"

"Are you speaking from experience, darling?"

"Cat!"

"She must know what she's doing," shrugged Feride. "She's not a child."

It was Kemal who began to wonder what he was doing, at the end of ten days in which he had blatantly displayed his attachment to Evelyn Barrett. True to his devious nature, he intended to kill two birds with one stone in his pursuit of Evelyn. He meant to have her; he had never wavered in that, but it was also vital to his greater plan, the plan which in its paper form lay in the locked drawer of his desk at Chankaya, to appear more absorbed in the seduction of a married woman than in the prosecution of the war, and although he often left the city to confer with his corps commanders, brought from north and south for these talks, he left in the dark hours before the dawn when not many people were about, and was next seen in his usual place in the Assembly. He arrived late at the various receptions. His practice was to greet his hosts, accept a drink and then make his way to Evelyn, bowing over her hand in such obvious delight that even the Russians hesitated to break the spell. How strong the spell was Kemal only knew when, taking Evelyn away after an hour—no longer—he walked with his arm around her up the lane to her little house. Sauntering, laughing (and they soon had a supply of private jokes), whispering, kissing her at the gate—it was like a boy's courtship, and as Kemal walked back alone to the waiting car he thought with amazement that he had never known anything like it in his life. "Falling in love" was an expression which on the lips of happily married men had made him roar with laughter, for love was not a word in his vocabulary. Long before, as a young military attaché in Sofia, he had been strongly attracted to a Christian general's daughter. He was not heart-broken when her father ended the affair. But even what the young Kemal had felt for Ditrimina was not the same as the happiness which warmed his cold heart when he thought of Evelyn.

On a night when he had worked himself into such a state of strain and nervous tension as he would have relieved, in other days, by sending into Angora for a girl from the Street of Red Lanterns, he left Chankaya at ten o'clock "for a breath of fresh air" and went hurrying down the hill to the poplar valley. Kemal was not unduly sensitive: that the only place to possess Barrett's wife was presumably Barrett's bed troubled him not at all; but when he went quietly up the lane and saw Evelyn sitting in the lighted room the disturbing new tenderness suddenly drove out desire. The August night was hot, and she had left the door as well as the windows open. She was sitting at the big table reading (Clausewitz?) with her fair hair rumpled and her chin in the palm of one hand, in an attitude which strangely reminded the man of himself as a studious boy. And within ten minutes the Commander-in-Chief found himself seated beside Evelyn at the trestle table, giving her a first lesson in the war game as his instructors taught him to play it at Harbiye. She was so close to him, sharing the petrol lamp, that he could feel her arm and shoulder in the white silk shirt, and the tautness of her thigh thinly covered by a cotton skirt, but Kemal made no move to embrace her. He took his perverse pleasure in watching her boyish hands in the moves of the game, and her boyish profile beneath the straight light hair.

"That was fun!" said Evelyn when the game was over. "I was right, it really is like chess!"

"Poker." Kemal was a born teacher as well as a born soldier. He drew a writing pad towards him and began to sketch illustrations to some of his theories, using the Gallipoli battles as his text. As always, he caught fire from his own words, and though he never boasted, and never forgot to praise the courage of 'Johnny Kikirik' and Johnny's brothers-in-arms, the Australians and New Zealanders, it was the tenacity of the Turkish soldiers which their former commander stressed as the blazing panorama of 1915 was unrolled for Evelyn. She heard Kemal tell of the April morning when he foresaw and checked, by a hair's breadth, the Allied landing at Ariburnu, now famous as Anzac Cove, and the three days and nights he spent in the saddle at the August battles for the Anafarta Ridge. He took her hand, and laid it on the scar on his breast, raised beneath his thin shirt, left by the splinter of shrapnel which destroyed his watch; and Evelyn sighed and listened, an American Desdemona, enthralled by her general's tales.

"More!" she said when Kemal stopped at last. But he laughed and got up, saying, "No more tonight, my child! I've got an early start tomorrow morning, and a speech for the Assembly to finish first."

"When are you going to deliver it?"

"On the eighteenth—Friday afternoon."

"May I come and listen to it from the gallery?"

"You, Evelyn? I don't address the Deputies in French, you know."

"I do know, but I believe I could understand some of it, if you'd permit me to be there."

"No permission needed. Several ladies have been admitted to the gallery; foreign visitors, and Madame Emine, who means to be a Deputy herself some day; and that Russian press attaché girl goes all the time."

"Oh, marvellous!"

Kemal laughed, and said in English, "Evelyn, you have the big mind. Marvellous to visit our Assembly! Tell me, why do you really want to go?"

"To see you. To hear you. To watch other people listening to you. To understand you better."

Kemal drew her up from the hard wooden chair, up into his arms, and desire rekindled as he felt her body against his own.

"There is another way of knowing me," he said. "A much, much better way—"

"No."

"Evelyn, I'm tired to death. Let me stay here. Let me sleep with you tonight."

"No."

"Never?"

"Not till I'm quite, quite sure."

"Sure of what?"

"That what I feel for you is true."

7

IN CONSTANTINOPLE the Emergency was at an end. The resolution of General Sir Charles Harington, commanding the Allied Occupation forces, and the arrival of massive naval support from the British base at Malta caused the Greeks to withdraw discreetly from the Chatalja Lines. The white fustanellas, the pompommed shoes and the fezzes of the Evzones faded into the Thracian landscape, and Constantinople breathed again.

To British diplomats like Mr. Elliott, submerged in paperwork, the Chatalja crisis was a matter for the military, not seriously affecting their own office routines. To their womenfolk, all more or less exasperated at being brought back from the Bosphorus resorts to the heavy heat of Pera, the return of calm was an excuse for seeking any kind of pleasure, and there were evening picnics at the old fortress of Rumeli Hisar and moonlight boating parties which were responsible for several secret adulteries and one highly publicised cross-petition for divorce. Some of the less dashing wives struck up friendships with the Turkish ladies who, even where the Sultan still nominally ruled, were enjoying a new liberty; these were said to have "gone native" by others who felt themselves isolated in Turkey and preferred the company of their own kind.

One who neither went for midnight sails nor took tea with Turkish women was Mrs. Gilbert Elliott, whose narrow social circle consisted of the senior ladies of the British High Commissioner's staff and her own daughter, Jean. With Jean in attendance, Mrs. Elliott was established at her favourite table in the Marquise tearoom in the Grande Rue de Pera on the morning of the fifteenth of August: an opulent Edwardian figure in a mauve dress and a flowered hat, the veil pushed up over the brim as Mrs. Elliott ate her way through a slice of baklava, a slice of chocolate cake, and a glass of iced coffee.

Her doctor had advised Mrs. Elliott to try to reduce her weight, by Banting if necessary, but Jean and her father believed that a reliance on sweet cakes and chocolates was preferable to the endless glasses of port, cherry brandy and crême de cacao which partly compensated Mrs. Elliott for her son's death as a prisoner of war in Turkey. Jean knew nothing about psychology, a study just coming into fashion, but she realised that the daily visits to the Marquise tearoom, for morning coffee or afternoon tea, were a reassurance to her mother that the world of Harrods and the Fuller teashops was not very far away. The Marquise was old-fasioned; its *art nouveau* murals named "*Le Printemps*" and "*L'Automne*" dated from the turn of the century, but it had dainty white tablecloths, electroplated tea services and a vase of fresh flowers on each table. The windows were draped with white muslin curtains, and concealed behind them Mrs. Elliott was able to pretend for an hour at a time that Turkey did not exist.

"I wish you had invited Mr. Munro to luncheon at home," she was saying in her peevish way. "I don't think he ought to have asked you to meet him in the city."

"But, mummy, you always say you don't like having guests at lunch, unless we're actually having a party. It's so much easier for everyone this way."

"Where *is* he taking you for luncheon, dear? Nowhere on the Stamboul side, I hope?"

"Oh no, of course not. A very special restaurant near the Galata Bridge. Somewhere convenient for the boat."

"The *Iron Duke*, Jean?"

"Oh, mummy, *no*, the Eyüp ferryboat. You know we're going to the Pierre Loti café."

"Well," sighed Mrs. Elliott, taking some lira notes from her silver mesh bag and laying them on the bill, "it sounds a very hot, unpleasant trip to me. But if you want to do it—"

"Oh, I do! Daddy wants to know what it's like now, at the top of the Golden Horn. He says if it's still as lovely as it used to be at the Sweet Waters of Europe he'll hire a caïque some evening and take you up there for a sail."

"You know where I really want to go to, Jean."

"To Chanak? It's a long way away, darling, and Daddy thinks everything has been too unsettled lately for us to take a trip like that."

"But now the Emergency's all over, ask him again, Jean. He'll arrange it if you ask him. Will you, dear?"

"All right." The girl was glad to get into the Rue de Pera and end the conversation for the time being. She was only too well aware of her mother's morbid wish to visit the Dardanelles and see the little town of Chanak, where Lieutenant Ronald Elliott, R.N., had been well treated by his Turkish gaolers before the death march to Afyon began. "Let's take the short cut," she said firmly. She knew her mother disliked the narrow cobbled alley running down to the Pera Palace hotel, but it cut off three sides of a square on the way home, and she wasn't going to be late for Archie.

They started down between the little Turkish shops where the vendors smoked their water-pipes sitting on the irregularly raised pavement, making their way through a crowd of Turks with loads on their backs or pushing handcarts of fruit and vegetables. Taller than any of the Turks, a young man with a bare dark head was forging his way uphill.

"Hallo, Mr. Barrett!" said Jean as he came abreast of them.

"Hallo, Miss Elliott, nice to see you!"

Jeff stopped politely and Jean introduced him to her mother. "Daddy was talking about you just the other day," she told him. "He was hoping you'd come and call on us again."

"Why, thanks, I'd like that. I've been under canvas at Chatalja for the past ten days, but I'm back at the hotel now. I'd like to drop by sometime, if I may."

" 'Drop by!' " said Mrs. Elliott faintly, when Jeff had said goodbye and hurried on. "What very casual manners! Who is he?"

"He's an American, mums, a journalist."

"That accounts for it, of course. But when did he ever call on us before?"

"Oh, one evening about two weeks ago. You had one of your bad headaches, you were lying down." Jean was too compassionate to say "You'd drunk three quarters of a bottle of cointreau and you were dead to the world," but she added as they reached the Rue des Petits Champs, "Daddy liked him. He told Daddy something important, of course I don't know what, but it was the night Mr. Trakas was murdered in the Pera Palace. You know, the Capitulations expert, the one they haven't caught his killer yet."

"I wish you wouldn't talk about such horrible things, Jean."

"I'm sorry."

Twenty minutes later she ran into the drawing-room, where her mother was reading *The Tatler* and her father *The Times,* and kissed them both impulsively before she left. They looked such miserable, bored old pets, condemned by the aftermath of war to sit waiting to be fed by their foreign servants, so far from England in their foreign room.

"Jean, where are your gloves? Where's your jersey coat?" exclaimed her mother. The girl had changed from her tussore silk coat and skirt into a blue and white striped dress, with a small white hat crammed down over the knot of red hair, as usual escaping from its comb.

"I'm all right, darling! Back for dinner!" She was gone in a flash. They heard her running feet, then the banging of the street door, and then a loud happy voice shouting "Taxi!" in the Rue des Petits Champs.

"She'll get one, too," said Mr. Elliott, laying down his newspaper. "Jean has a talent for taxis. Come and watch!"

They reached the balcony in time to see a flick of the striped dress, as Jean jumped into the taxi she had snapped up as it cruised down the hill from the British Embassy.

"Jolly as a sandboy, bless her heart!" said Mr. Elliott, but his wife sighed "To think that at her age I had a maid to accompany me every time I went out."

"When you were nearly twenty-one? Oh, come now, Victoria!"

"Gilbert," Mrs. Elliott changed the subject. "Do you really approve of Jean's seeing so much of Archie Munro?"

"I don't think it matters whether we approve or not," said Mr. Elliott. "Times have changed since you and I were courting."

"Courting! You can't mean he's *spoken* to you, Gilbert?"

"No, and I'm sure he hasn't spoken to Jean herself. Archie Munro has his head screwed on the right way; he knows he can't afford to marry yet. But that's no reason why they shouldn't enjoy themselves; after all, they've known each other since last winter, when your own sister introduced him to Jean at Malta."

"I'm sorry now we allowed her to go out to Georgiana and Tom at Malta. This Munro boy has nothing but his pay, and no prospects—"

"As far as prospects go, neither has Jean. All she has is a very pleasant disposition and a lot of common sense—"

"She'll have all that we can leave her, won't she?"

"If taxation goes on increasing, and the strikes and slumps go on at home, that won't be very much. She'll be all right. Always reminds me of my Scots grandmother, old Jeanie Hay, who brought up eight children on a little farm in Berwickshire, and lived to see them all make successes of their lives."

"Yes, but I don't want Jean to have *her* children in the kind of furnished lodgings they let to young naval officers," said Mrs. Elliott.

"If Ronald had come through the war he might be very happy with some nice girl in just that sort of lodgings now," said Mr. Elliott, and ignoring his wife's stricken glance at their dead son's photograph, he repressively took up *The Times*.

*　　　*　　　*

Lieutenant Archibald Munro, R.N., in his grey flannel go-ashore suit, was waiting for Jean at the Galata Bridge, where the clanking tramcars swung right for Tophane. His dark Highland face, high-cheekboned and severe, broke into a smile when the taxi rattled down the hill from Pera, and Jean got out.

"Hallo, Archie, isn't this fun?"

"Hallo, Jean, you do look ripping! Just like the girl in the Kodak advertisement!"

"She isn't wearing a hat, and I won't either." Jean pulled off her soft white hat. With the Brownie camera slung round her neck and the blue and white dress, innocent of jersey coat or gloves, she was not unlike the windswept Kodak girl of the magazines as she joyfully went with Archie down the greasy wooden stair which separated the pavements and trams of Galata Bridge from the teeming life of the landing stages below. Swung on pontoons, these moved slightly beneath the feet of the thousands who passed under the bridge each day, traversing a city within a city where shops and booths of all kinds were selling newspapers, bazaar trinkets, dates, nuts, figs and snack meals to the crowds waiting for the arrival or departure of the boats. The ferryboats plied up and down the Golden Horn from a berth on the east side, surrounded by caïques waiting for fares; the larger vessels going to the Princes' Islands, the Bosphorus and the suburbs on the shores of Asia left from berths on the west.

Archie, lightly holding Jean's elbow, stopped at a small, clean

114

restaurant under the overhang of the Bridge near the Island steamers.

"They say this place is all right," he said, "Not too rough for you?"

"It looks fine. But Archie, I suppose I couldn't persuade you to go on to the Stamboul side and buy us some of those fish sandwiches? You know, the ones you see the men catching the fish and frying them over wood fires in the bottom of the boats?"

"What, and stand there chewing in the open air, with everybody staring at us?" said the outraged naval officer. "No fear, Jean! Besides, those fishermen probably aren't very clean—"

"I just thought it might be fun to try." But Jean went quite happily into the dark little restaurant of Archie's choice, which had freshly-wiped oilcloth on the tables, blunt cutlery and tumblers of the cheapest glass; the menu was written in Arabic and Roman scripts on a blackboard. It was a delightful contrast to the Marquise tearoom.

"You can have fish here, if you like," conceded Archie. "It's fresh from the Bosphorus."

The grilled swordfish was served in small slices on a skewer, with cuts of tomato and bay leaves between each slice and an accompanying dish of succulent new potatoes, and after that they had a rice *pilav* with raisins and pine kernels mixed with the grains. Jean, with her mother's example as a warning, declined dessert, but Archie had a pastry called "twist of the turban" with the coffee. The little place was crowded with men, mostly Greek or Levantine, and both Jean and Archie had to raise their voices to hear each other above the noise of talk, but this was a minor matter, and they were well-fed and in high spirits when they left the restaurant.

"Now for the Golden Horn!" said Jean when they came out on the landing stage. And then, touching Archie's arm, "Look! there's Mr. Barrett again!"

Jeff, with a very pretty girl beside him, was just leaving the ticket office nearest the Island boat. He turned and smiled.

"I guess this is our day for meeting, Miss Elliott," he said. "How are you, Mr. Munro?"

"We met this morning, Archie," Jean explained. She beamed at the pretty girl in the smoke-blue coat and skirt who stood beside Jeff. "But you didn't tell me your wife had arrived from Angora!"

"Well, no," said Jeff without expression. "May I introduce Mademoiselle Mavros? We're off to Prinkipo for the afternoon, on what you Britishers would call a busman's holiday."

"You're on a job?" said Archie, clearing his throat.

"I've got to do an interview. Mademoiselle Mavros is coming along to interpret for me."

"Very nice," said Archie, seeing that Jean was silent with confusion. "Catching the two o'clock express boat, are you? We'd better not detain you. We've got to get to the ferryboat ourselves."

They all parted with smiles, and Archie conducted Jean through the dark tunnel to the ferry gate before he allowed himself to laugh.

"Jean, you're priceless!" he said.

"Oh gosh, I really put my foot in it, didn't I? But after all, he did tell me he was *married*—"

Drily: "You thought they looked like a married couple, did you? I didn't. But Mr. Barrett has a nice taste in interpreters."

"She's an awfully pretty girl," said Jean wistfully.

"Too much powder and lipsalve for my taste." Archie looked down at the innocent pink face beside him and pressed Jean's hand between his arm and his side as he helped Jean aboard the Eyüp ferry. With some difficulty, for the little boat was crowded with women enveloped in black charshafs and veils and carrying mysterious bundles, they found seats on a wooden bench against the railings. The boat left the Bridge and began its zig-zag course from one shore of the Golden Horn to the other. There was a dreamlike quality in the slow movement, the shuffling off and on of the anonymous black-clad figures, the passing of the great mosques and the tumbledown buildings of the old Phanar quarter on the Stamboul side. Opposite the Phanar, anchored and rusting near their former base at Kasimpasha, the surrendered ships of the Turkish Navy swung idly with the tide.

Among them was one battlecruiser, holed and barnacled, which bore the name of the Sultan Yavuz Selim. Archie Munro knew the story of the *Yavuz*, once the *Goeben* of the Imperial German Navy, which with her sister ship the *Breslau* had slipped through Admiral Troubridge's guard in the Mediterranean in August 1914. The two German cruisers had reached Constantinople, there to be offered as a German bribe to the Young Turks, a compensation for the arbitrary British seizure of two Dreadnoughts, ready for delivery to Turkey at Newcastle-on-Tyne, and paid for in advance by public subscription. Archie also knew the story of that example of Winston Churchill's dash and initiative (and also what it cost the Allies by the entry of Turkey to the war) but he was not interested in raking up ancient history as the ferryboat sailed past the *Yavuz*. To a young man of twenty-five, 1914 belonged to the past; only, he knew, to mourners like his own mother and Jean's mother, it was still the bitter and never-to-be forgotten present.

"Here's a Navy patrol boat," he said, as they passed Balat, and Jean took her Brownie out of its canvas case for a snapshot.

"Didn't we pass one already near the Phanar?" she asked.

"There's been a pretty heavy patrol service since the Emergency. I say! There's Eyüp ahead, but it's not the last port of call."

"I know. Daddy said get off here, and then walk up the hill to the place Pierre Loti liked, and from there by a path down to the Sweet Waters of Europe. We take the ferry back from Kagithane."

They went ashore at Eyüp and walked through the little old Turkish village, where the fine fretted bay windows of mashrabiya work leaned dangerously above the narrow street. It was crowded with people, including many children dragging their parents towards the toyshops for which the place was famous, for Eyüp, companion and sword-bearer of the Prophet Mahomed, was also the patron of every Turkish child. His mosque, where each Sultan of the House of Osman girded on, at his accession, the famous sword, was one of the sacred places of Islam. Archie and Jean looked at it curiously as they passed. Two minarets rose above the dome, and one of the storks which never migrated from Eyüp flapped lazily from its nest to the surrounding trees. In the outer courtyard, which they could see through the open gates, some of the pilgrims to the inner Tomb of Eyüp were scattering *yem* for the pigeons which, like cats, had been commended by the Prophet for especial care.

"It's peaceful, isn't it?" said Jean.

"To look at them now, you'd never guess these jokers could go on the rampage in a Holy War," Archie agreed.

They walked round the outer precincts of the mosque and found the path and broad stone staircase which led up the hill.

"I'm afraid I don't know much about Pierre Loti," Archie confessed, as they began the climb.

"He wrote a book called *Les Désenchantées*, which Daddy made me read before we came out here."

"In French? I know you read a lot of poetry, Jean; I didn't know you could read French."

"It was my least worst subject at school, thanks to Dad's coaching. But the Loti book's most awfully depressing. It's about three Turkish girls who were so fed up at having to marry chaps they never even *saw* before the wedding-day that they started a correspondence with a famous French novelist—"

"Correspondence being as far as they got, eh?"

"Sometimes they all met him for a nice talk in a cemetery."

"This cemetery?"

"I imagine so."

"Pretty cheerful outing you planned for us," commented Archie, for where the stone stair ended a vast graveyard began, filling the slope of the hill above the Golden Horn with stone tombs and gravestones, some of them with the fez, and some the turban hanging in sculptured lines from the moss-grown pediment. But Archie took Jean's hand as he said it, and smiled down at her, for after all there was nothing dismal in this quiet garden of the dead. It was not like the dreadful graveyard which lay beside the Rue des Petits Champs, choked with the refuse of Pera, for flowers grew here, and tall cypresses edged the grassy paths. Far below the waters of the Golden Horn, romanticised by distance, glittered in the August sun.

"Let's stop here for a breather," suggested Archie, when they came to a place where a rough stone bench had been hewed out beneath the terraced wall. "Your pal Loti must have been quite an athlete if he climbed up and down here every day."

"He'd been an officer in the French Navy, Archie."

"Ah, that explains it!"

Jean took a shapshot of him, sitting on the bench, and then Archie snapped Jean standing against the wall where tiny scented flowers grew between the stones and butterflies, blue as the stripes of Jean's dress, hovered above the flowers. ("Wouldn't it be great if I could snap this in colour!") He took a picture of a man on a donkey riding up the cobbled way while his woman toiled behind on foot, laden with their belongings. Then Jean snapped the view downstream, where the minarets of Constantinople rode in silverpoint through the summer air, although peering anxiously into the viewfinder she declared it was "too far for a box Brownie". Then Lieutenant Munro lit a cigarette and became serious.

"I heard a buzz today that we start our Adriatic cruise at the end of the month," he said.

Jean's face fell. "So soon?"

"'Fraid so. After all, we'll have been in port at Constant. for nearly eight weeks, and the Emergency's well over."

"It looks like it."

Archie put his arm round the girl. "It was the greatest piece of luck ever, meeting you at Malta last winter, and then to meet you again on my very first shore leave, at that tennis party at Therapia. After this you'll write to me, Jean, won't you?"

"Of course I will."

Archie hesitated. "I only wish I knew what's going to happen to me next. All those cuts in defence spending at home, to say nothing of that damned Washington Treaty, have played hob with a man's future in the Navy. Thanks to the Geddes Axe, one-third of all the Captains have been struck off the List in the past year, so why shouldn't they axe me too? And if they do, then what? I can't see myself chicken-farming in Surrey; too many decent chaps have gone broke that way already."

Jean was sympathetically silent.

"What the Government doesn't realise when it orders the defence cuts," said Archie bitterly, "is that the Great War's still going on! Look at this chap Kemal, fighting the Greeks while we hold the ring; look at all the trouble in the Ruhr! I tell you, when I saw the German Navy taken in to Scapa Flow I thought, we all thought, we'd won the war at last. We were the victors, even after Jutland, which was only half a victory, and now what are we? Nothing but a lot of traffic policemen! I tell you, Jean, I'm sick of it. Sometimes I don't give a damn if I *am* axed out. Since I met you I've wondered if I couldn't make a new start, maybe in the City. Twenty-five shouldn't be too old to learn about stockbroking, or some job where the real money is."

"But the Navy is your *life*, Archie!"

"It is and it isn't. Oh, the Munros have always been a Service family, but I don't feel about the Navy the way poor old Ian did. I imagine your own brother was the same. All those chaps who were in at the beginning of the war thought they were off to some great romantic adventure, didn't they?"

"Ronald wrote home when they were ordered to the Dardanelles that he was so thrilled to be going to fight in the last Crusade, to free Constantinople from the Turks."

"I know. Well, my crowd doesn't see things that way." Archie gave his shoulders a shake. "This is a pretty dismal sort of chat for a fine day! Don't you think we should cut along and have another coffee? Your little café can't be very far away."

It was farther than they thought, for the cobbled ascent changed to a path of beaten earth following the slope of the hill. The distant view, which had once framed the charming resort called the Sweet Waters of Europe, was not attractive now, for some ramshackle factory buildings hid trees and stream from view, but when Archie and Jean reached a grove of acacias they could see a wooden building surrounded by a dusty garden set with empty tables and chairs.

"We're here," said Archie. "Tired, Jean?"

"'Course I'm not! I say, let's climb up through the trees a bit and take some pictures before we have our coffee."

"More climbing!" said Archie, pretending exhaustion. "You're an energetic young woman, aren't you?" He followed her up a runnel in the scrub in which Jean's large, flat-heeled white suede shoes were soon stained with green. He took his jacket off at the top of the runnel and made the girl sit down.

"Here's as far as we go," he said, "or you won't be able to get a picture at all with that little box of tricks."

They now had a clear view of the small café where Pierre Loti had so often sat to muse on the beauty of sunset over Constantinople. The door lay directly in their line of vision while at the side a large bay window overlooked the Golden Horn. The garden was surrounded by a low stone wall on which pots of trailing geraniums had been set.

"Pretty!" said Jean, clicking the shutter, "but they're not doing much of a trade."

"Look at those two in fancy dress," said Archie, lowering his voice. The door of the café had opened. A young man and an unveiled girl stood on the doorstep, talking earnestly. They were dressed in the Greek costume of a hundred years back, the girl wearing a tiny round hat with a long tassel and a black bolero over her white-sleeved blouse, the youth wearing a red fez and baggy white breeches. He had an antique pistol in his scarlet sash.

"That should be a good one," said Archie, hearing the camera click. "Talk about local colour!" The young man went inside the café and shut the door, the girl ran out of the garden and down the path to Eyüp. Beside him he heard Jean gasp.

"Oh *gosh*! I forgot to wind the film!"

"Honestly—!" Archie took the camera from her hands and adjusted it. "That's your last frame," he said, "better make the next one good."

The café door opened again. The youth reappeared with a very tall man in a tussore suit, carrying a panama hat.

"They're moving!" said Jean. "It's too fast for my shutter speed!"

"You always say it's too fast or too far." The men stood still in the empty garden, the younger scowling and silent, the older talking with an emphatic nodding of the chin which made him look like a bad-tempered camel. Jean knelt upright, the Brownie held tightly to her breast. The man's face, with its close-set eyes and elliptical symmetry, came full into the viewfinder. She took her last picture and sighed with relief. "That one should be good," she said. "I think having people in it gives a picture life, don't you?"

"Oh Jean, you are a silly darling!" And Archie pulled her down into his arms and kissed her for the first time, full on the lips, under the blue butterflies of Eyüp, so that Jean sighed blissfully, seeing life stretching before her peaceful and happy, as if war and rumours of war had never been.

Nothing more was said between them, for Archie was afraid of saying too much and Jean could only think in terms of the poetry she loved, but they were both smiling and happy when they reached the now deserted garden of the small café. The youth appeared at the door almost as soon as Archie opened the gate.

"Engliss?" he said. "Very sorry, madam. Sorry, sair! The café is close."

"There's nothing here to say so," Archie replied.

"*I* say so!" said the boy impertinently. "*Allez, fermé! Geschlossen!* Café is close."

"Couldn't we just have a cup of coffee?" pleaded Jean. "We've walked a long way in the heat, and I'm *so* tired!"

"No coffee," said the boy, relenting slightly. "You stay in garden and I bring you sherbet. Orright?"

"All right," said Archie briefly. "— You're not really tired, are you, Jean?"

"Not a bit."

"Closed, indeed! Extraordinary way to run a pub!"

Lukewarm sherbet in sticky glasses appeared on a brass tray swinging by three brass chains from the young man's hand. He named the price, took the money and left them without further words. Jean sipped her sherbet dreamily. She was folding away all Archie had said about his future, and the memory of his kisses, to think about when she was at home alone.

"I don't see Daddy bringing my mother here," she said, remembering the purpose of their visit. "For one thing, he'd never get her up that path, and for another I'm sure the Golden Horn's a whole lot *dirtier* than it was in Loti's time."

"I'll bet it is."

"Dad raved about this little place, you know. I hate to go back and say we never even saw inside it. Couldn't we just peep?"

"I think the natives are distinctly hostile."

"Pooh! What harm can we do, just looking?"

"You do like to jump into things, Jean!" But he followed her up the steps and pushed the front door open. A wave of heat, thick with an unpleasant odour, rolled out to meet them. They were on the threshold of a single room, many windowed, with a long curtain in two folds down the left-hand side, and the usual cushioned benches running round three walls. Untidy blankets on one of them showed it was in use as a bed. A little dry stone bowl with a broken fountain attachment stood on a centre table and held the stub of a still smouldering cigar. An unlit oil lamp hung from the fly-blown ceiling. On the wall opposite the door there was a chromo of the very scene they had passed on their way, the cobbled pathway and the cypresses, with in the foreground a Turk with curling mustachios and a turban, courting a lady in a long *feraje,* whose amorous black eyes glowed above an almost transparent *yashmak.*

"I thought they didn't go in for pictures of human beings," said Archie in a whisper.

"These people are Levantines, that's why they're in fancy dress." Jean, too, spoke very quietly, and neither of them had moved from the door. But the subdued voices brought an astonishing response. They heard a hoarse cry from behind the curtain:

"*Mon commandant! Mon commandant! Ne me quittez pas!*"

"What the devil—?" began Archie Munro. But Jean had already pulled one of the curtain folds open with a great jangle of rungs. They saw an alcove, partitioned with thin wood, without a window but provided with a table holding a jug of water and a towel, a palliasse on the floor, and the youth in "fancy dress" crouching beside a narrow bed. On the bed, on top of a grimy blanket, lay a man flushed with fever under a heavy growth of beard. Over black trousers he wore a dirty shirt, the right sleeve of which had been torn off at the shoulder. The man's right arm, swollen to twice its normal size, was roughly bandaged from the shoulder to the finger tips.

"*Mon commandant!*" he moaned again, "*ne partez pas!*"

The Levantine boy uncoiled himself like a young snake. "You go now, miss! This not your affair!"

"Don't be so silly!" said Jean Elliott indignantly. "This poor man is very ill!"

Archie held the boy tightly by the shoulder. "Who is he?"

"Is my brother—is vair bad boy—was in a bad fight with an Engliss sailor—"

"And you couldn't put him into a nightshirt, or make him comfortable in bed!" said Jean. "Look at those filthy bandages!" The Scottish instinct to take charge, to boss, to do good to an unwilling victim, rose up strong and true in her heart. "Have you a knife in your pocket, Archie?"

He had, of course. "I hope you know what you're doing, Jean. . . . Now then, mister, you just stand still—"

"I've got my Red Cross certificate." But she gasped when the arm was laid bare, with the red lines of blood poisoning crawling into the armpit, where pus oozed from a long unhealed wound. The fingers were turning black. The sickening odour of gangrene filled the room.

"He must have been suffering for days," said Jean, aghast. "Have you no sterile dressings, nothing, for his arm?"

The youth indicated, on the other side of the bed, a box containing torn lengths of linen, and a bowl with a liquid which might have contained disinfectant.

"Where's the nearest doctor?" said Archie.

123

"My sister has gone to Eyüp for the doctor."

"And high bloody time too."

"Oh, that's good!" said Jean. She wiped the sweat from the sick man's face. "Poor fellow," she said in French, "how did you get such a horrible wound?"

He answered quite coherently, "It was the knife of Monsieur Trakas."

Archie asked, "Can you understand what he says?"

Jean, with her eyes fixed on the man in horror, answered "I think—that he must be—the Trakas killer." And looked round to find herself staring down the barrel of the antique pistol, which the Levantine boy had pulled out of his sash.

"*Archie!*" But Archie had the boy by the scruff of the neck, the other strong hand on the hand that held the pistol, which fell harmlessly on the straw palliasse. They struggled together, but only for a moment, reeling out into the big room and knocking over the ornamental fountain in their fury, and then Archie's trained strength mastered the sobbing youth.

"Make sure there's no one else here!" he gasped. Jean pulled open the other fold of the curtain. A primitive kitchen, empty, was revealed.

"Can't you see any rope? I've got to tie this beauty up—"

There was no rope. There was a roller towel on the wall, there were some dirty dish towels on a hook, all easy to cut with Archie's knife: the Levantine boy was tied up quickly to the kitchen chair.

"You're sure you heard him right? He *is* the man who killed your father's friend?"

"He said so—and then his arm; there was blood on Monsieur Trakas' knife."

"Can you go to Eyüp, as fast as you can, and bring up the police?"

"Archie, I've got to be the one to stay!"

"Do you think I'm going to leave you with a murderer?"

"*He* isn't able to do me any harm. And I understand what he's saying, and you don't; besides, at the gendarmerie they'll only listen to a man."

Lieutenant Munro had been trained to estimate a situation and take action. He knew that what Jean said made sense; he knew that every minute counted before the girl came back to reinforce her brother, with or without a doctor. He merely said "All right. Was that the gendarmerie, opposite the mosque, where the Turkish flag was flying?"

"Yes. Oh hurry, please."

"You're not scared?"

"No."

"You're a great girl." Then he was out, and running through the garden, down the path; Jean wondered if he would overtake the man who looked like a camel, and who that man was.

"*Qui est votre commandant?*" she said to the sick man.

"*Le commandant Cravache,*" he said at once.

"Was that he who was here just now?" But that set him off on the old tack, begging the major not to desert him, not to leave him in this hole, dying . . . until he fell into a kind of coma, and was still. Jean bathed his arm with the disinfectant liquid, laid the linen cloth over it and wiped his lips. She could think of nothing else to do until the doctor came—or the police, whichever came first. Archie had been gone for fifteen minutes.

She sat on the floor beside the bed. In the stifling, evil-smelling silence she became aware of a ticking clock. There was no sound from behind the kitchen curtain, and she began to wonder if the boy had lost consciousness in the struggle with Archie; certainly he had never spoken as Archie tied him to the chair. There was no sound from the garden: the café favoured by Pierre Loti might have been in a crater on the moon. She was beginning to shake with strain and anxiety.

"Madame Mavros!" said the sick man on the bed.

Jean had an inspiration. "Here I am!" she said.

He seemed to realise that it was a woman bending over him. He clutched at the front of the striped dress and begged her, begged Madame Mavros, not to send him away with the Syrians. To let him stay there in safety, in her nice house . . . after all, he had done everything the major told him. He had shot the old Greek, Trakas—but Major Cravache had never warned him that Trakas might draw a knife—and no one, he swore by Almighty God, had followed him to the scent shop, all wounded as he was—

"Was it Cravache who planned the Trakas murder?"

"Yes."

"If I write your confession down, could you sign it with your left—"

She was dragged violently backwards by the coil of her own red hair. The Levantine boy was upon her, lean and supple, beating her over the head and breast, swearing, choking, while the sick man screamed in the high voice of fever from the bed. Jean felt her senses going. But she was strong, with muscles developed by tennis and fencing, and the boy, who had already fought with Archie, was amazed to find her fighting back. They struggled together on the floor, each one attempting to rise above the other, and then Jean's bruised cheek fell upon the pistol on the palliasse. She managed to get one hand out of the boy's stranglehold, and seize it. She beat the butt of the antique pistol across his face.

Jean struggled to her feet. The man on the bed lay rigid, his eyeballs rolled back to show the yellowish whites. Blood poured from the nose and mouth of the boy on the floor. Jean's nerve broke as she fumbled and pulled at the closed door. "Help! Oh Archie, help!" Then the heavy boots sounded on the cobbles. Archie had done better than the Turkish gendarmerie. He had brought up reinforcements from the Royal Navy's Golden Horn patrol.

8

AT ALMOST THE SAME time as Archie Munro, on the landing stage at Eyüp, was blurting out his story to the officer in command of the patrol boat, the Island steamer was approaching the harbour of Prinkipo. Jeff Barrett and Leila stood by the rail, looking at the red roofs of the white villas scattered along the slopes of the largest of the Princes' Islands, and breathing in the scent of the *maquis* drifting out to meet the boat. Wild roses, lentisk and thyme were mingled in that perfume with the scent of flowers from the villa gardens, for the Islands, where so many Byzantine princes had been blinded and held captive by the rulers who dreaded their rivalry, were now a favourite summer resort of the wealthy Greeks of the capital. It was only since the downfall of Imperial Russia that a new race of princes, defeated and exiled, found their way to the Islands from Constantinople.

"Pretty, isn't it?" said Jeff, as the steamer's whistle startled a flight of birds from the pinewoods above the high red cliffs. He was not prepared for the deep feeling in Leila's sigh.

"Oh Jeff, it's beautiful! It's like the islands I am loving at home, at Smyrna!"

"Are there islands in Smyrna bay?"

"Yes, but far out, nearly in the Aegean; how do you say, in the Gulf of Smyrna. I am going with my family often; Uncle Homer would hire a boat, and we are taking food and wine, and going for the whole day to Doctor's Island, where the giant fig trees grow. A whole village of people would be living there under the trees."

"Camping out, you mean?"

"I guess so." Leila had picked up one or two of Jeff's expressions. "With straw mats strung between the boughs for roofs and walls, so that each family is having a little house by themselves, and all summer long they are working in the olive groves and tending the fig trees."

"Sounds wonderful."

"Oh, it was! There were many children, and I was swimming

with them in the Aegean Sea. It was so warm and so blue, just like here."

"And in winter, Leila, what did the folks on Doctor's Island do? Go back to town?"

"In winter they are going back to Anatolia."

To Anatolia—of course, he might have known the fig growers were not likely to be Smyrniots; their home village would be somewhere in the coastal plain, or even somewhere in the foothills of those mountains behind which lay Angora and Kemal.

"You think a lot about Smyrna, don't you, darling?" he said.

"I worry so much about my grandmother. She's so old and so frail—"

Jeff looked fondly down at her. Such a little thing, hardly reaching to his shoulder, and so easily swayed by the mood of the moment! She had been so gay over the luncheon table at Tokatlian's, so happy to be going on this trip with him, and now the thought of her poor old granny had actually brought tears to her eyes. He put his arm protectively around her.

"Don't let's be sad today, cutie. This is a sort of holiday, isn't it? Talking to Madame Tricoupis won't take long, and then we'll go and look for Vava."

"The prince?"

"Prince Ivan Vorosilov. You'll like him, Leila, he's a great guy."

"But first, I am being your interpreter with Madame Tricoupis?"

"You wouldn't enjoy it, honey."

"But you told those people—"

"I just said the first thing that came into my head."

Leila giggled. "They were thinking I am your wife! But can't I come with you to the house of Madame Tricoupis? I am wishing so much to meet the General's lady."

"I know, honey, but this is work. She mightn't like it if I took a friend along."

"Why are you writing about the Greeks now, Jeff?"

"Because the editor wants me to. Remember I told you about interviewing Hepitis, the Greek admiral, one of those days I came into town from the Lines?"

"I remember," she said, but not convincingly. Leila was not good at remembering the things he told her about his work, but then why should she be? She wasn't like Eve, with all the details at her pedantic finger-tips. He said,

"He was a funny little guy. I jazzed the story up a bit for Donnelly."

He had jazzed it up so well, in fact, that Mr. Donnelly—that master of hard cablese—had wired: "Hepitis fine send more stuff Greeks etrussrefs." It had taken even Jeff Barrett a few minutes to decode "etrussrefs" into "and Russian refugees".

"You are being so clever, Jeff." He doubted if Leila had quite understood, but she sure knew what to say to make a guy feel good! Jeff stepped between her and three hurrying sailors, for the steamer had reached the jetty now and the gangway was ready to be run out. Women in summer dresses and pretty Greek children in white were waiting to meet the passengers. The light frocks and parasols were the keynote of a scene which breathed brightness and gaiety by contrast with the sombre tones of the Turkish mainland. On the right of the waterfront a line of carriages was waiting for hire, on the left there was a miniature promenade with café tables set out along a low sea wall. The cafés and beach hotels on the other side of the narrow walk were not especially inviting, but their shabby exteriors were wreathed in green creepers and bougainvillea. Leila, at any rate, was not critical; she said it was "lovely!" as soon as they went ashore.

"You'll be all right here for an hour, won't you, sweetie?" said Jeff, as he settled her at one of the tables, under a pink beach umbrella. Leila smiled her thanks as he ordered coffee for her and brought her a fashion magazine and a box of *lokum* from the promenade kiosk. Leila had a passion for lokum, which Jeff knew better by the name of Turkish Delight.

He looked back at her before approaching the line of carriages, and was glad to see that she was already talking to two young women at the next table, one of whom had a baby on her knee. Jeff thought Leila looked "kind of overdressed" beside them in her smoke-blue coat and skirt and velvet hat, and her grey suede shoes with the three-inch heels looked more like Pera Street than Prinkipo. Poor pet, she enjoyed putting on her little bits of finery! He was trying to cultivate an indulgent attitude to Leila, to think of her as a kitten, or a little girl; for sleepless in the night after their emotional reunion at the Petits Champs he had told himself again and again that he mustn't let his feeling for the child get out of hand. And then he had been conscripted into the Chatalja press camp, and promptly came down with dysentery, like every second man there; so that he felt too weak to be ardent while the bout lasted. Once or twice, while the Emergency dragged on, it had been possible to arrange transportation to the city, with six or seven correspondents crowded into a ramshackle taxi; and then Jeff had a bath in the room he had kept on at the Pera Palace, several rounds of drinks at the bar, and gave Leila supper at the Petits Champs between her two performances. He had not yet asked her to go back to the hotel with him. He was pretty sure that she would come to his room if he asked her, but he couldn't do it, couldn't walk her through that lobby, up to that lift, under the familiar, cynical eyes of his colleagues, only to leave her in a couple of hours and go roaring back to the Lines with a bunch of raucous drunks. This trip to Prinkipo, now, was different. He didn't quite know what he expected to come out of that.

Most of the little carriages had been hired by passengers from the steamer, which could now be seen making its way to the last outbound port of call, Yalova on the Asiatic shore of the Sea of Marmara, and only one remained on the rank at the waterfront. It was too much to hope that the driver would be Vava Vorosilov, but the man was certainly a Russian, and had a familiar face.

"Haven't I seen you round the Pera Palace?" Jeff began. "I'm Jefferson Barrett of the *Clarion*."

"Boris Volkonski." The driver bowed ceremoniously over the reins. "Of course I know you by sight, Mr. Barrett; I often saw you with Prince Ivan Vorosilov, about a year ago."

"That's right. I'm told he's living on Prinkipo now; I'd like to see him."

"He's not only living, but working," said Volkonski with a wry smile. "At the moment he's having luncheon with his mother; would you like me to drive you to their home?"

"I don't want to disturb the Princess, and first off, I've got to get to the Villa Myosotis. Is that far?"

"Get in, sir." It was a little embarrassing to be driven up the hilly main street of Prinkipo by a former colonel of the Preobrazhenski Regiment, and to pay him off, with a substantial tip, at the door of the villa, but at least it wasn't a long ride, and the Russian drove off with a flourish of his whip, promising to get a message to "Vava" at what sounded like a corner in Kiev. Jeff turned his mind to Madame Tricoupis. He saw at once that there was nothing to be got out of her worth more than a line in his Greek story; the general's wife received him graciously, and appeared to be quite forthcoming, but she had learned the lesson of discretion well, and confined herself to predictions of a Greek victory in Anatolia, brilliantly led by her husband, of King Constantine's triumphal entry to Angora, and so on. To Jeff's more probing questions she conveniently raised the language barrier, although her English, when she recited the prepared lesson, was quite fair. Jeff noted that the villa was most luxurious, that the coffee service was of the finest Sèvres, and the lady herself elaborately dressed. He expressed the hope of meeting General Tricoupis himself in the near future, and took his leave. It was exhilarating to see, about a hundred yards down the road in the direction of the town, Prince Ivan Vorosilov lounging at his ponies' heads.

"Vava, you old horse thief!"

The Russian reared his great height of six foot six off the shaft of his little carriage and folded Jeff in a bear's embrace. The dandy of last year's *thés dansants* looked wilder than Jeff had ever seen him, with an untrimmed moustache and shaggy tawny hair drooping over a cotton blouse cut in the Russian peasant style; shabby trousers tucked into patched cavalry boots completed the Tolstoyan image. Prince Ivan Vorosilov, the last of his name, was barely twenty-four years old. He had been thrown into action as a boy soldier when Brusilov's great attack on the Austrians renewed Imperial Russia's hopes of victory in the summer of 1916, and he had been in combat continuously for four and a half years thereafter, until General Wrangel's final defeat at Sevastopol brought the hopes of the White Army to an end. Now he was one of the "russrefs" of Donnelly's cable: one of the most fortunate of the one hundred and twenty thousand thrown up in Turkey on the ebb-tide of the Great War's storm.

"Come and have a drink," he said, when the boisterous greetings and explanations were over. "Come on down to 'A Corner of Kiev!'"

"Oh, it's a bar, is it? I might have known!"

"Bar—restaurant—club—rooming-house; Igor Nelidov owns it, remember him? I've got a room myself at the 'Corner'; Irina and my mother are sharing a little house with some other ladies. But the 'Corner's' the place for gay bachelors like me."

"I'm game," said Jeff. "Can we go there by the waterfront? I brought a girl down with me for the afternoon."

"A girl for the afternoon. Same old Jeff! Who is it this time? One of your last year's loves?"

"Her name's Leila Mavros," said Jeff. "She's not much more than a kid."

"Any relation of the great Rosette? Not a daughter, surely?"

"She calls Rosette aunt, but it's not that close. Near's I can work it out, Rosette was Leila's mother's cousin. She's singing at the Petits Champs, so we've got to go back on the early boat," Jeff concluded, and the Russian's lips pursed in a soundless whistle.

"Let's go!" he said laconically, and the little carriage went rocking down the hill. It was not, as Mr. Braun had said, an araba, but what the Turks called a *fayton* and Jeff a surrey, the canvas canopy having a fringe that swayed with the speed of Vava's driving. He drove the two grey ponies as if he were competing in a trotting race under the eyes of the Tsar and the Tsarina, and his voice, when he turned to speak to Jeff, had the Cockney inflections picked up as a child from his father's English jockeys. His manner, when Jeff introduced him to Leila, was impeccable; the little singer and the prince in exile might have been greeting each other at a reception in the Winter Palace.

Leila was an immediate success at "A Corner of Kiev". They got there by a roundabout way, for Vava insisted on taking them on the five-mile drive round the Island first, and pointing out the beauty-spots. Leila leaned back in the fayton with her hand in Jeff's; she had taken off the unsuitable velvet hat, and the black curls which had been pinned up beneath it fell loosely on her shoulders. The reflection from the pink canvas canopy turned the nectarine of her cheeks to rose. She said Prinkipo reminded her of Smyrna; Vava said it reminded him of Cap Martin on the French Riviera, where his parents had a villa when he was a child. "Sold before the War, unfortunately, it would have been a home for my mother and sister now," he said with a nonchalant twirl of his whip. Prinkipo reminded Jeff of no place in particular; it simply relaxed him, and made him indolently happy to be driven through the warm afternoon with Leila's hand in his, along the red roads of this island of refugees from reality.

It was a lotus life on Prinkipo, Vava Vorosilov admitted when they were settled in a back room at the "Corner of Kiev" with a bottle of chilled white wine and a plate of fruit on the table between them. Personally he owed his life of comparative comfort to his mother, who had stopped him gambling away the last of the money they had brought out of the Crimea, in time to get them all to Prinkipo. He wondered if the old Jew still kept that room in the Pera Palace where he bought the diamonds, the Fabergé Easter eggs, the furs which the more fortunate refugees had brought with them. Shut up shop, had he? Ah well, the supplies were bound to be running low! Was General Wrangel still living aboard his private yacht, and did he still believe that the army of Russians he had led into exile would be needed to put down a revolution in Germany? Jeff Barrett had seen the *Luculle* anchored in the Sea of Marmara and planned to interview the White Army general as soon as possible. What Wrangel thought of Germany now was anybody's guess. As Jeff pointed out, the Genoa Conference had shown the strength of the "new" Germans, who seemed eager to co-operate with the Soviets.

"I'll back the Germans against the French any day," said the proprietor of the "Corner of Kiev". "If the French had had their way in 1920 we'd have been thrown out of Turkey and moved on to Brazil, slave labour for the *hacendados*. That, or certain death as guerilla fighters in the Caucasus."

There was a murmur of agreement, for the back room had filled with six or seven Russian ex-officers, eager to meet the American correspondent and hear his comments on the news. They brought with them two young Russian wives and some Greek girls, all of whom made much of Leila. "Everybody is being so sweet to me!" she whispered ecstatically to Jeff. She had a craving for affection, and Jeff knew that what made the cabaret life bearable and even pleasant to little Leila was that "all the girls in my dressing-room are being so nice to me!" It sounded improbable, given the reputation of the Petits Champs chorus, but Leila was full of prattle about the sweetness of Doris, Lili and Justine. When tall glasses of tea were brought in to the back room the girls were all gossiping together while the men continued to question Jeff: about Kemal's intentions, about the Greek initiative in Thrace, about his life at the Chatalja Lines in a tent city on that dismal frontier. They laughed loudly at his account of the

"Galloping Third", ferried across in horseboats from their fox-hunting in Ismid to hold the fifty-mile-long front with a very mixed defence force of Spahis, Senegalese and two companies of Ottoman troops. Jeff knew that some of the men who questioned him had fought all through the Great War from Tannenberg to the Crimea and had won every conceivable Russian decoration from the Anna to the Vladimir Cross. They might wear the blouse of the moujik as they plied for hire among the villas of Prinkipo, but they were still loyal to the regiments which would never fight again.

He began to block out his story at the back of his mind. He would lead with the horrors of refugee life in Constantinople: the court ladies reduced to prostitution, the noblemen fiddling in the dance bands of the nightclubs in Taksim Square. Then he would play up the work of the American Near East Relief Mission, which was feeding seven thousand of the Russian refugees and had found shelter for some of them in the Sultan's stables at Dolmabahce Palace, and use a quote from General Wrangel—when he saw him—to introduce the more sinister note of the thirty thousand men, most of them armed, in the great refugee camp on Gallipoli. And then, by contrast, he would describe the "Corner of Kiev", that little haven on the remote Turkish island—

Almost as if Vorosilov had read his thoughts, the tall young Russian said, too quietly to be heard by any of his friends:

"You think we're leading the life of O'Reilly here, don't you?"

"The life of *Riley*, Vava! Yes, I think you're pretty well fixed here at Prinkipo, for the time being."

"Ah, for the time being! That's the whole point, my friend—I don't think it can last."

"You ought to be doing something more active," said the American. "I told you last year you ought to apply for a U.S. visa—"

"I've had enough action to last me a lifetime, old boy! And this place suits me nicely. A fine open air life, and I earn enough to keep my mother and Irina," said Prince Ivan Vorosilov, once the heir of vast estates in Georgia and the Crimea. "No, the new master of our fate is your military friend in Angora. If Kemal Pasha throws out the Greeks, he'll throw us out along with them. His pals the Bolsheviki will insist on that."

"In all fairness, I've heard him say he would respect the special status of the White Russian refugees as Turkish residents."

"Was he sober when he said it?"

"Not very."

"Well, then!" Vava Vorosilov exploded in a roar of laughter. He stood up and stretched his tall body, his arms almost touching the low ceiling, and shouted to the landlord, "Bring vodka, Igor Ivanovich! Tell us what we're going to have for dinner!" And after that nothing serious was said in the back room of the "Corner of Kiev".

*   *   *

It was much later in the evening when Leila sang for them. The Russian husbands and their wives had left as soon as the meal was over, the Greek girls remained in the warm room, now full of cigarette smoke and the smell of the crude *retsina* wine which was all the cellar offered when the vodka and raki had gone round. There had been songs, and slow caresses given and taken when the balalaika music warmed the blood: they sang "Dark Eyes" and "The Red Sarafan" and all the soldier songs of 1914, good-bye my near ones, good-bye my bride. There had been toasts to Denikin, to Wrangel, to Winston Churchill, with Igor Ivanovich imploring them not to break the glasses after they drank. In the songs the sweetness of Leila's voice had been heard, and after she had shaken her head at the unfamiliar balalaika somebody brought in a Turkish *kitara* and she agreed to sing.

"But we mustn't miss the last boat, Jeff!" she said. The earlier boat had been missed before they ever started dinner.

"We'll make it, sweetie."

"Because there'll be a double fine to pay if I miss both the shows!"

"I don't suppose it'll break him, mademoiselle," said a voice from the shadows, and Jeff interposed, "Sing 'Maid of Athens', dear."

"That's a man's song," said Vorosilov.

"Like hell it is, she sang it when she was auditioning for the Kristal, didn't you, Leila?"

But Leila swept her small fingers across the strings and sang one of the old-style Turkish *gazels* which suited her voice so well:

135

"Row gently, let not the moonlight wake,
Let not the water, lost in a world of vision, wake."

The lyric had the ebb and flow of the ocean. Jeff gave himself up to
the seductive, coiling, gliding tune, and to watching Leila as he
remembered her first, not in the tinsels of the cabaret, but
curled up in one corner of a big sofa with her little feet in their
grey silk stockings just visible beneath her skirt. Her face was
flushed and the black curls clung in tendrils to her moist forehead; her mouth was like a summer fruit. Desire invaded Jeff's
body; he saw by their eyes that more than one of the Russians
desired her too.

Nobody spoke when the *gazel* was finished, and Leila, after
hesitating, and smiling at Jeff, said "Lord Byron's song!" and
began:

> *"Maid of Athens, ere we part,*
> *Give, oh give me back my heart;*
> *Or, since that has left my breast*
> *Keep it now, and take the rest!*
> *Hear my vow before I go,*
> Zoë mou, sas agapo."

"What a little beauty! You're in luck, Jeff," whispered
Vorosilov. Jeff made no reply, and Leila sang:

> *"By that lip I long to taste;*
> *By that zone-encircled waist;*
> *By all the token-flowers that tell*
> *What words can never speak so well —"*

"You're not taking her back to Constant. tonight, are you?"
murmured Vorosilov. "I'll give you my room here. Irina can fix
up a sofa for me at the villa."

"Thanks, Vava, but Leila wouldn't like it. You wouldn't
understand."

"What is there to understand? She's a pro., isn't she?"

"A *what?*"

"A professional singer, old top, what did you think I meant?"
said the Russian smoothly, while Leila ended:

136

> *"Though I fly to Istambol,*
> *Athens holds my heart and soul:*
> *Can I cease to love thee? No!*
> *Oh, my life! I love you so!"*

"And now we've got to hit the trail for 'Istambol'," said Jeff firmly, over the applause. He suddenly wanted to be alone with her, away from Vava's whispers and the watching eyes. The farewells, the thanks, the messages to friends, were quickly said. The "Corner of Kiev" was so near the little harbour that there was no need of a fayton: Leila even in high-heeled shoes made light of the distance. She was very quiet as they walked through the sleeping town. There was no moon, but the stars were bright above the Sea of Marmara, and in the distance, coming from Yalova, they saw the lights of the steamer for Constantinople. The only lights on the Prinkipo promenade, where all the beach umbrellas had been furled for the night, shone in the bar of a small hotel called the Calypso.

"I wish you didn't have to play that second show at the Petits Champs," said Jeff.

"I do too." He looked down at her; the small face, usually so vivid, was expressionless. He felt the warmth of her body against his own.

They had come to the end of the promenade, and the jetty gates were open in front of them; only three other passengers were waiting for the last steamer of the night. And Jeff watched the steamer coming, the lighted portholes growing in size, the figures now to be seen moving on the deck. He felt that this was the great moment of decision, that on what he said now more than one life might hang, that what he ought to do was walk on with Leila, present their return tickets at the jetty gates—

He stopped and caught her to him, with all the rising fever of the evening beating in his brain and in her flushed cheeks.

"Leila, stay with me tonight. Here, where nobody knows us— nobody in the world—let me be your lover—Leila, *zoë mou!*"

She was great enough—as it seemed to him—to offer no arguments and no resistance. For Leila only echoed his last words, and called him "my life"—"Jeff, *zoë mou!*" before she walked back with him to the Calypso Hotel.

*   *   *

About half past nine next morning a taxi took Jeff and Leila to the entrance of the Pera Palace.

"Honey, you'd better have some coffee while I check the mail and make a few phone calls," said Jeff. "The tea we had on the boat was horrible; and after that I'll take you home."

"Coffee would be nice," the girl agreed. Jeff was proud of her composure. He knew she was dreading the inevitable scene with Rosette, and he intended to take the brunt of that upon himself, but he admired the calm way Leila walked into the hotel, and the way she looked—wonderful for a girl whose only toilet articles had been a clean handkerchief and a pocket comb! He smiled down into her trusting dark eyes as the hall porter said,

"A cable for you, Mr. Barrett. Nothing else today so far." But the door of the assistant manager's office, which stood ajar, suddenly opened wide, and Albert Braun's shrewd face looked out.

"I thought I heard your name, Mr. Barrett—" He caught sight of Leila, stopped, and bowed. "Good morning, Miss Mavros. We haven't had the pleasure of seeing you at the tea dances for a while. Will you forgive me if I ask Mr. Barrett to give me five minutes of his time?"

"Right now?" said Jeff.

"Well, yes. It *is* rather urgent."

"Just let me order some coffee for Miss Mavros first," Jeff said easily. He took Leila into the ladies' drawingroom, at that hour as empty as the adjoining bar.

"Nobody is being here, Jeff!"

"No, but you don't mind that, do you, baby? They're all having breakfast in their rooms."

He told a waiter to bring her coffee with rolls and honey, and left her with a kiss. At the door he looked back: Leila looked very small in the huge tapestry chair, soft as a little dove in her smoky blue, but the smile she gave him touched Jeff to the heart. He thought of the tawdry bedroom in the waterfront hotel, and dawn breaking over the sea. He was as nearly sure as any man could be that he had been Leila's first lover, and yet the child had made love like a great big woman—! Jeff dragged his thoughts back to the present hour, and the urgency of Mr. Albert Braun.

When they were in his office with the door shut Braun began:

"Have you seen the morning papers, Mr. Barrett?"

138

"I didn't stop to buy one at Galata Bridge. Miss Mavros and I spent the night with friends at Prinkipo, and I knew she was anxious to get home. What's new?"

"The police have caught the Trakas murderer."

"My God! Where?"

"At a little café up the Golden Horn. He was brought back to Constant. about five o'clock, and confessed to the murder shortly before he died."

"He's dead?"

"He died not quite two hours later, of septicaemia and gangrene, resulting from a knife wound."

"Trakas and the paper-knife!"

"Exactly. There's a short account in the *Orient News*."

Jeff took the English-language paper. The two words *Missed it!* thundered in his brain. After having a clear world beat on the murder story, he was about fifteen hours late on the dramatic sequel. Donnelly would have taken the story off the Associated Press before midnight, Constantinople time. Hell! He scanned the story quickly. Jamil Riachi—Damascus—murder was plotted by a group of Arab terrorists— He said, "The *News* hasn't given it much of a play. What did the Constant. papers give it?"

"Banner headlines. According to my Turkish colleagues, the local press doesn't believe in the Arab terrorist tale. They say the whole thing was a Kemalist plot."

"Kemal gets blamed for more damned things—" Jeff thought of Hamdi Bey at the cabaret, on the night Trakas was killed.

"Do you know more about this than the papers do?" he asked abruptly.

"Yes, I think so, Mr. Barrett. You know we have our own police sources at the Pera Palace. Our information is that there is a great deal more to this affair than what was contained in the press release. For one thing, it wasn't the Turkish police who found Riachi, it was a British naval officer —the Allied censorship won't let *that* pass, and for another, far more important, Madame Rosette Mavros was arrested yesterday evening and has been held for questioning. Riachi said she gave him shelter in her flat before he could be got away up the Golden Horn."

"My God! "said Jeff again.

"The police are being very circumspect with Madame Rosette, because as you probably know she has powerful connections out at

139

Yildiz Kiosk, but they've set a police guard over the shop and her apartment, and—I'm sorry, Mr. Barrett—they went to look for Miss Leila at the Cabaret des Petits Champs."

Jeff drew a deep breath. "Between ourselves, Al, I wouldn't put anything past Rosette," he said. "But that little—Leila— she mustn't be dragged into a mess like this."

Mr. Braun coughed. "We have a single room vacant on your floor. Would you like to reserve it for Miss Mavros until we can find out how the police enquiry is going on?"

"A hide-out here? That wouldn't do much good." He thought of the porters, the waiter, who already knew Leila was in the hotel. A sense of guilt, of having got in too deep, stunned his capacity to think. Take her back to the Russians on Prinkipo? "Wait a minute," he said, "I had a cable. What the hell have I done with it?"

For some reason he had put it carefully inside his wallet. He opened the flimsy enevelope, and there it was: the solution to all his problems, Leila, Evelyn, the story he'd missed, contained in a few terse words from Donnelly:

"Proceed urgentliest smyrna assess greek military position stop halliday athenswarding for coverage greek government regards donnelly"

"I'm ordered to Smyrna," Jeff told Mr. Braun. "Is there a boat this afternoon or must I wait until midnight?"

Mr. Braun consulted a timetable on his desk. "You're in luck," he said, "there's a boat at noon. I doubt if you'll get cabin space at two hours' notice, though."

"I'll have the hall porter call the line and book two tickets right away."

"You're taking— ?"

"Sure. And if the police come nosing round, looking for Leila here—"

"I shall have no idea where she's gone."

9

"JAMIL RIACHI, 22, was arrested by gendarmes in the neighbourhood of Eyüp on Tuesday and charged with the murder of Mr. Hercules Trakas, the well-known entrepreneur, at the Pera Palace Hotel on July 31. Riachi, a native of Damascus, died in the hospital of the Central Prison two hours after confessing to the crime which, he said, was planned by an Arab terrorist group. Shukri Khalil, 19, also from Damascus, has been charged with harbouring Riachi in a café of which he is the manager."

"Is that all?" asked Evelyn Barrett.

"The very last para," replied Abdul the son of Riad, folding up the Turkish newspaper from which he had been translating brief news items from Constantinople.

"Not much in any of them."

"No."

"So shall we go?"

"You're impatient, Mrs. Barrett."

"I want to get a good place in the Listeners' Gallery."

Abdul sighed. "You'll be the only woman there." They were sitting in the dusty public garden opposite the Grand National Assembly building, and it was the eighteenth of August, the day when Evelyn was to hear Kemal address the Deputies.

"I *have* heard of women listening to the debates from time to time," she said.

"Yes, middle-aged ladies, experienced political ladies from Europe, not a girl like you," said Abdul bluntly. "The Deputies will think you shameless. They will stare."

"I thought one of the aims of the Revolution was to put Turkish women on an equality with men?"

"One of the Gazi's aims, maybe. The Deputies don't agree with everything *he* says. You'll see."

"Well, there's no point in arguing about it, Abdul. The Gazi himself gave me a card for the Listeners' Gallery."

"But *Mr. Barrett* never goes to the debates, he relies on me! He can't understand anything that's said, and neither can you!"

"That's why I want you to sit beside me, in case I need a translation."

"The Gazi is quite capable of speaking for hours. I've got to take his speech verbatim, for my own paper."

"Get one of your colleagues to spell you, then." Evelyn got up, smiled at her friend the ayran seller with the wonderful brass cart, and led the way out of the garden. As they crossed the road she took a fresh pair of white gloves from her handbag. The staring Deputies must not have an excuse to think her shameless in dress, at least, and with this in mind she had put on a dark-blue cotton frock with long sleeves, and arranged the wide brim of her hat to hide her eyes. Still she felt conspicuous as she passed under the gaze of the Laz guards at the entrance gate. They were waiting for Kemal, of course; their presence was a sure sign that he was going to take his place in the Assembly. For a fleeting moment she wondered if these two men had ever waited in the car on the highroad while she and Kemal walked up and down the poplar lane.

"This is the prayer room," said Abdul, when the doorkeeper allowed them to pass. Through a half-open door opposite the entrance Evelyn saw a miniature mosque, orientated towards Mecca, with rugs spread on the floor and a plaque with Arabic writing representing the *mihrab*. The door of Kemal's office as President of the Assembly was also open, revealing a desk and three leather chairs standing on worn linoleum. They walked on down a narrow corridor with the Cabinet and other conference rooms on the left-hand side. The chamber in which the Grand National Assembly met was on the right. The Young Turks had intended it for concerts, so it had two galleries, one used by members of the diplomatic corps of Angora, the other—called "the Listeners' Gallery"—by members of the press. The floor of the House was fitted with school desks and resembled an overgrown classroom with the Speaker's tribune in the place where a schoolmaster would stand. The rostrum beneath the two petrol lamps had been draped in black ever since the Greeks captured Brusa, a holy and historical city of the Turks.

Some of the Deputies stared as Evelyn came in, but the chamber was only beginning to fill up, and in the back row of the Listeners' Gallery she was not conspicuous—far less so than Masha Levin, the girl from the Russian press office, who thought a dirty scarlet sweater appropriate wear for the Assembly, and wore it defiantly in the very front row. Evelyn watched the Deputies coming in and taking their places at the uncomfortable little desks. There were a number of *hojas*, the Moslem teachers, in white turbans; there were greybeards in the long kaftans they were too conservative to lay aside; there were a few of the younger Deputies who might have been western businessmen. Finally there was Madame Emine, the widow of Fuad Bey, whose appearance in the Listeners' Gallery caused a great deal of rearranging places and moving along the hard wooden seats. Madame Emine, smiling her 'persimmons' smile, acknowledged the courtesies and the attention: the smile died when her eyes met Eve's. She bowed politely across the breadth of the gallery, but her expression was one of mingled exasperation and regret. Evelyn realised with annoyance that in acknowledging Madame Emine's bow she had missed the entrance of Kemal.

Somehow, she had expected the President of the Grand National Assembly, the *de facto* Chief of State, to enter to the sound of drums and trumpets. Kemal came in alone and accommodated his slim body to one of the little desks far more easily than most of the portly Deputies. He was out of uniform, wearing a kalpak and a black morning coat like several others present, but there was no mistaking the hawk's profile, nor the incandescent vitality which gradually made itself felt throughout the chamber. It was the presence of Kemal, and not the Speaker's bell, which stilled the restless Assembly.

"Doesn't he have a special place to sit, as President?" Evelyn whispered to Abdul.

"He sits anywhere he likes when he means to speak."

"What are they doing now?"

Abdul had his notebook open on his lap. He quickly printed in pencil: "Question time. Food supplies. The usual."

After the questions there were three brief speeches from the rostrum, each punctuated by heckling and interruptions, while Kemal sat motionless, his arms folded on his chest. The Speaker rang again and again for order. When the third man stepped down Kemal took a pencil from his waistcoat pocket and tapped on the lid of the little school desk. It was his way of asking for the floor, and the Speaker recognised him immediately. In a mutter of anticipation that was like the growl of summer thunder, the President took his place on the rostrum.

Evelyn had heard much, from Jeff and others, of Kemal's hypnotic power over the Assembly, and she had wondered if, in this other phase of the Revolution, the soldier would reveal himself a demagogue, a Svengali. When he told her the theme of his speech—an appeal for the unity of the National Pact made three years earlier at Erzurum, and for his own absolute freedom in the conduct of the war—she had thought it might easily be an excuse for melodrama; but nothing could have been quieter than Kemal's beginning. He spoke very slowly, his deep tones dropped to what one female admirer called "his Sarah Bernhardt voice" and filling the chamber with their resonance. He stood erect, hardly moving, with no gestures except once, when the long fingers of his right hand snapped in a gesture of disdain. The language he employed was far more complex than the simple Turkish Evelyn was learning to speak, and yet she thought she could almost follow what Kemal was saying. She watched a great variety of expressions on the faces of the Deputies. Some of them boldly interrupted the President's speech, notably the hojas, who rose from different parts of the floor to interject criticisms in high snarling tones which turned quickly to falsetto. They were backed up by two swarthy men, cramped into one of the front desks, whose heckling became a barrage the Speaker was powerless to control.

"From Trebizond. Hostile to Gazi," wrote Abdul, and Evelyn nodded. She saw Kemal, without hesitating, change his attack. The orator became the street-corner politician, the hawk turned into a vulture, and the apt insult he leaned across the rostrum to fling at the Deputies from Trebizond brought a roar of laughter from the House. The reporters laughed too, and looking along the gallery Evelyn could see that even Madame Emine was smiling. Smoothly, Kemal drove his advantage home. The short, biting sentences bullied his opponents into silence. The President had regained total control of his audience, and now he flung at them a new word, which reduced them all to an absolute stillness. Abdul wrote across his notebook:

"*Cumhuriyet* = Republic."

In the same quiet manner in which he had begun, Kemal concluded his speech to the Assembly. It had lasted for barely twenty minutes—time enough, in Evelyn Barrett's mind, for many things to fall into their proper place. When Kemal spoke, that pathetic classroom, badly lighted and smelling of petrol from the ceiling lamps as well as of packed human bodies, raucous with the contrary opinions of men of all classes and occupations, became indeed a workshop in which democracy was being forged. It was Kemal's genius for leadership which made his speech an emotional experience for everyone, and for Evelyn herself the acceptance of an elemental force of nature. She had been in his arms a score of times, had been subtly brought from rejecting his kisses to desiring them; it was only now, from the distance of the Listeners' Gallery, with a sea of heads between them, that Evelyn Barrett cried out inwardly:

"Oh, my God, I've fallen in love with him!"

*   *   *

She realised that the reporters were leaving the gallery, that Abdul was asking her to excuse him now, that Madame Emine had left her own seat and was saying:

"Good-afternoon, Mrs. Barrett. Do you find our parliament interesting?"

"Very interesting indeed, though I couldn't understand all of what they were saying."

"The Gazi was in excellent form."

"He certainly held his audience," Evelyn said quietly.

"When are you going to keep your promise to have tea with me?"

"Any time, madame."

"Then why not now? The Gazi has gone, you see; the fireworks are all over for today."

It appeared that Madame Emine had hired an araba for the afternoon. It was not a long drive to her home, and she talked very pleasantly on the way, pointing out a picturesque gypsy band leading a dancing bear into Angora, and the harvest gold beginning to colour the little cultivated fields on the edge of the great steppe. Nothing more was said about the Assembly as they drove across the Chubuk river, which the drought had reduced to a silver streak of water.

Madame Emine's house was within sight of the White Bridge, with the seven pointed arches which had stood for exactly seven hundred years. Like Chankaya, it had a ring of poplars behind it; in front of the low stone house, where a half-wild garden sloped down to the Chubuk, a line of willows with huge knotted trunks dipped narrow grey-green leaves to the surface of the water.

"What a glorious place!" Evelyn exclaimed as they drew up at the gate. "How fresh, how much cooler, everything seems to be out here!"

"I was so lucky to find a house like this, outside the city."

"Isn't it rather isolated?"

"In one way, of course, I *am* isolated now," said the Turkish lady, in the intense way which seemed to give all her words an inner meaning, "but no one could feel *lonely* here. There's always traffic on the White Bridge, and then I do a great deal of visiting among the humble peasant people, whom I love."

There were no humble peasants in the immediate foreground, but a manservant came out and directed the driver to take his araba to the barnyard and wait there for the Hanim Efendi's guest, and a woman appeared on the veranda of the red-roofed house. "That's my maid, Zala," said Emine tranquilly. "I told her to prepare tea as soon as I came home. Unless of course you'd prefer coffee?"

"Tea would be delightful."

"Be welcome to my house." The two women walked up the wooden steps and entered, by the open veranda door, a long low room, where as well as the Turkish divans with their embroidered cushions there were several deep velvet armchairs, low tables holding magazines and pots of flowers, and crowded bookshelves on one entire wall. Through an open doorway could be seen the foot of a low, wide bed with a violet satin spread laid over it.

"Books!" said Evelyn. "Oh, may I look?"

"Of course." As she spoke, Emine loosened, without removing, the long black silk scarf which covered her head and shoulders. A fold of black hair, streaked with grey, was revealed above her forehead; her face, with its too-large eyes, resembled a cat's face, watchful and intent. She watched Evelyn roaming about the beautiful room, touching the morocco bindings of books printed in several languages, looking at the mosaics framed in gilt and the silk Persian rugs hanging on the wall.

"I hear Zala bringing the tea-tray," she said. "Do come and sit by the fire."

"A fire, how welcoming!" said Evelyn. "I can't believe it's cool enough for that."

"The house is built of stone, and is never too warm; besides, the evenings have been cool here since the beginning of the week. Have you no fireplace, where you live?"

"No, but there's a charcoal mangal in the yard, that I cook on. I'll take it indoors if the weather turns cold."

"Be sure you have proper ventilation, then," said Emine, directing the maid in arranging the tea things on a table. "Charcoal indoors can be quite dangerous. But you'll have left Angora, I imagine, long before snow flies."

Evelyn reflected that her hostess must feel the cold, for the fire made the room almost too warm, but the pine logs smelt delicious, and it was pleasant to relax in a deep chair after weeks of Ayesha's spartan furniture. The smoky tea and tempting cakes were served from English Georgian silver; the fat rose-tipped cigarettes were offered in fine Lalique boxes from Paris. And Emine's voice was soothing as she led the talk to San Francisco, "which I know so well from the stories of Jack London and Frank Norris", drawing out the girl to talk about her father's house on Pacific Avenue, and the holiday visits to the Nevada ranch.

"It sounds a delightful life," she said. "You must find Anatolia very harsh and bleak, by comparison."

"It's not a soft life here," said Evelyn, "but this is a most wonderful moment to be living in Anatolia."

Sighing: "If only all the suffering would end ... Tell me, what did you really think of the Gazi's performance today?"

"Performance?"

"His speech, then. I call it a performance, because although I've never been inside a theatre, I imagine that's the way a first-class actor works."

"His appearance is very striking, certainly."

"Very striking, and of course he knows it! I hope you won't think I'm calling *you* theatrical, my child, when I tell you that you look rather like the Gazi yourself. I thought so in the Gallery this afternoon; it must be your fair hair, and your high cheekbones."

Evelyn was silent, with a sick feeling of having been spied on in a private experience.

147

"Yes, Kemal Pasha is a born actor," Emine went on. "I enjoyed him today, even though I knew he only took part in the debate because he has been under fire recently for his failure to take the offensive against the Greeks. That was why the hojas attacked him, in the first part of his speech."

"I imagine the Commander-in-Chief is more capable of drawing up a battle plan than a group of religious teachers!"

"The hojas accused him of wasting time over drink and women. You didn't understand what they were saying?"

"I only understood the key words in the Gazi's speech."

"What do you call a key word?"

"The one that shut them all up. Cumhuriyet. Republic."

"Ah, Cumhuriyet. Yes, that was very bold. Everybody knows that when Mustafa Kemal speaks of a Turkish Republic, he thinks of himself as its first President."

"Does anyone else have a better right?"

"It's not a question of right, it's a question of democracy. And *he* has all the instincts of a dictator."

"You say so, and yet you fled from Constantinople to join him?" said Evelyn.

"Not to join *him*, but as a gesture of protest when the British occupied our parliament and trampled on our few remaining liberties. I offered part of my fortune to the Revolution. I hoped to do my share in striking the old chains from the women of Turkey. I did *not* come here to help a Macedonian adventurer to become Turkey's tyrant!"

"Is that what you think of the greatest soldier Turkey has ever known?"

Emine did not answer. She got up to arrange a finely meshed fireguard across the hearth. Then she said softly,

"How long have you been in Turkey, Mrs. Barrett?"

"Only since the middle of June."

"Only a few summer weeks. Would you be very angry with me if I advised you to leave Angora—now—at once?"

"But why?"

"Because you ought to be with your husband now, or he with you."

Evelyn smiled. "I can't go with Jeff on all his assignments, Emine Hanim. Does that concern anybody but ourselves?"

"It appears to concern Kemal Pasha," said Emine. "The whole

of Angora society is talking about his attentions to you, and your appearance at the Assembly debate today will only add fuel to the fire! . . . Now wait, *please*! I was a student at the American College, I understand the freedom of American girls, I'm sure it all began innocently enough with a few morning rides on the steppe, but now—it's so public, it's so obvious what he feels for you! *He* won't trouble to hide it, he parades it, everybody sees it—"

"Do people say he really cares for me?" said Evelyn, in such a hushed and tender voice that Emine whispered "Allah!" before she sat down again in her great chair.

"My child," she said, "Mustafa Kemal has never loved a woman in his life. He only cares for two things, Turkey and himself."

The repeated "child" grated on Evelyn's ears. She knew it was a common Turkish phrase, she had heard Kemal say "my child" to his orderly when an American officer would have said "son", but she was not prepared to accept it from Emine.

"I wish you wouldn't keep calling me 'child'," she said. "I'm not a little girl. I'm twenty-five."

"How old do you think Kemal is?"

A lovely smile flowered on Evelyn's pale face. She said, "He once told me his true birthday was the nineteenth of May in 1919, when he landed in Anatolia to start the Revolution. He counts his real age from then."

"I know, I know, and it's what you Americans call a very cute story when you hear it for the first time instead of the fiftieth. I can tell you what his real age is. It's my own age exactly, almost to a month. He's forty-one."

"Oh, I could believe it of you, madame," said Evelyn pleasantly. "But *he* never seems to be any age at all."

"He's reached an age when most men in Turkey have been married for years, and have sons growing up around them. Kemal Pasha ought to marry now, Mrs. Barrett. If he aspires to lead this country after the war he must marry a Turkish girl, of the Moslem faith, to reassure our spiritual leaders that he means to keep Turkey within the Moslem fold . . . At one time I thought his choice would fall on Fikriye. Heaven knows she has adored him long enough!"

"Perhaps Kemal Pasha doesn't believe in cousins marrying?"

"Fikriye's not a blood relation. Kemal's mother, Zübeyde Hanim, married twice, and Fikriye was the stepfather's niece. I must admit she was very foolish when she came to Anatolia; she told too many people that she had come to marry him, and of course he was displeased. But now she's sick, and Kemal can't bear to have sick people near him. His mother's illness was a good excuse for getting rid of Fikriye—after you came to Angora."

"I hardly know Fikriye Hanim," said Evelyn. "But the one time I had coffee with them together at Chankaya I thought she was terribly possessive and jealous and *soft*. And I don't think Kemal Pasha cares for women who dramatise their troubles. What he admires is independence."

Her intention had been to destroy the self-righteousness on the feline face. She was not prepared for Emine's start of dismay.

"You're not thinking . . ? Oh no, that would be impossible. Haven't you been happy in your own marriage, my—dear?"

Evelyn looked into the fire. If Emine had asked that question earlier, when the girl was soothed and relaxed by the comfort of the beautiful Turkish room, it was just possible that she might have opened her heart to the older woman. But after the attack on Kemal all was changed, and Evelyn said only:

"Jeff and I married in haste, and have had plenty of opportunities to repent at leisure."

"You hadn't known each other long? Fuad Bey and I met for the first time on our wedding day, and yet we were very happy. We might be happy still, if it hadn't been for the troubles, and this—passion for killing."

"Mine was a war wedding too. Spring 1918 was a terribly emotional time, and I couldn't refuse Jeff when he talked about going to France, and wanting some happiness to remember over there."

"You obviously have a strong fixation on soldiers," said Emine thoughtfully. "But Mr. Barrett is a very charming man. What really went wrong between you? Was it a case of sexual incompatibility?"

"Forgive me," Evelyn said coldly. "It's second nature with me not to discuss that side of our marriage—even with my friends." She took her handbag from the floor beside her chair and stood up. "I mustn't keep the man waiting any longer. Thank you so much for giving me tea."

"I'm afraid I've offended you, Mrs. Barrett. Believe me, I only spoke out for your own good—"

"I detest being spoken to for my own good."

"Because you're afraid of being revealed to your own self, my dear. Have you ever read Freud?"

"Not since I was in college," Evelyn said. "We studied *Uber Psychanalyse* in class."

"Oh, so you *have*—"

"In our sophomore year we used to discuss our fixations and frustrations to a fare-thee-well; after that we more or less outgrew it."

Emine's white face flamed. "Very well," she said, "you use mockery in self-defence, but remember this: if you're fool enough to let him, Mustafa Kemal will use you for his pleasure as he's used a thousand others, and then desert you for his next fancy, as he deserted poor Fikriye for yourself. He sticks at nothing, not even murder; and he doesn't understand the meaning of the word loyalty. Friends and helpers like me are abandoned whenever we refuse to bow down to his will—"

"Emine Hanim," said Evelyn, "you understand Americans so well, I'm sure you know this New York saying: 'with friends like you, who needs an enemy?'"

*　　　　*　　　　*

Darkness had begun to fall earlier over Angora as August advanced, but the sunlight still lay gold over the apricot trees and the well-head when Evelyn returned to the wooden house among the poplars. By the time she had bathed and changed from the sober dark-blue dress into the freshly laundered yellow cotton, the quality of the light had changed as well, into the bronze and umber of a tremendous Anatolian sunset, which Ayesha declared must mean a change of weather.

There was something else that was different in the air, something Evelyn in all the confusion of her feelings was attempting to define when Ayesha came waddling along from the rammed-earth hut with her usual cheerful grin and greeting. She had two letters for the Hanim Efendi; there had been a mail delivery that afternoon while Evelyn was at the Assembly, and the girl had to listen to some account of Ayesha's repartee with the mailman before fetching her purse to refund the surcharge the woman had paid on the letter from San Francisco. It was one of Mrs.

Anderson's peculiarities that she invariably understamped her letters to Europe and the Near East, and her daughter sighed when, Ayesha having reluctantly departed, she read the California letter first. It dealt extensively with the "message" of a Swami called Vivekananda who had recently caught Mrs. Anderson's eclectic fancy; Evelyn read only enough to assure herself that everyone in the family was well before she turned to the other letter, which was from Jeff.

> "Pera Palace Hotel,
> August 16, 1922

Dear Eve [Jeff had written],

Donnelly wants heavy coverage on the Greek front and has ordered me to Smyrna. Halliday is being moved from Vienna to cover Athens.

I'm going south on the noon boat today, and before some busybody spills the beans I want to tell you that I'm taking Leila Mavros with me. Rosette is in a mess of trouble here and Leila wants to go home to her own family.

Remembering what you said to me before I left, Eve, I don't think you'll object to this, and if you want to make something out of it you can go ahead. I'll be at the Kramer Hotel in Smyrna, and if you're short of money please wire me there. I've cabled Donnelly to send you half my August pay check.

> Regards to Monseigneur,
> Jeff."

Halfway through the reading of this letter Evelyn started up with her hands clenched on the paper until it almost tore; at the end she flung it down on the red Angora goatskin, with all the resentment kindled by Madame Emine's interference flaring up into a blaze of anger. She was too furious to read between the lines of Jeff's bravado, which recklessly concealed his own guilt and confusion. "Regards to Monseigneur"—that jaunty ending was an insult to Kemal, and the offer of half his August salary an insult to herself. Send *her* money, while he went off with a cabaret girl! Evelyn had accounts with the Osmanli Bank both at Constantinople and Angora, and these were well looked after by her father, who ever since her marriage had made her an allowance which Jeff resented while he helped to spend it. Short of money, indeed! Telegraph Jeff Barrett for money! Never!

But Evelyn was too honest with herself to remain furious long. What Jeff had written was in essence true: she *had* told him, before he left Angora, that they were the wrong people for each other, their marriage a mistake. She ought to have realised that during their brief engagement, but now it was difficult to remember the Evelyn Anderson of that emotional spring of 1918, so ingenuously attracted to the young man who was soon going "Over There", so naïve to the point of ignorance about sex and marriage. If I'd gone away for just *one* weekend with Jeff before we went through that—that grotesque ceremony at City Hall, she thought, I would have known we would never be happy in that way together. Emine Hanim had been right about sexual incompatibility, but the girl who had read Freud and Clausewitz, and graduated from college *summa cum laude*, had then had no idea what those words meant.

It was just possible—and Evelyn had often thought this before—that if they had had a real home in the first months of their marriage, they might still have come together completely, but Barrett had been ordered almost at once to the training camp at Plattsburg, where his wife could only visit him for occasional Saturday nights in a tawdry hotel room. He had complained endlessly about being "holed up at Plattsburg", out of the firing line, and their first serious quarrel had exploded on the Saturday when Evelyn, in all good faith, had asked why, "if he felt so badly", her husband couldn't put in for a transfer to a combat outfit. The line Jeff had taken then was that she wanted to get him killed. And so it had gone on, from war into peace, from the sports desk to the Paris Conference, until here, in Turkey, they had come to the end of the road.

She had herself in hand, but only just, when Kemal came walking through the yellow dusk, far earlier than she expected him; and Evelyn flung herself into his arms with a new abandon which told him that the hour of his triumph was not far off. He was much too wary to press home his advantage, but instead—as he had been doing for three weeks past—kissed her tenderly, and told her she was lovely, *"iki gözüm"*—"my two eyes", and Evelyn smiled at the beautiful Turkish endearment which told her she was more to him than sight.

"But Kemal, have you been in Angora all this time?" she said in surprise, for he was still wearing the black morning coat of the Assembly debate. It looked oddly formal in the plain little living-room with the whitewashed walls and the deal floor.

"I held a Cabinet at four o'clock," he said, and flung his kalpak on to one of the divans. "And by the way, before it started I sent Sami Bey to find you and offer you the car. The Lazes at the gate said they'd seen you driving off in great style with Emine Hanim."

"She asked me to go home with her for tea."

"Did you enjoy yourself?"

"Not really."

"Emine talks too much," said the most tireless talker in Anatolia. "What had she to complain about today?"

"Oh, she rambled on . . . Kemal, was her husband under your command when he was killed?"

"Far from it. Fuad Bey was three classes ahead of me at Harbiye, and he was killed in the street fighting in 1909, when the Sultan Abdul Hamid was trying to keep his throne. Why? Does Emine Hanim blame me for his death?"

"Oh no, it was just an idea I had," said Evelyn discreetly.

"Emine's a feminist," said Kemal. ". . . Yes, raki, thanks . . . Come to that, I'm a feminist myself, at least so far as equality between man and woman goes; but I told Emine Hanim, when she turned up full of enthusiasm for the Revolution, that any woman who undertook to work for me must take her medicine like a man if the work wasn't up to standard. She said she understood that." He smiled reminiscently. "Of course the work I gave her wasn't quite grand enough for the lady. Her demotic Greek is very good, so I put her on to translating the Greek newspapers and propaganda sheets. But she was mortally slow, and one day I gave her the rough side of my tongue, as I would to any junior officer; and then we had tears and sulks and hysterics, and that was the end of Emine in the translation department."

"I wish I'd heard you," said Evelyn vengefully, and Kemal cocked an eye at the glass she held in her hand.

"Don't tell me you're taking to raki too!"

"I still think it tastes like a cough remedy," said Evelyn. "But it's got something, after all."

Kemal laughed. "You haven't told me what you thought of our zoo."

"The Grand National Assembly?"

"What else?"

Evelyn ignored the flippant tone and answered gravely: "I thought I saw a nation being born again."

Nothing she said could possibly have pleased him more. Kemal set down his glass and kissed her in silence, thanking and blessing her in his heart for the vision that matched his own.

"But—it's not an easy birth," she said when he released her. "You—you alone can bring it about; you swayed them, it was marvellous, but some of them hate you—don't they?"

"I know they do," he said indifferently.

"Especially the two Deputies from Trebizond."

"Filthy fellows, they'll have to be eliminated sooner or later."

"You mean in an election?"

Kemal's grin was savage. "Trebizond is on the Black Sea, and the Black Sea is notoriously dangerous. Did you ever hear of a Communist agitator called Mustafa Subhi, who disappeared from the deck of a ship in those turbulent waters? Something of the same sort might easily happen to those gentlemen."

Evelyn drew back. "Sometimes you frighten me," she said.

"Why?"

"Because you are so—ruthless."

"Never ruthless to you, Evelyn *mon amour*."

Kemal was so sparing of endearments, so unlike Jeff with his monotonous "baby" and "honey" that Evelyn was seduced by the love words. She let him take her in his arms again, and ask her very softly if she understood him better, as she had hoped to do, now that she had seen him at grips with his Assembly.

"I understand—oh, much better—all you have to do before Turkey is a free nation. You have to . . . inspire . . . and fuse all those different people, all those men . . . and the women you'll have to free and reach as well. You'll have to say 'we' instead of 'I' when you talk to them—"

"We?"

"Yes. Today you said 'I' all the time. *Ben, ben, ben, ben. I* think, *I* want, *I* say . . ."

"What I mean is this: I want everyone to do as I wish and command."

"Like Mussolini?"

"Don't compare me to that mountebank!"

"I'm only thinking of what might be the world's opinion."

The steel-blue eyes flashed fire. "I'm not concerned with the world's opinion. I act for the nation and my own satisfaction."

"But when you're the President of the Turkish Republic, and one of the world's leaders?"

Kemal struggled between amusement and annoyance, and amusement won. "Upon my word," he said, "you're heckling me like a hoja! I can't remember listening to a woman's advice before."

"Do you take advice from many men?"

"Not often . . . Perhaps from Ismet Pasha . . . But Ismet's a long way away, and you are here."

"And so happy to be."

The soft whisper intoxicated the tired man. Kemal drew Evelyn's fair head to his shoulder, and whispered in his turn: "I told you there was a better way for a man and a woman to understand each other. Have you thought about that, my two eyes?"

"Very much."

"But you still say no?"

Evelyn was silent. He laid his hand upon her breast.

"Have you never had a lover, Evelyn?"

"Never."

"Barrett was the first and only?"

"Wait!" said Evelyn in a voice that stopped the movement of the caressing hand. "There's something I must tell you. I'm going to light the lamp."

The yellow flame sprang up, the petrol was as pungent in the little room as in the classroom that was called a parliament.

"I had a letter from Jeff tonight," said Evelyn Barrett. "He's gone to Smyrna with a girl called Leila Mavros. He—won't be coming back."

Kemal sat very still. He thought, as often before, that a great part of the art of war lay in waiting for your enemy to make the first mistake. Not that Jeff Barrett was worth being called an enemy; he was merely a fool, but his classic error had given his rival the advantage. He said,

"Why Smyrna?"

"The paper sent Jeff there, and the girl went with him because her aunt, or cousin, or whatever she is, Rosette Mavros, is in some sort of trouble."

"She *was* in trouble," said Kemal. "She was held for questioning in connection with the Trakas murder. No doubt you've heard of that?"

"Had *she* anything to do with it?"

"Only as the tool of a man called Cravache. You asked me about him a couple of weeks ago."

"Jeff asked about him." Evelyn stood pondering, with her left thumb on her chin. It was one of several of Kemal's mannerisms which she had unconsciously begun to copy. Jeff's the one who's in a mess of trouble, she thought. I bet he fell down on the story, too.

"You mean this Major Cravache planned the murder?"

"He was the master mind behind it, certainly. The Constantinople papers are blaming me for it," said Kemal negligently, "but this time Cravache is the guilty man."

"But *why*? What harm had this old Greek done to him?"

"None whatever. But by eliminating Trakas Cravache did away with a great conciliator, the only man who could have got the British and the Sultan's government to see eye to eye on the Capitulations. With him gone, it will be possible to drive a wedge between the British and all the Christian communities in Turkey, and in the long run to destroy British influence all through the Near East."

"And don't the British know Cravache is responsible for all this?"

"Certainly they know it. An English girl found out that he was in it—she went to the Embassy, screaming for justice to be done."

"I thought the British were so strong on justice."

"But they daren't quarrel with the French. The French and the British are, on the surface, allies; Cravache is French; therefore the British are saddled with Charles Cravache to all eternity.'

"I think that's terrible."

"It's high politics, a question of expediency. And now let's forget about all that: tell me why you're so sure that Barrett isn't coming back."

"Because he told me if I wanted to make anything of his going away with Leila Mavros, I could. He remembered what I said the last morning he was here—"

"What *did* you say?"

"I told him there wasn't any sense in our marriage, and never had been. I said we were all wrong for each other—"

"And then?"

"And then you came." It was said simply, revealingly; Kemal got up from the divan and came towards her.

"You never told me this before," he said.

"It's only fair that I should tell you now."

In his arms, close pressed against his body, Evelyn felt the frightening outline of the pistol holster underneath his armpit, and once again she evaded his embrace, begging that they might ride tomorrow, begging him—for now—to go.

10

THE STORMY YELLOW SUNSET, as Ayesha had predicted, ushered in the first rain of autumn. All through the night, and well into the next morning, heavy rain and wind lashed the high plateau where Angora stood, and it was nearly three hours later than the time planned for their ride that Kemal rode through the Chankaya gates on one of the beautiful horses from Eskishehir and drew rein to wait for Evelyn.

A few paces to the rear of his master, Captain Riza shivered, and hoped the shiver would pass unnoticed. He had five hours of solid work behind him, for the Gazi was already in the study when Riza came on duty at six that morning, and remarked casually that he had gone to bed at three. It was a miracle how he stood the pace. Most of the Staff felt like men strung on a piano wire being pulled ever longer and finer and more taut; and even the Gazi, Riza observed, was showing signs of nerves this morning. He had pulled his left glove off, and was alternately stroking his fair moustache and thumbing his chin as if in indecision. Riza hoped the ride, and Mrs. Barrett's company, would do him good. Riza Bey did not think Evelyn Barrett especially attractive, he preferred plump, dark, giggling girls like his own Feride, but the Gazi's preference—of the moment—was obvious enough. It was Riza's opinion that very soon there would be hell to pay.

"Here they come!" said the Commander-in-Chief.

He was nervous, but it was not the nervousness of indecision. Kemal had just made one of the momentous decisions of his life. For three hours, while the roof gutters of Chankaya overflowed, he had lain on top of his bed in his shirt and trousers, lighting one cigarette from the stub of another, and planning for the future. It was not the first time he had passed a sleepless night, but never before in his life had he stayed awake to think about a woman, and that one the woman he now intended to make his wife.

What he felt for Evelyn Barrett could never be satisfied by a casual affair, such an affair as he had planned at the beginning. In

159

a few summer weeks she had become indispensable to him: her talk, her thinking was now as important as her exciting physical presence. And since Barrett had played the fool, and was off, there was nothing—he swore to himself, nothing—but a legal obstacle, easily surmountable, to their marriage.

Evelyn came up the muddy road laughing, with her mare's hooves striking up splashes of water from the puddles, and Kemal grinned as he moved forward to salute her. For the first time she had left off her hat and skirted riding coat, and he guessed that in her new mood she cared as little as he did for shocking public opinion. He saw two female figures coming away from one of the officers' chalets and stopping to stare at the American girl in shirt and breeches.

"Bravo, madame!" he said with his hand at his kalpak, "You've got the bit between your teeth, I see. We'll ride fast and far today: no holding back?"

"None!" Evelyn accepted his challenge gaily. They trotted through the plantation and broke into a gallop at the edge of the steppe. On the plateau where Evelyn was accustomed to stop, Kemal urged her on; it was Captain Riza, having his orders, who now halted there with the orderly who had escorted Evelyn from her home. Their figures grew small in the distance while Kemal led the girl on, though watchful of her as always, across the parched turf newly refreshed with rain, beneath the great skies of Anatolia.

"All right?" he called over his shoulder, and Evelyn called back, "Yes! Where are we going?"

"I want to show you something." They were riding uphill, along a faintly marked track past a stone where a little staring shepherd boy was sitting while his flock grazed twenty yards away: they scattered as the horses came among them. Then the track disappeared between the undulations of the steppe, and Evelyn saw that they had reached a cleft, too small to be called a valley, where a few little acacia trees already turning yellow drooped their shivering leaves above a tiny spring. Far overhead a hawk hung in the blue.

"How pretty!" Evelyn said as they drew rein. "Living water! I thought the steppe here was bone dry."

"This is the spring that waters my garden at Chankaya," said Kemal. "It goes underground further west, and when it appears again it's fed by other springs, but this is where it rises."

"And there's actually a patch of green here, so soon after the rain," said Evelyn, as Kemal helped her from the saddle and tethered the horses to a tree. "Now I understand how the camel drivers feel about an oasis."

"A real oasis has a well," objected Kemal. "Your little yard is *my* oasis."

"With Ahmed's well!" she said, delighted, and let him pull her down to sit beside him on a flat rock which stood beneath the shivering golden leaves. Their two heads, both so fair, were very close together, their shoulders touching, but Kemal made no move to embrace Evelyn. His narrow hands were tightly clenched. He was looking in dismay at his own riding crop, thrown down a few feet away. What had possessed him to carry it today? He had hurried out of Chankaya at the last moment, taking the first crop to hand from the rack where he kept such things, and where this blackened stick hung more as a memento than for use. It was the riding crop of Gallipoli, the crop he had raised at dawn on the heights of Chunuk Bair to launch the great holocaust in which fifty thousand men had died. It was the symbol of victory but also of death. Kemal had a superstitious streak in his nature: he was shocked at having carried such a symbol to this hour with Evelyn.

"What's the matter?" said her soft voice beside him.

"Nothing." He took her hand and kissed it. From somewhere in the distance came a thread of melody, tenuous as the murmur of the spring.

"What is that music?" whispered Evelyn.

"It's the shepherd boy, playing his pipe."

"Oh!" She laid her cheek against his shoulder. "If only it could always be like this!"

"It could be," he said.

"Our lives one long holiday, out on the steppe all day, instead of the rationed hours?"

"It *could* be so," Kemal repeated obstinately. "Look up, my two eyes, and let me tell you how it will be so."

The brown eyes, sparkling as he loved to see them, were raised to his, and the Commander-in-Chief, awkward as a boy, said in his careful English:

"I must say this to you in your own language. I love you, Evelyn. Please will you marry me? Please."

"Kemal!" He gave her no time to say more. He seized her in his arms and covered her face and throat with kisses.

"Kemal—I *am* married."

"Your marriage was as good as over, you said so last night, before you and I were ever once alone together."

"Still, it exists legally."

"A civil contract—it can be set aside. Will you, Evelyn? Will you divorce Barrett and become my wife?"

"*Your wife!*" she repeated, as if she hardly realised the future which he held before her. "Kemal, how can I? What would your friends say, what would it do to the Turkish Revolution, if you married an American divorcée?"

He damned his friends comprehensively, and included the Turkish Revolution; they could all go to hell, he said, the woman of his choice must be their choice too. "Only tell me this," he said, "if you were free now, would you choose *me*?"

"Oh, my darling," said Evelyn, and her eyes filled with tears, "if only I could!"

"You have!" Kemal said exultantly. "You will! Now let me hear you say it—"

"What more is there to say?"

"Only what you've never told me yet."

"But you know it already," said Evelyn, "that I love you too."

"Now I'm completed," said the Commander-in-Chief. And while Evelyn's emotion kept her silent, he—never at a loss for words—began to analyse their happiness, to tell her how love for her had risen in his heart "like that living water", how he could not say the awareness of love had come upon him more at one time than any other: perhaps when they played the war game together, perhaps when they danced at the Russian Embassy, or strolled in the poplar lane; but in fact it was the sum of all their hours together, this enchantment that she had laid upon him. . . . And then he asked to be told when Evelyn first realised that she loved him, and she replied in her straightforward way:

"It was only yesterday, when I heard you addressing the Deputies."

Then Kemal's tension broke, and he roared with laughter, the hearty laughter which often shocked the sombre Turks around him. "That's the best excuse for our zoo that I ever heard in my life!" he said. "Come along home to Chankaya, Evelyn, and let's drink to the future in champagne."

"I can't go to Chankaya dressed like this," she objected as they got to their feet.

"Why not? We'll have luncheon alone, there won't be any other guests this day of all days."

"But there'll be the servants, and your secretary, and the aide-de-camp on duty, and people hoping to see you—I can't eat lunch at Chankaya wearing my breeches and boots!"

Kemal nodded approvingly. Fastidious to the point of mania in his own grooming and choice of clothes, he knew Evelyn was right. He said, "Wear your pretty green dress, then, the one from Italy." He looked at her with fire in his strange blue eyes. Her small breasts hardly swelled the white silk shirt, and she was wearing a man's belt round her slender waist. He dug his thumbs inside it and pulled her body close to his own.

"This is the way I love you best!"

"Dressed like a boy?"

"Oh, my innocent Evelyn!"

*   *   *

The Commander-in-Chief was at all times capable of bathing and changing into uniform in fifteen minutes. On the day of his proposal to Evelyn Barrett he was dressed in twelve, scowling at his watch and wishing he had not said he would send the car to fetch her in an hour. For when she talked about their rationed hours she hadn't known that they were already limited to rationed minutes, and he must leave for Polatli at three o'clock.

He ordered his soldier-servant, Sergeant Ali, to bring him a glass of raki and a bottle of water, and when the man had obeyed and left him Kemal stood sipping the drink in his big airy bedroom, where a safe now held, folded in its map case, the map which he had kept in his desk drawer downstairs. All his paperwork was done, and certain papers were in a despatch box with the map case; every other detail was carried in his head. He looked at his watch again. He wished now that he had gone home with Evelyn: what did food or even drink matter at such a time, when it was vital not to let his influence over her slacken for a moment? Kemal knew quite well that although Evelyn had confessed her love for him he was still a long way from winning her promise to be his wife. *Not* because of Barrett! He was sure that Barrett was eliminated, and in a much simpler way than he proposed to eliminate the Deputies from Trebizond. It was when Evelyn began *thinking* that the trouble would start, and of course he knew the way her mind worked, well enough. When he praised her for possessing "the big mind", as he called it, he had really meant her capacity for seeing a political fact, like the spread of Fascism, in all its aspects, and she would certainly see their marriage in all its aspects too. Even in the first moment of their avowal on the steppe she had thought of it as affecting the Turkish Revolution, where another woman would have thought first of his family and hers. And from the Revolution it would only be a step to what he admitted was the real difficulty, compared with which a brief appearance in the divorce court was child's play.

He ran downstairs. Evelyn was right about one thing: Chankaya was always thronged with people. He had already said he would give no interviews that afternoon, so there was no one waiting on the red leather sofa in the anteroom, but the aide-de-camp on duty came smartly to attention and presented a staff captain who had problems about the train journey to Polatli; the secretary was as usual hovering in the background with a file. Kemal swore at them all and told them to solve their own problems; he sent for a servant and gave special orders about serving lunch. Then he shut himself into the study until he heard the car's tyres on the gravel and went out to welcome Evelyn.

He saw at once that she hadn't begun thinking yet. Her delicate face was glowing with the same rapture his words had kindled on the steppe, and in her green dress and green feathered hat she seemed to float beside him up the stairs. Kemal took her to a room behind the library where she had never been before, a small room with a bay window underneath Chankaya's conical tower, into which light poured almost from all sides, and the only view was of the poplar trees and greenery. His orders had been carried out exactly: the champagne was in an ice bucket, and two places were laid at a small lace-covered table, with food on a sideboard.

Kemal indicated the cold chicken, the dish of cold aubergines, tomatoes and onions in oil, the little almond cakes. "I hope you don't mind this," he said. "I didn't think we could bear to sit downstairs at the Table, with the servants coming in and out."

"I'm sure *I* couldn't," she confessed. "Shall I serve us both?"

"This is your home now, my two eyes; do whatever seems right to you."

She turned away at once, saying as she bent over the dishes, "But I'm probably too excited to eat anything!" while Kemal deftly uncorked the champagne, and filled the tulip glasses.

They drank to each other, and to the future, although Evelyn drank only "to the future victory", and made a pretence of eating the chicken and the vegetables. In fact, neither one had any appetite. So much had already been said between them that words exchanged over a luncheon table seemed formal and meaningless; Evelyn was reduced at last to saying insincerely,

"What an attractive room this is!" It was attractive only in being light and airy; the furnishings, like all the other furnishings at Chankaya, were banal in the extreme.

Smiling: "You don't think too highly of my house, do you, Evelyn?" said Kemal.

"It's an official residence rather than a home, isn't it?"

"I suppose so. But you know you can do anything you like to Chankaya, when you're the mistress here. We'll get modern furniture from Paris, new wallpapers, anything you want."

"Oh, Kemal!" Evelyn laid down her fork for good. "Are we really talking about getting married?"

"We are."

"Then it wasn't a dream, what we said out on the steppe?"

"I was never more in earnest in my life."

"But the steppe is a dream," she persisted, "and the living water and the shepherd boy's pipe are part of it. But now we're back in Chankaya, and it's for real, and it's not as easy as you think it is!"

"I know it won't be easy for you," said Kemal gently, "and the worst is, I'll have to let you leave me for a while, to arrange for your divorce. It could be done in Paris, couldn't it?"

"I think so. I don't know."

"And if there's any unpleasantness with Barrett, you must let me handle that."

"I wasn't thinking of Jeff," said Evelyn, "I was thinking about all the other people close to us. What would your mother say?"

Kemal smiled. "My mother has disapproved of practically everything I've done since I was five years old. She's a wonderful woman, but we've never lived in peace together, and she'll have no influence in the home I'll make with you."

"And Fikriye Hanim?"

"What about Fikriye?"

"Wouldn't your marriage make her terribly unhappy?"

"Possibly," said Kemal indifferently. "Fikriye is a very unstable girl. Her own marriage was a failure for that reason; I refuse to let her feelings interfere with mine."

"But she's a part of your family. She's living with your mother now."

"But not for much longer. They had another of their tremendous rows the other day—God, how I hate the sound of women crying!—and Emine Hanim has asked her to stay at Chubuk."

"Before that she lived with *you* for quite a while."

Kemal looked at her closely. Evelyn's face was calm, neither compassionate nor complaining, but he saw that her hands were trembling.

"My child," he said, "Fikriye came here to help with the arrangement of Chankaya when I bought the place. She stayed on at her own wish and not at my invitation; she never was in any way the mistress of the house. As for the rest—I'm a man of forty-one, Evelyn. If you love me you'll have to take me past and all, for good and ill, the way I am."

"We'll both put the past behind us," Evelyn said, and Kemal leaned across the table and took her hand. "What about *your* family, Evelyn?" It had to be said, although they were getting on to thin ice now.

"I think my father would be perfectly delighted." She could almost hear John Anderson rolling the words "My son-in-law, the President of Turkey", round his mouth with his after-dinner port.

"And your mother?" (That absurd mother, who changed her religions as she changed her hats, would she be on his side or against him?)

"Mother only wants me to be happy."

Kemal relaxed. "I'll make you happy in my love for you," he said. "And I know you'll come to love my country too. The Turkish people are not easy for someone like you to understand, but they are true, and once they're your friends they'll be your friends for life. You'll understand my country all the faster when we're living in a land at peace."

"I'm living for your victory," she said. "But Kemal—there is one terribly important thing." Evelyn hesitated, and Kemal held his breath. "You and I—we don't share the same religion."

"I told you, only the other evening, I'm not a religious man."

"But officially you're a Moslem."

"So officially," Kemal said with a lifted lip, "that when the Grand National Assembly was opened in Angora we began the proceedings with prayer in the Haji Bayram mosque—that, I accepted—and then with the sacrifice of two live sheep outside the Assembly building. Do you think I approve of such primitive mumbo-jumbo as that? I've been opposed to it all my life, just as I hate the Whirling Dervishes and all the other Moslem fanatics, have done since I went to school at Monastir. . . . Evelyn! I've told you already, I'm not one of the Faithful, but I believe in the One God: how do we know that Allah is not the same God as yours?"

"Would you say that in the Assembly, where the prayer room is next door to the President's own office?"

Kemal got up from the table. "Come and sit by the window," he said, "we can't discuss religion over the cake crumbs."

She sat down beside him on one of the little velvet sofas with which Chankaya was infested, and the familiar charm of his nearness so invaded Evelyn's being that she almost threw herself into his arms and cried "It doesn't matter! What does a difference in religion matter, as long as you love me!" But instead she sat quietly in her corner and waited until Kemal, cursing the luck which had brought this upon them now, marshalled his thoughts and said,

"Does your religious faith mean a great deal to you, Evelyn? Are you—I suppose you are—a Protestant? Do you go to church regularly, in your own country?"

She considered that "*Etes-vous pratiquante, chez vous?*" and answered it first. "I haven't been to church since I was last in San Francisco," she said honestly. "And then I went to please my father. We're Protestants—I was baptised and confirmed in the Lutheran faith."

"I intend that all Christians, all the religious minorities, including the Jews, shall be free to worship in their own way in the new Turkey," said Kemal. "Does that satisfy you?"

"You mean if and when a Protestant church is built in your new Angora, I would be free to worship there, whenever I pleased?"

"Evelyn, let me try to explain something to you. Islam is a great and terrible religion, which has conquered half the world. It has also kept Turkey in a state of enslavement to the religious leaders, who administer the law and most of the schools, and that is why I'm opposed to them, and that's why the hojas oppose me in the National Assembly. I'm not fighting a *jehad*, a Holy War, as the *imams* are forever preaching at me to do. I'm fighting a war for my country's independence under the Crescent and the Star, not the green flag of the Prophet. As soon as we're free, and I've the power to do so, I intend to secularise the State."

"But please answer my question," the girl said faintly. "I asked if I could continue to be a Christian, as your wife."

". . . No."

It was said, and Kemal wished he could unsay it, as he saw shock painted white on the face of the girl he loved. He said wretchedly, "It would be impossible, Evelyn. For a time, at least."

Her lips just moved: "How, for a time at least?"

Reluctantly: "Because in this one matter I daren't move too fast. What I wish to do for Turkey, in freeing the nation from the fetters of Islam, can't be done in a day or a month. It'll be easy enough to end the Sultanate. That old fool at Yildiz Kiosk will run like a scalded cat as soon as I've thrown the Greeks out of the country. But the Sultan is also the Caliph of Islam, the Shadow of God on Earth. If I abolish the Caliphate at the same time as I destroy the throne, I should lose the support of more than half my followers. A Prince of the House of Osman will have to be declared the Caliph, even if his honours last only for six months or a year. But when the Republic is firmly established, and Turkey's course is set towards the western world, then—"

"Yes, then?"

"Then you and I can each follow the dictates of our own conscience, Evelyn."

"But if you marry, your wife—if she's not a Moslem already — must seem, must be *seen* to be, a convert to Islam?"

"Yes."

"So what you're proposing is just political expediency," said Evelyn. "Another concession to high politics, like the British made for that awful man Cravache!"

Kemal kept his temper with an effort. The name of Cravache was a powerful irritant, but he was both patient and wary, and he believed time was on his side.

"My child," he said, "let me remind you that there is much of your Bible in our Koran. The Prophet Mahomed himself admired and respected Jesus of Nazareth, and accorded Him a place among the prophets who went before him. Will you promise to think this over seriously, and always in the light of our love for one another?"

"Yes, of course," said Evelyn, thankful for the reprieve. "Kemal, certainly I promise that!"

*   *   *

She thought so long, and of so many things, during her lonely evening that Evelyn slept soundly all through the night. It was a relief, after the emotional tornado through which she had passed in twenty-four hours, to find a full day's practical employment awaiting her in Angora. A large consignment of food and medical supplies had at last reached the American Relief Mission, and when Evelyn finished helping the two ladies to make an inventory and check it against the list sent from New York she went with George, driving the Ford truck, to distribute some of the goods in the settlements beyond Chubuk. It was not possible to visit a wider area, for the Mission's petrol supply was still very low. Evelyn went home in an araba as sunset reddened the long dusty road.

Kemal had said that he would come to her as soon as he was free after returning from Polatli; that might be early or late, so as soon as she had made tea and eaten some bread and fruit she bathed and dressed in the silk kaftan and gilt slippers in which Kemal had compared her to a Turkish girl. Evelyn's hair had grown long, for there was no hairdressing salon in Angora; she brushed it until it shone like moonlight, and put scent on her wrists and behind her ears. Then Evelyn sat down to wait for the man who loved her, possessed by a sensual anticipation such as she had never known before.

169

At the beginning of that day she had dreaded, while she longed for, their next meeting. Before she left Kemal at Chankaya she had said to him forlornly, "Oh, why aren't you just Captain Mustafa Kemal of the Turkish gendarmerie, stationed in some little Black Sea town where what we believed in would matter to no one but ourselves?" Kemal had laughed at the fantasy, and she knew he was right to laugh. He was what he was; and she had fallen in love with a man who was a great soldier and a dedicated patriot, not a captain of police. If their love brought with it a huge problem of religion and politics which she felt too inexperienced and ignorant to solve at once, she must wait for time to bring wise counsel—in that she was agreed with Kemal. But as the day wore on, and she was out on the steppe roads at the wheel of the old truck, a new resolve was born in Evelyn. Victory, divorce, the "fetters of Islam", might all lie in the future: there was no need for delay in the consummation of their love.

"If you get the name you can have the game"—it was something Jeff Barrett had been fond of saying; and Evelyn's lip curled at the thought of Jeff in Smyrna with the girl from the scent shop. She wondered if Jeff thought *her* frigid, and if he would allow *her* to have a child! But now it was Evelyn who had the name, and thus the right to have the game: "Angora society", according to Madame Emine, already believed that she was Kemal's mistress. Well, why not? And she said "Tonight!" in her heart as she swung the truck into the yard of the Mission; tonight Kemal's desire should be fulfilled.

Over the summer weeks, by the skilful bestowal and withholding of his caresses, Kemal had roused all of Evelyn Barrett's latent sexuality. The barrier of withdrawal which she had raised between her husband and herself soon after their physically disastrous marriage had fallen at the touch of a more experienced hand, and Evelyn with the coral tesbih twisted round her wrist waited restlessly for the lover who should deliver her to love. It was very quiet in the little house. As the hands of the small travelling clock moved on there came to be something ominous in that silence. At last Evelyn realised that one sound, so constantly heard as to be no more heeded than the wind, was missing from the evening air. The hammering from the railway workshops where old iron was hammered into bayonets, that *faux bourdon* to all the sounds of Angora, was no more to be heard.

170

As soon as she heard Kemal's step on the flagstones of the yard Evelyn had a premonition of a hard parting. He always walked so lightly on those evening visits, out of uniform, moving as softly in his English shoes as the brown retriever which sometimes padded at his heels. Tonight she heard the heavier tread of field boots, and even before Evelyn sprang to open the door she knew what she would see—a man in field uniform, wearing a greatcoat, the Commander-in-Chief on the way to his command.

He knew at once that she had understood, and without saying a word folded her closely in his arms, kissing her hair when she laid her head down on the rough material of the army coat and wound her arms tightly round his neck, as if to keep him there for ever.

"Evelyn!"

"Is it now? Is it tonight?" she said at last.

"I'm leaving for the front in half an hour."

"For your forward headquarters? I knew as soon as I saw your uniform."

"So did my mother. I went to see her before I came to you, and told her I was going to a party. All she said was, 'You're not the sort to go to a party in field boots, my little Mustafa!' . . . Ah, Evelyn, don't look like that! You knew it would be soon. I've always told you we hadn't much time together—until the victory —but I couldn't tell you when the time was up. I've kept such strict security on all the plans that though I trust you with my life I couldn't tell you when the final attack would open—too many other men's lives hung on it, as well as mine."

"You knew yesterday, when we sat beside the spring, that this would be the night?"

"Of course, my child. I hoped, I still hope, to have your promise to marry me, to take with me to the front."

"You have all my love instead."

"Is 'yes' so difficult to say?"

"It's an enormous 'yes', Kemal. And when I make a promise to you I never break it."

"I'm sure of that." Kemal pulled off his heavy greatcoat, and Evelyn, remembering even in this crisis the Turkish laws of hospitality, turned to the waiting tray.

"Raki?"

"Thank you, no. Drink and duty don't mix; I shan't have a

drink again until the whole thing's over. May I have a glass of water?"

She poured it steadily. "I think I knew what was going to happen when I realised the railway workshops had shut down."

"Yes, I ordered the night shift stopped at eight tonight. They'll start again at eight tomorrow morning, of course, but the end of the road's in sight now, Evelyn: in fourteen days I'll destroy the Greeks and drive them into the sea."

Kemal spoke coolly, even nonchalantly, but the light in his strange eyes betrayed his fierce excitement as he saw his goal at last in sight.

"We'll drink champagne together when we get to Smyrna," he said. "General Hajianestis may be crazy, but I hear he's quite a connoisseur of wine. We'll requisition his cellar as soon as we get there!"

"*We?*"

Kemal laughed outright at her expression. "But you're coming with me, iki gözüm! You didn't think I could leave you behind?"

"Come with you *tonight*?"

"No, not tonight," Kemal sat down on the hard divan, his knees and shoulders braced as if ready for a spring. "You're not a camp follower to be brought up to the line in a baggage truck. But I want you to come *to* me, a few days from now . . . and bear witness to the triumph of the Revolution, and the cowardice and cruelty of the Greeks."

"You're thinking of that other promise I made you, nearly a month ago, when we talked in the garden at Chankaya?"

"Yes."

Kemal watched her leaning back against the table with the map. It was one of Evelyn's moments of romantic beauty, with her hair shading her downcast face, and he enjoyed her fragility all the more for knowing what a burden he was laying upon her.

"Come to your headquarters as a journalist, writing the story of the Turkish offensive, as Jeff did at the Sakarya?"

"That was a defensive battle, but—yes, that's what I want you to do."

She straightened up and said briefly, "Where do I report for duty?"

Kemal jumped up and seized her in his arms. " I knew you'd do it!" he exulted. "My wonderful girl!"

"I'm just afraid that I won't do it well."

"Yes you will. And now I've got to tell you something no one in Angora knows: I want you to come after me to Konya. At Konya headquarters—Army Main—they'll arrange for your transportation."

"How do you say 'headquarters' in Turkish?

"*Karargâh.*"

"And then I'll follow you to Army Forward at Akshehir?"

"Probably."

"I always knew there was something funny about that football match you went to see at Akshehir."

"It was a good excuse to see my army commanders, and the Pashas too. But now the only problem is how to get you to Konya. Perhaps I should leave Hamdi behind tonight and have him bring you across the desert in the Benz."

"I could get to Konya on my own, if I had the gasoline," said Evelyn.

"Alone! That's out of the question."

"No, not alone, but with George the Relief driver in the truck. We were all round the Chubuk area today, and Miss Mabel was saying how she wished we could get some stuff to Konya."

"You're very resourceful, Evelyn." The admiration in his eyes filled the girl with pride. "But is this George a reliable person to take with you? It's a five-hour drive to Konya, remember; it's not like driving round the outskirts of Angora."

"George is all right. I'd feel safer with him and the Ford than with Captain Hamdi and the Benz."

"Talking of safety," said Kemal, "I brought you this." He turned to feel in the pocket of his greatcoat. "Have you any experience of small firearms?"

"I'm not a good shot, but I did learn how to handle a pistol in Nevada."

"The cowboys again?"

"The cowboys again."

"Very useful. See if you can handle this. I've got quite an arsenal up there at Chankaya, and I picked out a Mauser .32 for you. The Lugers we use are far too heavy for your little hand."

Evelyn took the weapon. "It's an automatic, isn't it?"

"Yes. Now let me see you load it." Kemal gave her a box of ammunition. "Quick and neat—that's good. Now unload it again and put it somewhere safe."

"Presently." Evelyn laid the wicked little weapon on the war map of Asia Minor, where the green pins had stood against the yellow for so long. Kemal was reminded of the night when she had told him "If I were a man I would have been a soldier"; again, the contrast between her grace in the long silk robe and the harsh facts of war moved him very much. He took her in his arms and said,

"Darling, am I asking too much of you? Are you afraid of the journey? It's not a good road to Konya, but it's a perfectly safe one; we've always kept it well policed. I came up that way only a few weeks ago, after the famous football match."

"It'll be easy," she said. "I'll be coming to you!"

He kissed her. "Now I'll give you a line for the commanding officer at Army Main," he said. "He'll send me a signal as soon as you get to Konya. And I'll write an order for the *benzin*."

He took out cards and a fountain pen, and sitting at her table wrote with his customary quick absorption in the task in hand.

"When do I start?" asked Evelyn. Her body, which had been heavy with the expectation of love, now felt drained and almost weightless in the stress of this most extraordinary of all their meetings.

"Friday morning."

"Not until Friday!"

"No. Now remember, Evelyn, nobody is to know that I've left Angora. Officially I'll be at Chankaya, working; Hayati is going to send out invitations to a reception there, later in the week. It's vital no one should have any idea that I've gone to the front."

"I understand."

He came round the table and took her in his arms again. "You're *sure* you're not afraid?" he repeated. "I need your help. God knows I need you always, but this I ask for Turkey—for my countrymen."

The girl saw that even in her embrace he was already with his men in spirit: it was the soldier, not the lover, who held her now.

"Evelyn," said Kemal, "if you believe in prayer, will you pray for me?"

"I'll pray for your safety, always . . . and your success, Kemal."

"For our success— *insh'allah!*"

"Go to victory," said Evelyn, and kissed him with dry lips. "Go smiling."

II

EVELYN'S PLAN FOR HER journey to Konya, so promptly
conceived, was almost shipwrecked on the strong opposition
of the two old ladies who ran the American Relief Mission in
Angora. They were frankly horrified at the idea of sending her off
alone in the truck with George through an area they believed to be
teeming with brigands, for George, they said, was useless as a
protector, and they could never face Mr. Barrett if anything happened to Evie. Miss Mabel and Miss Lily repeated these objections
separately and in chorus; Evelyn's weapon against them was the
frequent pleas from Konya for food and medical supplies. When
she countered the objection that George had no petrol for a three
hundred mile round trip by saying "A Turkish officer has given
me a chit for as much benzin as we'll need!" the two American
teachers had no more to say. Not, at least, to Evelyn herself, but
when she had gone to work in the storeroom at the far side of the
yard Miss Lily said to Miss Mabel with a sigh:

"I'm afraid there's no doubt who the Turkish officer is?"

To which Miss Mabel replied grimly, "No doubt at all, if you
ask me! And I must say I'm disappointed in Evie Barrett, letting
herself get talked about like this."

"We mustn't cast the first stone, sister. 'Twouldn't be very
Christian if we did."

"Oh, I'm not putting all the blame on Evie. We all know what
You-Know-Who's like; it was too much to hope that he would
leave a pretty girl like her alone."

"But it's such a shame for Jefferson Barrett, a nice clean-cut
American boy like him."

"Maybe this trip to Konya will do her good. It'll get her out
of *his* reach, and the Fisters will look after her all right."

"They'll be mighty thankful to get the pharmaceuticals and
the powdered milk," said Miss Lily. "It *is* good of her to offer to
deliver it." So Evelyn's morals were redeemed by Evelyn's useful-
ness, and presently the two ladies went fussing out with tea and

176

cookies for the girl who was checking stores with a sparkle in her eyes for which no powdered milk could ever be responsible.

Miss Mabel and Miss Lily believed implicitly that the Commander-in-Chief, that permanent threat to virtuous womanhood, was still in residence at Chankaya. They were among those favoured with invitations to his evening party on the twenty-sixth (which they accepted with pleasure) and they believed the press releases which announced that the Gazi was exceptionally busy and would grant no interviews, either at his home or in his office at the Assembly until the end of the week. It was not like him to stay away from the Assembly debates for several days on end, but Angora could readily believe that he was concentrating on the reports coming in from his corps commanders. There had been a resumption of activity at both ends of the western front, which was three hundred miles long: far to the south and west the Turks opened an attack along the valley of the Menderes, and the news of this move was actually received in the Nationalist capital after Kemal had secretly left Angora. Three days later, on the twenty-fourth, a communiqué from the northern sector reported Turkish attacks on the Greek outposts at Brusa. These seemed like the preliminaries to a real effort to liberate the holy city, the burial place of the founder of the House of Osman, and the bellicose Deputies were wild with delight. What pleased Evelyn was that nearly all the few American and British correspondents still in Angora went posting off towards Brusa to get the story.

For Evelyn, who knew that she was positively going to Konya and "probably" to Akshehir, where the Western Army's forward headquarters had been set up, the real objective of the Turkish offensive was easy to guess. From Konya the railway ran through Akshehir into the mountains, and then due west through the coastal plain to Smyrna, the centre of Greek power in Turkey and the one city which had to be liberated before Kemal's victory was won. North-west of Akshehir along the railway line lay the junction of Afyon Karahisar, the Black Fortress of Opium, from which the rails ran north to Eskishehir as well as west to Smyrna. Afyon had once been called the Turkish Verdun, and in the year since the Greeks took the ancient city it was said to have been made impregnable. If Kemal could take Afyon he would hold the key town on the road to the Aegean Sea.

Kemal had no need to swear her to secrecy, for Evelyn had her own reasons for keeping her departure quiet. She wanted to be not merely one of the correspondents writing the story of the new campaign, but *the* one; the only one filing copy to the United States. Her ambition was whetted by the arrival of a cable from Donnelly, the first received since Jeff went to Constantinople, and addressed directly to herself:

"jeff reassigned smyrna temporarily stop relying on you transmit any important communiques exangora best donnelly."

She put it with the cards written in Kemal's beautiful Arabic script. It was something official, something resembling an accreditation from the *Clarion*, though Evelyn intended to show Mr. Francis Xavier Donnelly that she could do a great deal better than transmit communiqués. "I always thought I could do as well as Jeff, if I only had a chance," she told herself. It was her great weapon against Jeff in that week of slow-passing days.

Without any particular feelings she annexed a haversack of Jeff's, left behind on top of the wardrobe, and also his old water bottle, when the time came to make practical preparations for the drive to Konya. To wear on the way she laid out an old suit of fawn-coloured, washable twill with a skirt much shorter than the current fashion, and a big square of white silk to keep the dust out of her hair. Ayesha, giggling, was called in to cut the ash-blond bob and did it badly, so that Evelyn had to trim it as best she could with her own nail scissors, achieving a rather short and ragged result; a shampoo with a camomile sachet on the last night made the fair locks tumble over Evelyn's forehead until she looked like a dishevelled boy. She had the white headscarf firmly tied beneath her chin next morning, when she walked down the poplar lane at six o'clock, with the haversack on her back, and Kemal's Mauser fastened to the money belt around her waist. The long coat she wore for riding was on her arm.

At that hour the highroad was quite deserted. Up on the heights some lights were burning in the windows of Chankaya, to keep up the fiction that the Gazi was still there, and Evelyn looked wistfully in that direction. She was not unduly nervous about the journey, nor indeed thinking much about anything but the safety of a Commander-in-Chief who invariably led his troops from the front, but in the last moments before starting on her way to join him she felt a longing to relive just one of the days behind them.

One more ride on the steppe, one more walk beneath the poplars in the moonlight, one respite before the great decisions had to be taken—and then she heard the grumbling of the Ford truck coming up from Angora, and time past turned into time to be. George had already extinguished his headlights, if indeed he had ever lit them, and he bucked the truck to a stop beside Evelyn with a dreadful grinding of brakes.

"Good-morning, George, thanks for coming to get me," said Evelyn, climbing aboard. "Let's go right back to the station and gas up."

"Bet you nobody awake yet," said George gloomily, hauling the wheel around.

"Bet you somebody is," said Evelyn. She was right, although so few motorised Army vehicles remained in Angora that there might have been some excuse for empty sheds. The duty sergeant, a fat man smoking an illicit cigarette, came to the door of what was called by courtesy a garage, and at the sight of the Gazi's order made haste to top up the tank.

"Ask him for some extra cans," suggested Evelyn. "We don't know what supplies will be like in Konya for the return trip."

"We have too much, we sell," said George, brightening. Evelyn walked round the truck while a young mechanic, wearing army fatigues with heelless bazaar slippers, checked the oil and water and clucked his tongue at the patched and worn out tyres. She made sure that the packages of Relief supplies were securely lashed between the floor of the truck and its tarpaulin roof.

"Okay, George, now the Konya road," she said, as they pulled away from the army garage. "With any luck we'll be there for midday dinner."

"What a hope," said George.

*   *   *

The first ten miles were easy going. The road south was no worse than the road to Chubuk or Kalaba; it led straight up to the steppe Evelyn loved, where the sun was beginning to burn away a fall of dew. Soon they were in a wilder country, where the summer drought had brought the turf to the uniform dun of a camel's hide, and one small camel train they did pass at a crawl, the drivers hanging on to their beasts' turquoise-studded bridles and cursing the strange noisy vehicle as it went by. They were members of a tribe of Yürüks, carrying their cone-shaped leather tents called *yurts*, travelling with their women and their flocks in search of new pastures north of their mountain home in the Taurus.

After they passed the nomads the road became a dusty track which, if the rains came early, would in a few more weeks be almost impassable. George drove slower and slower, and by noon, instead of coming near Konya, they were still only seventy miles outside Angora. They came to a Kurdish village of rammed-earth huts, and the tall women of the Kurds, dressed in blazing colours, came to their doors and stared over their veils at the fair-haired girl driving alone with an elderly man. There was of course no sight of an inn, nor any house where George felt inclined to stop.

"Much better we go on, missis," he said. "These not good people. Not educated. Not Christians."

About five miles from the village he stopped the truck and they ate the bread, cheese and pears which Evelyn had brought, and drank half the contents of the water bottle. It was very hot, sitting in the cab of the truck, and soon George fell asleep.

He slept while Evelyn started up the truck, and was still asleep when a back tyre blew out, thirty miles further on, but awake enough to give a most unChristian howl of "Allah!" when the heavily laden truck slewed wildly off the track and careened across the turf to end at a drunken angle against a boulder. It took time to change the tyre and get the truck back on the road. With no spare tyre left they drove more slowly than ever, each in a ten-mile turn at the wheel and stopping to consider every pothole, while the afternoon shadows of the great mountains, shaped like the domes and minarets of the mosques of Turkey, fell lower and lower across the steppe. They were travelling to the west of Tuz Gölu, the great salt lake, and all around them spread saline marshes and salt-encrusted vegetation. Evelyn's lips grew cracked, her face stiff with dust, while the cab reeked of benzin and the heat of the engine came up through the floorboards in sickening waves. It was an immense relief to see the ancient walls of Konya ahead of them as twilight began to fall, and in the swift darkness to drive through that beautiful city in its huge natural oasis of gardens and orchards, up the main avenue to the headquarters of the American Near East Relief Mission.

*　　　*　　　·*

180

While Evelyn was learning from the garrison commander of Konya, whose only western language was the scrappy army German he had picked up when General Liman von Sanders led the Turkish Army, that the Commander-in-Chief had ordered telegraphic communications to be cut all over Anatolia, Kemal was eating supper with the four commanders subordinate to himself in the coming offensive. They ate eggs and rice pudding and talked in lowered voices, as if they could be heard in the Greek lines now so near. They were nearly two hundred miles west of Konya.

Towards midnight Kemal allowed himself two hours of sleep. He lay down on the ground, under cover, wrapped in an old grey cloak which he had used many times on bivouac, and fell asleep at once, lying motionless and undreaming until Ali touched his shoulder and the barber came with his shaving tackle. Then, by lantern light, he drank coffee with Ismet Pasha, the general commanding the entire Western Army, and General Fevzi, the Chief of Staff. Both men had campaigned with Kemal for years. Each complemented, in some respects, Kemal's character as well as his military genius; neither man, single-handed or with the other, could have led the Nationalist Army to the supreme effort and the supreme sacrifice Kemal demanded, and both Ismet and Fevzi Pasha knew it.

They made their final appraisal of the reports coming in from the First and Second Army chiefs and their divisional commanders. Every unit and every gun had now reached its appointed position on the hills surrounding Afyon Karahisar. For several nights, since the arrival of Kemal from Angora, the Turkish troops had been moving forward in the dark of the moon from their base at Akshehir, without ever being challenged by a Greek outpost, picking their way with skill through the ring of mines, trenches and barbed wire which the Greeks had constructed outside Afyon. Turkish reinforcements from the northern sector had been filtering southward for a month, ever since the time when King Constantine and his generals made the fatal error of ordering two Greek divisions into Eastern Thrace, and this prolonged deployment, too, had been conducted in complete secrecy. Token forces were left behind to light campfires at night opposite the Greek lines at Eskishehir, mules and men moved about so as to indicate the presence of large forces: no Greek suspected the immense Turkish concentration in front of Afyon Karahisar. This was the result achieved by Kemal's consummate planning and his insistence on massive security precautions, and he was now about to mount an offensive of classic simplicity, in which Clausewitz would have enthusiastically concurred: the earlier feints at Brusa and along the Menderes covering the main attack on the centre of the enemy's lines.

As the sky began to pale, Kemal sent for horses and led the way up the slope called Koja Tepe, the Great Hill, one of the several *tepes* which ringed the town and the railway junction of Afyon. He dismounted, and the two Pashas watched in silence as Kemal paced up and down among the stones at the top of the hill, listening, bent forward with one booted foot on a boulder and his left thumb at his chin, for the slightest noise from the enemy positions. The only sound was the sound of his own sigh. A pale yellow light from the eastern horizon at their backs began to filter through the grey, and Kemal turned to face it. When the sun appeared above the mountains his hand moved once, and the full fury of the Turkish artillery barrage lashed across the startled Greeks.

*   *   *

About twelve hours after the dawn of that Saturday which was to pass into Turkish history as *Büyük Gün*, the great day, Evelyn Barrett was actually on her way by train from Konya to Akshehir. It was something which had seemed impossible at noon, when despatch riders on motorcycles came in with the news of a smashing Turkish victory on the heights above Afyon; the middle-aged officers of what was now Army Rear, trained in the conventional methods of Liman von Sanders, had proved unequal to the demands of what was apparently going to be a lightning war. The departure of the single train left at Konya was ordered and countermanded twice; the RTO was with difficulty persuaded to allocate a seat on it to an American girl "representing the Chicago *Clarion*". This was how Evelyn now described herself; she had ceased to be a voluntary worker for American Relief about ten o'clock on the previous night, when Mr. Fister of the Konya Mission learned to his dismay that the young lady who had turned up out of the blue with much-needed medical supplies had no intention of returning to Angora. "I just wish Mother was here!" he kept repeating, but "Mother", a practical nurse before she

182

married a missionary, was working among the sick of a little settlement along one of the canals which irrigated Konya from the lakes. It was evident that the gentleman, who was at least sixty, feared being compromised if he offered "Mother's" guest room to the attractive stranger for one night; but there was nothing else for it; Evelyn slept inside the Fister house and George with several other Armenians in the store rooms across the yard. George, to Evelyn's annoyance, was rather harder to handle than the missionary. He objected noisily to driving back alone across the great salt desert, and Mr. Fister had to promise to find companions for him among some men who wished to visit their relatives in Angora. Evelyn felt a little guilty at the thought of what Miss Mabel and Miss Lily would say when he returned without Mrs. Barrett: they would certainly believe her conduct had been underhanded. She didn't give a damn what they said. She was beginning to learn her lesson of ruthlessness from Kemal.

The troop train, with its wood-burning engine, jogged very slowly along the hundred miles to Akshehir. Sometimes it stopped for ten minutes at a time, and then the women of the region came up to the windows and handed grapes and apricots to the reservists going to the front. There was much singing as the wild rumours passed up and down the train. Everything was *büyük*, the great day, the great victory, the great Greek losses; even the surly army doctor who was Evelyn's escort joined in the general euphoria. It became cooler as the train climbed up into the mountains, and the summit of Aladag was diminished by the eight thousand feet high peaks of the Sultan Dag. It was twilight when they reached Akshehir station, and the doctor, who had resented being made to escort a foreign woman, touched his kalpak to Evelyn and left her alone in the crowd of soldiers struggling with their rifles and their packs.

Now for the first time the girl was in a hostile atmosphere, evident from the moment she entered the Transport Officer's room to ask the way to the karargâh. Even the production of the Gazi's card could not make the man understand her; what she said in Turkish merely made him laugh in her face, and it was his clerk who finally took pity on Evelyn and told her there was no karargâh now at Akshehir, because Army Forward had moved thirty miles up the road to Chay. He showed her a *han* not far from the station where she could find accommodation for the night . . . what!

was the Hanim Efendi crazy, to think she might go on to Chay by train? The train she travelled on to Akshehir had to go back within the hour to Konya, it was the *only* train now in service over this section of the line, the enemy had the monopoly of the rolling stock . . . and so on, and on, until Evelyn was thankful to escape to the crowded inn across the way.

There was hostility there too, suspicious looks from the inn-keeper and subdued laughter from the male customers thronging the downstairs room. Evelyn was taken upstairs to a room much worse than those she and Jeff had occupied in similar hans on their way from the Black Sea to Angora. There were three beds in the room already occupied by four Turkish women and three children, two of whom had been excessively sick: Evelyn supposed correctly that they were the families of some of the men downstairs. And the hostility of these veiled women was the worst of all to endure, because Evelyn tried so hard to be friendly; she met with nothing but averted faces and signs against the evil eye. The foreign woman alarmed them as much as a strange man would have done, and to share the evening meal with her was obviously an ordeal for them all. It was not so much served as put down on a leather square laid on the floor to do duty for a table, and consisted of beans and half-fried onions in rancid oil, and jars of the inevitable ayran. Evelyn declined to share one of the dreadful beds. She lay down on the divan beneath the window she insisted on keeping open, with her haversack for a pillow and her coat for a blanket, more discouraged than at any time since the start of her journey to the front.

Next morning she discovered the han had a neglected kiosk in a garden of sorts and insisted on having her coffee there, and after that good beginning there was an improvement at the station, where the surly RTO had been replaced by a more helpful man. The telegraph was still closed, but he promised to get a message to Chay by the next despatch rider if it was very simple; they settled on "Mrs. Barrett is at Akshehir station". After that the waiting began again (Clausewitz had said nothing about the waiting), waiting obstinately, sitting on her coat and haversack or pacing up and down the now deserted platform, listening like everyone else in Akshehir to sounds which came intermittently on the west wind in the early hours of the forenoon and then stopped, sending a small boy to fetch a glass of tea, growing hotter and more worried as the hours went by. But never leaving her appointed post: Mrs. Barrett was still at Akshehir station when a staff car came down the road in a cloud of dust, and Captain Riza jumped out and came running up to her.

"Madame!" Kemal's aide-de-camp exclaimed, "Allah be praised, you're here. When did you come and how long have you been waiting?"

"Just a few hours. Oh, Riza Bey, how glad I am to see you!" Evelyn gave both her hands to the young Turkish officer, who shook them fervently. He was obviously wildly excited, his smooth olive face flushed, and before repeating his questions to Evelyn he blurted out: "The Gazi's in Afyon! The city surrendered without a shot being fired!"

"Oh, Riza Bey!" she said again, "how wonderful! And is it true that you've all won a great victory?"

"On Saturday, yes, the great day; and even that was all over by half past nine in the morning. But, *chère madame*, when did you get to Akshehir?"

"Last night, about seven o'clock. Now please don't look so angry, it was all terribly confused and I don't think the RTO could understand me. If only I could have used a telegraph—"

"The telegraph may be working again tonight. Thank heaven someone had the wit to send your message on from Chay. I took it to the Gazi myself, and he sent Ali flying for a car at once. 'Find Evelyn Hanim and bring her here immediately!' Those were his orders, but now I've found you I'm going to take you to a decent restaurant and get you food. Where did you spend the night?.. That dump! Oh, Allah!"

Evelyn saw that another crime was to be laid to the door of Railway Transport. "It didn't matter," she insisted, "everything's all right now!" With the arrival of Riza she felt herself back in the Angora world, protected, among friends, and she was on the last lap of her journey to Kemal. Riza's driver, grinning, took them into the heart of what proved to be an attractive little town and to a restaurant much patronised by the Staff when Army Forward was at Akshehir, where they shared a platter of roast mountain lamb and vegetables, and a bunch of grapes. Riza ate quickly; he wanted to bring in his charge "immediately", but Evelyn kept asking questions which the young aide-de-camp was very glad to answer.

"The Greeks hadn't a hope in hell," he said of the battle begun at Koja Tepe, "they were totally taken by surprise. Some of the officer prisoners told us they'd been at a dance in Afyon until three o'clock in the morning, they were dead to the world when our artillery barrage began at half past four."

"Didn't they put up any resistance at all?"

"On one or two of the tepes they fought well enough. There was real trouble on our right flank at one time, but as soon as the Gazi got there himself it was all right. Allah, what a tongue-lashing he gave the men! 'I'd sooner see the sky fall than the Greeks win,' he said, and then he asked them to volunteer to die, and led them up the slope. Die they did by the drove, poor fellows, but they kept coming, and soon the Greeks abandoned the position and took to their heels. That was the end of the first line of defences, and we just walked through the second and the third."

"And the Gazi, was *he* all right in this terrible attack?"

"Madame, you know he bears a charmed life!"

"Yes, I've heard him say so. But Afyon? You said the city surrendered without a shot fired?"

"Well, almost. The enemy set fire to Chobanlar village in his retreat, but there was no defence to speak of—we took more prisoners than we can handle!"

"I thought I heard firing from the west this morning."

"That was our artillery trying to bag one or two Greek planes. They've been flying some air reconnaissance, hoping, I suppose, not to be surprised again, but Captain Fazil went up and scattered them . . . Mrs. Barrett, may I tell you something?"

"Certainly, what?"

"I think you're very brave to come all this way from Angora by yourself. I can't imagine my wife attempting it!"

"She could do it if she had to, just like me. I'm here on behalf of the *Clarion*, you know."

"Of course."

They drove off through the hot fag-end of the afternoon. The road at first was clogged with traffic going west, and with a long marching column of Greek prisoners, many of them bandaged, going east to Akshehir, but after they had gone about thirty miles, and were at Chay, the driver was able to make better time. At that town, so oddly named "Tea", a grinning Riza brought out a glass for Evelyn, who waited in the car while he talked to some of the officers in the temporary headquarters. It was being moved up that very night, he told Evelyn. "He's going like the lightning— *Yildirim Kemal!*"

Lightning Kemal. *"He asked them to volunteer to die, and led them up the slope. Die they did by the drove, poor fellows, but they kept coming"* . . . Evelyn shivered in the late sunshine. She remembered one of Kemal's theories on the art of war, expounded in comfort in her little house among the poplars: "The important thing is to keep coming—or keep going, whichever you prefer. The Royal Navy could have forced the Dardanelles in March '15 if they had kept going on after their ships were mined, because the German gunners standing to the Krupp guns at Chanak were almost at their last shell. The Anzacs could have beaten us in April at Sari Bair if they'd kept coming when they stumbled into me and the handful of men I'd taken on reconnaissance. But they stopped for a moment, and that was *my* moment; I'd just time to send for reinforcements, and the Anzacs were driven back . . ." "Were the casualties at Koja Tepe very heavy?" she asked Captain Riza, as he returned to the car.

"Pretty heavy on the right flank. Look, I got a pair of goggles for you, army issue. Put them on, they'll keep the dust out of your eyes. Are you fairly comfortable?"

"Quite, thank you." Evelyn settled again in her corner of the open car. She and Captain Riza were in the back seat. The jolting was terrible, but she was able to cushion herself a little by passing her right arm through the straps of her haversack and cramming it between her side and the side of the car. With her white headscarf tightly tied, and heavy gauntlet gloves she was as well covered as possible from the insidious dust. And Evelyn continued to ply Captain Riza with questions: where were the Greeks now, how long would headquarters remain at Afyon, how were the Supply problems working out, and so on. Riza told her that as part of the assault from Koja Tepe the Turkish cavalry had executed a flanking movement south and west and cut the railway line which was the enemy's escape route to Smyrna and the sea.

"We've pretty well got them where we want them," he said, "but I think the Gazi means to stay at Afyon for the next forty-eight hours. Now we hold the junction he can begin the liberation of Eskishehir and Brusa, although of course Smyrna is the main

187

objective. He and the advance party were just settling in at Afyon town hall when I came off to look for you."

"Is that Afyon up ahead?"

"Yes, that's the famous citadel. We haven't far to go now!"

The road, which had been so heavily encumbered with traffic of all sorts, with gun and lorry parks at intervals and pickets for the transport animals, now stretched clear ahead of them for a whole mile. *"Chabuk ol!"* said Riza to the driver, and to Eve, "You don't know that expression? I'm telling him to hurry up. You'll be glad to get to Afyon, madame!"

"Yes, I shall." They were climbing a road which led upwards through vallonia oaks to the plateau where a high, almost conical peak seemed to spring from the flat land, with an ancient citadel at its summit. While Evelyn looked, there was a throbbing sound, and what appeared to be a giant bird hung in the blue above the mountain top.

"Aircraft!" said Captain Riza, pushing up his goggles to see better. The driver did the same.

"Dushman!" he cried. "The enemy, sir!"

Evelyn pushed the dark goggles above her headscarf. She saw the enemy aircraft coming in low, and as the pilot banked almost above their car she saw the blue and white of Greece on the fuselage. He made straight for the lorry convoy which could now be seen about three-quarters of a mile ahead and swooped down firing his port and starboard guns. There were explosions and a burst of flame.

"Everybody into the ditch!" said Captain Riza. He leaned across Evelyn and flung open the right hand door. She was out of the car and running. The baked earth rose up to meet her and a sickening pain burst across her ribs. Instinctively she tried to shield her head with her arms and found her right arm was doubled underneath her, still passed through the straps of her haversack. There was a great rush of wind, another burst from the Greek pilot's guns, and spurts of earth and pebbles from the richochet broke around her head. Frozen with terror she burrowed her head into the ground.

Then there was the sound of moaning, close beside her, and daring to look she saw first an empty sky with a distant speck in it, flying west, and on the far side of the road the soldier-driver crawling dizzily out of the dry ditch, his face as filthy as her own must certainly be.

"*Yuzbashi'm!*" she heard him say.

His captain lay spreadeagled on the road not far from the car, which was riddled with bullets, with blood drenching one sleeve and the breast of his tunic; his face, unmarked, had already turned the colour of clay. Evelyn lurched unsteadily to her feet.

"Oh God, is he dead?"

She knelt beside Riza, while the driver tore his tunic open and nodded to tell her that the young man's heart was beating.

"We shouldn't move him—but we've *got* to move him, in case the gas tank blows—"

The Turkish driver understood not one word of this, for Evelyn spoke in English, but in their mutual terror he was able to make a sign to her, indicating that the ignition was switched off. And now help was at hand; an army lorry, at the head of a new convoy, was pulling up behind their car, and half a dozen soldiers were gesticulating round Riza's unconscious body.

"Afyon Karahisar!" cried Evelyn. "*Askeri doktor! Askeri hasta-hane! Chabuk ol!*"

A corporal, who appeared to be in command, exclaimed yes, yes; they would take the *yuzbashi* to the military doctor, the military hospital—and he said *Kizilay, Kizilay* several times, to indicate that the Red Crescent would take charge—but as for hurrying up . . . a wave of the hand indicated the confusion and the burning trucks ahead where the Greek had made his first successful strike. But Riza was lifted aboard the rescue lorry as gently as possible, and Evelyn brought her coat from the car as it was being hauled off the road, and spread it out for him to lie on. The floor of the lorry was covered with cigarette ends and spittle.

She sat down beside the wounded man, cross-legged, while the Turkish boys stared at her. None of them had the least idea what to do, but one youth sacrificed his clasp-knife to act as a lever when Evelyn used her white scarf as a tourniquet on Riza's upper arm. As far as she could see his right elbow was shattered. She took the water bottle from her haversack, which she was still grasping—and now she realised that she had fallen on the water bottle and bruised her side—and after giving a little to the driver to clean his face she used the rest to moisten Riza's lips from time to time as they waited for the blocked road to be cleared. She thought of the young wife waiting in the chalet near Chankaya, and how she wanted to show Riza Italy. "God, let them get to Italy! Please let him live to get to Italy," Evelyn prayed.

At last the lorry started rolling, very slowly, towards the town below the conical mountain peak. The corporal told Evelyn that there were only ten kilometres to go. *"Chabuk ol! Lûtfen, chabuk ol!"* she implored, for now the unconscious man had started coughing, little shallow coughs which brought up each time a thin bloody froth, coloured bright red, and she was too ignorant to know what this might mean. The Turkish soldiers, seated on each side of the truck, sighed and shook their heads. They were swarthy Anatolians, each clutching one of the old Mauser rifles with which the Germans had armed the Ottoman troops in the days of the Young Turks.

"It is kismet," said the driver, shivering in his torn uniform. "My captain will die."

Chabuk ol. Chabuk ol. At last they were in town streets, which might at another time have seemed beautiful, with ancient caravanserais and vine-shaded cafés where elderly Turks had gathered to celebrate the liberation of their city. Now ambulances painted with the Red Crescent were drawn up in a long line at the kerb in front of the cafés: the street led to Field Hospital Number One, a charnel-house of pallets laid two deep in the corridors, of choked sluices surrounded by pails of excrement and sodden dressings, of a morgue cleared for hasty burials and filled again at once with Turkish and Greek dead. Evelyn stood back appalled. A Turkish surgeon at once took charge of Captain Riza, still unconscious; a young doctor, scarcely more than a boy, who had some words of French, looked after the driver and Evelyn.

"Captain Riza is the Gazi's aide-de-camp," she told the doctor. "Can I send word about him to the town hall?"

"As soon as we've given you first aid, madame."

There was no fighting it, the message had to wait, but as soon as her bruised side was bathed and gauze dressings put on her bruised knees (her lisle thread stockings were torn to ribbons) Evelyn took a notebook and pencil from her haversack, where her blue cotton dress, underclothing and slippers were now in a hopeless jumble, and wrote a line indicating Captain Riza's whereabouts. She wrote in French, and signed herself Evelyn Barrett; there was no one she could address it to but Captain Hamdi, who

Riza had told her was already at the town hall. Then she waited, in one screened corner of a dreadful ward, while a sullen Greek girl brought her washing water and mended the rent in her skirt with a black thread. The girl was one of those who had been dancing until three o'clock on the morning of Koja Tepe. She had been conscripted for service in Field Hospital No. One. When she bit off her thread and gave Evelyn back her skirt she said with hatred in her black eyes:

"My lover died two days ago, *kirya*. I hope yours dies too."

"He's not my—" Evelyn stopped. There was nothing that could be said between two women penned together in one of the grim outhouses of the battlefield. She was glad to be alone, even to wait while another twilight fell, until someone came with a candle and ushered in a Turkish officer in early middle age, wearing the insignia of the Staff, who addressed Evelyn in perfect English.

"Mrs. Barrett? I'm Major Orman, at your service. The MO has told me about what happened, and I'm so distressed that you were hurt yourself!"

"I'm not hurt at all. Oh, thank heaven for someone who speaks English!" cried Evelyn. "I can't get anyone to tell me about Captain Riza. How is he?"

"He's going to be all right, they think. The right lung was in some danger, but they operated at once, and with luck Riza Bey will pull through. But now, Mrs. Barrett, I've got to get you to headquarters! Let me take your haversack—the car is at the door."

Major Orman was considerate enough to say nothing as the car drove them to the town hall. He gave Evelyn one or two friendly smiles, and she was grateful for his silence; she liked this man's lined face, and the grizzled hair above his ears, just visible beneath the kalpak. She was nerving herself for one more effort: to walk straight, to look calm, to speak intelligently when she went inside Kemal's headquarters.

There was a flight of steps, and the Lazes in their black uniforms—the Lazes again!—and first a lighted hall and then a big room where six officers sat at six desks, working by petrol lamps, and one of them was Captain Hamdi.

He got up at once and came to Evelyn with an air of great concern:

"Good heavens, Mrs. Barrett, are *you* all right?"

"Perfectly, thank you, Hamdi Bey."

"The Gazi and the Pashas are having a conference. My orders were to interrupt it as soon as you arrived."

Hamdi opened a door leading to an inner room—and that was the last room, the end of the fantastic journey—where the hum of voices stopped at once. Evelyn straightened her bruised body in the ruined fawn twill suit and came to what in a young man would have been attention, for the Commander-in-Chief was standing in the lit doorway with his hand lifted in a grave salute.

"Well done, soldier," said Kemal Pasha. "Welcome to the House of War."

12

THERE WAS, AFTER ALL, another room beyond the last room. It was the place where Evelyn awoke a few hours later, half dreaming, only half aware of her new surroundings. At first she thought she was back in the wooden house among the fruit trees, for she was lying on a mattress on the floor, but then she realised that this mattress was twice as wide as Ayesha's and spread with linen that was even coarser, although quite clean and fresh. Then the window was in a different place: instead of being at the foot of her bed it was at one side of the room which, as she could see by a diffused light coming from below, was very small and contained little but rows of shelves stacked with parchment scrolls and ledgers in old musty leather bindings. There was a low table, just higher than the pillow under which she had put her money belt and pistol. Her suit had been taken away by a young Turkish girl, who promised to wash and mend it properly by next day.

Evelyn lay luxuriously still. The girl had prepared a tub bath for her in a cupboard next to a lavatory with a cess-hole in the floor which Evelyn preferred not to remember, and there had been scented herbs in the hot water which soothed the bruises of her headlong fall. Her knees were healing, but the flesh above her ribs was swollen and tender, purpling with the colours of contusion. There had been one long scratch on her face beneath the dirt.

She sat up in bed. The Turkish girl had brought her a bowl of strong soup with meat among the vegetables and a strip of pide bread, but the bowl and plate had been taken away while she slept and the window opened. A light breeze fluttered the curtain bunched at one end of a rod. Evelyn could hear excited voices not far off, and the sound of a sentry's measured tread beneath her window. She remembered having climbed one flight of stone stairs.

That was after the talk in the inner room at Kemal's headquarters, when she told the story of the Greek plane's attack on the convoy and the staff car as briefly and as crisply as she could. She had to address the two Pashas with whom Kemal had been in conference, for the Commander-in-Chief stood slightly behind her instead of resuming his place at the head of the conference table. The Pashas looked curiously at the American girl. Of one she had heard much already, for General Ismet, so unassuming in appearance, was a Turkish soldier of renown. He was small and swarthy, with prominent dark eyes, and deaf enough to have an attentive way of listening with his head bent forward, which many people found appealing; Evelyn thought him more attractive than the Chief of Staff, General Fevzi, who was a broad-shouldered, burly Turk of the old school, brushing up his thick black moustache self-consciously while she answered Ismet's questions, and barely able to conceal what he thought of the presence of a woman at Supreme Headquarters. It was Kemal himself who ended the interview by saying, and thus making Evelyn turn round to face him:

"So! Now you've had precisely the same experience I once had on a road in Gallipoli, madame."

"But you're a lucky general, *Excellence*."

"Your luck was in too," said Kemal. "And your man didn't get away with it, while my man did."

"The Greek pilot?"

"Captain Fazil went up in a pursuit plane and shot him down not far from Ushak."

Ismet, watching the girl's face, said gently, "I think madame should have some food and a rest now. After all, tomorrow is also a day."

So now she was fed and rested, and the only discord in her peace was that sound of rapid hysterical voices from somewhere near, and also a high wailing echo from the liberated city which might have been a concerted cry of triumph or of grief. Evelyn, subconsciously, was listening for another sound. At last it came: she heard light steps on the cobbles and the sentry's challenge:

"*Dur! Kim o?*"

Evelyn heard the deep voice which replied, and shivered with anticipation. A gentle knock fell upon her bedroom door.

"*On peut entrer, madame?*"

"*Soyez le bienvenu, Excellence.*"

The door opened in the half-light. "Still *'Excellence'*?" said the Commander-in-Chief.

"Kemal." With a sigh Evelyn opened her arms to him, and Kemal knelt down on the floor beside her, straining her to his heart, lifting her clear of sheet and blanket to cover her scratched face with kisses. "Shekerim!" he said, *"mon amour!* Mine at last!"

"All yours."

It was her final and complete surrender, but for the epicure there were refinements of pleasure; Kemal said, "Evelyn! Isn't there a light? I want to see you, very much."

"There's a candle on the table right beside you."

Kemal rose in one swift movement. He struck a match·and lit the candle. He drew the curtain over the window and shot the bolt across the door. Evelyn saw that he was out of uniform, wearing a white shirt with the sleeves rolled up above his elbows. When he lay down on the mattress beside her the candlelight behind his head turned his fair hair to gold.

"My two eyes, you are so beautiful!"

Evelyn's pillow was propped against the whitewashed wall. She wore a nightdress of white Italian silk, much crumpled, with medallions of lace inserted below the square neck, in its luxury intensely provocative by contrast with her tanned face and ragged fair hair. Kemal slid one fold of the nightdress off her shoulder.

"You had a fall, my darling. You weren't badly hurt?"

"It hardly hurts at all now."

"I would have gone mad if—anything had happened to you." Kemal laid kisses like a necklace round her throat. "My God, but I was proud of you tonight! You were dead beat and dead game— and to think I couldn't be alone with you, even then!"

"We aren't quite alone together, even now. Where are we, Kemal?"

"In the Archives Department of the town hall, right behind headquarters. My soldier-servant's on guard down below. No one will get past Ali, he even challenged me! . . Oh!" as Evelyn inclined her head towards the window, through which still came the distant sound of voices, "I know what you mean. Hamdi and two of my staff captains are interrogating some of the Greek prisoners of war."

"And enjoying it, no doubt."

Kemal, with a long caressing movement, laid bare her other shoulder. "Not as much as if the prisoners were refractory. But they're giving us no trouble. Those Greeks would babble anything, betray their grandmothers as fast as their generals, if they thought it would save their own flea-bitten hides . . . Can't we take off this very pretty thing?"

The white silk nightdress, crumpled, lace-inserted, lay in a ring on the sheet. And the Conqueror surveyed his conquest, lying naked in the candle light.

But now it was Evelyn who wished to prolong the sweetness of the moment. When Kemal sat up to take off his own shirt she whispered,

"You won a great victory, on the Great Day—"

"I won *a* victory, and took Afyon without much trouble—"

"Kemal—that awful hospital was full of badly wounded men."

"Calculated losses, Evelyn."

"Captain Riza wasn't a calculated loss."

"Am I to be jealous of Riza Bey? He's going to pull through all right. I went to enquire for him myself an hour ago." Kemal was lying naked beside her, with the sheet and cover thrown off the makeshift bed, and his strong hands tenderly caressing her.

"You don't have to be jealous of anybody," she whispered, looking into those lambent blue eyes so near her own. "I only felt . . . it was so terrible today when Riza Bey was wounded . . . I knew he was only there because of me."

"If I said that! Oh God, Evelyn, if *I* said that!"

The lean face on the pillow beside her was suddenly drawn with pain, and Evelyn's last defences went down as she drew the fair head to her breast. But it was not in Kemal's nature to surrender to a woman's tenderness. With every touch of his hands on her naked body he had been learning Evelyn; now with an indrawn breath of dismay he saw the discolorations of her fall, and with the lightest touches of lips and tongue drew the pain away from her bruised ribs and knees until all the ache of the Afyon road fused into a new and melting ache in the core of her being. He divined exactly how she had been abused by a clumsy and selfish lover, and he waited, curbing his desire until he had made certain that hers would match his own. Then he kissed her breasts, and heard her moan when his moustache rasped over the soft nipples growing hard and urgent, while with one hand she traced the scar on his own breast, the legacy of Gallipoli; and then she lay beneath him while Kemal dragged the fair hair back from her temples, seeing in a spasm of narcissistic pleasure what others had seen in Evelyn's face, a fleeting resemblance to himself. Their identities merged and, with their bodies, became one.

13

WHEN KEMAL OPENED his offensive at Koja Tepe, Jeff Barrett had already been in Smyrna for ten days.

After the press camp at Chatalja, it was a pleasant life he led in the rich and self-indulgent city, although Jeff was industrious enough in the morning hours to file all the cable copy he thought likely to interest his publisher and editor. To his great relief they had not queried him on his failure to report the arrest of the Trakas murderer. For a few days after coming to Smyrna he had a waking nightmare of Red Donnelly saying, "Barrett fell down on the Trakas story. Barrett's slipping," and the Commodore, brandishing his Cuban cigar, barking out, "Then recall Barrett, Donnelly. Put him back on the sports desk and see how he shapes up." When no furious cable came from Donnelly he breathed more freely, and the next message which did arrive was encouraging: it was a word of praise for the Russian refugee story he had cabled as soon as the steamer docked at Smyrna, though without an interview with General Wrangel.

As far as the job went now his only headache was Burton Halliday, moved from Vienna to Athens, and punctiliously sending Jeff blacks of the stories he was filing out of Greece. Halliday was big competition to have in what Jeff had begun to think of as his own neck of the woods, and of course the *Clarion*'s chief foreign correspondent had immediately been received in audience by King Constantine. His profiles of the King, his brother Prince Andrew, and his prime minister Monsieur Gounaris had been given a big play in the paper. But Jeff scored, too, with an interview with General Hajianestis, the Greek Commander-in-Chief. He had to hire a boat and a boatman to get his story, for the black-bearded general had given up visiting his headquarters in Smyrna, and was commanding the Greek Army in Asia Minor from a luxurious yacht anchored far out in the Gulf. Over a tumbler of neat whisky he explained to Jeff that he was afraid to risk his footing on the Smyrna cobbles. His legs, said General

Hajianestis, being made of glass, a fall would be extremely dangerous. The *Clarion* ran Jeff's story under the headline "British Back Brittle General", with a cartoon of the British Lion looking ruefully at its own glass legs.

It wasn't any good trying to second-guess the Commodore, as Jeff well knew, but the pitch of that headline made him wonder if Mr. Weintraub's wayward fancy might not be straying in an anti-Greek direction. He put up a trial balloon after taking an eighty-five mile rail journey to Alashehir, the ancient Philadelphia, to interview General Tricoupis, the effective Greek commander in the field. Tricoupis, lulled by Jeff's charming account of Madame Tricoupis's discretion and kindness during his visit to Prinkipo, was trapped into blurting out that the Greeks had "no real interests of their own in Anatolia" as distinct from the Powers which had encouraged them to invade the territory. This was allowed to run in Jeff's printed story, from which it would certainly have been cut a year before, and the young man wondered whether, back in Chicago, his bosses were beginning to hedge their bets on King Constantine.

There was no doubt which was the dominating Power in Smyrna. The great British merchant families had had their roots there at least since Lord Byron's romantic championship of Greece. Their mansions were set among vast gardens at Bornova, six or seven miles outside the city; their villas in the seaside suburb of Karshiyaka, at a little distance beyond the Point. Jeff's first think-piece from Smyrna began, "British business is the mainstay of this beautiful city, a great Mediterranean harbour since the beginning of time", and even the geographical inaccuracy seemed to suit the image of Smyrna—smiling and acquiescent to her guests. If Eve had been typing up his copy she would have x-ed Mediterranean out, you bet, but no reader of the *Clarion* except a few Greek immigrants was likely to have heard of the Aegean Sea. Anyway, Jeff reasoned, Smyrna's trade was with the Mediterranean, and anyway, the place reminded him of Naples or even Genoa. It was the western grace of Smyrna which struck him most at first, by contrast with the dirt and corruption of Constantinople and the harsh verities of the Anatolian steppe.

His interviews with the British Consul-General and the Greek High Commissioner, Monsieur Sterghiades, produced only the routine assurances that the Allies would certainly settle the

Greek-Turkish "dispute" through diplomatic channels. His own Consul-General, Mr. Horton, was in an ultra-neutral position, since the government of the United States recognised neither King Constantine's régime in Greece nor Kemal's in Anatolia, nor had diplomatic relations with the Sultan's government as yet been resumed. Mr. Horton, however, was friendly and helpful in getting Jeff guest cards to the Sporting Club and the Cercle Européen, the latter a sophisticated meeting place for the rich British businessmen and their Levantine associates.

In the afternoon and evening, provided he kept checking on his news sources, Jeff was free to devote most of his time to Leila Mavros. He had taken her to her grandmother's house as soon as the boat docked: poor little pet, she looked so limp in the wrinkled suit put on to go to Prinkipo, but her jolly relatives hadn't criticised. They laughed and cried and kissed her, and embraced the kind American gentleman who had brought their little Leila back to them. A great deal of *retsina* wine was drunk in celebration.

Leila's old home was in the Greek quarter of Smyrna, in a street called the Rue d'Angoisse. The quarter was rich in cypresses, cedars and palm trees, and the Mavros garden was entered by a gate hung with luxuriant vines and creepers. The interior of the white two-storey house was less attractive, being in a chronic state of untidiness, with which a little Turkish servant girl called Güzel, "the beauty", never seemed quite able to cope. The poor little Beauty, who might have been all of thirteen, and whose black eyes were piteous above her womanly veil, was at the beck and call of two plump and idle ladies called Irene and Aphrodite who also answered to the name of Mavros, although Jeff once heard Irene addressed as Madame Naccache. The genuine Madame Mavros, Leila's beloved grandmother, was crippled by arthritis, but she must once have been very pretty and was charming still. The household was completed by the two blue-jowled men whom Leila called "the Uncles", and who had some minor employment in the Customs House. Jeff never worked out the exact relationship—by blood, for the other relationships were fairly obvious— of any one member of the Mavros family to the others, but he liked to amuse himself by assuring Homer and Sophocles, the Uncles, how well they would fit in to the American way of life. The Uncles were delighted, and Jeff did not elaborate: in fact, he saw Homer, who was powerfully built, as a possible bouncer in any speakeasy in Chicago's Loop, with Sophocles as a crimp on the San Francisco waterfront. He sometimes wondered if the Uncles were any better protection for his little Leila than the notorious Rosette herself.

Rosette was never mentioned when Jeff was in that house, where a fly-blown picture of Lord Byron had the place of honour on the parlour wall. He pled work as a reason for not going to Agony Street very often, and no objection was ever made to Leila's spending a great deal of time with him. The relationship between them seemed to be completely understood and accepted by her family, but the first time Leila stayed all night with Jeff at the Kramer Hotel her Uncle Homer turned up next day with a request for a "loan" of fifty dollars, which the American was well aware would never be repaid.

Jeff took a suite at the fashionable hotel. The living-room had a balcony above the sea, the bedroom, at the back, overlooked a garden where the privileged cats of Turkey lazed among the creepers and the flowers, and the protected pigeons, God's messengers to Noah, cooed and strutted on the walls. Leila liked to throw down crumbs for the pigeons: the cats were fed from the hotel kitchens, and lavishly. The suite cost money, and Jeff was drawing too heavily on his expense account, but at the start of his assignment in Smyrna he felt obliged to reserve a livingroom. There was enough of the American puritan in Jeff Barrett to make him want to preserve the fiction that Leila came to the Kramer to translate the Greek newspapers for him.

"I do wish I could be having some pretty dresses!" she told him wistfully. "All my nice things I am leaving behind when we run away from Pera!" So what could Jeff do but take her to a famous department store on Frank Street and tell her to choose what she wanted? He found that for such a simple, poetic child Leila had precise ideas on the satin lingerie, silk stockings, gloves, slippers and accessories needed to complete each outfit, down to the silver sandals Jeff gave her to wear with the new evening dress. It was made of clinging ivory crêpe de chine, cut on classical lines, with silver ribbons crossed to define her young breasts and tied in a girdle at her waist. The goddess Artemis might have worn such a robe, and Leila, who was not tall or grand enough to do it justice, spoiled the effect by carrying a fan made from a single ostrich feather dyed rose pink. But heads turned to look when Jeff took her to dance on the terrace of the Hotel Nain, which had the best orchestra in Smyrna, and this pleased him so much that he forgot the tawdry feather and saw only Leila's glowing face. After all, she was a little beauty, and she sure was in love with him. Didn't she prove that when they went to bed together? Leila was always warm and always willing, and he was sick of trying to melt an icicle like Eve.

Just the same, he would have liked to hear from Eve. He already regretted the letter he had scribbled to her in the haste and anxiety of that last morning at the Pera Palace, or at least he regretted the fatal sentence, "If you want to make something out of this you can go ahead!" Not, so far as his knowledge of the law stood, that there was anything to go ahead on. No man could be divorced on the grounds that he had escorted a young lady, on a passenger steamer, sitting in chairs in the first class saloon, from Constantinople to her family home in Smyrna! Still, it wasn't like Eve not to give him a line of her mind by this time . . . especially since what he had said about the money must have riled her.

Jeff Barrett was not usually sensitive to atmosphere, but in those August days there was an ominous feeling in the air, a calm before the storm, as he went from the Kramer to the Club, from the Club to the cable office, and from the Point back to Agony Street to pick up Leila. The storm signals went up one Saturday evening when he was working in his room, and Monsieur Mavros was announced: that one of the Uncles should appear at the Kramer was so unexpected that Jeff thought the page-boy had intended to say "Mademoiselle". But it was Uncle Homer, the potential speakeasy bouncer, who waited in the Palm Court of the Kramer, startlingly dressed in an electric blue suit and twisting the brim of a greasy fedora in his unwashed hands.

"Hallo there, Homer, how's tricks?" said Jeff. "Everything all right at the Rue d'Angoisse?"

"Sure, sure, boss," said Homer Mavros. "Sophocles and me just thought I should drop by to tell you about so'thing that come up today."

He looked suggestively towards the bar. Jeff didn't want to act like a tightwad; he also didn't want to be seen with a bum like Uncle Homer in the Kramer bar.

"I'm kind of busy tonight, fella," he said. "What's on your mind?"

"We gotta news from Cousin Rosette today."

"What's her story? Sprung her from the tank, have they?"

"She sent a telegram. She's on her way down from Constant., aboard the *Kléber*, going to Beirut."

"So what?"

"So she wantsa take little Leila with 'er."

"Hell no!" exploded Jeff. "She can't do that!"

"You say no?"

"What does Leila say?" Jeff temporised.

"We haven' told *la Leila* yet. Soph' and me, we wanna know what *you* think about it."

"I figure Leila told you about the kind of life she had in Pera," said Jeff. "You don't want her mixed up in that sort of racket in Beirut."

"She had a good job at the cabaret till you take 'er away with you. Now what 'as she got? Soph' and me, we ain't rich; we can't feed all them women all the time, and what can you do? Can you marry 'er?"

"I'm a married man," said Jeff. "I thought you all knew that."

"So was Leila's father a married man, when my cousin Helen died giving birth to 'er, in Athens eighteen years ago."

"Oh, Leila's mother was your cousin, was she?" said Jeff, diverted. "I always thought she was your sister."

"Was Aphrodite's sister," said Homer, and Jeff gave the tangle up. "What time does the *Kléber* dock?" he said.

"Ten o'clock, and leave for Beirut at noon."

"Tell Leila to pick me up here at half past nine and we'll go down to the harbour and have a word with the lady. But I don't want to see your brother and you hanging around, trying to pan-handle from Rosette."

"Lend me twenny-five dollars, boss?" said the opportunist.

*   *   *

Leila, clinging to Jeff's arm, picked her way along the Smyrna waterfront as daintily as a cat. Between the Kramer Hotel and the Point, and on to the garden suburb of Karshiyaka, it was one of the most beautiful waterfronts in the world, with the blue waves of the bay lapping against the sea-wall of a long promenade called the Kordon, where the Greek and European inhabitants enjoyed strolling in the warm summer nights. On the other side, towards the Customs House and the Konak Square, the business centre, the Kordon became a busy, noisy street with horse-drawn tramcars in the middle, the sheds and buildings of steamer lines along the water, and on the landward side block after block of commercial buildings, banks and the main post office, many with cafés and barber shops at pavement level. The pavement itself was encumbered with the chairs and café tables at which half the minor deals of Smyrna were transacted. The men sitting there were Levantines in white suits and panama hats, but there was a sprinkling of red fezzes among them, worn by the Turkish fruit brokers who carried their own amber mouthpieces to pull on the nargiles between sips of coffee, and fidgeted with the prayer beads on their wrists. Little shoe-shine boys knelt industriously at their feet. Samples of the fruit they had to sell were everywhere, for it was the moment when the figs, raisins and sultanas of the rich province were sold and shipped to foreign lands, and the fruit freighters were lying under many flags in Smyrna bay. Smyrna, on that August Sunday, when the bells of the Christian churches were ringing to prayer, was brimming over with good things. At every street corner vendors offered two kinds of melon, the golden and the pink; purple aubergines, peaches, oranges; grapes in all sizes and colours from mauve through green to the tiny yellow ones which were the sweetest of all; nougats and lokum for those with a sweet tooth, and for others black olives and mussels offered with a slice of lemon to be eaten off the half-shell. There was no end to the delights poured out of Smyrna's cornucopia. The city, in its ring of gentle hills, breathed prosperity and safety; it was only from the bay that a watcher could see the menacing high peaks of Anatolia.

The *Kléber* had berthed rather ahead of schedule. As Jeff and Leila hurried along the landing-stage they had to make their way against a tide of passengers, some followed by porters with their luggage, others going for a stroll on shore, and Jeff said,

"I can't see Rosette anywhere. Can she have changed her mind?"

"Why, there she is on deck!" said Leila, pointing.

Madame Mavros was indeed leaning against the rail, with the air of one who had no intention of joining the milling crowd on the gangway. Jeff was convinced that she saw them arguing with the French purser, who was most unwilling to let two strangers go aboard the *Kléber* without paying, but she gave no sign of recognition, apart from a wry smile, until they joined her on the deck. She was very well dressed, with a black silk cloak covering a rather short dress of the same material; the cloak had wide sleeves trimmed with monkey fur. Her small hat was of scarlet velvet, her mouth made up to match.

"Good to see you, Rosette," said Jeff ironically. "Taking off on a little trip?"

"*Toujours farceur, ce grand Jeff!*" said Rosette to Leila. "*Eh bien, mon petit*, you look very well. Your little *affaire* 'as done you good, I see; but come, *dis donc*, where is your luggage?"

"She isn't going anywhere with you," said Jeff.

"Oh, please," said Leila, "I am not liking to go to Beirut, *ma cousine*."

Rosette looked at them both, biting her lips and trying to be pleasant. "Look, Jeff," she said, "I don' want to quarrel with you. You wrote me a ver' cheeky letter, but you don' make me mad. I wasn't surprised when you didn' come back from Prinkipo, because Leila is a little fool, like 'er mother was a fool before 'er; and I was glad—you 'ear, *glad*, you took 'er away from Constant. before the police got at 'er. But now the drama is all over. I go free with a police apology, and I 'ave a good business opportunity waiting me in Beirut in the perfume and cosmetic line. So Leila 'ad much better think of 'er own future—"

"And Lebanon's under a French mandate now," said Jeff. "Did your pal Cravache fix up the new deal for you?"

"You write too many faked-up stories, Jeff."

"Oh, please!" said Leila again. "Please not to be quarrelling! Rosette, won't you come ashore? In a taxi we could be at home in ten minutes, and grandmother would like to see you!"

"There isn' time."

Jeff looked down the landing-stage. At the gates the Greek officials were examining passports.

"Maybe you're not allowed to go ashore?" he suggested. "You wouldn't by any chance be leaving Turkey under a deportation order?"

Scornfully: "You're not writing for the *Clarion* now, Jeff. I told you, the police apologise' for making a big mistake; if I choose to go to Beirut for a while, there will soon be many people wishing they could follow me."

"But you *did* have the Trakas killer hidden in your apartment on the night of the murder, didn't you?" persisted Jeff. "He was in a room down the corridor, and Cravache went to see him while you kept me talking in the salon. Right?"

Rosette laughed. "*Mon pauvre* Jeff, if the Ottoman police couldn't make me squeal, a big silly American like you needn't even begin to try . . . Leila! I ask you again, will you go home and get your things, and come back to me 'ere before the *Kléber* sails at noon? I ask you for your own good, because in spite of everything I'm fond of you, and if you stay 'ere there may be much suffering—"

"W-what?" said Leila, terrified. She shrank closer to Jeff. "Suffering?"

"You poor silly child, it's a matter of life and death. The Turks are moving, back there in the mountains, two days ago they were on the Menderes: we 'ear the *news*, back in Constantinople! And if Kemal Pasha beats the Greeks, and comes to Smyrna, 'e won't spare you rape and murder! He'll take 'is revenge for what 'appen here three years ago! You take my advice, and get out of Turkey while you can!"

"I want to stay with Jeff," said Leila with a sob.

*   *   *

Jeff took Leila back to the Kramer in a taxi, left her there, and took the taxi on to the Cercle Européen. The club was quiet, as befitted a Sunday morning, but more and more of the European members dropped in for drinks after church, and there was the usual sprinkling of Greek officers. Jeff talked to several people. The skirmishing along the Menderes was no secret, he had heard of it before he listened to Rosette's sarcasms, and no one seemed to think there was very much in it. Just the same—one of his favourite expressions—it might be a good idea to take a trip down the railway line to Aydin, and see what was really going on along the Greek right flank. There were no urgent despatches pinned to the bulletin board, but when Jeff came out of the club the news-boys were shouting an extra, and he bought several papers. Leila could have a shot at translating them for him after luncheon.

After lunch, which they ate on the shaded balcony, she wanted to go indoors. The *imbat*, which blew in from the sea every day at that hour, crossing the town from the south-west to the north-east, was gustier than was proper for the end of August, and Leila hated to have her plumage ruffled. She sat in Jeff's lap, rubbing her cheek against his in a way that usually roused him, but he was worried and anxious, and presently put her on the sofa with the newspapers and a box of her favourite lokum beside her. He wanted to drink a brandy and smoke a good cigar, and that wasn't possible with his little dove in his arms—the dove who wanted to stay in her nest beside him. He thought that at times a dove could weigh as heavy round a man's neck as an albatross.

Almost the only positive fact that emerged from Leila's botched translation was that the extra edition dealt with the afternoon's horse-racing. She persevered with the political pages, directly inspired from Athens (where Halliday was probably lunching with King Constantine at that very minute) and did it so badly that Jeff's teeth were on edge. Her mistakes in English grammar just weren't cute when he was trying to make sense out of some news item. As Leila hacked her way through "Many—clever—peoples—are—now—saying—" he could almost hear Eve translating crisply, "According to informed sources—" You could bet your bottom dollar Eve would have had demotic Greek hog-wrastled and thrown before she spent a week in Smyrna.

"Okay, baby, that's all for now," he said, getting up from the writing table and stretching.

"I am not being good?"

"You're being very good. But it's hot in here, sweetie, let's get a breath of fresh air, walk along the Kordon a bit, or something." The imbat had ceased to blow, but it hung in the shaded room like a hot breath from the fevered shores of Greece, and Leila's neck, when Jeff kissed it underneath the curls, was moist and over-warm.

"Shan't we go for a drive?" she said hopefully. "Up to the Velvet Fortress, that would be nice!"

"Let's go, then."

The way to the Velvet Fortress, Kadife Kale, lay right to the top of the hill the Greeks called Mount Pagus, where stood the ruins of an ancient fortress dating back almost to the time of Alexander the Great. They drove there in a little Smyrniot carriage painted pistachio green and pink, with pink spokes to the wheels, and pink beads in the horse's harness. People were coming out of doors now that the long midday meal-time and the blowing of the imbat wind were over, and there were the usual loiterers outside the Konak, the building where the government of the city and the province was carried on. A large portrait of Lloyd George in a massive gilt frame wreathed in laurel hung above the door of the Konak. It had been placed there on the day at the beginning of August when Smyrna heard the news of the British Prime Minister's speech implying military aid to the Greeks in Turkey. The Konak was the effective centre of the Greek civil power; King Constantine himself had entered it in triumph a year before, wiping his boots, as he did so, on a Turkish flag spread for that purpose across the step.

"I wish there was being a nicer way to the Velvet Fortress," Leila said. The only way led through the Turkish quarter, a rabbit warren of tiny houses built on the slope of the hill between the Konak and the summit, where the many evidences of utter poverty were only made picturesque by Smyrna's characteristic trails and trellises of creepers and wild grape vines. The men of the district were hanging about the wretched coffee shops; the veiled women and their pathetic children lurked in the alleys near their homes.

"Don't you think the Turks are being very dirty people?" Leila insisted as Jeff made no reply.

"Poor devils, they haven't much of a chance, the way things are. And I suppose it's their city, after all."

Leila never argued. Soon enough, they were through the Turkish quarter and on the open hillside, passing the blue cupola and the minaret of the Velvet Mosque. At the gates of the ancient fortress the driver asked eagerly if he might wait for them, and Jeff agreed. He had never visited Kadife Kale, and at first glance there wasn't much to see but a rather gloomy pinewood and a lot of mouldering walls. But Leila was tugging at his arm, prattling about the view, and when he had helped her up a steep flight of stone steps, there the view was, superb, the red-roofed city below them and the blue bay broadening into the Gulf of Smyrna.

"Say, this is great!" said Jeff. "Let's sit down and have a cigarette."

Leila hesitated. She was wearing a white dress, and the stones of the fortress wall were dusty.

Jeff laughed at her expression and took his jacket off to spread it on the wall. "Is that better?" He sat down and put his arm round the girl as Leila, relaxing, took off her small white hat and shook out her curls in the light sea breeze.

"My little maid of Athens!" Jeff said fondly. "Now you're like that verse in your own song, about the tresses unconfined—how does it go?"

> *"By those tresses unconfined,*
> *Woo'd by each Aegean wind;*
> *By those lids whose jetty fringe*
> *Kiss thy soft cheek's blooming tinge"*

sang Leila softly, and then Jeff interrupted the song to kiss those black lashes and the flushed cheeks they swept, and Leila sighed with happiness. But then Jeff took out his cigarettes, and before these were half smoked she was saying "Why are you so quiet this afternoon, *chéri?*"

"I was thinking about Rosette," he confessed. "Are you sorry you're not aboard the *Kléber* and on your way to Beirut with her now?"

"As if I ever wanted to leave you, *mon grand* Jeff!"

Jeff was silent. He couldn't find the courage to tell her that "all this" had got to end some day, that he couldn't stay in Smyrna for ever, and that perhaps the greatest kindness he could do his little maid of Athens would be to send her back to Greece, out of this troubled Turkey once and for all. But she was saying pensively:

"I wish some day we could be taking a boat to Doctor's Island, Jeff. Is so beautiful!"

"Baby, from what you told me it's way out in the Gulf, and I'm scared to take a whole day trip away from Smyrna. Remember what happened when we went to Prinkipo?"

"Oh, Jeff!"

He looked at Leila's blushing face and realised that she was remembering their first night together at the Hotel Calypso, whereas he had been thinking that the stopover on Prinkipo had made him miss the story of the Trakas murderer. With an odd mixture of guilt and boredom he kissed her and tried to say lightly:

"Not sorry you ran away with me, are you?"

"I am being so happy to be home in Smyrna, and with you . . . What a lot of ships in the bay!"

She was like a child, jumping from one idea to another, or like the little lizards, flicking out and in between the sunwarmed stones they sat on. To please her, he said, "See your two Greek battleships, lying between the Konak and the Point. Do you know their names?"

Proudly: "The *Kilkis* and the *Lemnos*, of course."

"Aha!" said Jeff. "They started out as the U.S.S. *Mississippi* and *Idaho*, built in Philadelphia just about twenty years ago."

"You mean they were being American ships?"

"Sure as you're born. The Greeks bought them from us to get parity with the two armed cruisers the Turks got from the German government."

But Leila, who had frowned at the word "parity", was still watching the summer sea.

"There are three big Greek ships in the bay now," she said.

"Your eyesight's better than mine, baby. I wish I'd brought the binoculars. That's the Greek flag, all right. Hell! it can't be the *Averoff*, come down from Constantinople?"

The third ship flying the blue and white, and the flag of the Royal Greek Navy, manœuvred into position beside her sisters. She came broadside on to the watchers at the Velvet Fortress, and even without binoculars Jeff could see the huge Red Crosses on the pale grey paint.

"My God!" he said, "that's the hospital ship that's be.n lying off Chios for so long. Coming into Turkish waters—that means trouble, and I don't mean maybe. So let's go hunt up that driver and get back to town."

14

THE TELEGRAPHIC MESSAGE informing the Greek government of the Turkish attack at Koja Tepe, which caused the nearest hospital ship to be sent to Smyrna, was almost the last to come out of Afyon Karahisar under Greek occupation. Kemal's flying column of cavalry, moving to outflank the enemy and cut the railway line to Smyrna, had orders to cut the telegraph wires at the same time.

Afyon was thus cut off from the outside world for the better part of two days. The speed of the Greek retreat had left Kemal with twenty-four hours in hand for the final liaison of General Nureddin's First Army with the Second, under General Shevki, which had come south from Eskishehir, and he spent the whole of his second morning in Afyon in conference with these two commanders. In the afternoon Kemal rode some distance west to inspect the progress of the labour and supply battalions which were already moving forward at the slow pace dictated by bullock and camel transport. Fortunately the Greek air reconnaissance was feeble and there was little or no attempt at bombing.

After a busy day, Kemal announced his intention of receiving the press corps at headquarters in the early evening. The little group of journalists was not particularly impressive, thanks to Kemal's own tight security precautions; the best of them were two middle-aged men from Angora who had been working at the Eskishehir front and followed the troops south when the Second Army began to move. The others had followed Kemal himself from Konya and onwards; they were local men, stunned by their new responsibilities. There were six reporters in all, and two photographers, all representing the Turkish press. The foreign press was represented by Evelyn Barrett, and it was perhaps on her account that General Ismet, hesitating, had addressed one of his gentle remonstrances to his headstrong chief.

"Pasha, don't you think this press conference, as you call it, rather premature . . ? Is this kind of a meeting usual, or even necessary . . ?" Those were the uncompleted sentences, the diffident hints, which sometimes worked wonders with Kemal, for Ismet's nature was in many ways the reverse and complement of his own. Today he merely barked that a press conference was a modern idea, and that an old soldier like Ismet (who was thirty-seven) must learn to march with the times.

"Pasha, is this quite fair to the lady?" Kemal had honestly no idea what Ismet meant. He had summoned the reporters precisely because he wanted to see the lady, it was as simple as that; and the European in Mustafa Kemal was amused, the Turk exasperated, to think he had to call a press conference in order to be with his young mistress, hear her speak, watch her smile, only a few hours after he had risen from her bed.

"Fair to the lady" indeed! The lady was like no other lady he had ever known, in the carnal sense or otherwise, and while Kemal exulted in his possession of Evelyn he was enraged to think that although he was the commander of a liberated city he could requisition no place where the woman he loved could wait in luxury for his return. He had seen her three times from a distance, once leaving the hospital where Riza was lying, then out and about in Afyon, talking to shopkeepers, soldiers, letter-writers, sherbet-sellers (and in what language, pray?) and he knew she had requested an interview with Ismet Pasha. He remembered the aftermath of his other victories, when he had enjoyed the warrior's rest in the darkened boudoirs of Pera. He couldn't imagine Evelyn as an *odalik,* a bedroom girl, lying loose-limbed on her couch to await her master, but—thought the future emancipator of Turkey's womanhood—there was, after all, a great deal to be said for the harem.

"What sort of questions did Mrs. Barrett ask you, when you talked to her this morning?" Kemal asked abruptly.

"She asked me about the night movements over the past month, and the secret concentrations to prepare for the attack."

"Is that still news?"

"She said she needed more background for her story. I must admit she asked some very searching questions! Quite a masculine intelligence—I was most impressed."

"She *is* very intelligent."

"Very effective, too. I hear the corporal who brought in Captain

Riza told the doctors she kept saying 'Hurry up! Hurry up!' all the way to Afyon."

Kemal smiled. "She may well have saved poor Riza's life, at that. But it looks as if his soldiering days are over for good."

Ismet saw that the subject was to be changed, and made one more effort.

"I hope Mrs. Barrett will be assigned to the rear tomorrow. A woman correspondent will be a great novelty to the men, and besides, she should be kept away from danger. That's a very vulnerable young lady, Pasha. I would hate to see her wounded . . . in any way."

Kemal rang a handbell for the duty officer. "Show the reporters in," he said curtly.

Evelyn Barrett walked in first. She was wearing her dark blue dress, which Kemal noted had been carefully pressed, and to replace the white square used on Riza's arm she had bought one of the black draperies, pinned beneath the chin, which Turkish women like Madame Emine wore as a substitute for the forbidden veil. On Emine the thing looked merely lugubrious, like exaggerated mourning, but anything more seductive than Evelyn's face framed in black, with just one lock of blond hair showing, the man who loved her had never seen.

Kemal began at once.

"I've asked you all to come here," he said, "because I understand there have been complaints about the lack of—er—transmission facilities in reporting the offensive begun at Koja Tepe and continuing with the liberation of Afyon. You, Hilmi!" he jerked his thumb at one of the men from Angora, "I hear you had a good deal to say when you found the telegraph office closed today. Would you care to repeat it to me?"

"The Gazi must remember we've a duty to our readers," said the man addressed. "Our job is to get the news to our editors as fast as possible." Evelyn looked at him beneath her lashes. He had struck the same heckling note as the hojas who baited Kemal in the Assembly, and Kemal reacted exactly as he had done there. With a bitter twist to his lips he said,

"I've a higher duty to your readers than you have, gentlemen. Mine is to free their country, and I won't fail in that duty to please the editors of Angora or any other city in Turkey. I've sent despatch riders with two communiqués to the capital already, and

that's all the outside world is going to hear from Supreme Headquarters until the Greeks surrender. Then the telegraph offices
will be reopened, and subject to military censorship you can use
the wires exactly as you please."

"Does that go for the foreign press as well?" said the other man
from Angora innocently.

"It goes for all of you. Come now, don't look so glum! I've
been patient for a year; surely you can be patient for two or three
more days!"

"Does that mean we can expect victory inside three days?"
cried a chorus of voices.

"The final victory—in Anatolia—will be when we clear the
Greeks out of Smyrna, and we're a long way from Smyrna still.
But"—relenting—"the decisive battle can't be long delayed.
General Tricoupis is preparing to stand at the village of Dumlu
Pinar. You can see the new Greek positions on this map."

They crowded round a side table. Upon a drawing-board, unrolled and pinned in place, was the map Kemal had prepared and
kept in his locked desk at Chankaya.

"Can you read this kind of map, Mrs. Barrett?" Kemal said in
French.

"I think so, sir." She was as close to him as when he sat beside
her in Ayesha's house to demonstrate the war game. But now,
though he knew every secret of the body inside the cotton dress,
and all the textures of her skin and hair, Evelyn refused to look at
him. She bent over the map with the palms of her boyish hands
laid flat on the table top, quite genuinely absorbed by the military
problem, and when she raised her head it was only to glance at
Ismet Pasha, who was watching them both. Nothing could have
excited Kemal's passion more than this cool aloofness from himself. He remembered the wild ecstasy of gratitude he had aroused
in Evelyn: he was suddenly frantic to rouse that gratitude again.

One of the reporters was asking a question, and judging by
Ismet's cough not for the first time.

"I was asking the Gazi if he hadn't expected Tricoupis to put
up a better defence at Afyon?"

"I expected him to stand in front of Afyon, probably at
Chobanlar, and took my dispositions accordingly. But as you all
know the enemy set fire to Chobanlar village and retreated to the
west. It's to be feared that these tactics, if tactics you can call

them, will be repeated elsewhere. The Greek officers we interrogated yesterday admitted that their orders were to pursue a war of extermination against us."

The reporters looked uneasily at one another. Kemal went on:

"Here you can appreciate the situation in terms of the terrain. (Mrs. Barrett, can you follow me, or must I translate?) Here is Dumlu Pinar, about forty miles away, and these are the Greek lines, held in depth. When I attack from the north, east and south, General Tricoupis has no alternative but to fall back on Ushak. He has only two ways west; one, across the mountains, which are impassable, or two, through the valley of Kiziljidere, where we . . . should have . . . no difficulty . . . in containing him."

The last slow words caused a silence to fall in the room. Kemal himself was the first to break it.

"And now, gentlemen, having made you a present of my plan of action, I intend to confine you all to your quarters until your movement orders can be issued. Captain Hamdi will be in charge of your transportation, and you'll draw army rations while you're at the front."

They thanked him and moved towards the door. Kemal was unable to stop himself from saying to Evelyn, more emphatically than he meant:

"*Vous m'avez suivi de très près—enfin, vous m'avez bien compris, madame?*"

"*Parfaitement, monsieur le maréchal!*"

Evelyn looked at him at last, with the sparkle in her eyes and the smile that made the Commander-in-Chief, every minute of whose day was precious, ache with longing for the hours of night. He went to the door and held it wide for her, shouting into the anteroom:

"Sergeant Ali, take the Hanim Efendi to her quarters!"

      *   *   *

As soon as Evelyn was back in her strange old room in the Archives Department, the Turkish girl who had waited upon her the night before appeared with a supper tray which had certainly not been prepared from army rations, since it included half a bottle of white wine and a basket of choice fruit. Evelyn did not dally over the meal. She ate with her left hand and wrote with her right—

quickly, for she instinctively knew that Kemal, when he came, would not be pleased to find her working—setting down in her notebook all the impressions she had gathered during that day. First, the interview with Ismet had to be transcribed, for Evelyn's shorthand was rusty and Ismet's French was halting, but she got the substance into longhand, and went on to describe the poppy fields which surrounded the strange peak which dominated the plateau where Afyon stood. Afyon Karahisar, "the Black Fortress of Opium", was, she noted, one of the centres of opium production in Turkey. "It is one of the aspirations of Mustafa Kemal Pasha," wrote Evelyn, "to secure Turkey's admission to the League of Nations, and so to place the opium traffic under legal and international control." And, since she was not sure what might happen to her notebook in the stress of the hours ahead, Evelyn resorted to shorthand to record one incident of the morning, when an old Greek woman who spoke some French had insisted on showing her the Armenian church at the foot of the mountain peak where English soldiers had been imprisoned during the Great War. "Turkish dogs!" said the old woman, and spat upon the ground. "Today's liberators! Yesterday's torturers! Two hundred skeletons, *kirya*, two hundred Englishmen dying from dysentery and starvation, they kept in this Christian church!"

The Turkish girl came back for the supper tray. She was carrying Evelyn's fawn coat and skirt, washed and neatly mended, and kissed the lady's hand in thanks for the money she was given. Then there was silence, broken only by the sentry's step below, in the little room which in spite of the open window still smelled of the musty parchments which might have dated back to the foundation of the House of Osman, but it was a silence held breathless within the four walls of the old courtyard. All round the block of the municipal buildings there was a hum of activity; occasionally Evelyn heard a shouted word of command.

"My darling!"

"Kemal!" He had come to her unchallenged by Sergeant Ali, padding up the stair as quietly as a great cat, and now she was in his arms again, sighing with delight.

"Happy?"

"Wildly, deliriously happy. And you?"

"*Follement, follement heureux!*" Kemal echoed her words. They heard drums beating somewhere near at hand.

"I call this the very strictest security," murmured Evelyn. "In the arms of the Commander-in-Chief!"

Kemal laughed with her, but his eyes were sombre. "Evelyn," he said, "are you sure you want to go up to Dumlu Pinar tomorrow?"

"I want to see the battle. I want to be with you."

"You can't be with me, at least not for very long, and the battle will be—not exactly as you picture it. Not a game of chess. Not even poker."

"I can take it," she said steadily. "I won't let you down, if that's what you're afraid of!"

"I'm only afraid of the possible danger—for yourself. Ismet wants you kept well in the rear—"

"I won't stay there!" she said indignantly, and Kemal laughed again, and called her insubordinate, a disgrace to the service, as he took off his belt with the pistol holster, and undid the high collar of his khaki tunic. There was only one chair in the little room, and he dropped to the wide mattress, pulling Evelyn down into his arms.

"When do we—leave?" she said in a small voice.

"I go at midnight, you about one o'clock."

"Then we haven't very long."

"No." Kemal took out his cigarette case, changed his mind, and laid it on the table by the bed.

"This is the bad hour before battle, Evelyn. The worst hour, that I've lived through so many times before, but never with a woman I loved beside me. Never with any woman! Is it you, so near me, so sweet and loving, who make me feel as I never felt before the horror of what lies ahead?"

Evelyn was silent. It was the first time she had ever known him in such a mood.

"Or is it what happened at Chobanlar?" he went on, almost as if he were speaking to himself. "But Chobanlar was nothing. The Greeks burned down the houses, but the people got away and took refuge in Afyon. What happens when there's no refuge to fly to? Will there be bloodshed all along the road to Smyrna?"

Evelyn slid her hand inside his shirt. She felt his heart beating fast and irregularly against her palm.

"My love," she said, "it's very nearly over now!"

"Yes," he said, and put his hand over hers. "I have to tell

myself that! I have to believe this is the last battle—and then Turkey will be free." He kissed her on the lips. "This is a dark hour I've asked you to share with me, my two eyes. But you're my light in the darkness!"

Then as if Evelyn were all the light he needed, Kemal struck out the candle flame.

"I wonder where we shall all be by this time tomorrow," she heard him say. "You and I—and Ismet—and thousands of our friends and enemies?"

He tried again. "How can any rational man believe in the Moslem paradise, an eternity of feasting and music and beautiful black-eyed virgins? And if there is no paradise after death, then what is there?"

"Perhaps the Light hereafter?"

On the night before, their first night together, Kemal had possessed his love in silence, using his hands and his lips and finally his whole body to rouse her to a wild sharing in his passion. Tonight he whispered to her, sometimes in French but more often in Turkish, using phrases she had never heard before, but which she knew by intuition were not the coarse sexual slang, the words limited to four letters, which Jeff had sometimes used in a vain attempt to excite his wife. In the rich complexities of his native language Kemal offered her the tribute of his heart, until Evelyn, clinging to him and murmuring *"Seni seviyorum,* I love you too," as he had taught her, was carried over the rapids into the dark pool of joy.

She slept in his arms, those lean and muscular arms which held her in security, so deeply that Kemal said her name twice over before she even moved her head on the rough pillow.

"Evelyn! Darling! Half past eleven!"

"Only half past—" She felt as if she had been asleep for hours.

"*Only!* I must go." She saw by candlelight that he was fully dressed and buckling his belt. He stooped and kissed her quickly, with no word of farewell except "Remember, when we're married there'll be no reveille!" and was gone. The drums were beating more loudly than ever in the streets outside.

Evelyn crept out of bed. A strong smell of tobacco smoke fought with the odour of the parchments, and there were several cigarette butts in the ashtray beside the bed. She realised that the

Commander-in-Chief had not slept at all, had lain awake beside her in that soldier's bed while she dreamed what had seemed like a long night away. She pulled her cotton dress over a body soft with satisfied desire, ran down the corridor to the dreadful lavatory, washed, and combed her hair. She put her dress and other belongings into the haversack and made herself as neat as possible in the clean coat and skirt. Then she hurried through the dark courtyard, round the side of the building and up the town hall steps.

The entrance hall was full of men, moving from room to room in an orderly confusion as the Staff made ready to follow the Gazi up the line. There was no sign of Captain Hamdi, but Evelyn's guide of the night before, Major Orman, came up at once and led her into a side room.

"I'm going to be your conducting officer, Mrs. Barrett," he said in his pleasant way. "Captain Hamdi is briefing the Turkish reporters now."

"What on earth's the matter?" The noise in the side room was considerable.

"They're being made to draw lots for their positions," explained Orman. "Three with the First Army and two with the Second. One photographer to go up to the front line. You, with one reporter and one photographer, go with the Staff."

"I'm very fortunate."

"I'm fortunate, madame; I get to ride with you in an automobile instead of plugging along in a lorry like the rest. By the way, I got a greatcoat for you from Supply. You don't mind wearing khaki? I noticed last night you had no overcoat."

"I left it in the truck—on purpose."

"I understand, but it's cold at night in the mountains. Let me get you a glass of tea."

Major Orman was too tactful to remark that Evelyn's teeth were chattering; she hoped he would only think she was feeling cold. In fact the chill of fear was creeping over her body at the thought that nothing now but some miles of mountain road separated her from the battlefield. Standing alone by the door while Major Orman went to look for a servant in the crush, she tried to think of nothing but the argument between her Turkish colleagues and the irritable Captain Hamdi. It was exactly like all the press rooms she had ever known (waiting in the background with notes or material for Jeff) with the same wrangles over priority, the same row about transmission; only in Europe the liquor was usually flowing freely by this time. The Turks were drinking the excellent Anatolian tea, and Evelyn was glad when the tea-boy bowed before her, swinging his little brass tray.

"Would you like anything to eat, Mrs. Barrett?" Major Orman had returned to her side. "I can't give you any guarantee when breakfast will be served!"

"Nothing, thank you; I feel as if I'd just finished dinner." It was a lie; she felt a nervous hunger, which she dared not satisfy for fear of being sick.

"I think we ought to be starting, then, if you're quite ready."

Evelyn picked up the haversack and slung it on her back. "I'm ready," she said.

*   *   *

She must have slept in the car as it went slowly up to the front. Perhaps she had fallen asleep first in the darkness under the trees in one of the leafy streets of Afyon during the long wait which preceded their eventual departure: certainly she remembered the Turkish reporter beginning to snore (it was the man named Hilmi, from Angora) and the photographer dozing and wakening to swear as his heavy camera slipped from his knees. But in or outside the town, Evelyn's sleep was so light that she was always aware of the silent marching columns beside which the ancient tourer passed. Major Orman sat in front beside the driver. His arms were folded on his chest for warmth. Evelyn had wrapped the military great-coat very closely around her. The mountains glittered in the starlight and there was a nip of early frost in the air.

Even when she was sure of being completely awake and aware of her surroundings there was a fluttering confusion in Evelyn Barrett's brain. She seemed to hear Kemal saying again and again, "Where shall we all be, this time tomorrow night?"—where shall we, where shall we be? said the wheels grinding in the dust, and that question blurred into another question, a verse from the poem called "The Isles of Greece" which she had once quoted to Kemal:

> "*He counted them at break of day*
> *And when the sun set where were they?*"

Where would *they* be at sunset?

> *"For what is left the poet here?*
> *For Greeks a blush—for Greece a tear."*

Evelyn tried to put Lord Byron's poem from her mind. But it came back with maddening reiteration, half remembered, the isles of Greece, the isles of Greece, where burning Sappho loved and sung, until Evelyn in desperation leaned forward and asked Major Orman to give her a cigarette. He turned round to talk to her after that, explaining that he was a professional soldier, an artilleryman, who had spent a year at Woolwich before the Great War ("That's how you speak such marvellous English, major!") and having been severely wounded in the civil war had now "a Staff job"—it was all told in a deliberately prosaic manner which steadied Evelyn's nerves. But there was the sound of gunfire up ahead, and the glow of fire in the paling sky: the Turkish newspapermen were wide awake now, and Hilmi predicted:

"Looks like they've fired Dumlu Pinar."

They had fired Dumlu Pinar, the village of the Cold Spring, which the Greeks had first fortified with machine gun nests and barbed wire entanglements, and then abandoned as the Turks came on in strength. But before they retreated they had set fire to every house in Cold Spring, and the inhabitants, unlike the villagers of Chobanlar, had no friendly town to take them in; some of them, born Greeks, had been dragged away "for their own good" by the Greek soldiers; the Turks were bayoneted as they fled. A burial party was already at work as the press car came up, and men from a labour battalion were hastily digging a common grave, but there were bodies still lying like bloody sacks by the roadside, and one demented girl screaming above the dead body of her child. The driver accelerated, the village of death was left behind.

"Are you all right, Mrs. Barrett?" asked Major Orman.

"Yes thank you." She had to be all right, although her hands and face seemed to have turned to ice and her mouth was full of salt water, for now it was dawn, and they were climbing the hills above the valley of Kiziljedere, the Red Stream, where Kemal had been confident of containing his retreating enemy. They left the car and climbed on foot to where most of the Staff had gathered round the Commander of the Western Army and the Chief of

221

Staff, General Fevzi. Major Orman motioned to his reporters to keep well back out of their sight. Even without binoculars it was possible to study the whole terrain by the light of the rising sun. There on the right flank were the Murad mountains, which Kemal had rightly called impassable, and on the left a range of hills so densely wooded as to be almost as difficult to traverse, and in the valley between, laid out as neatly as the chessmen of Clausewitz, some four divisions of the Greek Army, prepared to give battle at last to the Turkish enemy.

"Where is the Gazi?" said Evelyn in a low voice to Major Orman.

"He intended to lead the attack with General Nureddin."

"So bang goes Nureddin's chance of claiming this as *his* victory," said the reporter, Hilmi, and although he spoke in Turkish Major Orman shook his head, and made a quick movement of his chin in Evelyn's direction.

"Do you understand Turkish, Hanim Efendi?"

"I understood what you said just now, Hilmi Bey."

"Oh." The man looked disconcerted. "The Gazi always wants to be in the front of the battle. The men say it's because he bears a charmed life."

If only I could see him, Evelyn thought. But there was no distinguishing anyone through the smoke which billowed up to the slope where she was standing: Kemal was playing his overture in the form of a grand artillery barrage, which the Greeks answered with every shell they had. The air was full of discordant sounds, like an express train, like a door shutting, like the rattle of wooden slats on wood, varied by a crump and whizz-bang which shook the very ground beneath their feet. Then a light wind came up, and swept the valley clear of smoke, so that Evelyn could see the perfectly mounted diagram of a gigantic war game, the guns and the men diminished by distance into toys. But toys not made of lead, for here and there fountains of metal sprayed into the air, and with the metal what looked like red cloth torn into rags, and the rags were the fragments of humanity drenched in blood and . . .

. . . Clausewitz had never mentioned blood.

By mid-morning all the Greek batteries on the surrounding hills had been silenced, and a brilliant charge by the Turkish cavalry, with sabres swinging, had cleared almost half of the valley of the Red Stream. It was followed by an infantry advance, as two

222

Turkish divisions, the 11th and 12th of the Second Army, moved forward at the entrance to the valley. "Mehmedjik" was traditionally said to fight best on the defensive, but on this day at Dumlu Pinar, following an inspired leader, the Turkish soldier mounted a brilliant attack. It was in the middle of this phase of the battle that Evelyn saw the Commander-in-Chief for the first time.

He came running up the slope where the Staff was grouped, as lightly as a boy, with his fair head bare. His empty Luger was in his hand, for he had been firing in his own defence, and a heavy sheath knife swung at the other side of his leather belt. He made General Fevzi look heavy and slow, and General Ismet insignificant, as both Pashas sprang forward to greet him and his soldier-servant hurried to his side.

"Another near miss!" said Kemal cheerfully. "Ali, get me a kalpak, and reload this. Yes, Pasha, we're doing it at last, I think! Now I want to see that exit closed as fast as possible."

Kemal's binoculars were slung around his neck. He took them from their case and put them to his eyes, spoke to an aide-de-camp, scribbled an order on a pad, while the photographer took careful focus with his old-fashioned camera, and the Staff whispered and purred over the latest addition to the legend of the Gazi's charmed life. Evelyn, well in the background, dug her trembling hands into the pockets of her twill jacket. Two inches lower down, and not the kalpak but the fine forehead would have been hit, the extraordinary blue eyes blinded . . . A shell whistled above the slope, and struck behind them.

"Looks as if they've found the range, gentlemen," said Kemal cheerfully. He turned the binoculars on his left flank. On one of the wooded hills there was a flash of green, where a little group of imams had appeared brandishing the emerald flag of the Prophet. Above the sound of firing came their hysterical chanting:

"Kill! Kill! Kill! Death to the infidels! Death to the Christian dogs!"

Kemal's pale face flushed scarlet. "Send a runner to that tepe!" he flung at his Chief of Staff. "Order every imam to the baggage trucks! Tell them to save their religion until we bury the dead! And take away their flags — we fight for a free Turkey under the Crescent and the Star!"

"He is furious," whispered the Staff, uneasily.

"What in *jehennem* has happened to the Sixty-first?" was Kemal's next demand. "Their orders were to close the exit by eleven o'clock."

Ismet murmured something about patience, and looked at his wrist watch.

"Ah! here they come!"

At the far end of the valley, where the Red Stream was running crimson now, the flag of Turkey had appeared. The white Crescent and Star on the scarlet ground was displayed in the van of the 61st Division of the Second Army, as the Turkish troops wheeled into place to close off the Greek retreat. The enemy, fighting every inch of the way down the valley, now found himself caught in a trap from which there was no escape except surrender. Kemal, with a grunt of satisfaction, hurried off to join General Nureddin.

"I think we might have something to eat now," said Ismet Pasha comfortably. "Mrs. Barrett, I know you're there, and while I'd much rather you were in the rear with the nurses, I feel bound to offer you a cup of coffee."

"*Merci, mon général.*" Evelyn came forward diffidently. She had passed through several stages of physical discomfort during the long hours on the hill, and was now although without knowing it in a state of shock; she was thankful to sit down at the folding table which the soldier-servants hastily set round with folding stools. Some food was brought from a little field kitchen: pilav, she thought, and strips of pide bread and cheese, but now the smell of blood and death was so heavy above Dumlu Pinar and its fatal valley that the very thought of eating was sickening. She sat absolutely still, looking at the table top, it was something to focus her eyes on instead of that awful carnage of men and horses and mules which had been going on, hour after hour, and mechanically thanked the man who gave her a mug of coffee.

"The Gazi was right, they *have* found the range," said General Fevzi without undue concern. "Why can't we put that fellow out of action?" For once again the shells were coming over the slope where they sat, and falling in the rear: Evelyn found that her hands were shaking badly. To lift the enamel mug of coffee she had to fasten her left hand tightly round her right wrist. She hoped no one would notice, but Ismet Pasha said,

"Where did you learn to stand fire, madame?"

"On the road to Afyon, *mon général*."

Fevzi Pasha stood up suddenly, capsizing his canvas stool.

"Look," he said, "the white flag! Tricoupis has surrendered!"

15

As SOON AS A runner from General Nureddin's command post brought Ismet Pasha written confirmation of the Greek surrender, Major Orman took Evelyn back to the nurses' lorries in the rear. "I can only allow you half an hour," he warned her, "because Hilmi and the photographer are anxious to get to work, and I'm afraid we'll have to cross the battlefield on foot. Will you sleep with the nurses for the night, if we have to bivouac somewhere along the way?"

"Of course." Evelyn was grateful for the Turkish army nurses' friendly welcome. They were a pitifully small corps, because only since Kemal forbade the veil could adult women go among sick and wounded men; even as recently as the civil war little girls of twelve, still unveiled, had tried to do the work of women in the wards. The girls Evelyn now met had not been idle; they had been doing what they could for the survivors of the burned-out village of Dumlu Pinar, and they had even recruited a platoon from one of the labour battalions to dig out a small latrine and put up canvas screens. As the nursing sister in command of the corps observed realistically to Evelyn, the latrine problem was the real objection to the presence of women on a fighting front.

The water in Evelyn's bottle was not fit for drinking, having come from a tap in the corridor at Afyon, and she felt free to use it to wash her face and hands. One of the young nurses shared a small phial of rose-water with her, so that Hilmi, the Angora reporter, sniffed appreciatively when she rejoined the group, and told her she should have kept the scent for later. The imams, in spite of Kemal's embargo, were raising the chant of victory as Major Orman led his charges back through the baggage lines. "Praise be to him who is Allah of all the world!" The thin song pursued Evelyn like curls of gunsmoke as she began to cross the battlefield of the Red Stream.

The hojas who had accompanied the Turkish regiments were there already, praying over the dead with their hands lifted high to heaven. Major Orman told Evelyn they had found the Moslem death, *shehadet*, each man a martyr for the Faith; the Greek corpses, hastily tumbled into shallow trenches by the Greek prisoners, were the *ölü*, nondescript dead—she thought at once of the House of Islam and the House of War. Ten thousand prisoners had been taken, with all the heavy guns on the field and a huge quantity of rifles and small arms, and the Greek II Corps had abandoned all its wheeled transport, including one hundred motorised vehicles—a tremendous windfall for the Nationalist Army. Major Orman had already compiled a number of statistics, all of which Hilmi copied into a reporter's notebook, while the photographer fiddled with his plates. Evelyn decided to trust to her memory, at least until she was back with the army nurses. To her mind, already racked by the events of the day, there was something indecent in reducing suffering to numerals, in the course of this solemn procession across a battlefield. Because the numerals, the digits, the "effectives" were, or had been, human beings: they lay now, dead and at peace, or hideously maimed and helpless in their blood and excrement, men who had died for King Constantine's Great Idea, or for Kemal's vision of an independent Turkey, but individuals still, each with his own loves and hates, his family behind him. The girl nurses, the men who wore the brassards of the Red Crescent, moved after the army surgeons, alleviating pain where it was possible, while the farrier sergeants, in a task no less merciful, shot the writhing horses which had fallen with the cavalrymen and the mules which had dragged the howitzers into place. The field of the Red Stream still rang with shots as Evelyn came trembling to the exit lane. You wanted to see a battle, she told herself. You've seen it. And surely there can't be much worse to see than this.

But there was; far worse, for the next village on the way west had suffered the same fate as Dumlu Pinar, and this time there was no task force to shovel the dead out of the way before the advance caught up. In that great retreat of the Greeks which from the hill where the Staff watched had looked like a dam bursting fully as many had escaped as had been taken prisoner: with what vehicles they had left, with what jaded horses, they were fleeing west to Smyrna, and as they went they took their hideous vengeance in rape, arson and murder. The Turkish troops, reformed and on the march, broke ranks as girls with bloodied garments knelt by the road and begged revenge for their virginity; the army nurses, in despair, put field dressings on the scorched bodies of old men and children. Evelyn worked with the nurses as best she could. The smell of burned flesh was over everything, and in that village—she never learned its name—as the sun set on the day of battle she fought with her own nausea until the moment came when, like many another, she leaned above the choked ditch and vomited. She had seen, lying beneath what had been a fruitful vine, the body of a girl with the corpse of her unborn child torn from her belly and run through with a Greek bayonet.

Much later, when dusk was falling over the mountains, the convoy in which the nurses were now travelling entered the ruins of yet another settlement, and word was passed down the line that the Gazi himself was there. There was a brief halt, for everyone wanted to see the victorious commander, and the order was given to bivouac about five miles further on. Evelyn, who had been sitting in front with the soldier-driver, remained alone in the cab of the lorry. Major Orman had thoughtfully brought her army greatcoat, and she huddled into it; Kemal himself, she could quite clearly see, had what looked like a long grey cape slung round his shoulders. He was sitting on a folding stool with people all about him, while closest to his feet was a ring of kneeling women, dishevelled, bruised, with smoke-stained hands and faces, alternately screaming and sobbing as they begged for vengeance on the Greek destroyers. The girl who loved him winced with pain at the expression on his face. The gay, confident mood of the morning was gone, and her lover was again the care-laden man she had comforted in the night hours. Kemal gave his hand to the women, and one by one they made the Moslem obeisance, lifting their finger-tips to their breasts and foreheads and reverently kissing his extended hand. Then the officers of his entourage gently motioned them away, and Evelyn saw, where the trampling feet had been, a rag of white and blue that had once been a Greek flag.

Kemal seemed to notice it for the first time. "Don't walk over that flag, you fool!" he said to someone whose face was hidden from Evelyn, "whatever we may think of *them*, it's the flag of a free country. Give it to me!"

He stood up, taking a few paces with the stiffness of utter exhaustion, and holding the Greek flag clear of the dirt, hung it on the wheel of a capsized limber which had been dragged off the road. Then he returned to his seat, pulling the grey cloak round him, and gave the signal for the halted convoy to proceed. Darkness came down on the field of Dumlu Pinar, and on the valley of the Red Stream, while in the cab of an army lorry Evelyn slept uneasily, waking again and again to remember that motionless figure of the victor in the dust.

*   *   *

The Turkish forces moved forward slowly after the decisive battle of Dumlu Pinar. It was soon found that General Tricoupis, after the official surrender, was missing, and it was rumoured that he was among the many who, fleeing beyond the point at which the Turkish cavalry had cut the railway line, were able to use the rolling stock in the sidings at Ushak and other westward stations for fast transportation to Smyrna. The ten thousand prisoners had to be fed, the wounded taken to the rear, the mountain road was clogged with traffic by day and by night. Kemal jolted ahead with his Pashas in an open touring car which the hard road from Angora to this stage on his journey had turned into a heap of old iron not much better than the famous Benz. As he drove the word came back down the marching columns that the Gazi was raging and Ismet Pasha choking between tears and curses as they passed through hamlets and villages where the retreating Greeks had passed. As it had been at Dumlu Pinar, so it was at Kutchuk village, at Islahanlar, at Elvanlar: everywhere the ruins of smouldering homes, the tale of Greek Christians dragged away weeping from their burning houses, of sobbing violated Turkish girls, of the mutilated bodies of women and old men.

During the two days and nights following the battle Evelyn Barrett had scarcely seen her lover. On the last day of August he got out of his car and rode on horseback all the way down the columns to the rearguard, with an aide-de-camp ahead of him forbidding the troops to cheer. They sang instead, invigorated by his presence and the few curt words of praise he spoke here and there as he turned his horse occasionally and rode forward talking to officers and men. When he reached the Red Crescent ambulance where Evelyn had found a place that day, and was sitting beside the driver, he pushed up his goggles and rode beside her for just long enough to say unsmilingly:

229

"*Ça va, madame? Allez, bon courage!*" His face, like her own, was drawn and grey with dust.

The dust lay over everything. The Turks marched like a pack of grey wolves, the cavalry always out ahead, hunting down the Greeks intent upon destroying the soil, the homes, the people of Anatolia; every day finding the harvest fields blackened ahead of them, losing time as they waited for the mules carrying fodder. The rations grew shorter and bread was a forgotten luxury. But the men marched without military music; many of them carried flutes which looked almost like penny whistles, and when the thin fluting stopped for want of breath a thousand voices took up the freedom song:

> "*Let us march, friends!*
> *Let our voices be heard by the earth, by the sky,*
> *By the water,*
> *Let the hard ground moan from the harsh tramp*
> *Of our feet!*"

Evelyn Barrett watched them tirelessly. She noted in her book the names of the weapons they were carrying, the Mausers of 1898 with which the Germans had equipped them, the French Lebels, Italian Mannlicher-Carcanos and Russian 3-Lines which Kemal had been able to purchase after making treaties with Turkey's former enemies; some of the Kurdish and Circassian troops were even armed with the old black powder rifles of the Eighteen-Eighties. She noted the broken boots, the feet without socks, the frayed uniforms; she noted the spirit in the burning dark eyes. Sometimes she remembered with shame her own military fantasies: the study of Clausewitz, the lovingly prepared maps, the foolish words to Kemal, "*If I were a man I would have been a soldier*" —how empty they seemed now that she had looked into the grim face of total war. And yet as the time passed she felt less shame. She was standing up to the ordeal as well as anyone, she hadn't collapsed or fainted, still less had she given up and asked for transport back to Afyon. Slowly, the dreadful excitement of the victorious pursuit possessed her utterly.

When they reached Ushak, she was able to look on unmoved at a lynching in the square, when several Greeks in the last stages of physical humiliation paid the penalty for the sins of others, and was eating with no loss of appetite a strip of pide bread and half a can of sardines when Major Orman, who had never lost touch with her on the march, suddenly appeared before her.

"Hallo, major," said Evelyn, "what have you done with the other boys?"

"Your Turkish colleagues? They're holding some sort of protest meeting in the schoolmaster's house. I came to find out whether you wanted to be present."

"I probably wouldn't understand half of what they said. What are they protesting about, anyway? Transmission?"

"Exactly. The photographers are very worried about getting their pictures out."

"I don't blame them," said Evelyn thoughtfully. "I've been trying to figure out what to do about my own story. Are we going to stop over in Ushak tonight, have you any idea?"

"We most certainly are. The first town we've come to with two-thirds of the buildings left intact! You're going to have a proper billet all to yourself tonight."

"Hooray," said the *Clarion* correspondent, licking her oily fingers. "Can we go there now?"

"I believe Sergeant Ali will take charge of you."

"Oh. But what about the nurses?"

"There are beds for all of them at the hospital. Ushak is—was—a prosperous town, you know, important for its carpet industry."

"I hope *you'll* sleep in a bed tonight, major."

"I'll settle for a decent wash."

Evelyn laughed. She liked her conducting officer. He was a man of about forty who, unlike Kemal, looked older than his age, with wings of grey hair above his ears. His humorous dark face, now as grimy as her own, was marked by laughter wrinkles and by the deep lines carved from his nose to the corners of his mouth.

"What about tomorrow?" she asked. "Do we march at first light?"

Orman hesitated. "I don't think so," he said. "There may be some sort of ceremony here in the morning—I really don't know much about it."

"An important ceremony?"

"Mrs. Barrett, I'm not at liberty to say. You may hear about it from—other sources, and then you can decide what you ought to do. But if I were a journalist with a big story to tell, to-morrow morning is when I would try to get to the nearest cable office."

"Using what for transport?"

"If I were a journalist, and didn't mind a rough trip—though not *so* rough as the one we're on—I would try to get down to Afyon on the *derzin*. What's the English word? the trolley, yes, trolley. The railway inspector is going to take one back up the line tomorrow to check what the repair gangs have done since last Tuesday."

"And from there could I get a train to Konya?"

"Yes."

"Do the Turkish reporters know about this? No? Then thanks for the tip-off, Major Orman."

*   *   *

Although it was true that the Nationalists had reached Ushak before the Greeks had time to raze the town to the ground, enough damage had been done to present a fearful scene of ruin, through which Sergeant Ali led Evelyn to a little house in what had once been a pleasant garden district. Most of the neighbouring houses had been gutted, and in the yards lay the corpses of cats and dogs, goats, pet lambs and one child's pony—victims no less innocent than children of the perverted fury of the Greeks. A fatigue party was gathering up these pathetic bodies for burning outside the town.

Ali had already been busy in the little stone house. There was water in a primitive washing place, a charcoal fire burning in the kitchen stove, and a wood fire on the hearth of what must have been a sittingroom, and now contained nothing but a wide sofa, a table, and a pile of firewood so charred that it might have been chopped from the beams of a burned-out house. Kemal's soldier-servant pointed all this out with pride, showing Evelyn the pilav and cooked vegetables in covered containers on top of the charcoal mangal, and the Thermos flask of tea. Cups and plates had been set out on the kitchen table with a bottle of raki and two glasses.

"You take raki, don't take water, Hanim Efendi," Ali warned. The Greeks had polluted the wells, and the army had to fill its water bottles from mountain streams and springs. Even so, there was some danger of an outbreak of typhus, and dysentery had already started.

"I won't touch the water, except to wash in, sergeant."

Ali saluted. "The Gazi comes!" he said, with the rare smile that brightened his dark face. Evelyn was left alone. The house was warm—too warm, but if she opened the windows a dreadful smell of blood and burning entered. She saw a smear of blood on the newel post of the front door, and wondered what tragedy had been enacted there. Where, now, were the people who had lived there, called it home? The place had been ransacked, if not gutted, but Evelyn found one clean sheet in a cupboard, which she spread upon the sofa, and one clean towel, torn almost in half, which she took for her own use. Her pocket mirror showed a thin face deeply tanned, with white rings round the eyes where the goggles had pressed. "He won't call you beautiful now," she said aloud, and instantly was possessed with the desire to be beautiful for him, scented, wearing silk, somewhere far away from this anteroom of death. She put on her one clean shirt and went into the kitchen. She poured half a glass of raki and drank it at a gulp. It was fiery and stimulating; she still disliked the taste of aniseed, but the spirit was an antidote to the brutalisation of the past few days. Evelyn was quite aware of the hardening process going on in her own mind. She had seen too much suffering in one short week to feel pity and terror any more: the strongest human instinct still at work in her was sexual desire.

Kemal, with subtlety and force, had brought her so far and fast along that road that the very thought of their last embraces in the book-lined room at Afyon had disturbed Evelyn's hard-won rest on the journey through the mountains. Now, waiting in the anonymous house, she was ready for him before she heard his quiet word to the sentry and his hand upon the latch.

Kemal came in. By the firelight she could see that he was wearing the grey cloak which he wore on the night of the battle, and underneath it a white shirt and dark grey slacks. She flung herself into his arms, drinking his kisses, exulting in the fury of the passion which leaped to master her own. Without a word spoken they fell together to the broad sofa, tearing at each other's clothes, locked immediately in the closest of all embraces, making in the desert of death which lay around them the grand affirmation of new life to come.

"I adore you," said the Commander-in-Chief. He pulled the grey cloak over their naked bodies.

"And I adore you," sighed Evelyn. ". . . What *is* this thing you've taken to wearing now?"

"It's the cloak I wore in last year's fighting. Many a night it was my blanket when we bivouacked on the ground. I've *never* put it to a better use than this!"

"But darling, let me get up now." Evelyn sat up in his embrace, with the rasp of the cloak's rough material falling over her bare shoulders. She reached down to the floor for her shirt. "Ali brought food for both of us—or have you had something to eat already?"

"Not I." Kemal lay back on the sofa, watching her. "I told the Staff I was dining with the city fathers, who proposed to kill and roast a sheep in my honour, and I told the city fathers I had to be alone in my room to meditate. What sort of food did Ali bring?"

"Rice and raki. And please don't even *talk* about killing sheep."

"Are you really developing a taste for raki?"

"I thought he brought the bottle for you."

"I told you, no drinking till the campaign's over. Did he bring washing water too?"

Presently they were sitting side by side on the sofa, eating the modest supper, while the fire crackled companionably, and the pillaged room took on an illusion of home.

"I've dragged you into some queer places, Evelyn," said Kemal, looking about him, "but this one isn't quite as bad as Afyon, is it? I wish I could show you *my* billet—it would make you laugh."

"Tell me about it."

"Well, after far too many speeches from the leaders of the carpet industry, who appear to think I went to war to save their looms, I was solemnly housed in the residence set up for King Constantine after the Greek advance last year. And I must say the Son of the Eagle did himself very well. He actually had an air raid shelter installed (he obviously didn't know much about our air force) as far underground as they could dig, with electric light, and a very grand bed, and all sort of luxuries. I said I'd had enough of dug-out living on Gallipoli, so they escorted me to another apartment prepared for His Majesty, with a white satin bedspread and cushions embroidered with those purple flowers, what d'you call them?"

"Irises?"

"That's it. Well, all tucked up in white satin and irises, that's where I'm supposed to be meditating now."

Kemal laughed, and Evelyn laughed with him; it was so wonderful to find him in a light-hearted mood. "I don't suppose King Constantine will ever see his irises again," she said.

"M-m? Oh no, he'll be travelling pretty fast in the opposite direction, before the month is out. But he knows the ropes well, because he already abdicated in 1917, so he only has to take the old escape route. Corfu first, to pick up the stuff they keep for emergencies at Mon Repos, and then the road to Rome. Maybe he'll fetch up in Holland, with his brother-in-law the Kaiser, but anyway, this is the end of the Great Idea for all time."

He produced his cigarettes, and Evelyn carried the tray back to the kitchen. When she returned she saw that Kemal had put two more billets of charred timber on the fire, and had lit their cigarettes with a blazing splinter.

"*S'il vous plaît, madame.*" He handed one to her politely. "I think it's time for me to tell you the great news. General Tricoupis has given himself up."

"Oh, Kemal! When, and where?"

"A few hours ago, to a flying column of our cavalry. He and General Dionis had had enough of skulking in the woods and quarrelling with what's left of the Greek Staff. The Venezelists and the Royalists are at each other's throats now, as I knew they would be; they don't know if they're at war with each other or with us."

Evelyn realised that this was the news at which Orman had discreetly hinted. "Tricoupis surrendering! Oh, have you seen him, darling?"

"Not I! I mean to make him wait until early morning, and accept his sword in a public ceremony. Excellent for the morale of our troops." Kemal grinned suddenly. "What Tricoupis doesn't know yet is that he actually is the Commander-in-Chief of the Greek Army tonight. According to Intelligence, General

Hajianestis has been superseded in the supreme command, he's halfway to the Piraeus by this time. He'll be hanged in Constitution Square before the month's over, if I know anything about the clemency of the Greeks."

"Then, if the Commander-in-Chief himself surrenders, does it mean that the campaign is over?"

"I wish it did. But the commander of the Smyrna garrison may receive orders to defend the city, and then of course we'll have to fight our way in."

He threw his cigarette butt into the fire. "If I had *only* a little more mobility, Evelyn! If only the whole army could keep up with the cavalry, and stop this—wholesale slaughter that's going on all the way down the line! You can see for yourself what mood the men are in now, and can you blame them? They see this wanton death and destruction all about them; how can I—even I —keep them from reprisals?"

"Kemal, you *must*. Beat the Greeks in the field, you can do that whenever they stand and face you, but don't, don't let your victory degenerate into a massacre!"

Kemal swore. "That's up to the Greeks," he said coldly. "If they choose to defend Smyrna, and it falls, then Ottoman law gives the victorious troops the right to sack a stormed city for three days."

"You haven't lived by Ottoman law since the beginning of the Revolution. Oh, Kemal, I implore you, be a merciful conqueror! Don't stain your name with crimes like those we've seen ever since we reached Cold Spring!"

Kemal kissed her hand. "You say 'we', my two eyes, as you taught me I should say more often. Let's talk about *our* life instead of the capture of Smyrna. It's going to be dull, don't you think, when all the fighting's over? We'll have to find some new excitement, Evelyn!"

"Such as?"

"Such as our marriage."

"Oh, my darling," Evelyn said faintly, "I still can't quite believe in that!"

"Even though you belong to me now?" said Kemal. "But I tell you it must be so, my child; what can possibly come between us now?"

With his arms around her she still found courage to

say, "But there is one—one just cause and impediment—"

"Barrett?"

"You know what."

Scowling: "Religion? I thought we'd agreed not to discuss that, for the time being."

Evelyn was silent. She longed to say, "But we must discuss it! Talk to me about the Moslem faith, which I see every day, everywhere we go, has so much meaning for so many! You were furious when the flag of the Prophet was carried on to the field of the Red Stream, but there must be more to Islam than your politics! Make me see what beauty and truth must be in that faith, convince me if you can because I long to be convinced, but don't treat me as one agnostic to another!" It was not possible at that hour, in the middle of war's desolation, to trouble Kemal with her complaints. And besides, Kemal himself was saying:

"I will not be parted from you, Evelyn, by a—set of religious scruples which have no validity for you and me and the world we live in today. I feel for you what I have never felt, and never thought to feel, for any woman. Sometimes, and this is a crazy thought, I almost see in you my younger, better self. And yet you're all woman—God, how you proved that tonight! and my wife you *shall* be, by man's law and before whatever God there is."

"Oh, hush!" she begged him, "don't say any more! Give me time to think, to try to decide what's right, and let us talk about it when we meet again in Angora—"

"In *Angora*? Why not in Smyrna, after the victory?

"Because I must go back now," she said desperately, "I want to go back to Konya tomorrow."

"Evelyn, have you lost your senses? Do you think I'd let you go back by *that* road, now I have you here with me? I need you by my side in Smyrna, sharing in our triumph—"

"In public?"

"Certainly in public, what do you suppose?"

"Kemal, you know that's quite impossible. In Smyrna the Allies will *have* to treat you as a Chief of State; they mustn't be able to say that you're living with a woman who's still legally the wife of another man."

"You're not afraid of plain speaking, Evelyn."

"I'm only thinking of the future. If I'm ever to appear by your side in Constantinople, nobody must be able to say we were sleeping together in Smyrna."

"You admit, then, that you *will* be my wife in Constantinople! Ah, my darling, if I were the Sultan I would give you every palace for your own: Topkapi Saray, Dolmabahce, Beylerbey! But there will be no more Sultans, and Angora will be my capital; can you be contented with Chankaya for your home—and me?"

She yielded to his kisses then, quite helplessly, and Kemal, whispering "I've got to be back at Constantine's dugout by five o'clock!" lifted her bodily on to the sofa, and made love to her again. And this time, too, was different from all the other times, love in a slower, drowsier, more healing rhythm, released in a warm gentle tide that washed away all their problems, so that Evelyn, drowsing in her lover's arms, could only whisper:

"Kemal!"

"M-m?"

"It *does* mean 'perfection'!"

She felt his moustache move against her cheek as he grinned in the darkness, and they slept. The mountain stillness fell upon the desolate town.

Kemal was sleeping heavily when Evelyn awoke. There was enough light from the dying fire to let her see the time on the gun-metal wrist watch Kemal wore on campaign: a quarter past four in the morning.

She got up noiselessly, put on shirt, skirt and shoes, and quietly opened the front door. At the gate of the ruined garden Sergeant Ali, rifle in hand, was keeping his tireless vigil. Evelyn called to him:

"*Chavush!*"

"*Buyur, Hanim Efendi!*"

"Please bring some coffee for the Gazi."

The man saluted and hurried away. Evelyn turned back into the room. Kemal had not moved on the couch. His naked shoulders were bare, and one lean arm reached almost to the floor. She put another piece of charred wood on the fire, and pulled the old grey cloak of the Sakarya higher on her lover's breast. Evelyn, bending over him, saw that in this extremity the look of youth had gone from Kemal's face. The heavy windburn from the open car, the disfiguring mark where the goggles had been, could not disguise the lines of stress: it might have been a man of sixty who lay there, disarmed before her. She sat down on the floor beside him, with her lips just tracing the engorged veins on his hand, and the tears began to fall as the charred wood caught, and Evelyn's nostrils filled with a dreadful smell of burning.

16

ON SATURDAY, SEPTEMBER 2, the new Greek Commander-in-Chief gave up his sword to Kemal Pasha, who at once communicated the news by despatch rider and telegraph to his capital at Angora. From Angora it was relayed to Constantinople and from there to Smyrna, thus putting an end to the feverish speculation prevailing in the great seaport for several days.

There had been no firm news from the Greek front since the telegraph wires were cut between Afyon and Smyrna, but a tide of rumours had risen since the first Greek hospital ship sailed into the bay from Chios. She had remained discreetly at her anchorage until midnight, when under cover of darkness Jeff Barrett and other foreign newspapermen saw the first of the wounded from Koja Tepe carried aboard her; after that she berthed openly at the Smyrna waterfront and loaded casualties until a relief ship arrived and the first ship sailed for the Piraeus. Then the trainloads of sullen soldiers began arriving at Alcansak, the Point station; Greeks without arms, without boots, ready to mutiny against their officers, bringing stories of the surrender of Afyon Karahisar and the shattering defeat of Dumlu Pinar. The first of those arrivals were suspected of being deserters and as such were hustled out of sight by the Greek military police. The next detachments were accompanied rather than led by officers as broken and exhausted as themselves. They too were hustled away and taken down to Chesme, a harbour at the tip of the peninsula which protected the eastern shore of the Gulf of Smyrna, and from there, as fast as ships could be sent across from Greece, to Chios Island or the Piraeus.

Then the refugees and the animals began to arrive in Smyrna. By the day Tricoupis surrendered the stream of Greek troops had become a torrent, no trains could carry them all, even when men were clinging to the footboards or riding on the roofs of the coaches, and many tramped in with the refugees by road. The refugees were the Greek Christians, dragged from their village homes with what they could carry on their backs so that their fellow-countrymen in uniform could burn their homes behind them and leave nothing but scorched earth for the advancing Turks. By the third day of September there were ten thousand homeless refugees camped on the pavements and docksides of Smyrna, dependent on the charity of the inhabitants, and presenting a problem which the Greek civil authorities seemed to be powerless to solve.

The animals, army horses and mules for the most part, were in worse case, for the departing troops hamstrung them, or cut their throats, or gouged their eyes out, and flung their carcasses into the waters of the harbour.

When these scenes of horror began to unfold, the foreign merchantmen discreetly left the port. The ships loading the dried figs and citron peel, the currants and raisins which would go into thousands of Christmas puddings battened down their hatches and sailed with half their cargoes taken aboard. In their place the Allied battleships came in. The Royal Navy flagship HMS *Iron Duke* was followed by HMS *Ajax* and *King George V*, the Frenchman *Edgar Quinet*, with the flag of Admiral Dumesnil, was accompanied by the *Jean Bart*, the *Ernest Renan*, and the *Waldeck-Rousseau*. Italy sent the cruiser *Venezia* and a flotilla of destroyers. The Americans, while insisting upon their neutrality, sent four destroyers, the USS *Edsel*, *Laurence*, *Litchfield* and *Simpson*, which anchored in the Gulf beside the British. This formidable array lay at the entrance of the beautiful Bay of Smyrna, a grey line of guns completing the ring made by the Anatolian mountains which rose above the town.

On the day after the *Iron Duke* arrived, Jeff Barrett went to the Cercle Européen on one of his regular calls to check the bulletin board on which news received by ships' radio was posted. The Greeks in their gaudy uniforms had disappeared from the Club now, and the new guest members were British and American officers, dressed in tropical whites. Among them, standing at the bar and looking thoughtfully at an empty glass, Jeff found Lieutenant Archibald Munro, RN, last seen at the Galata Bridge on the day of his unlucky visit to Prinkipo.

"Hallo, Mr. Munro, remember me?"

"Of course, Mr. Barrett. I didn't know you were in Smyrna."

"Oh, I get around. What about you? Come to watch the fireworks?"

"That's about it. We were on our way to the Adriatic when all this blew up. That fellow Kemal seems to be winning all along the line."

"Looks like it. What are you drinking—pink gin? Let me get you a refill, I need a drink myself."

The bar was crowded, but they found two chairs in a corner and lit cigarettes. Jeff began the routine questions: did the Navy intend to evacuate British nationals if the situation got worse, and would Admiral Brock take aboard all and sundry in the case of a general evacuation? Did the British think Kemal would put Smyrna to fire and sword, or was there any hope that Lloyd George's government would arrange an armistice between Turks and Greeks? To all these questions Archie of course returned negative answers. Matters of policy, he declared, had nothing to do with him; but at the same time he was more forthcoming than at their two brief meetings in Constantinople, and Jeff felt encouraged to ask, "How's Miss Elliott?"

"All right, I believe. I've only seen her once since the day we met you on our way to the Eyüp ferry."

"Oh yes?"

"Her mother took her off back to Therapia the next day, and I've only had Therapia leave once since then."

"I thought she liked Therapia, playing tennis and all that."

"She didn't like the way she was shunted off up there." The sulky Highland face reddened, as if Archie felt he had said too much, and something clicked inside Jeff Barrett's brain. The trip to Eyüp! The British naval officer who brought in the Trakas murderer! He said casually:

"I suppose this is what you British call bad form, but was the Therapia trip intended to get her away from you?"

"I call it damned bad form, but no, I think the idea was just to get her out of Constantinople for a bit. Rotten climate in summer, of course."

"Did she find out too much about the man who killed Trakas? Or the man who planned the killing—Charles Cravache?"

There was no doubt now about Archie's flush. "Sorry, Mr. Barrett," he said, rising. "I got the bottle of a lifetime from my

242

Captain over that business; I've learned just enough not to discuss it with the press. But thanks awfully for the drink."

"See you around," said Jeff. So his hunch had been right, and if he ever met the girl again he might make something out of it, although the Trakas affair was so much water over the dam now. The big story was in Smyrna, and he was filing copy every day as the situation deteriorated. After the recall of General Hajianestis, the High Commissioner for Greece was the next important official to become a refugee, as Monsieur Sterghiades sought protection aboard the British flagship until such time as he could get a passage to Constantinople. By the sixth of September there were forty thousand homeless refugees in Smyrna, and sailors and marines were landed from the British ships to keep a semblance of order among them. The light cruisers *Cardiff* and *Concord* left Malta for Smyrna, and all through the eastern Mediterranean Lloyd's signals went up summoning every available steamer, every battered ocean tramp to proceed to Smyrna to evacuate the refugees.

The problem was where to take them. The nearest Greek island was Chios, and Chios was still crammed with Greek troops awaiting repatriation: the situation there was too explosive to admit more civilian refugees. Some of the more fortunate got away to the Piraeus, but the terrified thousands still camped on the waterfront and all along the beautiful Kordon, clutching their tattered bundles, under a blazing sun which turned the stones they lay on into ovens. The British evacuees pushed past them to the Navy cutters taking them out to the battleships; they, at least, were sure of a refuge in Malta, although in the first stage of the British voluntary evacuation most of the "British nationals" to go were Maltese and Cypriots by birth. The men and women from Britain who had made their lives in Smyrna were unwilling to leave their businesses and their beautiful homes, and refused to yield to the hysteria which was sweeping over the Levantine population. Mr. Lloyd George's government was bound to take some action, they believed: come to terms with this bandit fellow from the mountains, this Kemal, whose name nursegirls used to scare their charges . . . negotiate an armistice . . . or something. But the September days went by, and Kemal came nearer and nearer, his pursuit growing more relentless as the Turks swept into one ruined city after another. The banner inscribed "Hurrah for

Lloyd George!" which had been carried to the British Consulate by the Greeks of Smyrna was seen no more; his portrait disappeared from the front of the Konak, and the catch phrase of the moment, which swept the refugees on the waterfront, was "Bad times for George!"

Jeff Barrett chafed at being kept in Smyrna. He had made one or two sorties from the city with a British correspondent named Lyons, who was always anxious to split the expenses of a car, because it was impossible to go anywhere by train now. The Greeks had torn up as much as they could of the railway line into Smyrna and set fire to the rolling stock, and as a last act of sabotage they also put the branch line from Smyrna to Aydin out of action. Jeff and Lyons drove down the peninsula to Chesme to see the last of the Greek troops embarking, and on another day went fifteen miles up the hill road to Manisa, the Magnesia of the Trojan war, which report said had been completely devastated by the Greek troops. That day their Levantine driver lost his nerve half-way, and refused to take them any further. As they went higher into the mountains, he swore, the greater was the danger of meeting bandits and being killed or held to ransom: Anatolia was swarming with them now, the lawless men who had evaded service with the Nationalist Army but were now following it as self-styled "Irregulars". Jeff was anxious to try again, and above all to reach Kemal's army: it was a terrible come-down to be checking radio news bulletins at the Cercle Européen after having seen action for twenty-two consecutive days at the battle of the Sakarya. Since the Prinkipo mischance he was determined never to leave his post again without permission, and cabled to Donnelly for his approval of a trip to the front. He received a garbled message in reply:

evelyns fine story dumpling sufficient combat coverage stop want you remain smyrna report kemals arrival etref problem regards donnelly

Evelyn's fine story? Evelyn not merely holding the fort in Angora but filing stories, or a story, which appeared to have been printed? And what was "dumpling"? When he read the cable for the second time Jeff understood that the garble meant Dumlu Pinar, Kemal's decisive victory. Writing about that from Angora? She must have been faking, then, getting Abdul to translate from the Turkish papers, and Eve was usually death on fakes.

The rush of events in that first week of September had left Jeff with much less time to devote to Leila Mavros. She pouted and sulked when he said he was too tired to take her dancing at the Nain: for the gaiety continued in the big hotels, the music played, the champagne corks popped as if Kemal and his men were three hundred instead of thirty miles away. But Leila herself was tired as the days went on, for Güzel, the little Turkish servant, had run off to the warren where her family lived on the hill beneath the Velvet Fortress, and Irene and Aphrodite, two idle fat women, saw to it that Leila did most of the housework in her stead. In his heart Jeff felt that their afternoon at the Fortress had been their last really happy time, when the Aegean wind ruffled the hair of his maid of Athens—the day he had refused to let her go to Beirut with Rosette. He wished now that Leila was in safety in the Lebanon. If the Turks came in to Smyrna determined on vengeance for the devastation of Anatolia, then girls like Leila might be in great danger. Leila in danger and Evelyn getting stories into the *Clarion!* Jeff needed action, and when the ships' radios announced that the Nationalist headquarters had moved on to Nif, where Kemal would be visited by the Allied Consuls, he anticipated the consular party and left the city.

It was an easy drive to Nif, and his chauffeur of that day made light of the bandits, who were not likely to appear in the green and fruitful valleys which lay behind Smyrna, where the advance guard of Kemal's army was already pushing on towards the sea. The countryside itself was so little altered in this, the last lap of the Greek flight, that the sight of Nif village was a great shock to Jeff. It was only what the Turks had seen in every town and settlement from Afyon to Smyrna, smouldering ruins, mutilated animals, women tearing at the piles of stones which the Greeks had flung on the bodies of the Turkish dead: at Alashehir, at Sahlili, at Kassaba, at Manisa, so now at Nif. Jeff walked through the horrors to the house where Supreme Headquarters was established.

None of the duty officers was known to him, and his request for an interview with the Gazi was politely refused. He asked for Captain Hamdi, and Hamdi came; a changed man from the little dandy whom Jeff had last seen at a cabaret table—gaunt and hollow-eyed, as they all were, from hunger and sleepless nights.

He was friendly, he was sly, as always, but he was absolutely positive that the Commander-in-Chief would receive no representatives of the foreign press that day.

"He won't talk to anybody until he's seen the Allied delegation," said Hamdi. "Can *you* tell *us* when these gentlemen are likely to appear?"

"Last I heard, they were quarrelling about precedence," said Jeff. "They can't make up their mind who's going to do the talking."

"The Gazi's going to do the talking, my dear friend," said Hamdi. "He was livid with anger when he got their message about handing over Smyrna. 'Whose city are they giving to whom?' he shouted; do you blame him, after all that we've been through?"

"The Consuls want him to promise to spare the Christian population," said Jeff.

"We're not a bunch of murderers, you know; we leave that to the Christian and civilising Greeks."

"They've made a shambles out of Nif, I can see that."

"This is nothing compared with some of the towns we came through—Alashehir, for instance, just a heap of ashes . . . I must say I admired Mrs. Barrett's courage, when she was with us last week."

"You mean my wife was actually with the army? I had a cable from Chicago about some story she wrote, I just couldn't believe it—"

"She was with us from Afyon to—Ushak, I think it was. I didn't see much of her after the first day, but I know she was at Dumlu Pinar. I saw her off to the front myself, with Major Orman."

"Who the hell's he?"

"One of our English-speaking officers. Unfortunately he's not here today, we had to leave him in a tent hospital at Sahlili, down with dysentery, or he could certainly have told you more about Mrs. Barrett at the front."

"Would he know where she is now, for instance? Do you?"

Hamdi Bey shrugged. His smooth face, so oddly unlike itself in its new sunburned gauntness, was alive with the old malice. "I have no idea," he said. "She went off to cable to your editor, I was told. But wherever she is, I'm sure she will be well protected. After all, when she was with us, she was the Gazi's—very—special correspondent."

*   *   *

The Conqueror entered the city of Smyrna on Sunday, the tenth of September, in one of a procession of five cars wreathed with laurel and olive branches, with a division of Turkish cavalry as his escort. The entire Turkish population, it seemed, was in the streets to cheer him; poor and oppressed for three years under the Greek occupation, they were frantic in their joy as they hailed the liberator. The leaders of the Turkish community presented him with a motor car and a rowing boat, while outside the Konak, where he set up his headquarters, an ox was sacrificed in his honour. Kemal had to watch this ceremony from the balcony of the Konak, trying to conceal his disgust at the barbarity, and acknowledging again and again the cheers from the vast crowd of men in Konak Square. Then he worked for an hour with General Nureddin, outlining plans for the government of the city, and was at last free to savour his triumph in his own way.

First he sent for Sergeant Ali and his barber, had a hot bath run and fresh clothing laid out by the servant, and gave himself into the barber's hands. That morning, very early, he had shaved himself with his old cut-throat razor; now he told the barber to shave him again and trim both his hair and moustache. With his nails cleaned and filed he felt as if he had shed some of the grime and weariness of the campaign. Immaculate, dressed in a fresh uniform, he sat back in his armchair and closed his eyes.

The mischief was that he could not relax. Behind his eyelids he saw that agonising procession of burned-out towns, in his ears he heard the inhuman cries of those poor bereaved women and the thunder of his cavalry which, try as they might, had never quite succeeded in catching up with the fleeing Greeks. He wanted to talk to someone who knew, because she loved him, that he was not the cold-hearted tyrant of his own legend: that he had a capacity for sorrow, for compassion with human suffering. . . . He wanted Evelyn.

Not to take her to bed with him—though he wanted that too—but just to sit and talk to her, tell her all that had happened since she left him, all he had still to do. Watch those brown eyes light

247

up at his words, those hands clasped so calmly round her slim knee . . . He opened his own eyes and saw Ali, at attention, watching him from the closed door. He could have sworn the sergeant knew what was passing through his mind.

"Who's on duty?" he asked. "Lieutenant Aslan? Ask him to come in."

The lieutenant, who had been waiting nervously in the ante-room, hurried in. He was the junior aide-de-camp, very thrilled that the duty roster had given him the chance of being with the Gazi at this moment of glory, but very much afraid of doing something wrong. The Gazi's temper had been, not unpredictable, but predictably bad since the army left Ushak.

"You understand French, don't you, Aslan?" said Kemal. "I want to send a signal to Mrs. Barrett, through Army Rear at Konya."

"Yes, sir." The young man whipped out his notebook and wrote to Kemal's dictation. Sergeant Ali went off with the message to the newly installed signals room, and Kemal got up and stretched.

"So here we are in *güzel Izmir*," he said. "One day late! I promised to drive the Greeks out in fourteen days, and this is the fifteenth. My old schoolmaster wouldn't think much of my arithmetic now!"

"But the advance guard entered Smyrna yesterday, sir," protested Aslan. "It was the Allied Consuls who delayed your own arrival till today."

"And they never showed up after all!" said Kemal derisively. "Still, it's high time we started celebrating. Let's go out and find a glass of raki, child."

"May I be allowed to fetch a bottle of raki for the Gazi?"

"I said let's go and find it! In the town!"

"Have I leave to inform the Pashas—"

"You have not."

To Lieutenant Aslan's huge relief, there were Laz guards on the side door of the Konak, but the tall men in their black turbans and tunics merely saluted and looked straight ahead as the Com-mander-in-Chief came out. The street beyond, which led into the Turkish bazaar, was seething with men on their way to join the crowd in the Konak Square, where the sacrificial ox, roasted on the spot, was now being devoured.

"Sir, won't you take your bodyguard?" begged Aslan, looking back at the immobile figures of the Lazes on duty.

"Why not a cavalry division?" jeered Kemal. In a few steps he was lost in the crowd, just one more Turkish officer, sprucely dressed, with a badly scared young man at his heels.

"Sir, is this wise?" whispered the boy, as they shouldered their way through Konak Square. "If some of those *gâvur* devils recognise you—think of the risk!"

"I've been taking risks for years, and so have you," said Kemal. "Let's enjoy ourselves for half an hour!"

"At least come away from the waterfront, sir," said the boy, \ and Kemal allowed himself to be persuaded. The waterfront was in chaos, as the milling crowd of refugees moved slowly into some sort of order under the directions of a detachment of Royal Marines.

"The British Navy has quite a task in hand," said Kemal with indifference. "Do you know how many refugees there are in Smyrna now?"

"Fifty thousand, sir?"

"Seventy-five thousand, Nureddin Pasha says." Kemal led the lieutenant into a quieter street behind and parallel with the waterfront. Away from the yelling Turks and the distracted refugees, the broad, handsome street, lined with cedars of Lebanon, looked very peaceful. The buildings were fronted with white marble, the window-boxes spilled over with flowers. This was *güzel Izmir*, Smyrna the Beautiful, at its splendid best, and Kemal looked about him appreciatively. It was the Christian Sunday, and for this reason as well as for security the luxury shops had run down their steel shutters, but he recognised the name of a famous Paris jeweller, and decided that next morning he would buy a gift for Evelyn. Lieutenant Aslan walked alongside him with his hand on his opened pistol holster, and his eyes scanning the curtained windows on each side of the boulevard. Just one shot . . . ! What the hell, he wondered bitterly, possessed the Gazi to play Harun-al-Rachid in the streets of what had been, till yesterday, an enemy city? And now Kemal was looking in at the trellised doors of one or two sidewalk cafés, which seemed to be filling up again in spite of the day's alarms. Looking for the raki bottle! No, swore Aslan, only over my dead body will he go into one of those dark holes with no exit! "Sir," he said desperately, "the Kramer isn't very far away, and I believe it's one of the best hotels in town."

"Let's go there."

They had to cut back to the waterfront to find the main entrance, and walked through the hotel lobby into the Palm Court. There was nothing there, on this Sunday afternoon, to indicate that a mighty convulsion had passed over Anatolia, for the tea tables were set with spotless damask and silver cake baskets as usual, and the Palm Court was crowded with well-dressed men and women. A European string band was playing "Destiny" in an alcove at the foot of the hotel stairs.

The Greek headwaiter came forward without haste. He saw a slim, fair, youthful-seeming man in the uniform of the Turkish Army, with a young friend at his elbow; he saw neither epaulettes nor insignia, and he failed to recognise, on Kemal's collar, the field-marshal's five pointed star in its wreath of laurel. The headwaiter said, as impertinently as he dared:

"Table for two, sir? I'm afraid all our tables are reserved this afternoon."

"Whoa there, George!"

Jeff Barrett was coming, not too steadily, down the last steps of the stair. He said, but in a quieter tone, "You better find a table for this gentleman, George, if you know what's good for you. This is Mustafa Kemal Pasha, Gazi, Field-Marshal, and boss of Smyrna from here on in!"

Then, under cover of the music, he said with his face close to Kemal's, "What have you done with my wife, damn you?"

Kemal's eyes were icy. He said, "Mrs. Barrett is safe with friends in Konya. Now smile, you fool! For her sake, don't force a quarrel here!"

"You took her away from me, you bastard. You let her risk her life and her reputation—"

"We can discuss that calmly in some less public place. My headquarters are at the Konak, as no doubt you know." He looked over Jeff's shoulder, and a smile dawned on his own grim face. Jeff swung round and saw Leila, graceful in a pink dress, with one hand on the banister and the other at her lips.

"Don't let me keep you from your charming companion," said Kemal. He sketched a salute to Leila. *Mes hommages, mademoiselle!*

"Get back upstairs," said Jeff to Leila roughly. "What the hell did you come creeping after me for?"

"Please, darling, you were promising we should have tea in the Palm Court on Sunday and listen to the music."

"Not this Sunday, for God's sakes!" They were back in his sittingroom now, and Leila plucked up courage to say:

"Was that really Mustafa Kemal? He is being very handsome. Much more handsome than in his photographs. And he seems so nice! Perhaps he will not be so unkind to us after all."

She slipped out to the balcony, Jeff supposed for another sight of the handsome conqueror. If so, she hadn't long to wait. Lounging in the hot interior of the room, already regretting his outburst and the brandy he had drunk after watching Kemal's triumphal entry and the sacrifice of the ox, Jeff listened to the considerable fanfare which accompanied Kemal's departure from the Kramer Hotel. Reckoning by the man's usual drinking speed, just two of the ritual rakis could have been consumed.

"Come on, baby," Jeff said impatiently. "Let me take you home. I'll buy you all the tea and pastries you can eat tomorrow; things may have settled down a bit by then, if the Turks don't start acting up."

He found, when he came back from the Rue d'Angoisse, that the Kramer had been summarily requisitioned to billet a number of Kemal's staff. The manager met Jeff lamenting and wringing his hands: it was the headwaiter's fault, he said, his insolence to the Gazi had brought this infliction upon them. He had saved Mr. Barrett's bedroom—"I said, sir, that a famous American correspondent must have somewhere to sleep!" but three Turkish officers now occupied the livingroom and the connecting door had been bolted and locked.

"Is the Gazi staying here himself?" asked Jeff.

"Ah, no, sir. God is merciful!" breathed the manager. He explained that a house had been placed at Kemal's disposal out at Karshiyaka, away from the disturbed and anxious city.

The city rumbled ominously during the hours of darkness. Firing was heard from the heights round the Velvet Fortress, where a company of Greek troops tried a last ditch stand, and the

Royal Marines guarding the gasworks reported some robbing and raping in that district. But the next day dawned, the evacuation of British nationals went on by lighter to the battleships, and Kemal was in conference with the flag officers of the Royal Navy and other Allied personalities. The Levantines began to breathe more freely. The tide of war had lapped over Smyrna and might soon flow in another direction. The holy city of Brusa had been liberated on the same day as Smyrna: might not the Gazi find Brusa a convenient base from which to try for the greatest prize of all, Constantinople? Yes, said the café politicians, that's what he'll do. He'll come to terms with the Allies here, place his own men in the Konak, and then he'll be off to capture Constantinople.

But the foreign newspapermen thought otherwise. There were more of them now than when Jeff Barrett first arrived in town, for every ship to anchor in the Gulf of Smyrna seemed to bring its quota of correspondents from all the capitals of Europe. On September 12 Ward Price of the London *Daily Mail* and John Clayton of the Chicago *Tribune* (who was, by far, Jeff's most serious 'competition') were reported to have had interviews with the Gazi. Immediately, and in view of a serious incident which had just taken place, the whole press corps of Smyrna requested that Kemal should present his views and policy to all of them.

Kemal consented to see the newspapermen on the morning of September 13. They assembled in a hall at the Konak, nearly two hundred strong, sceptically noting the very formal preparations made for them: the Turkish officers on duty in parade dress, the Laz guards at attention, two on each side of a big desk behind which stood a Turkish flag. The formality seemed to call for a blare of trumpets for a Commander-in-Chief; more than one man was surprised when Kemal walked in wearing a dark blue suit instead of uniform and without any entourage of Pashas or aides-de-camp. He remained in front of the desk, half sitting upon it, with his hands in his trouser pockets and the air of a man prepared for a pleasant chat with friends.

"Crikey," whispered Jeff's English friend, Bill Lyons, who affected a Cockney accent, "'e ain't 'arf got class! Like a Guards officer in civvies, if you arsks me!"

Kemal himself, as he changed out of khaki, had remembered Evelyn. It was one of the last things she said to him, as they drank their coffee over the fire at Ushak, before she left him:

"Darling, do make yourself available to the press when you get to Smyrna. Everybody will want to interview you, and it's terribly important for Turkey that you make the right impression!"

"My child, I'm fighting a war—"

"But the papers can help you to win it, as far as the world's opinion is concerned. You even asked for *my* help, don't you remember? And there'll be men at Smyrna who can do far more for you—and for Turkey—than I can ever do."

She kept saying "for Turkey", his clever Evelyn, because she knew that would always make him listen. Advice from a woman, after all those years! But this was something that she knew about, and Kemal had said,

"I'll give a press conference, if I have to—"

"Then don't bark at the boys, like you barked at us at Afyon Karahisar."

"Any more suggestions?"

"Don't wear uniform, wear one of your London suits."

"Not wear my uniform? Evelyn, since I was twelve years old I've believed that to wear the uniform of the Turkish Army was the proudest honour any man could have!"

"Yes, I know, darling, but you look so particularly well in ordinary clothes. Try to be photographed that way. Your pictures never do you justice—I don't think the kalpak suits you very well."

"You should have seen me when I had to wear a fez."

So there he was, studying his civilian reflection in the wardrobe mirror. Dark suit, white shirt, plain dark blue tie and black shoes —not bad! Evelyn! In an inside jacket pocket he had the jeweller's case which held the diamonds he had bought her. It took up less space than a shoulder holster, but he was more conscious of it than of any weapon when he faced the journalists, and encountered the sullen dark eyes of her husband.

"Gentlemen!" said Kemal, into a profound silence. "I shall speak to you in French. There are interpreters present, and you may put your questions in any language you prefer."

A New York correspondent spoke up at once. "This murder of the Greek Archbishop, Mr.—uh—General. Are you going to— uh—will the folks who did it be rounded up and punished?"

"Not by my orders," said Kemal calmly. He sensed the ripple of feeling in the room, and smiled. "Suppose we examine the record of Archbishop Chrysostom. Three years ago, when the Greeks occupied Smyrna, the reverend gentleman encouraged and applauded their brutalities. He said that Nureddin Pasha, our military governor, should be shot instead of being allowed to go back to Constantinople. After we entered this city four days ago the Archbishop repeatedly asked the Allied naval commanders to fire upon us from the sea. A bellicose priest, don't you think? It was the judgment of Nureddin Pasha, now happily returned to Smyrna, that such a firebrand deserved to be hanged. Unfortunately the mob took the law into their own hands, and gouged out Chrysostom's eyes before they lynched him. Regrettable from a legal point of view, but if a Christian Archbishop chooses to interfere in politics and war, there shouldn't be many complaints when he has to pay the bill."

The reporters muttered among themselves, and a voice with a Southern drawl enquired, "What about all the looting and raping that's been going on in the Armenian quarter?"

"There's been remarkably little rape and looting since we entered Smyrna, compared with the atrocious scenes we saw along the way, but I've now made every such offence punishable by death if committed by a Turkish soldier."

"A soldier of the Kemalist army, you mean, sir?" said the same voice, and Kemal's eyes grew cold.

"I prefer the expression Nationalist Army, or Army of Independence," he said. "My men enlisted in the national cause, and not as my private troops. But allow me to draw a distinction between my—our—well-disciplined forces and the so-called Irregulars who followed us into Smyrna. I've sent for detachments of the gendarmerie from all over Anatolia to deal with *them*."

Someone asked a question in Italian, which was translated.

"Do I believe there are *agents provocateurs* at work among the Armenians?" Kemal repeated in French. "Yes, there are, and have been for years. They're being encouraged to bomb my men; some of the minor outbreaks of fire we've handled in the last few days have been caused by the Armenian passion for the manufacture of inefficient petrol bombs."

He got the ripple of laughter he expected, and turned to face attack from another quarter.

"What are you going to do about the refugee problem?"

Kemal shrugged. "It's none of my concern. Those poor devils

you see in Smyrna were dragged from their villages by Greek troops, who've now left them to their fate. Let the British look after the refugees; it's the British, in the first place, who are responsible for their plight."

"How do you mean, responsible?"

"In the name of common sense," said Kemal, "how could the Greeks have landed in Smyrna at all, without the help and good-will of the British?" His voice deepened, and he paused. The few Turkish reporters present exchanged discreet smiles; they knew the Gazi was about to move into top gear. He said,

"Believe me, gentlemen, I am not insensitive to the sufferings of these unfortunate people. I want to see them taken to shelter and some degree of comfort as soon as is humanly possible . . . Remember, I have had the refugee problem brought sharply home to me in my own family. Ten years ago, when the Balkan Powers attacked Ottoman Turkey, the Greeks captured my birthplace, Saloniki, and drove out the Turkish population . . . I came back from the war in Tripolitania to hunt through the inns, the streets, yes and the *waterfront* of Constantinople, to look for my mother, my sister, and my mother's young niece. I found them cowering in a corner of the courtyard of a mosque . . . hungry, ill, protected from the rain by sacks. No one had organised help for *them*. And I hope the British, when they take charge of the Smyrna refugees, will do a more efficient job than they're doing in that same city of Saloniki, where I hear they have one doctor to look after twelve thousand White Russian refugees."

The British newspapermen looked angry, and one of them said,

"Do you consider yourself at war with Britain, sir?"

"Not yet."

There was a concerted gasp, and the pencils flew.

"I want to make it clear to you," said Kemal, "that as far as the Smyrna situation is concerned I am in complete understanding with the British. Admiral Brock has promised me that he will embark only British nationals on the ships under his command, and I am grateful for the work his sailors and Marines are doing in helping to preserve order in the city. *But*"—he paused—"although the Greeks have fled from Anatolia, they are still present in Eastern Thrace, and from that province they must withdraw before I can send my envoys to a peace conference. I don't intend to make exorbitant demands. I have no desire to go to war to restore the old frontiers of the Ottoman Empire, which are part of a vanished world. But I *will have* Adrianople, which was once a Turkish capital, and all of Eastern Thrace to the River Maritza; I *will have* the withdrawal of all the occupation troops, and I *will have* Constantinople as a Turkish city in an independent Turkey."

"And if Greece refuses?"—"If the Allies refuse?" said half a dozen voices.

"Then I have no alternative but to wage war."

Lyons, the British reporter sitting next to Jeff, asked what Kemal meant by having no alternative.

"Let me put it this way," said Kemal. "I am the Commander-in-Chief of the Army of Independence. But, as I've already said, it's not a private army. I command it only by the vote of the Grand National Assembly of a free Turkey, and that Assembly, like myself, is bound by the National Pact to which we all swore at the start of the Revolution. One of the objects of our movement was to restore our national frontiers and our independence, aims which are recognised as legitimate in every land but ours. Since the Great War the Finns, the Esthonians and other Baltic peoples have successfully claimed their independence. The French have spilt blood and treasure recklessly to regain their natural frontier on the Rhine. Even peoples which in 1914 were part of an enemy nation—an enemy of the Allies, I mean—are now admired for their emergence as the independent states of Czechoslovakia and Jugoslavia. I have sworn that the new Turkey will never be enlarged at the expense of other nations, even of the Greeks. But I —we—claim independence in our heartland, and with it the restoration of our national identity and our pride. . . . Gentlemen, that is all I have to say to you."

The senior British correspondent spoke a word of thanks. Then the stampede from the hall began, as the newspapermen rushed out to tell the world that Mustafa Kemal Pasha was ready to take on the Powers in a final struggle to free his country. But one of the immaculate officers stopped Jeff Barrett at the door, and said in a low voice:

"The Gazi would like a word with you, monsieur."

The Gazi, still lounging against the big desk, had dismissed the Lazes and lit a cigarette.

"Well, Mr. Barrett," he said, "I've been expecting a visit from you."

"Have you, though?"

"Judging from your behaviour when you accosted me on Sunday, I thought you intended to challenge me to a duel."

"I'm not one of your gunsels," said Jeff. "I'm not going to shoot it out with you."

"I told you I was always to be found at the Konak."

"Would I have been admitted to the presence if I'd come?"

"Certainly."

"I don't know," said Jeff. "I didn't get to see you when I went out to Nif."

"Oh, were you at Nif?" said Kemal easily. "I didn't talk to any press men there."

"You were more accessible at the Sakarya, Marshal."

"Ah, but we've come a long way since the Sakarya."

"Both of us?"

"All of us."

"I see."

Kemal glanced at his wrist watch. "I won't beat about the bush, Mr. Barrett. You'd been drinking on Sunday; I'm the last man to hold that against you, and I'm prepared to overlook your offensive words. But I want to make it clear that Mrs. Barrett spent a few days with the army in the capacity of a war correspondent, and after General Tricoupis surrendered she insisted on returning to Konya to send her story to Chicago; her conduct at the front was above all praise. You accused me of taking her away from you. How dare you say so, when you yourself chose to bring your marriage to an end?"

"Did Eve say that?"

"She told me about the letter you wrote when you left Constantinople with Mademoiselle Mavros."

"She showed it to you?"

"How little you understand Evelyn," said Kemal coldly, "if you imagine she would let me see a private letter. But she told me that your words implied she could take legal proceedings against you. I'm not familiar with your western divorce laws, and it's possible that such a letter may not be real grounds for divorce. So, just to make sure, one of my officers took a sworn statement from the manager of the Kramer Hotel about—what shall I say? your continued association with Mademoiselle Mavros under his roof."

"You're a careful son of a bitch, aren't you?"

"I find it pays."

"And if Eve divorces me, what then?"

Kemal hesitated. It had been hard enough, at the beginning, to say "I love you" to Evelyn; he could not say "I love her" to the man still legally her husband. He said in his careful English: "I have become very deeply attached to—to Evelyn. I have asked her, when her divorce is granted, to do me the very great honour to become my wife."

Jeff wanted to shout "But that's impossible! She's an American and you're a Turk! You're a boozer and a womaniser and a bully and a murderer, and she—" But what *was* Evelyn? He didn't really know. He said, "Does Eve want to marry you?"

"I hope so."

"But you don't know so?" He saw the blue gaze waver, and attacked. "She hasn't said she would, has she? I don't believe she will, not when she comes to her senses! Chasing all over the country, calling herself a *Clarion* correspondent, getting herself talked about! Where the hell is she now? Who are the friends she's staying with in Konya? Are they decent people, or just pals of yours?"

"Your anxiety does you every credit," said Kemal. "But it's come a little late in the day, don't you think? Evelyn is with your American Relief Mission people in Konya. She's quite safe there, and I made her promise not to go back to Angora until she could travel in an armed convoy."

"Right," said Jeff. "I'll see her in Angora, then. And if Eve tells me herself she wants a divorce, then okay. But I'm not going to clear out on your say-so, Marshal. Not on your life!"

*   *   *

Jeff went to the telegraph office as fast as a fayton could drive him, and transcribed the notes taken at the press conference into a thousand words of hard cablese. He was loading the copy, playing up Kemal's intransigence, his determination to carry the war into Europe, and his cynical comments on the murder of the Greek Archbishop. While his fountain pen raced across the cable forms his ears were ringing with other words, not for publication:

"We've come a long way since the Sakarya."

"Both of us?"

258

"All of us."

All of us—that meant Eve, of course, meant she had gone the limit with that hard-faced, arrogant gangster who now coolly told her husband that he wanted to marry her! Eve of all people! Evelyn the Icicle, who hated sex, who could be relied on to do everything for her husband except make him happy in bed! What had Kemal got that he, Jeff Barrett, hadn't got? Just the same, he hadn't got Evelyn yet, not for keeps, and Jeff Barrett meant to see that he never did. Inwardly raging, he went to the United States Consulate, obtained some information and a letter from the Consul, and then hurried down the dreadful quays to the berth where the Consular launch was moored. It took him out to an American tramp steamer, the *Hiawatha*, which had answered the Lloyds signal for assistance and arrived in the bay of Smyrna overnight. After that he had just time to drive to the Rue d'Angoisse, where Leila was waiting to be taken out for lunch.

For once she was dressed and ready, and refusing her invitation to come in he put her into the little carriage and told the driver to take them back to the Kramer. What he had to say to Leila had best be said first to her alone, without any weeping from Granny or yapping from Irene and Aphrodite and the Uncles, who were always at home for the midday meal. Leila whimpered about "the poor Archbishop" all the way to the hotel, but she cheered up when they were once more in the soothing atmosphere of the Palm Court, although Jeff told her they would have luncheon in his room.

"We'll do better with the floor service," he said. "The restaurant's not a restaurant now, it's an officers' mess."

"Turkish dogs!" said Leila.

The floor waiter was commendably prompt with his tray of cold dishes, fruit and wine, and Leila ate with appetite. Beyond the locked door Jeff could hear the voices of the Turkish officers now occupying what had been his sittingroom. They were either going down to the "mess" or out on duty, for there was a good deal of door-slamming and coming back for some forgotten object, sought for with much creaking of the bureau drawers. Jeff was relieved when silence fell. The proximity of these men got on his nerves; he wondered if one of them had taken the statement from the hotel manager about Mr. Barrett and his mistress.

If you get the name you can have the game. Now he had the name *and* the game: it was sitting opposite him in the charming person of Leila Mavros, whose face seemed to have become all eyes, great black eyes which followed Jeff's every movement as he offered her the basket of fruit or filled her glass.

"You don't want coffee, do you?" he said, when the man came to clear the table. "There's something—uh—I want to have a serious talk with you, Leila."

"Yes, please, I am listening, Jeff."

Jeff got up and closed the louvred shutters across the window. The imbat wind had risen and was blowing into the room.

"Baby, it kills me to say this, but I want you and your grandma to get out of here and go to Athens."

"*To Athens?*"

"Yes. I've got berths for both of you on board an American ship, the *Hiawatha*. She's sailing for the Piraeus at noon tomorrow."

"But, Jeff, what would we be doing in Athens?"

"You've got cousins, haven't you, right there at the Piraeus? They'd take you in and look after you until you get a job, wouldn't they? And then there's Halliday, my colleague on the *Clarion*, I'll send him a cable and have him meet you at the boat."

"But Granny—you know Granny isn't fit to travel!"

"She can move around a bit, and we can carry her aboard."

"The Uncles will never let her go."

"To hell with your uncles." She was in tears by now, of course, he knew there would be tears, and Jeff picked Leila up from her chair and sat down cradling her in his arms.

"Listen, baby," he said, "I only want to get you into safety." He thought of Burt Halliday and his way with women, and wondered what sort of safety he would provide. But Halliday would soon be off back to Vienna . . . "Sweetie," he began again, "I'm worried to death about you and the old lady here in Smyrna. Things are going to get a lot worse here in the next few days. Kemal told us this morning he means to carry on the war, and the Turks are crazy drunk with power and triumph. If there's any kind of rising—"

Leila was not listening. With her soft mouth against his ear she was whispering, "Jeff, couldn't *you* take me to Athens?"

"You know I can't leave Smyrna now—not till I'm ordered."

He hardened his heart, and said what he had to say: "And cutie, you know it had to end sometime."

"Oh-h!" Leila sobbed, and pressed herself against him. "Are you going back to your wife, Jeff?"

"I don't know. Looks like she's made other plans."

"Then let me stay with you!"

It was all wrong, he knew, but the habit was too strong for him, and anyway she was very sweet and loving: Jeff took Leila to his bed. And while he made love to her he thought of Eve in Kemal's arms, writhing and moaning in her pleasure like this child beneath him, and jealousy made him brutal, so that Leila for the first time said "Jeff, you're hurting me!" and there were tears on her cheeks when she closed her eyes and slept. Jeff slept too, but not for long, the watch on the bedside table stood at ten minutes past three when he awoke. He pulled the sheet higher over Leila's creamy shoulders; at the hour of the imbat it was not wise to lie naked in a draught. Then he realised that there was no draught, that the current of air had stopped blowing through the room, which was hot; there was a powerful smell of smoke. He reached for his dressing gown and went to open the shutters. The hotel garden was as peaceful as ever, the pigeons were still strutting but the cats had disappeared. He leaned far out over the balcony and looked east towards the Konak. A pall of black smoke seemed to be drifting west and there was a sound of shouting and running feet.

Jeff shook Leila's shoulder. "Get up!" he said urgently. "The town's on fire."

*　　　*　　　*

She wanted to run home at once, and he prevented her. Of all the muddle-headed decisions Jeff Barrett had taken since the night he stood in the Grande Rue de Pera, a free man, and chose to go on to the house of Rosette Mavros, this one was to be the worst, and for all that remained of that terrible thirteenth of September he blamed himself for not setting off with her to the little house on Agony Street. But the first reflex of alarm, which had made him tell her to get up and dress, was soon spent. Dressed himself, Jeff went down to the lobby, which was crowded with people who had come in from the street, and heard reassuring comments. The fire brigade was at work, so were the Turkish troops, so were the

British sailors: the fire would quickly be under control. And so he wasted nearly an hour, trying to pacify Leila, while the flames, fanned by the imbat wind, sprang from street to street across the European quarters of the town. The little ghetto where the Jews lived, the Armenian quarter where the "Irregulars" had spent days and nights in molesting the inhabitants, finally the pleasant streets where the Greeks of Smyrna lived, went up in showers of sparks and falling timber. The fire brigade, once smart in scarlet skull-caps and jerseys, ran hither and thither, operating antiquated hand-pumps on poles carried on their shoulders, which were no more effective than soda-water siphons in extinguishing the flames. It was soon rumoured that when the firemen went to their station they found all the rubber hoses cut. The fire had been planned by the Turks, said some: look how the Turkish quarter on the hill alone was spared! The fire was started by the Armenians, said others; they had been seen throwing fire bombs at the Irregulars. The Greeks began it, was a popular cry; they had left their saboteurs behind them when they left the city, to ensure that Kemal's enjoyment of Smyrna the beautiful would be short-lived. These were the reports which ran as fast as the flames, while seventy-five thousand refugees, gathered like cattle on the water-front, cried and groaned as they saw machine guns set up and Turkish gunners moving into place. Kemal will butcher us! We are lost!

By the time Jeff consented to take Leila home, the streets of Smyrna were almost impassable. The British colony had panicked at last, and were claiming their right to be taken aboard the battleships; as Jeff and Leila fought their way into the back streets of the town they met crowds of well-dressed men and women, carrying children, ashen-faced, with money and jewels in satchels or knapsacks on their backs. They stood aside for a party of British sailors and an officer, who were carrying women from the European maternity home to safety: the home itself was already in flames. Finally, Jeff and Leila ran, for the fire, with showers of incendiary sparks, was licking closer to themselves. Jeff had a fore-boding of disaster long before they reached the Rue d'Angoisse. One street away, they were halted by a Turkish gendarme, one of the first of the force which Kemal had ordered in from Anatolia. Neither Jeff nor Leila could understand a word he said. But they understood what was before their eyes: the flames now so close that the smoke stained their faces and their clothing, the people running to safety in charred garments, carrying some useless household objects in their arms, and they heard the inhuman cries of those trapped by the fire. Jeff held Leila back by main force.

"Better get the lady out of here, sir!" gasped a British sailor with two children in his arms.

"Can we get through to the Rue d'Angoisse?" cried Jeff. "Her grandmother—her family's there!"

"Roo what, sir? Agony? Not an 'ope in 'ell for anybody there!"

Holding his hand over Leila's ears, as he pressed her face to his body, Jeff heard the last shrieks as the blazing roofs fell in on the Street of Agony.

. . . He had to spend another hour with her in his darkened bedroom, soothing, telling lies ("they'll be all right, sweetie baby, the girls must have got your grandma out in time") before the bromide the terrified chambermaid brought them took effect, and Leila slept. Then Jeff went out; every able-bodied male was needed by that time if loot and pillage were not to be added to the horrors of the fire. He was put to work for a time on an attempt to construct a fire-break, using the garden of the Hotel Nain where he had so often danced with Leila, but it was no use, the flames raged on from one closely built section of the city to another. Kemal, remarking grimly that he would be blamed for the fire too, set his Pashas to organise the task of keeping order, but neither Pashas nor Royal Navy could control the maddened mob of refugees, now spreading from the waterfront into the Customs House, the Post Office, the banks, ripping and tearing at anything and everything which seemed to promise shelter, until the public buildings themselves went down in the great conflagration. The lighters still came up to the jetty, four at a time, to embark the more fortunate refugees, and under the threat of the Turkish machine guns—beside each one of which now stood an English sailor—the embarkation was orderly enough. The steamers which had taken on their quota of refugees, and sometimes twice their quota, weighed anchor and sailed out into the Gulf. Jeff thought it would be impossible to reach the *Hiawatha*.

Late in the night, when Smyrna had become a burning fiery furnace, he changed his mind. The order was given to evacuate the Kramer, because the hotel was doomed. He went back to his room for Leila. She was in a state of complete shock, but quiet and docile; she only nodded apathetically when Jeff outlined his plan.

"Look," he said, "it's too late to start looking for your folks tonight. We've got to get away ourselves, and I hear there's just a chance, if we go out to the Point, to get a boat to row us out to the *Hiawatha*. Can you walk that far?"

"Yes, Jeff."

"Fine. And if we can't get a boat we'll go on to Karshiyaka, we're sure to find some place there to spend the night."

This was another lie, for he was sure the suburb must be bursting at the seams already, but Leila seemed not to notice. She stood waiting while Jeff put into his pockets all the papers and money he wasn't carrying already, and they went out together into the blazing night. The Kordon, westwards, was a seething mass of humanity, but Jeff shouldered a path through it, and stopping twice to let Leila rest on the sea wall, they made their slow way towards Alcansak. The sea was the colour of copper, reflecting the flames of the burning city, and dead bodies, human and animal, were drifting near the shore.

They were within sight of the Point, and Jeff's hopes were raised by seeing one or two rowing boats pulling away from the jetty, outward bound towards the American ships, when the shuffling crowd seemed to bunch together and press into a jumble of even more closely packed and groaning bodies. The pressure came from a Turkish army lorry, filled with Kemal's black-uniformed bodyguard, facing out towards the people and holding pistols in their hands.

"Kemal! Kemal comes!"

The cry rose like a concerted moan of terror from the crowd. The threat, so often used to scare children, was now made visible: the lorry was clearing a way for the open touring car immediately behind, in which Kemal sat with his Pashas, his face impassive. He had remained at the Konak until the last possible moment, until indeed his own life was in danger, and then, realising that not all his talent for planning and improvisation could cope with the disaster, he had consented to be driven to his borrowed house at Karshiyaka. The car was forced to go so slowly that every haggard line of his face was visible; his arms were crossed tightly upon his chest. There were men in the crowd who still had the strength to yell a curse at him, and Jeff Barrett was among them, but the cry which rose at the Conqueror's passing was more like a sigh than a howl of enmity. He, no less than the fire, was recognised by that sigh as an elemental force of nature.

"There's Uncle Homer!" Leila cried.

It was the Greek, swept alongside them like a piece of human flotsam on the tide released when Kemal's car went by. The crowd surging between them took Homer from their sight for a moment, but he fought his way back to them and seized Leila by the hand.

"You're safe, Leila? You're not hurt?"

"Granny?" There was anguish in her cry, and Homer's ugly face was distorted as he heard it.

"Gone—they're all gone in the fire—the girls too—and Sophocles—"

"Shut up," said Jeff, "she can't take it all at once!"

"Shut up yourself, mister," said the Greek savagely. "You've brought us nothing but bad luck!"

Half a dozen frantic men and women surged between them then, but Homer held tightly to his niece's hand, and Jeff, leaping after them, saw Leila's beautiful black eyes turned back towards him in a wild appeal.

"You're hurting her, you son of a bitch!" He had his arm round her now, with his body braced between Leila and the sea wall.

"Leila, where's he taking you?" Homer's words came out with a splutter of saliva.

"Out to a ship which will be taking us to Athens—"

"You got a passage?" Homer flung the words at Jeff.

"I sure have. And now get the hell out of here, Homer, *I'm* looking after Leila."

"You give me the tickets, mister. I'll take our little girl to Athens; you stay here and do your job!"

He grasped Leila by the waist, and the girl shrieked.

"Jeff, don't leave me!"

"Let go of her!" cried Jeff. In the surge of the crowd they struggled together, falling up against the wall, while Leila screamed. Jeff struck the Greek a heavy blow in the face. He saw a knife gleam in the man's hand and struck again. Homer fell against them, slipped to the ground, and was trampled on; Leila collapsed against Jeff's arm.

"Baby, are you all right?"

"Yes," she whispered, with her head against his shoulder. "But be quick, Jeff. Be quick and take me to the boat."

*   *   *

Aboard a larger boat, the great ship called HMS *Iron Duke*, officers and men spent the evening hours in a state of concealed anxiety. As many British refugees as possible had been embarked, and made reasonably comfortable below; as long as Admiral Brock respected his pledge to Kemal to take aboard none but British nationals nothing could be done to help the other refugees to safety. Much had been done, and was still being done, to keep order ashore, but the Navy routine had to go on, and most of the *Iron Duke*'s officers dined as usual in their white mess jackets, while the Marine band played popular music in the flat outside.

After the meal the watch below joined the watch on deck, for the ship's rail was like a magnet, drawing the whole company to stare across the bay at the sight of a fire now two miles long, raging across the desert which had been a city. The landmarks which some of the old hands had known for years disappeared one by one, the French Theatre, the hospitals, the crosses on the Christian churches — and beneath two of the churches, Aya Triada and Foti, it was discovered too late that the Greeks had stored explosives when they held the city. Searchlights trained from the deck of the *Iron Duke* and other ships revealed a sea now red with blood as brother fought brother for a place in the lighters which were still trying gamely to take off a few hundred of the thousands on the shore. At last, when midnight came, Admiral Brock decided that no pledge to Kemal could stand in the way of giving help in what was now almost an international calamity. He ordered all the picket boats, with the cutter and the whaler of the flagship and her sister ships, to proceed to the town and save as many lives as possible.

Archie Munro, like every officer aboard, raced to his cabin to change from his white mess uniform into Navy blue. Armed with a truncheon, he took his place in one of the boats, which carried Marines with rifles, and the sailors pulled for the shore.

It was on the third trip that he saw, by the glare from a searchlight, an overturned boat to which a group of men and women were feebly clinging, and ordered the crew to row in that direction.

"Looks like they took too many aboard, sir, and capsized," said one of the Marines. "Not the first time we've seen that tonight."

"This lot's not fighting, 't any rate," someone muttered.

"Come on, chums, cheer up, soon 'ave you aboard now!" was the word, as the sailors helped the exhausted refugees to climb into the boat. Archie Munro gave his hand to a tall man with black hair, and recognised Jeff Barrett.

"Good Lord, Barrett, how did you get here?"

"Is Leila there?" said Barrett faintly. "I didn't think—I could hold her up much longer."

"The girl? This girl here? Yes, she's all right, she's only fainted, I think."

"Look after her," said Jeff, and vomited sea water.

"I'll take her down to the sick bay myself."

But what the Surgeon-Captain said when Archie carried his light burden down the companionway made the Scotsman sigh, and shake his head. He went back to the place where Jeff had dropped on the quarter-deck, the flagship's sacred quarter-deck, now fouled by a hundred helpless refugees. Jeff was lying spread-eagled, his eyes fixed on the copper glow in the midnight sky, but he raised himself on one elbow when he recognised Munro.

"How's Leila? Where is she?"

"I'm awfully sorry, Barrett," said Archie Munro awkwardly. "They—they say she never had a chance. She had a knife wound in her side—I'm *sorry*, old man! She was dead before we brought her in."

17

"3922 from evelyn barrett at army rear headquarters konya
turkey am filing exclusive story greek defeat at dumlupinar
and greek atrocities under byline evelyn anderson repeat
anderson—"

EVELYN COMPOSED this cable in her head while the trolley
jolted east. It was probably far too "clear" for Donnelly's liking,
but she couldn't risk mutilated cablese; indeed, the chief reason
for going on from Afyon was that Konya was the only town in that
part of Anatolia with facilities for handling overseas cables. She
wrote the story itself on the next day, in the train from
Akshehir, using the three notebooks she had filled at the front.
Condense as she might, it still ran to three thousand words, but
she had plenty of money in her belt, and it would be worth every
penny of it to tell the true story of the Turks and the Greeks.

And the story of Saturday morning! She had watched and
listened with the Turkish reporters in the hall at Ushak, hastily
cleaned and swept and adorned with a single Turkish flag, when
the two Greek generals came in to make their formal surrender to
Kemal. He, standing with his Pashas, was vibrant with vitality,
for the fatigue over which Evelyn mourned while he lay sleeping
had been wiped, as by an unseen hand, from his face. In his plain
khaki he presented a strong contrast to the Greeks in their
bedraggled finery and rows of medal ribbons, and it was clear that
General Tricoupis, his face twitching with nerves, hardly knew
what to make of him.

"I didn't know you were such a young man, General," he
blurted out, as Kemal took his hand and held it for a moment in a
friendly clasp. That handshake, a mere expression of military
courtesy, must have encouraged Tricoupis, for he burst out with a
recital of his woes: the political differences in his command, the
indiscipline, the insanity of General Hajianestis, all came out; nor
had General Dionis any scruples about interrupting and con-

tradicting his superior officer. The Turks looked scandalised, but Kemal stroked his moustache once or twice, and Evelyn knew he was struggling to keep from laughter. At last he stopped the sorry performance by saying kindly:

"War is a game of chance, General. The very best is sometimes worsted. You ought not to be too distressed!"

"Oh, General!" cried the Greek, gesticulating like a bazaar seller, "I haven't done the last thing I should have done. I haven't had the courage to commit suicide!"

Kemal's blue eyes froze. "That, of course, is something which concerns you personally," he said, and motioned to the guards to take the prisoners away. Evelyn only saw him once after that, when he came up to the car which was to take her to the railhead, and with a hundred men watching, kissed her hand and thanked her for the service she was doing to the Turkish cause. That, Evelyn supposed, was military courtesy too, although for many miles of her long journey she thought she could feel the warmth of his lips on her skin.

At Konya, where Kemal had told her to report at army head-quarters, Evelyn was received with enthusiasm, and in scraps of several languages told the Turkish officers much that they wanted to know about the great battle and the Greek surrender. She was escorted to the telegraph office and helped in the despatch of her long cable. But there was no prospect of an armed convoy leaving for Angora within the next few days, nor could the soldiers approve of a foreign lady trying to live alone in any of the hans of Konya. There was nothing for it, Evelyn admitted, but to throw herself on the mercy of the Americans at the Near East Relief Mission, and to the gate of their compound, at nearly ten o'clock at night, she was driven in an army car.

"So you're the bad girl who ran off with the soldiers!" was how Mrs. Fister greeted the unexpected guest. She was a tall, raw-boned New Englander, with a little grey topknot of hair skewered with the largest metal hairpins Evelyn had ever seen, and she had already told her husband that if the Barrett girl came back to Konya she was going to give her a real good dressing-down.

"The Miss Livermores were worried sick about you," she said severely, as she ushered Evelyn into a pleasant lamplit living-room. "When their driver went back to Angora alone they like to died! They've sent three telegrams asking for news of you, and what could we tell them other than that you'd been and gone?"

"I'm very, very sorry," said Evelyn. "I had a job to do for my husband's paper, and I didn't know where I might have to go until I came to Konya."

"Why didn't you tell Mabel Livermore about your job, then? Seems kind of underhand to me, young lady! And where's your husband at now, pray?"

"He's still in Smyrna. I'll apologise to Miss Livermore and her sister as soon as I go home, indeed I will—"

"You won't get the chance. Their man drove them both to Mudanya to help in the refugee camps there, and dear knows when they'll get back to Angora."

"All the way to the sea coast in the truck! But what refugees are there at Mudanya?"

"Greeks from Brusa, of course. They thought they'd all be massacred when the Turks came in. Seems they're in terrible shape at Mudanya, waiting for transport across the sea to Thrace."

"You know something, Mother?" Mr. Fister intervened. "I think what this girl needs right now is something to eat and a good night's sleep, instead of a scolding."

"Humph!" But Mrs. Fister, in spite of her grunt of disapproval, took Evelyn off to the room she had occupied before, which had a narrow white bed with a striped afghan folded at the foot, white crochet mats on the bureau, and a sampler sewn with the words "Thou God seest me" above the door. She brought the exhausted girl a bowl of bread and milk flavoured with sugar and cinnamon, clucked at the sight of the stained khaki haversack and the Turkish army greatcoat laid on a polished pine chest, and left Evelyn in as completely American a setting as could be found in any foreign land.

There was no scolding in the morning, for Mrs. Fister was disarmed by Evelyn's offer to work in the Red Crescent hospital where the Fisters had spent most of their time since the ambulance convoys started rolling down from the mountains. She got out her sewing machine at once, and "ran up" two white cotton dresses for the new recruit, explaining to Evelyn that she would be given a Red Crescent brassard at the hospital and must at all times wear her flowing black headscarf in the streets of the town. The Fisters were accepted in Konya because they distributed food and medical supplies, but a foreign girl would not find it easy to go about alone, said Mrs. Fister: as often as possible they would all drive to the hospital together in their own truck.

Remembering the ghastly hospital at Afyon, Evelyn dreaded her new work, but the Red Crescent had organised their establishment well, and most of the patients there were on the way to recovery. There were no horrors for the new ward maid to shudder at, but a great deal of patience and gratitude for small services which made Evelyn remember that Kemal had told her she would find it easy to love his fellow-countrymen. One thing she found especially lovable was "Mehmedjik's" absolute devotion to the Commander-in-Chief. Time and again she was told by some wounded man who had shed his blood at Kemal's orders that the Gazi bore a charmed life, and was always in front when he led his troops to battle.

His own signals to her came in daily. They could be little more than reports of the army's progress, but they were very precious to Evelyn—precious in a quite different way from the cable from Chicago which arrived on the morning of September 6, and read:

congratulations your great story which led paper yesterday stop story ran verbatim bylined anderson stop using army nurses story featurewise stop keep it up stop best regards donnelly

Which led paper yesterday! All three thousand words of it! Evelyn tried to visualise the *Clarion*'s front page with Evelyn Anderson's three-thousand-worder in the lead spot, and turned a smile of such pure joy on the young officer who brought the message from headquarters that he went away dazzled, and not at all surprised at the rumours which were going about. That evening she was so gay at the Fisters' supper (baked beans and Brown Betty) that the childless couple, who had thought her too reserved to be quite frank and open, felt their hearts warming to the "lovely American girl" to whom they had given shelter. After supper Mrs. Fister showed Evelyn all her little treasures, chiefly souvenirs collected by her brother, who was also a missionary. There was a ring of Burmese gold, too small for Mrs. Fister's powerful hand; a carved box made of olivewood, "said to be" from the Mount of Olives; there was also a necklace of translucent white beads which Mrs. Fister called "chipped stones from Palestine". As Evelyn played with the string she realised that the "chipped stones" numbered thirty-three, and that good Mrs.

Fister's necklace was in fact a Moslem rosary. Thirty-three stones for the divine Names of Allah, then three times thirty-three, she thought, letting the cool stones trickle through her fingers. And then the Final Name, which is Unnameable. . . .

From that moment the old trouble and the old doubt, suppressed during the wild hours of love and war through which she had lived, came back to Evelyn. Everything in Konya conspired to remind her of the power of Islam, and of how deeply, in spite of any laws Kemal might make to secularise the future state, the Moslem religion was ingrained in the Turkish people. From her bedroom window she could see the conical blue-green dome of the great Tekke of the order of Whirling Dervishes—Kemal's especial hate—and sometimes fancied she could hear the wild flute music to which they abandoned themselves in the dances in which they sought complete union with their God. Lying in bed, she could hear the muezzin's call to prayer each morning from the minaret of the Selimye mosque: "Prayer is better than sleep! God is great! There is no God but Allah!"

She timidly questioned Mr. Fister about the religion which Kemal had failed to show her as a thing of beauty. The American was better educated and more cultured than his energetic wife: he had been a missionary in Constantinople for more than ten unproductive years, and was by way of being an Arabist. When Evelyn asked if he had a copy of the Koran he rather boastfully told her that indeed he had, but written in Arabic; he had never read the Koran in an English translation.

"And what do *you* want with the Koran, young lady?" he enquired.

"I'd like to know more than I do about the Moslem religion," said Evelyn.

"Yes, well, you'd find the Koran rather hard going, even in English," said Mr. Fister. "The Prophet declared that it was divinely revealed to him by the Angel Gabriel; in fact, it's a queer mixture of the Talmud and the Christian gospels. Islam is what scholars call 'a revealed religion', the religion of the Book; but the rules for living in the Moslem world are perfectly straightforward and uncomplicated."

"What are they, please?"

"Let me see . . . A Moslem must pray five times daily, give alms to the poor, go on pilgrimage to Mecca, keep Ramazan—

just as some of us keep Lent—and also keep himself bodily clean. Not a bad set of rules, for those who believe in them!"

"But what do they pray *for*, Mr. Fister?"

"In the mosques? They confess their faith that there is no God but Allah, and that the Prophet Mahomed is his apostle."

"I see." It was said so pensively that Mr. Fister felt obliged to say,

"You're not a doubter, are you, Evelyn?"

"I don't know *what* I am."

The old missionary rose and took a Bible from the bookshelf. "Read the Good Book, my dear," he said. "Read St. Paul. He preached in Konya once, you know, along with Barnabas, and he also wrote a letter to your friends in Angora, it's called the Epistle to the Galatians. That'll do you more good than twenty Korans."

Evelyn did read the Epistle to the Galatians, by candlelight, sitting up in bed, and a dry bad-tempered letter it turned out to be. All about circumcision! What possible light could that throw on her own problem? She put it aside for one night more, and lay down to dream erotic dreams of Kemal, and long to be in his arms once again.

Next day the news that the Turkish advance guard had entered Smyrna ran like wildfire through the town of Konya. The Fisters, who refrained from expressing any political opinions, looked very grave, and went home early from the hospital, driving circumspectly through streets in which every elderly man and adolescent boy in Konya seemed to be abroad. But if Konya was elated on Saturday night it was nothing to the frenzy of Sunday, when news came that the Gazi himself had entered Smyrna, again the Conqueror, the hero who had driven the Greeks from Anatolian soil. All morning, all afternoon the noise increased. It swirled from the Mevlana Tekke to the Selimye mosque and broke in waves against the stone walls of the mission compound. At four o'clock Mr. Fister asked Evelyn to help "Mother" to make up some shakedown beds in the store-room across the courtyard.

"We invite our Christian friends to supper here on Sunday nights," he said. "Maybe some of them will want to stop over until tomorrow morning, with the town in such a state."

"I'll be glad to help, but . . . are your guests really afraid of going home?"

"Most of them are Armenians, and they know only too well

what a great Turkish victory can mean to their race," said Mr. Fister. "The people here may very easily run amok tonight after their celebrations, and then the killing starts."

"But Kemal Pasha promised there would be no excesses—"

"Maybe so, but he's not here in Konya," said Mrs. Fister, who was counting sheets. "And from what I hear he's got more than his own share of human frailty."

"Remember I've been with the Turkish Army," said Evelyn proudly. "All the atrocities I saw—and reported—were committed by the Greeks."

"You don't know what you're talking about, young lady," said Mr. Fister. "Mother and I were in Constantinople all through the terrible Armenian massacre in March '15, when the Turks were celebrating the British retreat from the Dardanelles. We sheltered as many Armenians as we could in our own house, while the blood bath lasted, not knowing when it would be our turn next. . . . I never want to live through scenes like that again."

"You're both very brave people," said Evelyn.

"In the strength of the Lord! Amen!" said Mr. Fister.

*　　　　*　　　　*

The Armenian Christians came by ones and twos, till there were ten of them, filtering unobtrusively through the roaring streets to the Relief Mission. Almost the first request they made was for the heavy gates to be closed for their protection, but Mr. Fister tranquilly said,

"The gates will be closed at the usual time. We mustn't let our Turkish friends think that we don't trust them."

The Armenians, grey-faced, looked as if they trusted nobody. Evelyn, helping to serve the fried chicken and apple pie, thought it was all faintly ridiculous. Did these poor creatures really think there was going to be a massacre? They were huddled together like the English people she had read about in some old novel about the Indian Mutiny, crowded inside the Residency at Lucknow. She had implicit faith in Kemal's authority, though Kemal was hundreds of miles away at Smyrna, and how she longed to be with him there, or at the least out in the Konya streets, celebrating with his own people! But after supper was over, and Grace said, and the yard boy had shut the gates at last and come in to join in the worship, the little gathering in the Fisters' parlour, with the rocking chairs and the quahog shells on the sideboard, assumed a new dignity. Just so, she thought, might a little company of Christians have gathered round Paul and Barnabas in Konya nineteen hundred years ago; and she composed herself to listen while Mr. Fister read the Twenty-third Psalm and then engaged in prayer.

"Almighty God, we pray that peace may come speedily to this war-weary land, and that he who is today the victor may show clemency and pity to the vanquished—"

It was exactly what Evelyn had begged of Kemal on their last night together: to be a merciful conqueror. She felt the tears rising, and bit her lips to keep them back. God! Give him compassion!

Mrs. Fister took her place at the squeaky old harmonium which stood against the wall, and propped Sankey's *Sacred Songs and Solos* on the rack. "Let's all sing one of our old favourites," she said. "Number eighteen in your hymn books."

> *Tell me the old, old story*
> *Of unseen things above,*
> *Of Jesus and his glory*
> *Of Jesus and his love.*

Immediately Evelyn was transported back fifteen years in time and thousands of miles in place to a mission hall in downtown San Francisco, where her mother in an evangelical-revivalist phase had taken her several times to sing hymns and listen to a hellfire and brimstone preacher. The jingling rhymes, the sweet lilting tune, brought her childhood back:

> *Tell me the story slowly*
> *That I may take it in,*
> *That wonderful redemption*
> *God's remedy for sin.*

Then the tears were uncontrollable, and Evelyn ran out of the room. Mrs. Fister was considerate enough not to follow her. But when the Armenian guests had been housed for the night, and the Fisters were alone in their own room, she said as she unskewered her grey hair:

"That's a deeply troubled girl, Dad. What are we going to do about it?"

"I just can't seem to reach her, no matter how I try."

"It's the husband, I suppose; she hardly ever mentions him. I don't know what the modern generation's coming to, I really don't."

"We must take it to the Lord in prayer, Mother."

"We will." But before the good woman got down on her knees she opened the bedroom window wide.

"The town seems quieter now. Maybe it's all blown over for this time."

"Please God it has. But I wonder," said Mr. Fister heavily, "how they're making out at Constantinople."

18

AT CONSTANTINOPLE THE explosion of joy at Kemal's victory rocked the seven hills of the city.

Tramcars, taxis, cabs and carts were brought to a standstill as the students poured out of their classrooms and took over the Grande Rue de Pera, which became a solid mass of young humanity as the boys shouted and cheered for Kemal the liberator. The Greeks and Levantines of Pera ran down their iron shutters and barricaded themselves against looting and massacre, and Wrangel's Russian refugees felt themselves soldiers again as they prepared to take their stand against the Bolsheviki. Even on the Stamboul side, fallen for so long into cobwebs and dust, there was a new effervescence of life in the dingy streets, and the mosque of Aya Sofia was crowded with the Faithful whose hearts opened in gratitude for their deliverance.

The Ottoman police were quite incapable of keeping order in such mass uprisings, and since Kemal had his agents among them their efforts were half-hearted. It was the British troops who policed the roaring streets, watching for the signs of a crowd running amok, of arsonists, of the hotheads who would touch off disaster by screaming for a jehad, a Holy War against the Christians. The small British Army of the Black Sea, dispersed all through the Neutral Zone, once again had to concentrate on Constantinople.

In the grounds of the British Embassy all was calm. The sentries were on the gate, the gardeners at work with watering-can and rake, but Mr. Gilbert Elliott, seated at his official desk, had no illusions about what was going on beyond the preserves of His Britannic Majesty. Kemal had won, and Kemal had made exorbitant demands of the Allies, which would sooner or later have to be met, and the days of the Occupation were numbered unless the British were prepared to fight again. Gilbert Elliott, whose only son lay in a nameless grave in Turkey, wanted no more war. He wanted, indeed, a far more peaceful life than he had lived in the past few weeks.

Mr. Elliott rang the bell for his secretary. Miss Kellas came in, Scots, red-haired, efficient and *quiet*, just what he had hoped his daughter would turn out to be, with her notebook and pencil in her hand.

"Can't you get through to Kilia at *all*, Miss Kellas?"

"I'm very sorry, sir. Even the Kilia exchange doesn't answer, let alone the IWGC. I tried Chanak a quarter of an hour ago, and Chanak doesn't answer either."

Repressing the words "God knows what's going on down there!" Mr. Elliott said, "Thank you, Miss Kellas. I shall be going out presently; if any message comes in from my daughter will you telephone it on to my flat?"

"Certainly, sir."

Mr. Elliott fiddled with the objects on his desk. Pen tray, In and Out baskets, punches and green silk tags, the Foreign Office List and the Statesman's Year Book—all the orderly paraphernalia of his official life, which would presently be ending. It had been reasonably successful, diligent, and always pitched in a low key—until the day a few weeks ago when in this very room his daughter Jean, with her hair down and her face bruised and swollen, had made a noisy, sobbing, violent scene about that miserable man Cravache.

"It's not fair, Daddy! It's not fair, I say!"

"Jean, listen to me—"

"Riachi—Riachi told me Cravache planned the murder, and Madame Mavros gave him shelter. Why should the Ottoman police arrest Madame Mavros and let Cravache go free?"

"Because he's an Allied officer. He isn't subject to their Ottoman law."

"But couldn't the French court-martial him?"

"They could, but they won't."

"Are you going to let them get away with that?"

"The decision isn't in my hands, Jean."

"The Syrian boy at the café—that police captain said he would get a stiff prison sentence—"

"Upon my word, he's safer in prison than at your tender mercy, Jean. Do you know you nearly killed him when you whipped him with that pistol butt?"

"I only wish I had. Daddy, you know Archie Munro saw Cravache at the café—you *know* I took his photograph—"

278

Mr. Elliott took the negative and six prints, hastily processed, from his blotter. "This is *a* picture of Cravache talking to Shukri Khalil outside the Pierre Loti café. There is nothing to prove that he went inside the café, or talked to Riachi, nor even *when* he was there. He could say he went up there from Eyüp for a walk and a cup of coffee, just as you and Archie did—"

"Daddy, don't be so *reasonable!*"

"It's my profession to be reasonable, Jean."

"Haven't I told you and told you Riachi named Cravache as his paymaster?"

"We've only your word for that, unfortunately."

"*What?*"

"There was no witness to what you say he told you, and he was delirious, you admit that yourself. Come now, Jean, you must let me be the best judge of this. The killing of Monsieur Trakas was a disaster, it destroyed our prestige with all the Christian communities in the Near East, but we simply cannot let it develop into a major row with the French."

"Which there would be, if Cravache were accused?"

"He's on the High Commissioner's staff, Jean."

"But it's so *unfair!* The newspapers have been saying for days that the Kemalists planned the Trakas murder, and now we know it was Cravache."

"I don't suppose Kemal Pasha will lose any sleep over it. He, of all people, who took the trouble to send me a message warning me against Cravache!"

"Did he really?"

Mr. Elliott recollected himself. "Come along now, Jean, we've been over all this again and again, and it's time I took you home. What Mummy is going to say about today, I really do not know!"

"Will she be angry with Archie?"

Mr. Elliott saw his advantage. "Probably. I'm not too pleased with that young man myself. But he's bound to be in serious trouble with his Captain already. If you go on making a fuss about an—incident—that was closed when Riachi died, you could get him into worse trouble still, and you don't want that, do you?"

"Of course not." Jean drank a little water from the glass they had brought her when she arrived at the Embassy, dipped her handkerchief in what was left, and rubbed it over her moist face.

"I left my handbag in that awful police station," she said, trying to smile. "No powder!"

"We'll get it back for you tomorrow . . . What are you doing with that?" For Jean had picked up one of the prints of her last snapshot and put it in the pocket of her dishevelled dress. And for the first time in her life she answered "Daddy" impertinently:

"I'd like to keep it for a souvenir."

Next day Mrs. Elliott took Jean to Therapia, and when she came back the bruises on her face were gone, her red hair was bobbed, and she had played enough tennis to shed a good deal of the puppy fat. When Jean Elliott next faced her father in the office where she had learned her first lesson in political expediency she was perfectly calm and collected, but very firm in a new request she had to make.

"Mummy seems to think we might be going back to London soon."

"It's possible."

"Then before we leave Turkey I honestly think you ought to let her go to the Dardanelles. She really longs to see the place where poor old Ronnie—"

"It's morbid, Jean."

"I think it would do her good."

Mr. Elliott reflected. The country was in a most unsettled state, but the city was equally dangerous for two Englishwomen who liked to move about freely, and they would be safe enough with the Imperial War Graves Commission people on the European shore of the Dardanelles. Besides, both his womenfolk had become rather difficult to live with, Victoria always sulking and sighing, and Jean in her present mood about as amiable as a tiger cub. So he let them go on Monday, the day after Kemal entered Smyrna, on the understanding that Jean was to telephone to him every morning and bring her mother back on Friday night.

Today was Thursday, and there had been no phone call from Kilia at all.

What there had been, was the letter Mr. Elliott now took from his wallet and read again. It had been brought to his apartment on the Rue des Petits Champs by a messenger who merely pushed it into the maid's hands and fled. It had been enclosed in a rather grimy commercial envelope, sealed with a plain seal, but inside there was a second envelope of the finest cream-laid vellum, addressed to himself in an exquisite Arabic script. He spread the single sheet open on his desk. The letter ran:

"If Mr. Gilbert Elliott wishes to do an old friend a favour, he will come to Topkapi Saray in the strictest secrecy at four o'clock this afternoon."

It was signed by the Sultan of Turkey, Mehmed VI Vahed-ed-din.

To call him an old friend was surely a polite equivocation. No European could really make friends with the two pathetic princes who were the half-brothers of Abdul the Damned, while Abdul was on the throne of Osman. Mehmed V Reshad, who succeeded Abdul after the Young Turks' *coup d'état*, had been virtually the Sultan's prisoner for thirty years, cultivating an interest in painting; Vahed-ed-din, whose appeal lay before Mr. Elliott now, and who had come to the throne almost in the hour of Turkey's defeat and occupation, had cultivated an equally harmless interest in Sèvres china. Mr. Elliott had seen him only twice since returning to Constantinople, when as a matter of diplomatic courtesy he had attended the Friday *selamlik* out at Yildiz—had seen a little man in an army officer's greatcoat with a star on his breast, cowering behind his bodyguards.

But—they had been young men together, in the days when young men, even princes, went by caïque to the Sweet Waters of Asia, and studied the forbidden beauties drifting by on the Bosphorus behind the curtains that so often were transparent. The days when Turkish ladies really were beguiling, with their beautiful black eyes burning above the chiffon yashmaks, the long flowing ferajes merely hinting at the languid bodies underneath. The Sweet Waters of Asia were a public pleasure ground now, complete with sherbet, ice-cream and gramophone music. Mr. Elliott sighed, and took his homburg off the mahogany hatstand. Topkapi Saray at four, in the strictest secrecy! Both he and Sultan Mehmed VI were too old to start playing at Red Indians.

He took a fiacre across Galata Bridge to the Stamboul side of the city. There were groups of demonstrators waving Turkish flags all the way from Galata to the Sirkeci station, but no one molested Mr. Elliott, who with his sallow face and dust-coloured clothes looked not unlike a Turkish schoolmaster of the more educated sort. He dismissed the cab near what had been the Sublime Porte, in his young days the seat of government, whose *firmans* made the Great Powers bend their attentive ears: the pavements around the Porte were cracked and grass-grown now. It had been here, somewhere here, if he could only identify the street, that Gilbert Elliott had lived the best hours of his young manhood with a Turkish girl who had risked her life to take him for her lover. People talked nonsense about the locked doors of the harem! There were some who dared to open them, and it could be done: the anonymous correspondence by poste restante, the faithful old nurse who had a little room in one of those tumble-down wooden buildings of Stamboul . . . That girl! Her lovely Turkish name meant Water Lily. Nilüfer, *quelle gentillesse.*

The Sultan's summons had taken Mr. Elliott back into his own past. The Sultan, at sixty-one, was still very much in the present: he had a son aged ten, and report said he had a new wife, aged just fifteen. But so much of what went on at Yildiz Kiosk could only be a matter for conjecture; it was years since the Sultans, in their paranoic fear of assassination, had hidden themselves among the gardens and pavilions of the Star. They said their Friday prayers and held the Friday selamlik at the Hamidye mosque in the Yildiz grounds, and no Sultan within memory had used the great door to Aya Sofia, which Mehmed II, the Conqueror, had turned from a Christian church into one of the great mosques of Islam. Mr. Elliott, passing the lion-coloured mass of Aya Sofia, with its heavy dome and buttresses more like a fortress than a church, remembered days when the imam would ascend to the *minber* at noon (young Elliott with his shoes off, wearing a fez, kneeling among the men at the back of the mosque) and the imam was dressed in a robe of strawberry satin and a white turban, holding a drawn sword in his right hand. Behind him would be two green flags, the emblems of the Prophet and of conquest. Those were the days, and what had such days done for Turkey? With a continuing sense of stepping into the vanished past, and of regretting that past, Mr. Elliott passed through Bab-i-Hümayun, the Imperial Gate, into the precincts of Topkapi Saray.

The English preferred to call it the Old Seraglio. The name had a sexual overtone of the harem and the voluptuaries who had anticipated the joys of the Moslem paradise here on earth, but there were no ladies of the harem at the Old Seraglio now. They had been liquidated, in the sense that they were sent home, when the Young Turks took over the government in 1909, but some, who had neither home nor friends, were allowed to grow old in the haunts where they had lived only to gratify a Sultan's capricious desires. There was of course no sign of them on this hot September day, but a white eunuch, a real survivor of the harem days, was waiting for Mr. Elliott by the second gate, Bab-i-Selam, the Gate of Salvation. He was an enormously fat man in a black frock coat and a red fez. He bowed gravely to Mr. Elliott, and signed to the Englishman to follow him into the Courtyard of the Divan.

Here there was a faint stir of activity, for there were gardeners at work beneath the tall cypresses which edged the paths, and the result of their work could be seen in the great beds of roses, of all imaginable scents and colours, which filled the huge courtyard. "How beautiful!" said Mr. Elliott impulsively. He spoke in Turkish, but the eunuch made no reply; Mr. Elliott thought with some disgust that the creature had probably been muted as well as castrated. They came to the Bab-üs-Saadet, the Gate of Felicity, which led to the Throne Room. Here Mr. Elliott had expected to meet the Sultan, for here official audiences had taken place, and once long ago he had gone there in the entourage of his Ambassador. He remembered his romantic thoughts on that far-off day: of the Sultans coming forth to the courtyard of the roses to mount the Golden Throne on the days of their accession, while the Sheikh-ul-Islam pronounced their new titles before the rulers went by caïque up the Golden Horn to the mosque of Eyüp, there to be girded with the sword of Osman. The splendour and glory of those days! Now the vast palace, to which each Sultan had added his own library, treasure house, school, kiosk or fountain, had knelt in the sanctuary of the Prophet's Mantle, was like a great clock that had run down, and an Englishman, who like all foreigners had never had the right to penetrate beyond the Throne Room, was being led on by a eunuch past arches and gardens and blue pools to an exquisite courtyard which seemed almost to overhang the sea.

The eunuch, with another bow, indicated that Mr. Elliott was to wait in this courtyard for a few minutes. He was glad to rest, for the walk and the memories of the past had both been tiring, and he sat down unbidden beneath the little gilded canopy called

283

the Baldachin of Ibrahim. From there he had an unrivalled view over the mosques of Stamboul and the grey masses of Galata shimmering under a clear blue sky reflected in the waters of the Golden Horn and the Sea of Marmara. The Allied battleships lay at anchor, not as many of them now since the trouble started at Smyrna, but still an impressive sight. Wasn't it said to be sixteen miles long, the convoy which Admiral Calthorpe led into the Bosphorus in November 1918, when Turkey was beaten to the ground? Mr. Elliott had forgotten the exact figure, but he vivdly remembered Mustafa Kemal Pasha, on the day they first talked together in the Pera Palace, saying of those Allied ships, "As they have come, so shall they go!" Only four years ago . . . and now Kemal was in a fair way to making his vow come true.

The eunuch returned, bowing. He led Mr. Elliott past an apple tree laden with ripe fruit to a kiosk on which a pattern of yellow tulips brightened the walls of blue Iznik faïence, shining in the sun. Inside, a wave of heat seemed to leap at Mr. Elliott. He was amazed to see that a log fire was burning in the copper fireplace. The old man—for the Sultan looked much older than his age—warming his cold hands, wearing the greatcoat and fez of his Friday selamliks, was Mehmed VI Vahed-ed-Din, the Commander of the Faithful and the Shadow of God on Earth.

"I'm very glad to see you, Mr. Elliott," the Sultan said. "It was good of you to respect the need for secrecy, and come to meet me here at Topkapi Saray."

"The honour is mine, your Majesty," said the diplomat.

"I am so spied upon at Yildiz Kiosk, my visitors are all so marked and followed . . . besides, I had a fancy to see my Topkapi again . . . The roses are at their best now, don't you agree?"

"They're beautiful. And this must be the loveliest of all your Majesty's pavilions."

"The Bagdad Kiosk," said the Sultan. "My ancestor Sultan Murad VI built it when he took Bagdad in 1638. The dome is considered to be very fine."

The interior of the central cupola was a glory of rose and gold, pale orange and blue, from which a lighted lamp was hanging on a long gold chain. The lamp was deep rose, enamelled in gold and encrusted with turquoises, the same colours being repeated in the priceless carpet on the floor. The whole effect was exquisitely light and gay, in contrast to the cringing creature by the fire.

"Let us sit down, Mr. Elliott," said the Sultan, "We are old gentlemen now, and need not stand on ceremony here."

They sat down on a sofa in the eastern alcove of the little kiosk, beneath a blue wall inlet with shelves of mother of pearl.

"There have been many changes since we last met," began the Sultan.

"Very many, Sir."

"You lost your son at the Dardanelles, I was sorry to hear."

"My only son, Sir."

Vahed-ed-din sighed. "What a tragedy, that war! What a horror for Turkey that the Young Turks drove my brother Reshad into it! And now Kemal threatens us with another world war . . . as if yesterday's calamity at Smyrna were not horror enough! A disastrous fire, and half the population massacred!"

Protesting: "A calamitous fire, undoubtedly, but so far we have no reports of a massacre—thank God."

"Mr. Elliott, I've had enough of killing."

"So have we all."

"But Kemal will stick at nothing to gain his own ends. Do you realise that he actually demands Constantinople?"

"He certainly made his claim public, Sir."

"To think I once trusted that man! To think that I even took him with me as my aide-de-camp when I went to Germany in December '17! And do you know what he did when we were at Imperial Headquarters?"

"Sir?"

"He contradicted the Kaiser."

Mr. Elliott permitted himself a faint smile. "Many Englishmen would have liked to do the same," he said.

"I sent him a telegram of congratulations on the victory of Dumlu Pinar," said the Sultan drearily. "He didn't answer it."

The log fire crackled in the silence.

"I feel the time has come for me to leave the scene," said the Sultan. "It is kismet. I can't endure the thought of another war, or of Kemal ruling in my place . . . Would the British grant me asylum in Malta, until I could make more suitable plans for a residence abroad?"

"I'm sure that could be arranged, Your Majesty."

"I want you to arrange it, Mr. Elliott. Quickly, and in secrecy, or the Kemalists will try to take me prisoner. Talk to the

High Commissioner, talk to Sir Charles Harington. Get me out of here on a British battleship—I shan't feel safe till I'm on British soil."

"I'll do my best, but we shall have to do some careful planning. Whom shall we deal with on your side, out at Yildiz Kiosk?"

"My bandmaster. The only person I can trust."

This time Mr. Elliott managed to conceal his smile. The trustworthy bandmaster—and the Sultan expecting a message of thanks for congratulations from a man he had outlawed and condemned to death! The abdication of the Sultan was degenerating into farce.

"I must warn you, Sir," he said, "that the departure of a large company from Yildiz, with the usual amount of bags and baggage, is hardly likely to pass unnoticed by the agents you say are watching you."

"Who said anything about a large company?" said the Sultan irritably. "The ladies will have to take their chance later on. Only two of us need to seek an immediate refuge—myself and Prince Ertugrul."

"I've seen the Prince," said Mr. Elliott gently. "He semes to be a fine little boy."

"He's a good child," said the elderly father. "Perhaps some day he will wear the sword of Osman . . . but I doubt it very much."

Mr. Elliott doubted it too. When, after some more talk about plans and communication, he was permitted to withdraw, he was quite sure that he was taking leave of the thirty-sixth and last Sultan of the House of Osman. The long story of the Ottoman Empire, sometimes glorious and sometimes horrific, was over. As he followed the emasculated male through the gardens of the dead palace, he thought again of Mustafa Kemal's prophetic words about the Allied ships.

"As they have come, so shall they go!" Mr. Elliott remembered Kemal's hard young face, his intense vitality of purpose, and thought regretfully that not for the first time, and probably not for the last, the British had backed the wrong horse.

19

WHILE MR. ELLIOTT made his sentimental journey into the past, his daughter Jean was doing her best to cope with an urgent problem of the present.

She was sitting in a motor launch in which her mother, flushed and fevered to the point of delirium, was being taken to hospital at Chanak, on the Asiatic side of the Dardanelles where Mr. Elliott had forbidden his wife and daughter to set foot.

They had been at Chanak once already, on Monday afternoon, after the eight-hour sail down the Sea of Marmara and into the Narrows, but only for long enough to transfer to the launch operated by the Imperial War Graves Commission, the only organisation in the whole of the Neutral Zone which offered hospitality to occasional visitors.

"I hope you don't mind sleeping in a Nissen hut, ladies," drawled the limping young Australian army captain who had come to escort the Elliotts to Kilia. "We're not quite up to the Ritz standards, but we're a whole lot better than the London Hotel at Chanak!"

"I think it'll be fun," said Jean zestfully. Her mother winced. For Victoria Elliott this was a pilgrimage of mourning, and she looked back wistfully at the ugly little Asiatic town from which all the activity of the Great War seemed to have ebbed away. Her son had been kindly treated in the hospital which the Australian pointed out to her on the rising ground above the flat roofs of the dusty town and the rotting landing stage.

Jean, characteristically, was looking forward. In Kilia Bay, three miles north of Chanak on the European side, they saw the wreckage of war in the hulks of three Turkish transports sunk by a British submarine, and on the hills above a honeycombing of Turkish gun emplacements was clearly visible. But immediately behind the bay a small community was rising, entirely British in appearance, with little cottages dotted among the Nissen huts, and this was where the Commission, headed by an Australian officer, was organising the new cemeteries for the soldiers of the British Empire who died at Gallipoli.

"Have you any idea where you want to look tomorrow?" the Australian captain asked Jean two hours later. He had invited her to come for a stroll after her mother, who had quite willingly sat down to supper in the communal restaurant, had gone to unpack and rest in the hut assigned to the two ladies who had arrived with special recommendations from the British High Commission.

"Look?" said Jean.

"Yeah. Do you have any details about which cemetery your brother's likely to've been buried in?"

"Oh dear," said Jean, "I hope there hasn't been a misunderstanding. My brother died in Anatolia as a prisoner of war. He was captured at the Dardanelles, months before the Gallipoli invasion; mother just wanted to see the place where it all happened, before he was taken on that dreadful march into the interior, and died."

Captain Colson clucked his tongue sympathetically. "Over there?" he said. There was still a faint reflection of the sunset on the Narrows, and the town lights of Chanak were unexpectedly bright.

"Yes. It was the worst possible luck, because actually there were very few casualties at that time. Ronnie was in the *Ocean*, one of the old battleships which tried to force the Narrows on the fifteenth of March. She struck a mine, and they abandoned ship in a few minutes, but Ronnie was a very poor swimmer, and they didn't pick him up in time. He drifted down to a place called Erenköy, where some Turkish soldiers brought him ashore."

"And that was that."

"He was in hospital at Chanak for a while, but—yes, that was that." They walked on along the newly made road between the cottages, and Jean, in her impetuous way, burst out: "I hope this trip will soothe my mother; if it doesn't I just don't know what I'll do! She's brooded on it all so long, and read all those horror stories about how cruel the Turks were to their prisoners, at Kut, and Afyon, and how they left them to die in the desert, and she works herself up thinking that's what happened to Ronald, and she *cries*—"

"Ah," said Captain Colson, "it's tough on the mums, all right. But it takes them all different. Now you look at *my*

288

mum's sister, Auntie Agnes back in Melbourne; she lost two boys in Gallipoli and one in Flanders, and I never saw her shed a tear. She's saving up to come over here next year and see where Jack and Ned are buried. We should have the monuments up and the cemeteries looking real nice by that time. Ten quid we give the Turks, for every corpse or skeleton they bring in."

"I just don't seem able to get away from cemeteries," said Jean forlornly. She was thinking of the horrible graveyard opposite their temporary home on the Rue des Petits Champs in Constantinople, and that other, more tranquil city of the dead through which she had walked with Archie on the way to the Pierre Loti café.

"How long are you two ladies going to stay at Kilia?' asked Captain Colson.

"Why, do you want to get rid of us already?"

"I wish you could stay for ever," said the Australian gallantly. "We don't see many pretty girls at Kilia! No, but seriously, I hope you're not planning to be here too long. Too many reffos round about for my taste: the Russkis first and then the Greeks from Brusa, and now that old Kemal's in Smyrna you never know what may happen here!"

"But Smyrna's in Asia Minor, and over two hundred miles away!"

"Yeah, but when old Kemal starts going, he doesn't half go!"

*   *   *

The town lights of Chanak burned bright across the Narrows that night because the officers of the little British garrison were going through an urgent reappraisal of their task as defenders of the Neutral Zone. Reports were coming in of Nationalist forces moving north from liberated Smyrna, and General Sir Charles Harington, the Allied Commander-in-Chief at Constantinople, had already sent Colonel Shuttleworth, commanding the 83rd Infantry, to make an appreciation of the military situation at Chanak Kale, the ancient fortress whose modern batteries, complete with Krupp guns and German gunners, had formed part of the Inner Defences of Constantinople. Now, if Kemal meant to drive on to the Sea of Marmara, it would become vitally necessary to defend Chanak on the landward side.

None of this activity was evident to Mrs. Elliott and Jean, as they went on their first morning walk through the scrub oaks on the hills above Kilia Bay. There seemed to be a number of ships lying off Chanak, but that was nothing out of the way; all ships had to stop there, by law, for examination on their way to Constantinople, and the Elliotts were not experienced in reading flags or signals. They found a warm, peaceful place to sit, and Jean read aloud from a guidebook which told them they were now looking at the Hellespont, at Nagara Point beyond Chanak which was the site of Abydos, and at Sestos on the European side, while Mrs. Elliott seemed quite interested in talking about Leander's famous swim, and Lord Byron's equally famous repetition of the feat. Jean led the conversation to the plains of Troy and the old wars; she only remembered a little about them from her school-days, but she wanted to keep her mother from thinking about another young swimmer, struggling for his freedom in the dark waters of the Hellespont on a March night seven years before. The long sauntering walk through the heather, the frequent rests and chats with the English and Australian gardeners who were making a battlefield into a place of tranquil beauty, seemed to please and soothe Mrs. Elliott. In a flash of insight Jean realised that caring for Ronald's grave, if that had been possible, would have been an immense solace to her mother.

The only unfortunate incident, as they made their way back to the restaurant for lunch, was that Mrs. Elliott was bitten on the ankle by some insect. The bite smarted and turned red, but Jean rubbed the place with alcohol and the little swelling appeared to subside. Captain Colson drove them as far as Cape Helles in the afternoon.

Next morning Mrs. Elliott had a headache and was sure she had caught a chill the day before. As the Centigrade thermometer had stood at 25 degrees all day, this hardly seemed to be likely, and by lunch time Mrs. Elliott said she felt warm again, in fact quite hot. She developed a flush which turned into a dusky red as the day went on, and by nightfall—their third night at Kilia—she was alternating miserably between chills and fever.

That was the thirteenth of September, the day when the Smyrna fire began, and also the day when the first Nationalist advance parties reached the line of the Neutral Zone south of the Chanak area. The Turks came up close to the villages of Ezine and Biga and stood to arms, witnesses to the utter sincerity of Kemal's threat to cross the Sea of Marmara if the Allies refused to give him Eastern Thrace and Constantinople and bring the occupation of Turkey to an end. Against these advance parties Colonel Shuttleworth could only muster the 1st Battalion of the Loyal North Lancashire Regiment, which had passed the winter in the Yildiz Barracks at Constantinople and garrisoned Chanak since the month of May. They were reinforced, on that thirteenth of September, by "B" Squadron of the Third Hussars and the 92nd Battery of the Royal Field Artillery from Constantinople. It was difficult to land the guns on the rotten old landing-stage at Chanak, and the only transport in the town, either mechanised or horse-drawn, was that belonging to the Loyals.

Next morning Jean Elliott tried hard to get a doctor for her mother. There was one medical officer at the little British cantonment at Kilia, but he had been summoned to the camp occupied by Wrangel's refugees, where typhus threatened. A little Greek doctor came up from the village of Maidos on foot, stroked his beard, and said the lady had been bitten by a sandfly and in consequence was suffering from "the three day fever". He prescribed patience and castor oil. But after he left the poor woman became so alarmingly ill that Captain Colson, acting for the commandant, said she must be taken to hospital in Chanak.

"Yes, I know you think you can nurse your mum yourself," he said to Jean's protests, "but you see we haven't got the right medicines or anything for her here. The Scotch doctor at Chanak is a bit of a tartar, but he knows his job about one hundred per cent better than old Diplodoukis, and he'll look after her all right. Now you take her over in the launch and I'll keep trying to get a message through to your Dad on the field telephone. There's no use trying on the office switchboard, it's fairly jammed with calls today."

*   *   *

Fate and a sandfly's bite had brought Mrs. Elliott to a bed in the very hospital where seven years earlier her beloved son had spent his last days of comfort, and Jean, seeing her asleep under sedatives, was almost beyond dreading what her mother's reaction would be when she awoke. She told the whole story to the "Scotch doctor", who hailed from Fife, and was not disposed to be sympathetic to what he called "the consequences of stravaigin' about the countryside like twa great wuddiefoos!"

"I don't understand you, doctor."

"Aye, ye understand me fine, or ye shud do, wi' a good Scots name like Jean Elliott. Did you put anything on to this bite o' yer mither's?"

"Rubbing alcohol."

"Anither time, try ammonia . . . Aye weel, I doubt she's in for something a bit waur than the three day fever. Lat's houp it's jist a simple dengue."

"You mean it could be something very serious?"

"Lassie, if I had the brains and the laboratories o' a Walter Reed or an Ehrlich, I could tell ye mair about insect bites and their results; but in the lichts o' an M.D. o' Edinburgh University I'm going to try her wi' antimony. And you'll have to do the donkey work as lang as she's in hospital; I canna spare a Greek girrl for the nursing, forbye they're all to be evacuated the morn's morn. What a carry on, and all for that blackguard they ca' Kemal Pasha! I'm promised army nurses down from Constant., but whaur to put them when I get them is mair than I can tell."

"I did a Red Cross course in London, Dr. Lauder. I'll try to help you all I can."

"That's mair like the thing, We'll maybe have our hands full wi' the Smyrna victims before this day's done."

The sun moved down the sky towards the Islands of the Blest, while at Chanak Colonel Shuttleworth and his officers grappled with the problems of defence. It seemed imperative to get all Greeks and non-Moslems out of the town—the legend of "Turkish atrocities" was dying hard—and ferried across the Narrows to Maidos; but Maidos, like Chios near Smyrna, was already overcrowded, and the unfortunate evacuees were left to swelter in the ferry barges. For those who remained, food was already in short supply. A section of the 55th Field Company of the Royal Engineers arrived from Constantinople and at once began to work on an alternate system to the pumping station which brought water to Chanak from the Koja Chay river. Colonel Shuttleworth now had seven hundred men under his command, all British: there were still no French or Italian reinforcements to be seen. The Turkish gendarmerie was disaffected to the point of being, it was thought, Kemalists to a man; they could not be relied on to keep order if the Turkish troops advanced. So far, the Turks stood with rifles reversed, and even fraternised with the British pickets on the frontier of the Neutral Zone.

There was little sleep for anyone in Chanak or Kilia that night. The fire still raged at Smyrna, and the armada of mixed craft toiling to take off an army of refugees which had now swollen to two hundred thousand on the burned-out waterfront was plying from island to island of the Aegean Sea trying to unload their wretched passengers. The British battleships wasted no time in the Aegean. They were under new orders, and Jean Elliott, when she drew the flimsy hospital curtains on the morning of the fifteenth of September, was overjoyed to see the White Ensign flying off the decrepit Chanak piers.

"Isn't that the flagship?" she said to Dr. Lauder, who had just returned from a conference with Colonel Shuttleworth.

"Aye, that's the *Iron Duke*, and the *Benbow*'s lyin' out in midstream. They're going to unload stretcher cases from the flagship first, so I'll need you in the wards, lassie; just look in on yer mither when ye can. She's some better this morning, and I jalouse we'll see an improvement by the aifternoon."

Jean went to work with a lighter heart. One or two of the Greek nurses had refused to be evacuated, and there were a few Turkish girls, uncomfortably veiled, to help, as well as a fatigue party of the Loyals. There were not, fortunately, many stretcher cases to handle. Most of the sick from the *Iron Duke* were suffering from burns and exposure, and could be laid on mattresses placed in the corridors, but the little Nightingale Hospital was soon very crowded, and there were still patients from the *Benbow*, *Marlborough* and *Ajax* to come in. Jean kept glancing at the door; it was too much to suppose that Archie Munro would be able to leave his ship and come ashore at such a moment, and yet come he did, in charge of the last convoy of walking cases and one man lying on a stretcher.

"Archie!"

"Jean! Good heavens, what are you doing here?"

This was very different from their constrained meeting at Therapia, under Mrs. Elliott's disapproving eye, which had followed their escapade at the Pierre Loti café. With war and its human wreckage all around them they had a new sense of freedom, of being no longer an impecunious young naval officer and a girl

293

very much in subjection to her parents: if life was still to be given them, they would fashion it to suit themselves. All that was implied in one quick handclasp, and then Archie, after hearing what had brought Jean to Chanak, said,

"How about your father, Jean? He must be terribly worried about you both!"

"They were going to try to reach him by field telephone from Kilia, yesterday afternoon."

"But you haven't heard from him?"

"Not a word."

"Would you like me to ask permission to get a radio message off to him from the flagship? I could make it official, through the High Commissioner's office."

"You'd be an angel to do that!"

"*Jean!*" came a shout from the harassed doctor.

"Archie, I must go!"

"Just a minute. That stretcher case we brought in, he's somebody you know. Barrett, the American correspondent."

"Was *he* at Smyrna?"

"Picked him out of the drink myself," said Archie laconically. "He's badly concussed. The boat he was in capsized, and he thinks some wretched Greek beat him over the head with an oar while he was trying to right it: they were all crazy that night, and fighting each other like mad dogs. And you remember that girl he was with, that day we went to Eyüp? She was killed while he was trying to get her away from Smyrna. Barrett says her own uncle pulled a knife on him, and the poor kid got in the way—accidentally or on purpose, nobody will ever know."

"How absolutely terrible! . . Yes, I'm coming, doctor!"

"Jist like a' the nurses—aye ready to waste time at the sicht o' a uniform!" came the rough Scots growl, and Jean hurried to take the doctor's orders. Washing—wash the lot o' them wi' Lysol, blanket baths for this one and that one, and mak' the rest wash theirselves—it was clear that there were to be heavy demands on the new RE pumping system. But the doctor found time to transfer Mrs. Elliott to his own bedroom, with a shakedown for Jean on the floor, and to examine Jeff Barrett very carefully: his was the only case of concussion so far. Jeff was lying quietly in his blankets, his pulse still weak and slow and his respiration shallow; his case history, passed on from the sick bay of the *Iron Duke*, stated that he had lost consciousness soon after his rescue and had remained unconscious for most of the night. However, he recognised Jean Elliott, though without showing any surprise at her presence in Chanak, and Dr. Lauder was satisfied with the way his eyes reacted to light.

"Ye're not so bad," he said, "twenty-four hours' rest and ye'll be a new man." Jeff nodded. He lay with relaxed limbs in the warmth and eventually in the quiet which the doctor imposed on his refugee patients, sometimes dozing, sometimes sure that he was back again on the Kordon with one arm round Leila while Homer, with the madness of that night of terror in his eyes, drew the knife which her soft body received instead of her lover's . . . Jean was sometimes near him when he woke from that nightmare, and once the doctor spoke to him so vigorously, and in such a dialect, that when he was again aware of Jean's gentler presence, Barrett said,

"Who's the old Scotch cut-up?"

"Oh, be quiet! That's the MO, Dr. Lauder."

"First name Harry, I suppose?"

"You're getting better, Mr. Barrett."

"I wonder why," said Jeff. "It was your beau who brought me in, wasn't it?"

Blushing: "Archie? Yes."

"He should have let me drown."

"You mustn't talk like that, you know."

Jeff said drowsily: "Are you a refugee too?"

"Sort of."

"And no chaperone?"

Next morning, Mrs. Elliott's condition had improved greatly, and the doctor rejoiced that it had been "naething but a wee dengue aifter a'". Jeff was well enough to be shaved, and after the midday dinner to get out of bed. Jean came to talk to him in whispers when most of the patients in the refugee ward had fallen into an uneasy sleep; she explained about her mother's illness, and the radio message received that morning through the flagship which told them that Mr. Elliott would come to Chanak as soon as his wife was able for the trip back to Constantinople.

"So you did have a chaperone after all, eh?" Jeff managed to smile.

"Why do you keep harping on my chaperone?"

"Because your father asked you who was going to chaperon you at some party you were going to with Munro, the night I was at your house in Pera. It seemed kind of funny to me—I mean, a girl your age—"

"Julia Windsor's dinner—I remember now. Doesn't it seem like a long time ago?"

Jeff remembered standing in the Grande Rue de Pera, making up his mind . . . He closed his eyes. Jean said, even more softly than before:

"You've had a very sad experience, Mr. Barrett . . . haven't you?"

"Did Munro tell you . . . about Leila?"

"Was that her name? Yes."

He began to talk then, low and fast, still with his eyes shut, telling Jean Elliott the story of that dreadful night. Some of the things he said appalled and frightened the girl, but she was strong enough to take Jeff's hand, and endure the pressure of his nails driven into her now roughened palm, while he talked out the loss and shame which came over him whenever he thought of Leila and what in his incurable sentimentality he believed to have been her self-sacrifice. He had convinced himself that she had deliberately thrust herself between that murderous knife and him. And if only—the last of all the *if onlies* in the long tale of his responsibility for Leila's fate—he had got her out of that crowd on the Kordon somehow, got help for her somehow, instead of carrying her to the rowboat from which, in ten minutes, they had all been thrown into the water. "She never spoke to me again!" he said emotionally, and opened his eyes on Jean Elliott's sympathetic face. Its pink, innocent roundness was tauter and more mature now, and while he talked the tears had come to her eyes.

"You were very, very fond of her, weren't you?"

"Yes. She was so—so little and sweet—"

"I'm *so* sorry."

Jeff groaned. "If only there was something I could *do*."

Unexpectedly: "There is one thing, of course. If I were as clever as you are, I'd want to do it!"

"What?"

"Write her story. Oh, not the private bits, not even her name; but what it was like to be on the Kordon that night, and about the Navy . . . And then about the people here at Chanak, and all the others scattered up and down the islands, and what war means to the refugees—"

Jeff smiled wryly. "That's my job. And my editor is probably going mad, waiting for the Smyrna story. You say there's no cable office here at Chanak?"

"Only a telegraph station, and the army commandeered it when the Emergency began. Oh, do you really think there's going to be another war?"

"Kemal's only bluffing. I used to play poker with him, night after night up at Chankaya, and I should know . . . What about the field telephone? If I could just get through to Constant., there's a guy called Braun at the Pera Palace who would cable my stuff to Chicago."

"I'm sure they won't let you use *that*. But when you're better, when Dr. Lauder discharges you, you could take a caïque over to Kilia, couldn't you? There's an Australian officer called Colson who I'm sure would let you use their phone."

"Jean, you're a great gal," said Jeff. "And Archie Munro sure is a lucky guy!"

Jean blushed and put a finger to her lips, for some of the sleepers in the nearby beds were rousing from their short siesta. She bent over Jeff's chair to murmur,

"Mr. Barrett—forgive me, but is your wife still in Turkey?"

"So far as I know, yes."

"You're—quite out of touch with her?"

"Well, I walked out on her, you see."

"But she ought to know how ill you've been. Why don't you write to her and tell her where you are?"

"I wouldn't blame her if she tore the letter up."

"But surely she wouldn't do that if you just said—you were sorry?"

*   *   *

If Jeff Barrett really believed that Kemal was bluffing, he was the only person in Chanak who did. The sailors from the *Iron Duke* had already been digging trenches two miles inland for twenty-four hours; the crew of HMS *Benbow* had manhandled a battery of naval 6-inch guns up to the heights above Kilid Bahr on the opposite shore. The *Benbow*'s effort was intended as a deterrent to the Turkish gunners, should Kemal's artillery be placed on the hills

297

surrounding Chanak town, for the guns aboard the great grey battleships in the Narrows were not regarded as capable of giving close support to troops less than a mile away on shore. Barbed wire was put up along the perimeter, where "Johnny Turk" and "Johnny Kikirik" faced each other once again as at Gallipoli. For the time being the Turks were not present in great strength, but the British command knew that Kemal had over fifty thousand men at his disposal in the First and Second Armies now based on Smyrna, and over ten thousand in the Ismid area, facing Constantinople. The urgent need was for Allied reinforcements, and while the French General Charpy and the Italian General Mombelli assured the Allied Commander-in-Chief at Constantinople of their urgent desire to co-operate with him, only token forces were despatched to Chanak.

The Greeks, whose insensate ambitions abetted by the Philhellenism of Lloyd George had been the cause of all the trouble, were of no help to the Allies in this crisis. The troops who left Brusa without being able to carry out their plan of burning the holy city to the ground (thanks to the intervention of Tirnaksis, a Turkish brigand chief) had now crossed the Sea of Marmara to Rodosto, where they celebrated their arrival by mutinying against their officers. The Greek flagship *Giorgis Averoff* sailed from Constantinople without Admiral Hepitis aboard; when Hepitis came alongside in his barge the crew threw down a message saying they felt they would be happier without him. In Athens the government of Monsieur Gounaris, whose days were numbered, seemed to be powerless to do anything for the Smyrna refugees.

While British troops were on their way to the Dardanelles from Alexandria, Malta and Southampton, a contingent of seventy Italians arrived at Chanak from Constantinople. Unfortunately they had forgotten to bring with them their national flag, but this was rectified, and the French, when their force arrived on September 16, were at least showing the Tricolore. The band of the Loyals went down to the docks to play the French in. The contingent consisted of one company of the 66th Infantry Regiment and twenty-four Spahis, and to the disconcerted observers there seemed to be almost as many bandsmen as there were French. But in spite of the feeble response of their Allies, the British government decided to resist Kemal's demands by force.

The Prime Minister, David Lloyd George, was of course

smarting at the defeat of his Greek protégés, and the Colonial Secretary, Winston Churchill, declared that to allow the Turkish Nationalists to take over Constantinople and reoccupy Eastern Thrace would be an insult to the victors of the Great War. Telegrams were sent to the Dominion Premiers, asking for military support against Kemal, and assistance was also solicited from the Balkan Powers. The Dominion response was tepid, only Australia and New Zealand being really eager to fight again on the heroic battleground of 1915, although there was some enthusiasm in Canada, notably in Newfoundland and Ontario. In the Balkans Roumania and Jugoslavia were both prepared to fight rather than see the Turks returning to the line of the River Maritza, and Czechoslovakia agreed to stand by the Jugoslavs. When these favourable replies were received in Downing Street the two hotheads, Lloyd George and Churchill, published an independent communiqué on the situation, and on September 18 the British public awoke to the news that the Turks were on the march, the Balkans aflame, and the young men of the British Empire being asked to volunteer for the misery and sacrifice of another war.

By then Jeff Barrett had discharged himself from the Nightingale Hospital. With a letter from Jean Elliott to Captain Colson, he hired a caïque and crossed the Narrows to Kilia, where the Australian, with a fine disregard for Pommie red tape, allowed him to use the Commission's line to Constantinople for half an hour. So Jeff got out his Smyrna story, and began the remarkable series of despatches from mutinous Rodosto, from Prinkipo (where the Russian colony was preparing to move on to Bucharest) and again and again from Chanak, which caused Donnelly and the Commodore, back in Chicago, to rub their hands with satisfaction.

"Jeff's hit his stride at last, that knock on the head must have done him good," said Donnelly.

"Knock be damned, it's the competition from his wife," said the Commodore. "He's crazy jealous of that girl; always was."

Donnelly knew better than to argue; he reflected that it was just this snide knowledge of base motives that had brought Weintraub from a Lake Erie scow to the publisher's office at the *Clarion*. What really mattered was that Barrett was going great guns at last, and that his stories, like Evelyn's from Dumlu Pinar, were being picked up by the agencies and given world-wide

299

publicity. The world, as yet, could hardly believe in the tragedy which lay ahead.

Britain believed in it. A wave of anger swept the country at the very thought that the Dardanelles and Gallipoli might see another disaster like the defeats of 1915, and all eyes were turned to Chanak, the little dusty town which seemed cast for the role of another Sarajevo. Meantime, the Cabinet sent voluminous instructions to General Sir Charles Harington, who had done so well in the earlier threats to the Neutral Zone (threats which very few in Britain had taken seriously), and on September 19 all civilians were ordered to be evacuated from Chanak.

"Weel, Mistress Elliott, I've been a bit forehanded with ye," said Dr. Lauder, entering his own bedroom on the morning of the nineteenth, "I've jist had a word with your goodman on the field telephone."

"With my husband? How is he? What did you say to him?" Mrs. Elliott laid down the bandage she had been incompetently rolling and looked almost animated.

"He's fine. He was askin' for you and your girrl and said to tell you he was thinking long to see you."

At this cool Scots translation of Mr. Elliott's anxious questions his wife looked surprised, but Dr. Lauder gave her no time to speak.

"He's taking the High Commissioner's launch down for you now, and ye should be ready to go aboard about five this afternoon. Aye, you'll be in yer own bed in Constant. sometime in the wee sma' hours ayont the twal', and that'll be a fine change, eh?"

Mrs. Elliott, who seldom understood more than half of what the doctor said, replied graciously: "Of course I shall be delighted to get home again, Dr. Lauder. But I want to tell you how grateful I am to you, for your care, and for giving up your own room to me. It was very kind!"

"There's nae great merit in curing a case of the dengue fever." Dr. Lauder hitched up a chair with his foot and sat down. "Wumman, I only wish that I could cure your mind."

"*Really*, doctor!"

"Aye, I mean what I say," said Dr. Lauder. "Could I but minister to a mind diseased? Pluck from the memory a rooted sorrow . . . isn't that the way it goes? They tell me this psychology is all the go nowadays, but in spite o' what Professor Frood may say I think a good dose o' cascara is worth an hour o' psychoanalysis for the maist o' folk. But I've thought a lot about your problem, mistress. I wud like to see ye sort it out—for that nice lassie's sake."

"Doctor, you don't understand—"

"I understand fine, Mrs. Elliott. Ye lost yer only boy, and it was a sore hertbrak, but ye had no right to loss your grip on livin', you that has a man and a girrl to live for still. Jist look at you! Seven pounds and a bittock, a good half-stone, we've taken aff your great creeshy carcase since ye had the fever, and if you would stop eatin' fancy pieces and nippin' away at the bottle and loss another twenty, ye wud be a fine figure of a wumman still."

"Have you been discussing me with Jean, Dr. Lauder? She has a mania about losing weight—"

"And she's trimmed down verra nice herself since I set her to scrubbin' floors. Na, I didna need to discuss your habits wi' yer daughter. I've been practisin' medicine for forty years, and I can read ye like a book." He leaned forward. "Ye're jealous o' the lassie, aren't ye? Because she's alive, and her brither's deid? Because the lad she fancies is a sailor like your Ronald, and ye canna thole to see him in his uniform? Now, my advice to you, mistress, and it's worth its weight in gold, is to gie the young folks your blessing and find some work to occupy your days till you're a granny. Because Jean and her sailor lad are full o' life, God help them—if war doesna' take him from her afore they've had a chance to live."

* * *

While Dr. Lauder expounded his homespun psychology to her mother, Jean Elliott had his permission to leave the hospital for an hour. She had a list of supplies to purchase in the town, for one or two Moslem shopkeepers were keeping their foodstores open, and the army was not yet able to fill all the Nightingale Hospital's needs. She also had the hope that if she made a detour by the harbour there would be a chance of seeing Archie Munro, for picket boats were constantly coming and going to the flagship, that majestic grey presence still anchored in the Dardanelles. All shore leave was cancelled, but they had been able to snatch a few minutes together in this way once before.

It was impossible to hurry in the narrow streets of Chanak, now as crowded with Tommies, their weapons and their vehicles as the villages of Picardy, of which Jean remembered seeing pictures during the Great War. "Johnny Kikirik" was laughing still, of course, and while waiting for another round with "Johnny Turk" was very willing to whistle and wave at a big red-haired girl in an improvised VAD uniform, striding through the streets of the sleepy town which had turned almost overnight into a symbol of Britain's prestige in the world. Jean laughed and waved back. It was odd how cheerful she felt at the thought of a coming war. Archie had always declared that there would be a second world war in their lifetime—"not that the Great War's ever been really over," he said—and if it came now she intended to get a hospital job in Constantinople. As a VAD if need be; but administration, such as she and Dr. Lauder were improvising at the Nightingale, was the branch of service which really suited Jean. Taking charge of other people, becoming involved with their lives, was more fun than tennis or fencing or sitting with Mummy in the Marquise tearoom, though somehow she didn't think there would be so much of that any more.

Chanak was such a little town that in spite of the throng of servicemen Jean quickly reached the harbour. More guns were being landed from the lighters, and Jean heard an army officer say that the 1st Battalion of the Gordon Highlanders was almost due to arrive from Malta. With a lift of her heart she saw Archie Munro, with two other lieutenants from the flagship, waiting on one of the quays for the return of the picket-boat. She stopped in the shelter of one of the tumbledown sheds, willing him to look in her direction, and presently Archie saw her and came hurrying up, his serious Highland face bright with delight.

"Jean! I say, this is a bit of luck!"

"Daddy's coming to get us this afternoon," she said quickly, for there was no hope of more than a few minutes together. "We're going back to Constant. in the High Commissioner's own launch."

"Wonderful! I'm glad you're getting out of here, and maybe we'll be together again quite soon. The buzz aboard is that the Admiral's needed for a conference in Constantinople."

"A conference—you don't mean a peace conference?"

"No such luck. No, this is a pukka crisis, Jean. Perhaps we'll see some active service yet."

"But Kemal Pasha has no Navy!"

"What if his Bolshie friends come through the Black Sea, and join in?"

"Oh, heavens!" said the girl. "It can't be that bad!"

"I don't know, but look, just in case I *don't* see you for a bit —there's something—I can't explain it properly, but do you remember how I once said I might as well leave the Navy before I was axed out, and try to earn some money in the City? Well, I've made up my mind to stay in now, if they'll have me. Because the Navy did some good at Smyrna, even if we were only ruddy policemen, and not the heroes we thought we were going to be."

"I know how you feel, Archie."

"Would it make any difference to you?"

"Your not being a rich stockbroker? I'd rather you stayed in the Navy."

"Even if there's another war?"

"Especially if there's another war."

Archie averted his dark eyes from Jean's candid face. The temptation to kiss her had to be mastered at all costs. He said, "You're being a brick about all this, dear. Your mother, and the hospital, and now me. Really a Trojan!"

"Perhaps because we're so near the plains of Troy?"

"Ah, don't make fun of me, Jean. Don't you know I—don't you know all I want to say?"

"Some day soon I want to hear you say it."

She looked up at him, her inhibited, clumsy, Highland sweetheart, not as well groomed as usual in his Number Three uniform, tired as every man was who had a part to play in the Chanak Emergency, and was utterly content with what she saw. It was going to be all right with her and Archie. And then Jean Elliott stiffened at the sight of a launch coming smartly up to one of the ramshackle piers, flying the flag of the Allied High Commission, and along with it, the Tricolore.

"Archie, do you see who that is?"

Two officers of the tiny French force at Chanak stepped forward to greet the first passenger to leave the launch. He was a tall man with a small head craning on a long neck, a pouting mouth under a black moustache, and features curiously arranged in a series of ellipses. He carried a brief-case and a riding whip, for he was now in uniform, although the last time Jean and Archie saw him he was in civilian clothes, standing in the garden of the Pierre Loti café.

"Major Cravache," said Archie through clenched teeth. "What brings *him* here?"

"Trouble," said Jean briefly. Her rosy face had become very pale. "Wherever that man goes there's trouble."

The three French officers shook hands and walked away quickly towards the town. "You really hate him, don't you?" said Archie Munro.

"I hate him for what he did, and because the people at our Embassy put up with it," said Jean . . . "Archie, there's something I've been meaning to tell you. I couldn't at Therapia, when Mummy never left us alone for a minute, but—do you remember that snapshot I took of him outside the café?"

"I'll never forget anything about that day," said Archie. "I'm the n.o. who couldn't tie a knot in a dish towel, remember?"

"I sent a copy of it to Kemal Pasha."

"Good God, Jean! You wrote a letter to that fellow?" Archie gasped.

"Not a letter. I just wrote on the back of the print, 'Pierre Loti Café, August 15th, 1922, 4 p.m.' and posted it to him at Angora."

"But what *for*?" persisted Archie.

"Well," said Jean, and her eyes were on the Hellespont, where so many ships, so many craft had gathered to prevent Kemal from crossing into Europe, "it was something my father said that gave me the idea. I'd a hunch, as Jeff Barrett says, that if our own people were scared to tackle Charles Cravache, why—Kemal Pasha might be just the man to do it."

20

"WELL, GOD BLESS Winston Churchill's impulsive heart, I think he's done the trick for us!" said Kemal with a laugh. He was sitting on the veranda of a beautiful old house in Bornova, reading the despatches which a staff car had brought up from Smyrna, and discussing their contents with General Ismet. The third person on the wisteria-wreathed veranda was the daughter of the owner of the house, a plump young Turkish woman dressed in black, whose eyes never left Kemal as he talked.

"The reports from Paris say Poincaré is furious," said Ismet. "When he puts Curzon on the carpet for all this, the noble Lord will regret his high and mighty attitude to *our* envoys."

"The French are realists; they won't go to war for Constantine, or even to keep us out of Thrace," said Kemal. "But I would give something to have seen Colonel Shuttleworth's face when Cravache, of all the French in Constantinople, arrived at Chanak to announce that the French contingent was to be withdrawn."

"Who's Colonel Shuttleworth?" pertly asked the young woman presiding over the breakfast table, and Kemal's bristling eye-brows drew together for a moment. But he answered her with his usual courtesy: "Colonel Shuttleworth is the British officer commanding at Chanak, Latife Hanim. A very fine soldier, like the Allied Commander-in-Chief, General Harington."

"Pasha is so generous!" gushed Latife. Her hard, thin-lipped little mouth, which contrasted oddly with her chubby face, was wreathed into a smile.

Kemal got up. "Time for work," he said briefly. "Ismet Pasha, are you ready?"

"Certainly. My warmest thanks, again, Latife Hanim, for inviting me to dine and sleep."

"Do come back again tonight, General!" said the girl. "Pasha'm—" to Kemal— "what time may we expect you back this evening?"

305

"I'll dine at the Konak tonight, Latife Hanim," said Kemal, picking up his gloves. "We mustn't disorganise your household more than we can help." He cut short her protests, bowing over her hand, and when they reached the foot of the marble steps and were out of earshot (although Latife, leaning over the rose-hung balcony, followed him with her eyes) he muttered to Ismet:

"Women! What a problem!"

"Not exactly a new one for you, my friend."

Kemal laughed. A staff officer was waiting beside the car, and very little was said on the seven-mile drive into Smyrna. Kemal read his despatches, and one personal letter, for the first part of the way, and the last, which took them through devastated Smyrna, offered nothing to encourage conversation. The only hopeful sign was that now, four days after the fire was extinguished, some effort was being made to get the street car rails relaid.

The duty officers leaped to their feet as the Pashas entered the Konak. It had not suffered in the fire, but like every other standing house in Smyrna it reeked of burning whether the windows were kept open or closed. Kemal nodded to Major Orman, who had now rejoined the army from Salihli, and told the senior officer present that he would see no one until his interview with General Pelle at half past nine.

"Bring coffee!" he snapped at Sergeant Ali as he entered his own room.

"Not for me," interposed Ismet Pasha. "Not so soon after that excellent breakfast!"

"I never think it's too soon for a cup of coffee."

"I know you don't." And better that than raki, Ismet thought. Kemal was drinking again since the Smryna fire, though not seriously; he lived, these days, by coffee and chain-smoking, and was already lighting the sixth cigarette of the morning.

"Is Yusuv Bey here?" he asked Ali, when the soldier-servant brought the coffee tray. "He is? Good. Tell him, half past nine." As the man went out he said to Ismet, "Yusuv, as Foreign Minister, will have to be present at my talk with the French General. I know he's an unofficial envoy, but I'd like to go through again the gist of what I'm going to say to him." He leaned back in his chair and enumerated the points on his long fingers. "One, I don't recognise the existence of a Neutral Zone. Two, I claim the right to march my army to the Sea of Marmara and then cross into Thrace in pursuit of a retreating enemy. Three, I won't attend any peace conference until all my conditions and terms have been accepted. That's about it, isn't it?"

"You haven't decided to tone it down a bit, since we talked at Bornova last night?"

"Not I," Kemal said lightly, and Ismet sighed. He stood by his chief through thick and thin, but this time the risk was horrible, the possible consequences unthinkable. Kemal was walking a tightrope over the gulf of a general war.

"I suppose I'd better have an interpreter for Yusuv Bey," said Kemal. "And a shorthand clerk to take it down verbatim. A communiqué must go off to the Assembly as soon as possible, so, Ismet, if you have private messages for Angora, get them ready. I'm going to send Orman up with the staff car today."

"Orman?"

"Yes. I want to send a reliable and tactful officer who can attend to some personal matters for me." He paused, frowning. "The fact is, I had a letter from Fikriye's doctor today."

"How is she?" asked Ismet sympathetically.

"Worse, if anything. But her doctor has been able to arrange for her to spend the winter in a German sanatorium, so we'll have to get her off to Europe."

And out of the picture, thought Ismet. He said compassionately, "Poor Fikriye Hanim! I don't believe she'll agree to leave Turkey for anyone but you."

"And I can't leave Smyrna—Orman will have to do his best."

"Is it *so* urgent that it can't wait until you're back in Angora?"

"Better for Fikriye if I'm not there at all." Kemal blew a ring of smoke. "I'm not in the mood for any hysterical scenes . . . And, by the way, you happened to mention Bornova. I'm going to have a word with the Vali and see if he can find me a place to live nearer town."

"Leave Bornova!" said Ismet in surprise. "But . . . it seemed such an ideal place for you, when Karshiyaka was mobbed on the night of the fire. At least you can spend your nights in quietness and country air."

"It's too far from the city and the Konak."

"The Muammer family will be very disappointed if you leave the house Latife Hanim put at your disposal. Not to mention the young lady herself."

"She's become very possessive since I moved out there. Did you hear her asking what time I'd be home for dinner?"

"Oh well, that's very natural. She's young, and excited at having the Gazi in her parents' house . . . And you must admit she makes a very charming hostess."

"She'd give a party in my honour every evening, if I permitted it. I told her the fire had put entertaining out of the question. Ismet, I don't mind being called the brigand chieftain, or the grey wolf of Anatolia, but I'm damned if I'll allow myself to be called the Turkish Nero, fiddling at Bornova while Smyrna was in flames!"

Or the man responsible for starting the second world war, thought Ismet, and breathed a silent prayer to Allah.

"Latife Hanim is a very attractive girl," he persisted. "*Turkish*, but educated in Europe, and of our own *faith*, and rich as well . . . I think she shows a great deal of poise for such a young person."

"When she wants to," Kemal said, getting up to indicate that their talk was over. "I was annoyed with her yesterday—her little pretentious ways, and her rudeness to that English lady who came out to Bornova and asked if she could sculpt my head—"

"They all want something of you, Pasha!" said Ismet. Kemal grinned as the door closed behind him. Yes, they all wanted something, except the one girl—the one who eluded him, who had given him everything but her promise that she would be his wife, the one with whom, as he now knew, his life would be fully and wonderfully completed. Evelyn! It was over two weeks since they parted at Ushak, and since she left Konya for Angora it was more difficult than ever to communicate with her. The telegraph installations had been destroyed in the great fire, and his own means of communication with the outside world was via the radio shack on the French Admiral's flagship in Smyrna Bay. He knew Evelyn was safe and well, and that had to suffice, but he longed to know what was going on at Angora, and if Barrett—lost sight of since the fire—had turned up there to importune her. At least, Orman's was a sure hand to carry a letter and the diamonds.

He rang his bell and sent for Evelyn's conducting officer. Major Orman came smartly in; he still looked pale and unwell, but his keen face was as humorous as ever, and Kemal, who had so many anxious faces round him, looked up at the man with pleasure.

308

"Orman Bey!" he said informally, "how long is it since you reported for duty at the Konak?"

"Four days, sir."

"Do you feel equal to a trip to Angora?"

"Anywhere the Gazi orders."

"Good for you. I want you to leave this afternoon with despatches for the Assembly. The replies are to be sent back by the regular courier service, and you will remain in Angora to carry out two personal and absolutely confidential missions for me."

"Sir."

"The first is to take a letter and a small package to Mrs. Barrett."

"With respect, sir, I don't know where the lady lives, in Angora."

"She has a rented house out at Kavaklidere. But judging by the press digests I see every morning, you're more likely to find her in the Listeners' Gallery of the Assembly."

Kemal looked up with the sudden smile which could be, when he wished, so charming, and Orman ventured to say, "It'll be a great pleasure to see Mrs. Barrett again, sir."

"Quite so." Kemal paused. "The other mission will take a little longer. My mother's niece, Fikriye Hanim, is seriously ill, and must spend the winter in Germany. You will escort her from Emine Hanim's house, where she's living at present, down to the railhead at Ismid, and put her aboard the train for Constantinople."

"It will be possible to pass the check point at Ismid, sir?"

"I'll arrange that with the British authorities here, later in the morning. And of course Fikriye Hanim will be met at Haydar Pasha station and taken to the Orient Express. Your job is to get her as far as Ismid—that's all."

"Very good, sir. But—"

"But what?"

Major Orman cleared his throat. "How soon must we leave for Ismid, after I get to Angora? Ladies take a long time to pack their personal belongings. If my wife were leaving for a winter in Europe, she'd take a week to get ready."

Kemal smiled again. "You may give Fikriye Hanim forty-eight hours—no more. I'll arrange the train reservations accordingly."

He lit a cigarette. He was thinking of the girl who, in a mountain dawn at Ushak, had neatly packed everything she owned into a haversack in ten minutes by his watch, in readiness for the gruelling journey back to Konya. He got up impatiently, and Orman, expecting his dismissal, was surprised to hear the Gazi say,

"Mrs. Barrett will have a great many questions to ask you about the state of matters here. Tell her things are not nearly as bad as some of her American colleagues make them out to be."

"I will, sir."

"Those fellows who're holed up in Athens now, or Cairo—and especially the men who've never even left Paris—are making a great to-do about the refugee problem."

Kemal had moved over to the window and was talking with his back to Major Orman. Across his shoulder Orman could see over the devastated Konak Square to the waterfront, where between fences of barbed wire the endless stream of refugees was being shepherded by Turkish gendarmes and sailors of the Royal Navy to the lighters which still came and went to the steamers in the bay. At that moment of time there was no sadder sight anywhere in the world. Kemal had published a harsh decree that all refugee males between the ages of eighteen and forty-five were to be taken to temporary camps behind Smyrna as a precaution against their being drafted into the Greek Army when they arrived at the Piraeus. It was a military necessity, but the suffering it caused when families were torn apart was hardly measurable in human terms. Kemal bleakly surveyed the scene.

"May I make a suggestion, sir?" Orman was bold enough to say.

"Certainly."

"I'd like to tell Mrs. Barrett what a fine job the American Near East Relief people are doing in providing clothes and food for the refugees. I think she'd like to hear that."

Kemal turned round. "Yes, she would," he said. "But above all, Orman, impress upon her that there has been no massacre. I've already had more than enough of the fiction of the Smyrna massacre."

"Yes, sir." Orman had just seen the figures, compiled by neutral observers, of the loss of life during the fire and the accompanying disturbances: they added up to two thousand dead.

In Turkish terms, it was a long way from a calamity, and he could truthfully say that there had been no massacre at Smyrna.

"Report to me personally at two o'clock," said Kemal. "That's all, Orman."

Alone, he sat down at his desk and pulled writing materials towards him. He had fifteen minutes before the first appointment of the day—just time enough to write a letter to Evelyn. "*Ma bien-aimée*," he began with confidence, and then sat wondering. He had never written a love-letter in his life.

"My beloved, at last I can send you a letter by a—"

A tentative knock fell on the door, and the senior duty officer came in.

"What is it?" Kemal snapped.

"The Foreign Minister has asked to see the Gazi."

"I'm seeing him at half past nine, with General Pelle."

"Sir, the French general has not arrived, and the Minister says the matter is very urgent."

"Show him in."

Kemal had just time to slip his letter into the desk drawer before Yusuv entered, wearing morning coat and kalpak, and taking his position as the Assembly's representative very seriously indeed.

"Pasha, something extraordinary has happened," he burst out. "A French officer has arrived from the flagship with a message that General Pelle is indisposed, and is still at Constantinople. We're asked to receive this officer as his representative."

"A naval officer?"

"Army—and only with the rank of major."

Kemal scowled. "If they think we're prepared to receive any underling who comes with letters from Constantinople, they're very far mistaken. He *has* got letters, I suppose?"

"Oh yes, Pasha, the accreditations are quite in order, as far as that goes; they've been examined in the anteroom. But the insult to you—sending a man of that rank as their envoy—!"

"What's the fellow's name?"

"Major Charles Cravache."

Kemal had been sitting with his elbows on the desk, moving his left thumb across his chin. Now he sat up as alertly as a royal tiger moving to its kill.

"So!" he said. "Fresh from his recent successes at Chanak— Monsieur Cravache! This should be interesting, Yusuv!"

"But surely you won't see him, Pasha? What if I talk to him, with an interpreter?"

Kemal laughed. "No, my friend," he said, "We'll do it the other way around. We won't increase Cravache's self-importance by granting him an interview with you present, and an interpreter and a stenographer to record his immortal words. I'll have a chat with him myself, but strictly off the record. Ask them to bring him in at half past nine exactly."

Five minutes left. Kemal closed his eyes, and turned his enormous powers of concentration on his mental file of Charles Cravache. One tangible item had been added to it since he discussed the Frenchman with Evelyn Barrett, and he visualised the envelope now in his safe at Chankaya, and the little snapshot it contained. He was ready for the encounter, though apparently working on his papers, when *le commandant* Charles Cravache was announced.

"Cravache, representing the High Commissioner of the French Republic, your Excellency," was how he announced himself, standing at attention in front of Kemal's desk. He was not invited to sit down.

"Major Cravache, it's a long time since we met," Kemal replied, and the Frenchman raised his eyebrows. He was in parade dress, wearing medal ribbons and a *fourragère d'honneur*; in his gloved hand, instead of the riding-whip, he carried a small brief-case.

"I have not had the honour of meeting your Excellency before," he said impassively. Kemal smiled.

"Perhaps not," he said. "The Great War left its mark on everybody, and some of us may no longer be—recognisable. And now I come to think of it, the French tourist I arrested for disturbing the peace in Syria, and had deported from Latakia, was a civilian. He went by the name of Charles Ventoux."

"Your Excellency has had a very varied life," said the Frenchman. The arrogant mask of his face had not altered in the slightest; he might well have been prepared for Kemal's inconvenient memories of the past. Only his eyes, small and shrewd as an elephant's, went darting about the room, from Kemal to the window and back to the papers on the desk.

"Your own life has not been without variety," said Kemal. "I hear you went to Chanak two days ago, to inform the British

312

garrison that their gallant allies were deserting them and would withdraw their force—which was only a token force—from Chanak town."

"The withdrawal was ordered by the government at Paris, sir."

"But you enjoyed carrying the order, didn't you? Tell me, how did you feel when you saw the Tricolore hauled down at Chanak? Shame—or jubilation? When the British were left alone to face whatever may be in store for them—for of course the Italian jackals followed after you—did it compensate you for the day, four years ago, when Allenby's officers put you under close arrest for desertion in the face of the enemy? And that didn't happen to Monsieur Ventoux, it happened to Captain Cravache: I heard the whole story at Nablus, after you broke your parole at the ford of the Jordan."

"This is a pure fabrication!" said Cravache, flushing red. "Sir, you are insulting France in my person!"

"France in your person!" said Kemal. He tilted his chair back on two legs, and his hearty laugh rang out as he looked up at the tall Frenchman. "That's a good one! You think of yourself as France already, do you? Tell me, is it true what they say in Constantinople, that your friend Monsieur Franklin-Bouillon is urging you to leave the army and go in for politics?"

"Some approaches have been made to me," said Cravache icily. "I have not yet decided what is best for the French people."

"If the French people are fools enough to fall for the kind of lying you've been doing for the past few minutes, then they really will deserve you," said Kemal. "However, that's none of my business. Have you brought anything in writing from the High Commissioner?"

The gloved hand opened the brief-case and handed a letter across the desk to Kemal. He lit a cigarette, taking his time, before he opened and read it.

"You know the contents of this letter?" he said, looking at Cravache with his eyebrows drawn together in a scowl.

"I do—Excellency."

"The gist of it is that the French, speaking through the High Commission, ask me to respect the Neutral Zone and withdraw my forces from what they're pleased to call its frontier. In return, they assure me of their support at the peace conference, whenever it takes place."

"That is correct."

"Support Turkey against the British and the Greeks, that is? Even though the British are officially your Allies?"

Cravache was silent. His mind, tenacious and unscrupulous though it was, had not the speed in argument of Kemal's.

"Go back to Constantinople, Commandant Cravache," Kemal was saying. "Tell the High Commissioner that this document is entirely without value, because I refuse to recognise the existence of a Neutral Zone. I will pursue the enemy until they sue for peace, and at the conference I will make no bid for the support of France. Tell the Commissioner the French can't buy me: I am not to be bought."

"You were thankful enough for French support last year, when Monsieur Franklin-Bouillon helped to negotiate the Treaty of Angora."

"But that *was* a treaty, open and above-board. There were no secret offers of connivance, such as you were chosen—most appropriately—to present to me."

Kemal got up and walked round his desk to reach the Frenchman. Cravache was six foot four in height, he towered over the smaller, slighter man, and yet he instinctively stepped back a pace, away from the furious energy of the Commander-in-Chief.

"I want to give you a word of advice," Kemal said softly. "If I were you, I should ask at once to be posted back to France. That will save you the humiliation of being declared *persona non grata* in Turkey as soon as I assume the power."

"On what grounds do you threaten me?" grated Cravache. The strange lines of his face were concentrated in hate.

"On the grounds of your complicity in the Trakas murder," said Kemal. "You were careless, Major Cravache. There were two reliable witnesses to your presence at that café before Riachi died, and one of them took a confession from him there. This witness also took a photograph of yourself with the Syrian, Khalil. That photograph is now in my possession, and will be produced in evidence if and when I decide that the case should be reopened."

Cravache opened his mouth, but no sound came. After a moment he said, "I don't believe you."

"You'll believe me when you see the photograph," said Kemal

genially. "In court, that is. In the new Turkey there will be no special conditions for foreign criminals. You'll have to stand your trial like the rest."

He stubbed out his cigarette and reached for the handbell. "Get out of Turkey, Cravache," he said. "Give the people of France the pleasure of your company. We've got troubles enough of our own without having to put up with *you*."

*   *   *

On the day a convoy of discharged wounded, all armed, left Konya for Angora with Evelyn Barrett in one of the trucks, the news of the Smyrna conflagration was beginning to leak out to the world. She heard about it as soon as she entered Kemal's capital, for the citizens were running beside the convoy, shouting the news to the excited men, and there was so much cheering and laughter that she could hardly believe the tale was true. As soon as she went to the Osmanli Bank to draw on her account, however, the news was confirmed by the Bank's Swiss manager, Mr. Bruno Rossi.

"It's only too true, Mrs. Barrett," Mr. Rossi said. "What a calamity! What a ghastly end to Kemal Pasha's victory! I understand that practically every possession of the European community in Smyrna has been destroyed."

"But the people—what about the people? Was there much loss of life?"

"The Constantinople papers talk of massacre, but we must hope it wasn't as bad as that. Mrs. Barrett, how white you are! Let me get you a glass of mineral water—"

While he was getting it, Evelyn struggled for self-control. A destructive fire was bad enough, but *massacre*! The one thing that would stain Kemal's name for ever, the one thing she had begged him to prevent! She remembered the slaughter of Armenians in Cilicia, about which he had spoken so coolly, she remembered the old Greek woman's tale of Turkish cruelty at Afyon Karahisar. But the habit of concealing her feelings in public was so strong that when Mr. Rossi came back she was able to say:

"Do forgive me. I saw the start of the San Francisco fire when I was a little girl, and it left me with such a horror of burning . . . Besides, my husband was in Smyrna. I must try to find out what has happened to him."

315

"Oh dear! I thought Mr. Barrett was in Constantinople. Perhaps he got back there before the fire started. Some of the foreign correspondents must have left just after the Gazi's press conference."

"What press conference?"

Mr. Rossi handed her a copy of a French-language paper. "Read this at your leisure," he said. "Kemal Pasha's remarks are well worth pondering. And remember, if you want to join your husband in Constantinople, don't hesitate to let me know. Head Office sent us a very good automobile recently, and it goes down to Ismid every Saturday at noon. With a Swiss or an American passport one can easily pass the check point, and get a seat on the train."

"Thank you," said Evelyn. She hardly took in what the banker was saying. But when she found an araba she made the man drive to the telegraph office first and sent a cable to Donnelly. "Back at Angora," she wrote. "What news Jeff since Smyrna fire?" Then she went home, or to all that she could call a home, and in spite of a lively welcome from Ayesha and her husband it was strange and lonely to be back in the little house at the end of the poplar lane. After her solitary supper Evelyn took the yellow pins out of the war map on the table, and studied the positions of the Allies—now only the British—in the Neutral Zone. Kemal's demands had shocked her, in their implications, almost as much as the story of the Smyrna fire. There was of course no reason—given his passion for security—why he should have told her of his plan to invade Thrace, and yet she felt saddened, as if he had shown some lack of confidence in herself, whom he said he trusted utterly. She realised that when Kemal told her he would never carry the war across the Aegean, he had said nothing about fighting on the European side of the Sea of Marmara.

Next day a cable from Donnelly ordered Evelyn to assume the full duties of the *Clarion*'s correspondent in Angora but made no mention of Jeff. She walked into the city, weary with anxiety. Jeff and she were finished, and yet Evelyn had loved him once, as she understood love then, and the thought that he might have died a dreadful death in the Smyrna fire was extremely painful. She plunged into work: the director of the Angora press arranged at once for her accreditation to the Listeners' Gallery of the Grand National Assembly, and complimented her on the "magnificent

316

story from Dumlu Pinar". Evelyn had hardly understood until then that her first by-lined story in the *Clarion* had been picked up by the news agencies and widely circulated; much of it had appeared, though in a garbled form, in the Angora papers. She found this had improved her status with the stringer, Abdul, who no longer sulked at having to work for a woman. Evelyn Hanim was the Lady of Dumlu Pinar, who had written the story of the Greek atrocities for all the world to read, and incidentally had beaten two of Abdul's hated rivals to the story with a good forty-eight hours to spare. Mrs. Barrett, who now mysteriously appeared to be called Anderson, was treated with great respect by every Turkish reporter in the Gallery.

The Assembly was in session all round the clock, for Kemal scrupulously referred to it in every phase of the new situation developing since the Greeks fled from Anatolia. The Deputies fell upon his messages with shouts, tears of joy, wild arguments and even gunfire; Evelyn twice had to duck beneath the level of the balcony when some excited legislator, drunk with the desire to go to war with Britain, emptied his pistol into the air. Once a lamp, fortunately not lit, was shot to fragments in a shower of petroleum which cooled the squabbling Deputies wedged into the school desk directly underneath. The reporters roared with laughter, the French "observers" in the opposite gallery shook their heads. The National Assembly, in the absence of its lion-tamer, was more like a zoo than ever.

The Assembly missed Kemal, and Evelyn Barrett missed him, body and soul. She loved him with a passion all the more devouring because Kemal had given her the first complete experience of physical love she had ever known. But her mind, which meshed as easily with his as their bodies had joined in fulfilment, was still alive to the one great obstacle to their happiness. The victory of Turkish independence was being celebrated all through the East— but not as a triumph for nationalism. The Moslems of Egypt were chafing against the British protectorate because of a Moslem leader's victory. The rich Moslems of Calcutta had bought an aeroplane for Kemal's own use; the poor Moslems of all India had subscribed money for a presentation sword, sent with an address of congratulation so eloquent that in London the Secretary of State for India saw trouble ahead for the British Raj. Kemal had shaken the world, and Evelyn, who had once compared him to Garibaldi, now saw that he was hailed as a *Moslem* Garibaldi, whether he liked it or not.

On the seventeenth of September she cabled again to Donnelly, saying she had no news of Jeff, and asking what he had heard. It was three days before an answer came, and then it read:

"jeff now unhospitalized etfiling great copy exchanak stop want you continue send color stuff deputies horsing around etcetera regards donnelly"

So Jeff had been in hospital! Jeff was at Chanak, where the big news story was! Evelyn Anderson wrote so well that afternoon that Donnelly sent her another cable of congratulation. He then looked up the profile of Mussolini which she had written in the spring and to which the *Clarion* had tagged Jeff's by-line, and read it very carefully indeed.

The Turkish reporters were now almost the only people Evelyn could talk to in Angora. The diplomatic receptions had stopped in Kemal's absence, pretty Feride had gone bravely off to Afyon to be with her wounded husband, and the American ladies were still working in the refugee camp at Mudanya. There was literally no one to whom she could confide her anxieties about religion, for the Rossis, who often invited her to their house, were Catholics, and at the same time preoccupied with events in Italy, where the Fascists had taken over the city government of Milan. Evelyn nursed her problem in silence, wishing she knew more about her own faith and whether it could be reconciled at any point with Islam. There was something harrowing in reading her mother's letters, for Mrs. Anderson would have accepted the Prophet Mahomed with the same alacrity as she had already accepted Buddha and Mary Baker Eddy; but the Norwegian blood, the blood of the sailor from Bergen with its heritage of stubborn Lutheranism, did not come to Evelyn from her mother. She worried herself thin and white-faced, the army suntan all worn off in the Assembly, and Ayesha killed one of the scrawny fowls and made her eat.

On the day when, as Kemal had predicted, two Greek generals staged a *coup d'état* against King Constantine, Evelyn greeted an old acquaintance outside the Assembly.

"Major Orman! How good to see you again!"

"And I'm delighted to see you, Mrs Barrett. I came up from

Smyrna with despatches for the Speaker of the Assembly, and heard you were in the Gallery. Your—stringer, is it?—told me you would be leaving shortly, so I thought it better to wait here. The Assembly seems noisier than ever!"

"They're all going wild over the news from Greece. You've heard it, I suppose "

"Have I not! But we've been expecting it for days. At Smyrna we're able to keep a close watch on Chios, and we knew the two Generals—Gonatis and Plastiras—were plotting to lead a revolt against the King."

"The Gazi predicted that King Constantine would soon be in flight from Athens . . . How is the Gazi, Major Orman?"

"It's his energy that keeps us all going."

"I know."

"I have a letter and a package for you. May I drive you home and hand them over?"

"I have to file my cable first. It won't take ten minutes, and then can you come back with me for supper?"

"I wish I could, but I have to go on to Madame Zübeyde's house. We'll go right down to the telegraph office."

Major Orman dismissed his driver and took the wheel of the staff car himself. He could see that Evelyn was trembling with impatience when she came out of the office, and when they were only half-way to Kavaklidere he pulled in to the side of the road and stopped the car. It was a desolate spot, with only a small boy herding goats to be seen, and sunset beginning to glow on the mountain tops.

He handed Evelyn Kemal's letter and the jeweller's case, its white paper wrapping creased now, but the red wax seal intact, and saw how she flushed and folded her hands over the things Kemal had sent her. "I'll open these later," she said, not looking at him. "Talk to me now, Major Orman. What are things really like in Smyrna?"

"These have been hard times for everybody, Mrs. Barrett. I missed the worst of it, because I was fool enough to come down with dysentery and was in hospital at Salihli; the fire was more or less under control by the time I got to Smyrna. The whole city is gutted, except the Turkish quarter, and the Gazi is talking already about the new city he'll build where the old Smyrna stood."

"So he's going to build a new Smyrna as well as a great Angora?"

"I don't know if you can see it from our point of view, but the old Smyrna was such a symbol of foreign occupation—European commerce and latterly the Greek invasion—we aren't too unhappy at the idea of starting again with a clean sheet."

"But the loss of life—the suffering—"

"Was a great deal less than might have been expected. The refugee problem, of course, has always been acute, but the Gazi gave the Allied commanders in the bay an ultimatum to get the whole lot off by the thirtieth of this month, and they're really moving now."

"The Deputies have been talking about a massacre of Christians."

"The wish is father to the thought with some of them, I'm ashamed to say! Of course there wasn't any massacre! The refugees went crazy, and there was some stabbing and shooting as they fought for places in the boats, but the Royal Navy kept splendid order on the first night and until the fire was over."

"Thank heaven for that!" said Evelyn. "But Major Orman, who did start the fire?"

"God knows. The Greeks blame us, of course, and we blame them, but however the first spark caught, it was the wind that fanned it. The imbat wind, madame, blowing always in the same direction—the imbat was the real arsonist of the Smyrna fire."

Evelyn was silent. Major Orman, compassionately studying the down-bent, ash-blond head and the hands clasped protectively round Kemal's offerings, said gently:

"May I add my word of thanks, as your conducting officer, for the story you wrote about Dumlu Pinar? The wonderful story, which made us all so proud! I had the privilege of being with the Gazi when he heard it for the first time."

Colour came into Evelyn's pale face. "I knew it reached Kemal Pasha," she said. "He sent me a telegram of thanks. But I didn't know how it got to Smyrna."

"The full text was cabled on to us as soon as it appeared in Chicago, before the fire of course. I had the honour of translating it for the Commander-in-Chief."

"What did he say?" breathed Evelyn.

"He was very much moved. He sat quite still until I'd finished reading, and then he said 'The truth at last, thank God! You get the truth from Evelyn Hanim!' "

✻   ✻   ✻

Evelyn parted reluctantly from Major Orman at the entrance to the poplar lane. There was still so much she wanted to hear, about the nurses, and about Captain Riza, and always, more about Kemal. But what she wanted to know most of all, Kemal's real intentions towards the British, she could not possibly discuss with one of the Commander-in-Chief's own staff officers, and in any case, she was impatient to read his letter. The days were growing shorter, and she had to light the lamp to read the sprawling lines.

> *"Smyrne, le 21 septembre 1922*
> *Ma bien-aimée,*

At last I can send you a letter by a trustworthy messenger, and with it a gift I bought for you the day after I entered Smyrna. I've had to carry it with me ever since, thanks to the disagreeable incidents of which you know. Wear it for me until I can give you a wedding ring.

My Evelyn, the time seems long without you, and it is hard to be patient when we are apart. I am trying also to be patient with the British, to allow them to withdraw from their present attitude with dignity, but Mr. Lloyd George seems determined to renew the war on a major scale. However, Sir Charles Harington is a man of sense and must realise the sympathy of the world is with us now. The next few days should decide the matter. I embrace you—K."

Evelyn was smiling as she read. The letter was so exactly *him*—the precision, the sparing words of love, the mingling of the great theme of his life with their own affairs, that Evelyn looked up involuntarily, half expecting to see Kemal sitting on the comfortless divan, with a glass of raki in his hand. Looking back at the letter she wished, as so often before, that she could read Arabic script, and so understand what he wrote to her in his own language. In French, she thought, he had not been able fully to express his horror at the Smyrna fire. "The disagreeable incidents of which you know"—the holocaust which destroyed a city was *surely* more to him than *des incidents désagréables*! Kemal was ruthless

321

to his enemies, she knew, but *surely* not to the homeless and the weak!

Surely—it was the operative word, the hopeful word; it encouraged Evelyn to open the little package and look at the gift he had chosen for her. Inside the paper was a red morocco leather box, with the jeweller's name stamped in gilt on the white satin lining of the lid. His shop must be a heap of ruins now.

On a bed of white velvet lay a diamond brooch in the form of a crescent, about three inches long from tip to tip, made of three rows of beautifully graduated stones. Evelyn laid it on the palm of her hand. She knew something about diamonds, for John Anderson had given his wife many beautiful jewels, and their daughter was sure that these were diamonds of the first water. This was no ordinary present: it was the gift of a Chief of State to the woman of his choice.

It was also a little old-fashioned, a little heavy, like the furnishings of Chankaya; Evelyn had seen some of her mother's older friends wearing similar brooches in their lace jabots. But for those wealthy San Francisco matrons the Crescent had no religious significance. What significance did Kemal mean it to have for Evelyn?

He chose the first thing that appealed to him and I love it dearly, she told herself, holding the brooch up to see the many-faceted diamonds sparkle in the lamplight. But she knew that Kemal was far too subtle to have chosen such a gift without reflection: the diamonds formed the Crescent which had been for over a thousand years the adversary of the Cross. Evelyn's head went down in despair on her hands. Could she do it? Even for Kemal, could she renounce the Cross?

After that Sunday night at Konya when the Christian message, so humbly presented, had struck home to her heart, Evelyn Barrett had unconsciously made a bargain in her spirit, and had prayed as so many had prayed before her for a sign of the will of the One God. If a child were to be born of those secret hours snatched from the battle, would not that solve all the problems of her change of faith, and join her life irrevocably with Kemal's? Reliving every moment of their nights in the book-lined room at Afyon and in the little house at Ushak full of the smell of burning, it seemed to Evelyn incredible that she should not have conceived. Unlike Jeff Barrett, whose crude method of denying life had been responsible for much of their disharmony, Kemal's perfection had been in the completeness of his love. But three days after her return to Angora, the dream was over for that time. It was kismet. And Evelyn thought of Freud, whose teachings she had affected to despise, and wondered if "subconsciously", that favourite Freudian word, her whole reckless journey to the front had been in search of a father for her child?

She put the brooch away at last in the locked attaché case in which she kept her passport and cheque book, and also Kemal's other gift, the tesbih of red coral. She stood running the beads through her fingers, in the bedroom now faintly lit by the new moon. The crescent moon, shining for Kemal! Ninety-nine beads, three times the thirty-three divine names of God, and the One Hundredth Name, which is Unnameable—

Was it possible, she wondered, to persuade herself that the Final Name was the Name of Christ the King?

21

THE NEW MOON BROUGHT with it a change in the weather. Rain and wind lashed the Angora plateau for a day and a night, and the first snows of winter were seen on the summit of Mount Elma. At night, lying in bed, Evelyn could hear the howling of wolves on the steppe, and thought of the shepherd boy's song on that golden morning when Kemal asked her to marry him.

He had written that the next few days might settle the situation in the Neutral Zone. The following day he took his own steps towards a drastic settlement by ordering his troops to enter the Neutral Zone at Ezine, a village to the south-east of Chanak. No shots were fired on either side, although British troops were at once in contact with the Turks. Kemal let it be known that his men had orders not to attack the British: they were officially in pursuit of the Greek enemy, and on their way to the sea at Erenköy. He repeated that as he refused to recognise the existence of a Neutral Zone the Turkish troops had violated no frontier. They were on the march across their own country in the legitimate pursuit of a flying foe.

Although the tiny Italian contingent had left Chanak at the same time as the Tricolore was hauled down and the French left the British in the lurch, Britain without her Allies continued the build-up of armed force at Chanak town. The aircraft carrier *Pegasus* was ordered to the Dardanelles with seven Short seaplanes aboard to join the five capital ships and nine destroyers already on the scene at the time of the earlier Emergency at the Chatalja Lines. The garrison had been reinforced by Scottish troops from the Abbassia barracks in Cairo, and the 2nd Battalion of the Rifle Brigade was due for embarkation at Southampton. But Ismid was still vulnerable, and Kemal's forces were now there in strength.

As the revolt of the Greek generals spread to the mainland, the monarchy and the government were living through their final

324

hours. Lloyd George's government, too, was hurrying to its doom, as public feeling hardened against Britain's engagement in a major war. On the same day as the "frontier" was crossed the British Cabinet sent Kemal an invitation to a meeting at Mudanya to discuss terms for an armistice, and this invitation he ignored. He insisted that his just demands should be satisfied before he took part in any form of peace conference.

This firmness of course delighted the Assembly. Evelyn listened to speeches declaring that Kemal should be "ordered" to pursue the Greeks not only into Eastern Thrace but westwards across the line of the Maritza, to fight in Macedonia, to liberate his own birthplace, Saloniki, from the Greek usurper, and for all her confidence in his judgment she wondered how long he could resist that steady pressure from the men whose votes he needed to maintain him in power. Yet if he went to war with Britain he might well lose everything, all the power and glory he had already won: the Sultan would be confirmed on his throne, the dream of a Turkish Republic shattered, and Mustafa Kemal again an unemployed general, the man who had risked the peace of the world for—what had he once said? "the nation and his own satisfaction".

In the middle of those crucial days Evelyn received a lengthy cablegram from Donnelly:

"jeff going visit liberated cities then probably angorawarding stop would like you now consider following proposition . . ."

The proposition which followed took Evelyn aback. It almost, but not quite, distracted her thoughts from the information that Jeff was in all probability already on his way to Angora. The liberated cities (and the cable was so long that Donnelly might well have used two more words to identify them positively as Brusa and Eskishehir) sounded like an odd assignment, and she wondered how Jeff liked being pulled out of Chanak at such a time, but as things were going in Athens it was Halliday who had the big chance now. For under the pressure of the generals the Greek King abdicated, as Kemal had foretold, on the twenty-seventh of September, and took the well-worn road to Rome. The Prime Minister and General Hajianestis were indicted, and would probably be executed in the near future. When this news reached Angora Evelyn stayed in the press gallery just long enough to see the Assembly's first frenzy of exultation, and then went out.

325

Events were racing forward now, just as they had raced forward from the opening of Kemal's offensive to the Smyrna fire; Jeff and Kemal himself might both be in Angora soon, and she had hardly any time left to make her great decision.

She walked uphill, away from the Assembly, and into the bazaar. It was comparatively empty; the usual strolling, chaffering crowds were hanging round the outside of the parliament building, scaring the tethered horses and hoping to hear more sensational news—perhaps of Lloyd George's downfall, following King Constantine's. There was pathetically little to buy on the food stalls: the sacks of peas and beans were folded down in rings over the small quantities on sale, and the dress goods in bright colours of purple and red were thin and shoddy. This was Angora, the loyal city, which had given its all for independence, food and clothes and even shelter, and where the people had a fierce pride which made them look haughtily at the foreign woman walking by in her yellow cotton dress. Evelyn was wearing the black headscarf bought at Afyon Karahisar. It was more comfortable than a hat in the windy weather, and besides it had special associations with the days when she wore it above a soldier's greatcoat, and followed the Crescent and the Star.

The muezzin was chanting the early afternoon call to prayer from the minaret of the Haji Bayram mosque. The chant rang out over the old city, Come to prayer, come to security! God is great! There is no God but Allah! And Evelyn's heart replied Tell me, tell me, tell me, to the sweet jingling tune, made for the Salvation Army tambourines, which had never been long out of her head since that Sunday night in Konya:

Tell me the same old story
When you have cause to fear
That this world's empty glory
Is costing me too dear

Only there was nobody to tell her, and the Sankey hymn (it was odd how she remembered every word of it) was almost the only weapon she had to do battle for Christian convictions nourished on little, so far, but her recollections of a Lutheran Sunday School in San Francisco, and visits with her father to a quiet church with cool grey walls and a statue of Melancthon in one window bay. Who was Melancthon, anyway? If he could be set

326

down here in the steep streets of Angora's bazaar, could he help Evelyn Barrett to define her true faith? Or should she rest her faith in Kemal Pasha, who had no faith of his own?

"Lord, I believe; help thou mine unbelief." Those words came back from somewhere, and Evelyn thought it was the Bible. There was no Bible in the hundred books on Ahmed's clumsy shelves, books she had carefully selected in Rome and Constantinople as interesting and necessary. *Clausewitz on War*, of course: she had brought that all the way from America; why had she brought Clausewitz instead of a New Testament?

Evelyn was through the bazaar now, and climbing up the road leading to the citadel. It was little more than a track, made through the centuries by millions of work-worn feet to the gate in the double walls, in some places twenty feet thick, which the Galatians built between the ancient towers. The inner citadel was a city within a city, where picturesque houses with wooden balconies and mud walls stood lopsidedly on narrow streets where children played with broken marbles depicting the heads or hands of long-forgotten gods. Women came to their doors to look at Evelyn above their veils as she made her way to what seemed to be a high place in the northern part of the citadel. It was Ak Kale, the White Fortress, and as she sat down to rest among the stones Evelyn thought of all the wars through which Angora had lived from the time of Tamerlane to the days, just a year in the past, when King Constantine had come so near the city. What God had they worshipped, those old inhabitants, before St. Paul scolded them about circumcision or Gabriel revealed the Koran to Mahomed? Who was the God of the Sumerians, or the Hittites? In what heaven were the souls of those who in this place had worshipped the Moon god, or the nature goddess, Cybele?

Lord, I believe; help thou mine unbelief.

Evelyn was sitting not far from the edge of the cliff which fell from the White Fortress in a sheer drop to a little river three hundred feet below. When she looked south she could see right across the empty plateau to Chankaya on its hill, the chalets all hidden by the vines and fruit trees, and nothing between Chankaya and the red roofs of the town but that waste land where from Major Orman's car she had seen no human being but the little goatboy leading home his flock. And suddenly she thought of Chicago, and the towers which had sprung up round the log hut which marked where Fort Dearborn once stood, and in a moment of vision Evelyn was able to picture the fine city Kemal would build upon this waste: the tree-shaded boulevards, the University, the stately Parliament, the Opera House. At the thought of the Opera House Evelyn's spirit faltered. What would it be like to be present at the opera in Angora, wearing her diamond crescent, the wife of the President of the Turkish Republic? The vision faded, there was nothing left but the dusty fields, the distant steppe, but the great temptation was still powerful. From the heights of the citadel Evelyn had seen all the kingdoms of the world and all the glory of them.

"I must find out something for myself," she said aloud, and left the broken columns and stones of the White Fortress to walk back down the hill. There was one place where, she thought, she could learn more about Islam than Mr. Fister's prosy explanation had told her; it was in a mosque, a place she had never ventured to enter, and almost in her path lay the Haji Bayram, where the muezzin had chanted his call to prayer. She knew this was the place of worship to which Kemal had been forced to go before the inauguration of the Grand National Assembly: she had not known that the side road leading towards it ran through one of the most pleasant quarters of the town, where a few old trees grew, that rarity in Angora, and little quiet shops sold tesbihs and copies of the Koran in a variety of bindings. The mosque was small, and stood beside the ruins of yet another cult—the temple raised in the second century before Christ and converted by the Romans to the worship of the Emperor Augustus. Mosque and temple, holy man and dead Emperor, were sunk together in the golden depths of a September afternoon.

Evelyn entered the courtyard. It was between the prescribed hours of prayer, and there were no men gathered round the ablutions fountain. A few women, veiled in black, were standing close to one of the walls, with their hands lifted in prayer, and two of them were crying. For what? For whom? For some soldier dead at Dumlu Pinar, for a child to be born without a father? Evelyn looked at them uncertainly. Had Moslem women no right to go inside a mosque? She pulled her own scarf half across her face, and went up to the main door. The aged guardian made no attempt to stop her, but indicated that she must take off her shoes. She pushed open the inner door leading to the place of worship. There were only two old men in the tiny mosque, dressed in the turbans and kaftans of a vanishing Turkey; they both looked up angrily when Evelyn came in. But she knelt down so quickly, and at a distance from them, putting her veiled head in her hands so humbly, that the old men were mollified, and returned to their own silent prayers. When Evelyn dared to look through her fingers she saw, first, an expanse of emerald green carpet, the Prophet's own colour, and then light coming in through stained glass windows, just as in a Christian church. There were unfamiliar things like the minber, and the mihrab oriented towards Mecca, and ancient porcelain tiles glowing in scarlet, mauve and terra-cotta, but the whole mosque breathed restfulness and a curiously light-hearted peace. Evelyn sat back on her heels, with her hands folded in her lap. So this was the heart of the mystery, this peace, which must surely come from submission to the will of Allah; this right to pray alone, unprompted by a priest, this Quaker quietude! I can accept it, she thought, as she yielded to the second temptation; I can keep in my heart what I believe to be the Final Name, I can have Kemal. And then, as if she were a predestined apostle on the Damascus road instead of a perplexed and passionate girl, light-headed from overstrain and lack of food and sleep, it seemed to Evelyn that she heard a Voice not of this world proclaiming:

"I am the way, the truth and the life; no man cometh unto the Father, but by me."

It was only an instant of revelation, and it left Evelyn with no sense of having undergone a mystical experience. But the splendid words stayed in her shaken heart as she slipped out of the Haji Bayram mosque as quietly as she had entered, and set out on foot along the road back to Kavaklidere. They came and went, illuminating her mind, as she walked along in the gathering dusk to the rhythm of the hymn tune which had been haunting her for days:

> Yes! and when that world's glory
> Is dawning on my soul,
> Tell me the old, old story
> "Christ Jesus made thee whole."

No man cometh unto the Father, but by me. It all seemed so far away, the day when Evelyn Anderson might see the glory of the life to come, the Christian heaven, and all she wanted on earth was so very close to her; yet the words of the Saviour were explicit, and she knew now that she could never deny them. She was in tears as she went up the lane between the poplars, and saw Ahmed rounding up his poultry in the pear orchard. Evelyn hurried on, she was in no mood to chat with Ahmed then. But somebody— unveiled and wearing what looked like a kaftan, was waiting for her in the shadowy patio, leaning against the coping of the well.

"Is that you, Ayesha?" said Evelyn uncertainly.

The woman stood up, and spoke in Turkish. "It is Fikriye," she said. "You and I have an account to settle, Evelyn Hanim. Christian bitch! You made the Gazi send me away from Angora."

"I think you'd better come indoors," said Evelyn. "You're not very well—you're shivering, Fikriye Hanim."

Repeating "I am well, I am well, I *am* well!" the Turkish girl followed Evelyn into the livingroom. By the light of the petroleum lamp she was seen to be wearing not a kaftan but a long black coat with a fur collar, and carrying a soft leather bag. She had nothing on her head or hands, and Evelyn saw that those hands were scratched and bleeding. She also, and in one look, took in the ruin of Fikriye's beauty: the eyes reddened by constant weeping, the whole face sharpened and emaciated by the progress of her disease. Fikriye's voice, when she spoke, was hoarse with tears.

"You sent that man to Emine's house, to tell me I must go to Europe, to a sanatorium—"

"What man?"

"Major Orman."

Orman—who brought the diamond brooch from Smyrna, the love-gift of a man who, secret and devious as ever, had used his trusted servant for two errands! Aghast, Evelyn said,

"Believe me, Fikriye Hanim, I didn't know that Major Orman intended to see you. But he is a good man, you can trust yourself with him, if he is going to take you on a journey you will be safe with him. And in the sanatorium you will be well again—"

"If Kemal were here now I would kill him," said the girl. "He knows that I have worshipped him all my life. He discarded me for you, and now you have persuaded him to send me away from Turkey!"

"No one could persuade Kemal to be so cruel," said Evelyn. "I am sure his only concern is for your health."

"You made him do it!" again Fikriye said. "*I* know how you've

330

thrown yourself at him! You even followed him to the front, like a common soldier's prostitute—"

"Oh, hush!" said Evelyn. "You don't know what you're saying. You must have walked a long way, and you're exhausted. Did you come from Emine's house at Chubuk now?"

"I came from Chankaya, which used to be my home," the Turkish girl said proudly. " But Emine—yes, I remember now— Emine said she told you to go away from Angora and leave Kemal alone. Will you do it? Will you give him back to me, and go?"

"Not because you say so," said Evelyn. "Fikriye Hanim, I beg you to sit down and rest. Your hands are badly scratched. Let me get some water and a clean towel and make you comfortable, and then you'll feel much better."

She tried to speak as calmly as possible, but the feeling of alarm at being alone with a sick and possibly deranged woman was growing strong. Evelyn moved towards the bedroom door. She had the knob in her hand when she heard a little click behind her and turned round. Fikriye had taken a Luger from her handbag, slipped off the safety catch, and was aiming it, at no more than two yards' distance, at the girl she thought of as her rival.

"I mean to kill Kemal," said Fikriye hoarsely, "but I will kill you first!"

Evelyn stood motionless. Death and the life hereafter, which she had thought of as so far off, had come very close to her, as close as the movement of Fikriye's finger on the trigger. She said, still in the same calm voice, which now in her own ears sounded very far away, "Put that gun down, Fikriye, and try to behave like a sensible woman."

They had been speaking in French since they came into the house, and Evelyn was not sure that Fikriye had understood her. For the Turkish girl only repeated "I will kill you. I will kill you unless you give him up, and go. Will you promise?"

The heavy weapon wavered dangerously in her hand. But Evelyn saw a flash of colour at the open door, and took courage. She said contemptuously,

"Give him up at the gun's point? Never!"

Then Ayesha launched herself into the room, and with all the strength of her fat body pushed Fikriye against the trestle table and seized the hand that held the gun. The Luger went off, the bullet embedded itself harmlessly in the deal floor. And

331

Fikriye collapsed on the red goatskin, huddled in her black coat, unconscious.

"Oh, Ayesha, thank God you came!" sobbed Evelyn. She snatched up the gun, took out the remaining bullets, put them in the pocket of her dress, and knelt down beside the prostrate girl. "Is she dead?"

"She faints," said Ayesha. "I knew she meant no good when she came here and asked for you, Hanim Efendi. So I hid among the apricots, and when I heard what she said to you out there, I came to the door, and waited."

"You saved my life."

"Help me to lift her on to the divan," said Ayesha practically. "Ahmed has gone to Chankaya to fetch the bodyguard."

"You know who she is, then?"

"Of course. She used to drive past in her carriage and pair—proud and foolish—"

But Evelyn thought less of Fikriye's pride and folly, but more of her unhappiness and the great love of her life, as she put a cushion under the dark head, and watched intelligence coming back to the red-rimmed eyes. Nobody spoke as Fikriye came back to consciousness. Time seemed to have stopped in the little room now filling, through the still open door, with the sweet air of evening.

"Help comes!" Ayesha said at last. They heard the sound of men running, Ahmed far outdistanced by two of the Laz guards from Chankaya, and the Lazes themselves well behind Major Orman. He burst into the house, white-faced, and before Evelyn could speak Ayesha greeted him with a torrent of Turkish.

"Tried to kill Evelyn Hanim!" said Major Orman, stupefied. "You men"— to the Lazes— "take Fikriye Hanim to the car!"

"Oh, be gentle with her," begged Evelyn. "She's really very ill." She helped Fikriye to get up from the divan. The Turkish girl looked at none of them. In silence she allowed the guards to take her by the arms, and like a sleepwalker moved between them to the door.

"I'll be court-martialled for this," said Major Orman, "and I deserve it."

"No, no, you won't be court-martialled," said Evelyn. "But I want to know how it all happened. Ayesha, would you mind leaving us alone?"

332

"My orders were to put Fikriye Hanim on the train to Constantinople tomorrow," Orman began. "It's been the very devil of a job to get her to go. Emine Hanim kept telling her she should wait to see the Gazi, and so on—"

"Trust her!"

Major Orman, in his embarrassment, could hardly find words. "Finally, I produced the Gazi's written order," he said. "I didn't want to, for it was very stiff, but when those two women read it they were afraid to disobey. This afternoon her bags were packed and we started off in the car. Then Fikriye Hanim said she wanted to say goodbye to her dear aunt, and when we were on the way there she insisted on going up to Chankaya to see if her cats were being well looked after. When we got to the house she locked herself inside the Gazi's study, and Hayati Bey and I could hear her . . . crying and talking as if—as if—"

"I understand," said Evelyn. "Go on."

"We forced the door at last and she was gone. Out of the window, over that high sill!"

"That's how she scratched her hands," said Evelyn. "But she knew where the Gazi keeps his guns, all right."

"It was a gun she—"

Evelyn indicated the Luger lying on the old war map.

"Allah! She threatened you with that?"

"If it hadn't been for Ayesha . . . but Major Orman, she also threatened to kill Kemal Pasha."

"Come down to the car with me," said Major Orman. "I'm afraid to let her out of my sight."

"Take her handbag with you," said Evelyn. "Make sure there isn't any poison in it before you give it back."

"Allah!" said the man again. They hurried down the lane together. At the far end, walking very slowly, they could see the dark figures of Fikriye and the two Laz guards.

"What a damned fool I was," said Orman. "I went to Zübeyde Hanim's house instead of coming here."

"So the Gazi's mother knows Fikriye was missing?"

"She shouted with laughter, just the way *he* does, and said 'Good riddance!' "

"The fewer people who know about all this, the better," said Evelyn.

"The Gazi will have to know as soon as possible."

"Oh please, please wait until you've put her on the train at Ismid. There's no need to worry him about it right away."

"I'm taking her straight down to Ismid now."

"Tonight? But surely she's not fit for a drive across the mountains."

"I have my orders, Mrs. Barrett. I can't wait for a medical opinion. Threatened to kill the Gazi, did she? I won't close my eyes until I hear she's out of Turkey."

They had reached the end of the lane. A soldier-driver stood beside the car, and one of the Lazes had his hand on the rear door. Evelyn knew that the other must be inside with Fikriye.

"Are *you* all right, Mrs. Barrett?" said Major Orman. "You've had a nasty shock, you know. I don't think you ought to be alone tonight."

"I'll be all right with Ayesha. After all, she's a veteran of the Sakarya!"

She managed to make the soldier smile at that, as he saluted her and said goodbye. But Evelyn, when she ran back up the lane, found that Ayesha was of the same mind as Major Orman.

"I am making tea," she said importantly, for she was proud of having learned how to use the spirit lamp, "and I am going to come back by and by and sleep on one of the divans. The Hanim Efendi ought not to be alone tonight."

Evelyn smiled. She felt absolutely drained as the energy she had summoned to meet the crisis ebbed away. She drank the sweet tea gratefully.

"You were scared, poor little Hanim Efendi." Ayesha's rough hand was very gentle as she stroked the dishevelled fair head. "This was a bad woman."

"Oh, Ayesha!" said Evelyn from her heart, "I wish I knew what to do!"

"Wait for the Gazi. It is you whom he loves, Hanim Efendi; wait until he can hold you in his arms again."

"Did you know, then?" whispered Evelyn.

"Ayesha has always known," she boasted. "But this is one thing I shall never tell! I only pray— *insh'allah!* —may the Gazi come back soon!"

*　　　*　　　*

334

He came a few nights later, when the fresh smells of early autumn filled the little house, and Evelyn could hear the sound of his car over the rustle of the first yellow leaves across the stones. She heard it stop, she listened for the sound of footsteps in the lane, and when they came she ran across the yard and flung herself into Kemal's arms.

It was just light enough by the waxing moon for him to see, as he kissed her hungrily and said "It's been an eternity!" that Evelyn was wearing a black dress with something that sparkled on the shoulder, and he could feel as he caressed her that she was even more slender than before. But when he looked at her in the living-room she had flushed to such a beautiful colour beneath his kisses that Kemal told himself she was well and strong, and had survived the ordeal that was over now.

"You look lovely," he exulted. "I never saw you wearing black before."

"I wear this old dress to show off my diamonds," she told him. "Kemal, how can I ever thank you for such a wonderful gift?"

He saw that what sparkled was his brooch, and he touched it, pleased. "You like it?"

"I adore it. I wear it every night—it's been such company for me."

"I was sure that diamonds were the jewels for you. Cold and sparkling—and then you hold them in the right light, and they flame."

He took her in his arms again, and at the mere touch of that spare burning body the tide of desire broke out in her own. With parted lips Evelyn took her lover's kisses. "I'll have this at any rate, just once more," she told herself, and then, "if it's once more it'll be for ever," and she slipped from the circle of his arms.

"But, darling, I thought you were in Smyrna," she said. "Where have you come from?"

He named a village about twenty miles away, on the railway line to Eskishehir. "I left the Staff bivouacked there, and looking as if they thought we were starting out for Koja Tepe all over again. After supper I couldn't wait. I changed out of uniform, got Ali to bring up a car, and came right off to see you."

"But why the bivouac? Why not Chankaya?"

"Because I've got to make some sort of official entrance tomorrow morning. I'm going to address the Assembly at ten o'clock."

He was looking at her with a slight smile, and Evelyn caught his meaning instantly.

"Perhaps you've got some good news to tell the Assembly?"

"What would you like me to tell them, Evelyn?"

"That you've agreed to come to terms with the British," she said. "That you won't let the Assembly push you into a major war."

"I should very much like," said Kemal softly, "to see the Assembly try. But the news is good—in fact it's much better than good. Yes, I've sent word to Sir Charles Harington that we agree to a meeting to discuss peace at Mudanya within the next few days. Because, my two eyes, the British will promise—after a lot of talk to save their faces—to give me what I asked for when the Greeks left Smyrna. Constantinople—Eastern Thrace to the Maritza—and very soon, the end of the Occupation."

"Oh, Kemal! Kemal! You've really done it!"

"Yes, it's done." He dropped to the divan. "I don't mind telling you, I'd rather fight Dumlu Pinar all over again than live through the last few days. It was the waiting—the knowing that some damned young hothead on either side could forget his orders in some silly little flare-up on what they've the nerve to call the Zone frontier, and loose off his rifle . . . I kept telling myself it would only take one shot to start a major war."

"But still you wouldn't give in to the British Cabinet."

"No, but let's give some of the credit to General Harington," he said. "Our envoy in London, Dr. Reshad, knew quite well that Lloyd George and his Ministers sent Harington an ultimatum, telling me to get my troops out of the Zone by the thirtieth, or else . . . and Harington had the wits to sit on it until I was ready to talk . . . Some day I'd like to play poker with Sir Charles Harington."

"I think you've both played a great game already," said Evelyn. She sat down beside Kemal, noticing how thin his wrists were under the white shirt cuffs, and how sharply his shoulder blades were outlined beneath the dark blue suit. "You're tired, my darling," she said tenderly. "You'll have to rest now, for a while."

336

"With the Mudanya meeting, and a peace conference in Europe coming up?"

"Do you intend to go to Mudanya yourself?"

"Not me! There'll be nobody there above the rank of a general officer," Kemal said arrogantly. "Ismet Pasha will be our representative."

"But you'll have to write the script for Ismet, is that it?"

"Something like that." He took Evelyn's hands, as he loved to do, and kissed the finger tips. "I'm not tired now that I'm here with you. I used to think about this room every morning, and every night around ten o'clock. Evelyn's hour, I called it to myself. I thought about Ahmed's well, and the yard with the fruit trees. My oasis! . . Do you remember our last room, at Ushak?"

"With the awful smell of burning," Evelyn said, and instantly regretted it.

"But we've put fire and fighting behind us now," he said. "I've done all that I set out to do, and now Turkey will be free, and whole again, and I can fit my country to take her own place in the western world . . . I want our enemies to be reconciled with us, and we with them. I said years ago that the Young Turks should never have entered the Great War against Britain, and *my* Turkey will be Britain's friend. I'll make peace with Greece and keep it: I'll even shake hands with Venizelos if I have to, and mark my words, now that the generals have chased out Constantine, Monsieur Venizelos will soon be back in Athens."

"And then what?"

"Then I shall try to solve the problem that's bedevilled Greece and Turkey for a hundred years—the minority nationals in each country. There's only one way to put an end to the refugee problem, and it's a drastic way, but I'm going to take it. I shall send every Greek left in Thrace and Anatolia back to the motherland, and bring every Turkish citizen in Greece back home in the next few months."

"But won't that mean a lot of hardship, with the winter coming on?"

"If you had seen the sights I saw on the waterfront at Smyrna, you'd think repatriation was the only answer to a problem that's handicapped Turkey for over a century. One clean break now, and it's done."

337

"Won't people blame you again, for the inevitable suffering?"

"People blame me for everything, anyway," Kemal said coolly. "But I'll have the whole operation supervised by an Inter-Allied Commission, don't you worry!"

She was beyond worry, where he was concerned. She saw the excitement in the strange blue eyes, felt the wild energy which no fatigue could quench, and believed him equal to his formidable task. She brought him raki, and waited on him ceremoniously; this was the future President who sat with her, not the soldier-lover of the Smyrna road. He said abruptly:

"Have you heard from Barrett?"

"Not from him, no. But the editor sent him to visit the liberated cities, and probably he'll be coming on to Angora."

"Hamdi Bey was right, then," said Kemal. "He swore he'd seen Barrett in the crowd when I was addressing the people at Eskishehir."

"Eskishehir—that's not so very far away."

"I talked to him at Smyrna, Evelyn."

"Did you? What did you say?"

"I told him I'd asked you to marry me. And he said, if you told him personally that you wanted a divorce, he wouldn't stand in your way."

"I'll tell him that," said Evelyn.

"Good! Then the sooner he gets here the better. I think I'll check, and make sure he's coming in from Eskishehir." He hesitated. "Evelyn, did you know Leila Mavros was dead?"

"*Dead!*"

"Yes. I don't know what happened, but there's no doubt about it. I saw her name on a list the British Navy published, of people who actually died aboard the battleships, and I had it verified. She was buried at sea, early on the fourteenth, off a place called Doctor's Island in the Gulf of Smyrna."

"Poor Leila!" whispered Evelyn. "Poor Jeff!"

"This won't make any difference to your divorce, my child. I have a sworn statement from the manager of Barrett's hotel about their association, and *he* survived; he can be made to give evidence on your behalf, if necessary."

"Did you tell Jeff about this statement?"

"Of course."

338

She almost felt a pang of sympathy for Jeff, so hopelessly out-gunned and out-manœuvred by the Commander-in-Chief. Who said,

"So you see, it's all plain sailing. You'll have a talk with him, you'll go to Paris—where we'll take care that your petition goes to the top of the cause list—and as soon as you come back we shall be married. What's the matter?" For Evelyn had risen to her feet and was looking down at him.

"Kemal—oh, my dear love! There's something I—it kills me to tell you—but I can't marry you."

With one uncontrollable movement of the muscles of his face, as if he had received a blow, "Why not?" said the Commander-in-Chief.

"I can't abjure my religion to become your wife. I love you better than my life—and my life's worth nothing, yours is the life that counts—but I will not recant. I won't give up the Christian faith I was baptised in, even to marry you."

"And this is your final decision? You've thought it over carefully?"

Evelyn moved her hand as if to brush away a superfluous question. "I'm not a very good Christian, Kemal," she said. "I haven't cared as much about it as I ought. But I do know that men, and women too, have died for their Christian faith—the martyrs and the Crusaders and the prisoners of conscience—and so I—I just can't take the easy way out."

Then, since he was silent, and only sat looking at her with his fair brows drawn together in a frown, Evelyn went on: "Do you remember what you said when Tricoupis gave up his sword to you at Ushak? You said even the best generals couldn't win all the battles. Well, you're the best general in the world today—but this is one battle even you can't win."

At that Kemal smiled. "It's good generalship to anticipate your —adversary," he said. "I've expected, ever since Ushak, that you would tell me this."

"You *have*?"

"I admire your spirit, Evelyn, I always shall. And I respect courage wherever I meet with it. You are right to stand by your religion as I stood by my country, and you deserve to win. Let's forget all those grim words like recanting and abjuring, and let's forget, which I would be happy to do, about Islam. Marry me as a

Christian, worship when and where you please, and the hojas can go to the devil."

"Kemal, you know what you said to me about the Caliphate, and the need to keep those who do believe in Islam on your side."

"They'll all accept anything that I do now," said Kemal. Evelyn saw that in this moment of his double victory, in his triumph and his arrogance, he honestly believed it. She stood before him doubtfully, hardly believing that her long heart-searchings could be solved by a few generous words from him.

Kemal got up. "I must go," he said, "the Staff will be sending out search parties. And you're the one who ought to rest, my Evelyn. I can see you've worried too much, and worked too hard while we were parted, but remember, the parting is over now. Tomorrow we'll celebrate the real start of our lives together."

"Here?"

"No, at Chankaya of course, we'll have dinner alone, and make plans for the future."

"Chankaya will be as busy as the railway station, all day long."

"I'll take care that it isn't," Kemal promised her. "I shan't go home myself until all the rejoicings in the town are over. If you'll allow me to send a car for you at seven o'clock, I think that would be about right. They can't celebrate for ever, even in Angora, but there's to be a review of troops in the afternoon and I believe I'm to be given the freedom of the city." Kemal laughed. "You talk about martyrs; what about the martyrdom ahead of me, having to listen to so many addresses of congratulation?"

"That's part of the price you'll pay, now that you're certain of your place in history."

"Wasn't I, before?"

"Only of your place in legend."

Kemal smiled. "This is what I've been missing," he said. "The coolness of you, Evelyn, like spring water in the steppe. Do you remember how often you said 'No!' to me, in this very room? I sometimes thought you'd never heard of the word 'Yes'." He kissed her and held her close. "But you were right, of course. Better Afyon, better Ushak, than this place here. But tomorrow, Evelyn, at Chankaya, which will be your home . . . you'll be my love again . . . Because I love you, my two eyes, I was so lonely when you went away. I need you with me to tell me when to say 'we' instead of 'I', and not to bark at the

340

reporters, and when to wear my London suits . . . Now promise me that you'll be there tomorrow morning. There won't be any sacrifice of sheep this time, and I've sent word that I want to speak to the people, very briefly, before I read the Message to the Deputies. Because this is the people's triumph quite as much as mine. I want them all close to me tomorrow, the men and women who made independence live—and you."

"I'll be there," she said. "I promise you, Kemal." Then, before he realised what she meant to do, Evelyn Barrett touched her fingers to her heart and brow in the Turkish obeisance, and kissed his hand.

"May the One God guide you, my Pasha," she said. "Go smiling."

22

NOW THIS WAS THE last temptation, and the worst; and if Evelyn had called apostasy "the easy way", how much easier it would be by accepting Kemal's solution to keep both the man who loved her and her new and painfully achieved religious faith! When he left her, Evelyn was too completely under the spell of his personality to think coherently. The joy of being with him again, and the knowledge that by refusing the challenge to make war Kemal had proved himself a statesman of international stature came before any other consideration. For an hour before she slept Evelyn indulged herself in the fantasy that what Kemal had promised could in fact come true.

But at four in the morning she awoke, hearing rain on the leaves, and at once all the devils of doubt were back again. Kemal's plan for their future was too smooth, too simple for their situation. For herself, a brief interview with Jeff and a discreet visit to France for the fashionable "Paris divorce" need not attract attention. The eyes of the world would be on Kemal for weeks to come, and Evelyn was sure that in the shortest possible time he would abolish the Empire, drive the Sultan into exile, and pluck out of obscurity some other elderly bewildered prince of the House of Osman to play—temporarily—the role of the Caliph of Islam. But if, while these revolutionary doings were still news, the President of the infant Republic announced his marriage to a divorced American woman of the Christian faith, as far as the press of the western world was concerned the roof would fall in.

It would be the perfect "human story" for the Chicago *Clarion*.

About five o'clock Evelyn got up and made some coffee on the spirit stove. The rain had stopped, but it was cold in the little house; her hands and feet were icy.

If she gave in to this great temptation, Kemal himself would ultimately be the one to suffer. To be a nine days' wonder in the world press would disturb him not at all, but what about the propaganda to be made out of it by his enemies? Evelyn had no illusions about the welcome she would receive even from the friends he needed to help him in his tremendous task. Rauf, Refet, Fevzi had been courteous to her but aloof; Ismet the kindest, but could even Ismet remain kind? And Kemal's declared opponents, furiously jealous of his rise to glory, wouldn't they start a whispering campaign about the Gazi's choice, the shameless woman who had once followed the Turkish Army? From there on, doubt and disappointment in their hero would grow in the hearts of just those humble people he wished to see surrounding him today.

You have the big mind, he had told her once. She knew that instead, for weeks past, her mind had been preoccupied by the petty crisis of her own conscience. Even at the White Fortress three days before, she had thought of the future city of Angora and her position in it rather than of the men who must toil to raise that city from the waste land. Deliberately she let her thoughts range over the Turkish people as she had known them: the beggars of Stamboul, the dissipated merchants of Pera, the hardy mountaineers of Angora, the gipsies with their dancing bears, the Yürük nomads with their black tents, the Whirling Dervishes of Konya, the veiled women in the han at Akshehir who had greeted her with the sign against the evil eye. There were Turks, too, of whom she as yet knew nothing. The survivors of Smyrna, the fishermen of the Black Sea, where accidents overtook the politically unwary, the tribes of the far east beyond Erzurum and Kars, the villagers of the warm Mediterranean shore. All these diverse peoples had to be welded into a reborn nation, one and indivisible, by a man uniquely qualified for the task. A task in which she could only be his handicap.

The American woman, the Christian wife, would be blamed for every least error of Kemal's judgment, every untimely modernisation, every unwelcome introduction of western ways. Evelyn had no doubt that Kemal could break the political power of the religious leaders and substitute a civil judicial system for the Sheriat, the Holy Law of Islam. But even he could not challenge the spiritual power of the Prophet, rooted in the hearts of men who, secure in the House of Islam, would forever despise her as a tenant of the House of War.

343

Ten o'clock at night would always be "Evelyn's hour". Then Kemal would talk to her at Chankaya as fully, as intimately as they had talked in their oasis, and make love to her in a bedroom innocent of the smell of burning. But all day long this complex man, who had the talents and intellectual curiousity of five men in one, would be surrounded by Turkish males who, if they chose, could insidiously denigrate the woman in his life. At last he might be unfaithful, or come to blame her for the difficulties inherent in his great position. And if he ever loved me less than he does now, thought Evelyn, I would only want to die.

One clean break now and it's done. Evelyn remembered what Kemal had said of his plan to uproot and transfer two minority populations in Turkey and Greece. One clean break, and to hell with the suffering! I'm a calculated loss, she thought. I must write myself off, and go. She pulled a pad towards her, and began her letter.

"My beloved Kemal," Evelyn wrote in French, "I am going away now, because I love you far too much to stay." That was the beginning, which said it all; but Evelyn wrote on steadily, trying to explain, trying to find words which would alleviate his pain and anger. It all sounded futile, an unnecessary martyrdom, but with tears she accomplished it, and before she signed her name wrote in a flash of inspiration:

"Once you said to me, 'Well done, soldier!' I hope that some day, long before your great work is over, you'll feel able to say that of me again.'

She heard Ayesha moving in the yard, and called the woman in. In Turkish no longer halting she quietly told her friend that she was going away, and made some practical arrangements; then she took up the sealed letter to Kemal and showed it to Ayesha.

"I want you to take this letter to Chankaya, later on today," she said. "It is a message for the Gazi. Can you do that, Ayesha?"

"Of course, Hanim Efendi."

She didn't want to hurt Ayesha's feelings by asking if they had a clock. She said, "Take it to Chankaya when the moon rises above the apricots. Give it to nobody except the Gazi himself. If you tell them it is a letter from Evelyn Hanim, they will allow you to see him, for he has come back."

344

Ayesha's look of delight and pride faded as she put the letter in her breast. "Is it to tell the Gazi you are going away?"

"Yes, Ayesha."

"And never coming back?"

"Never."

"Oh, Hanim Efendi, but you love him so much!"

"That's why I must go, Ayesha."

*   *   *

Evelyn had bathed, had dressed in her black dress, had drunk more coffee before she heard Ayesha in the yard again. She had even finished packing one suitcase and her small attaché case, to be picked up later: her books, with the war map, had been packed in a wooden box. She was trying to write another letter, no less difficult than the first, when Ayesha's knock fell on the half-open door.

"Hanim Efendi!" said Ayesha, and her sunburned face was oddly strained, "I think—the Bey Efendi is coming up the lane."

Jeff! Evelyn reached the door in time to see him as he approached the gate, and put his hand uncertainly on the top bar.

"Hallo there, Eve!" he said.

"Hallo, Jeff. Where have you come from?"

"Polatli, the last hitch."

"By train?"

"No, I drove. I bought a car in Brusa, one of the army cars the Greeks left behind them."

"Well, come in. Would you like coffee and something to eat?"

"No thanks. I stopped off at the station and had coffee there. I didn't want to bother you."

"I was sorry to hear you'd been in hospital. What happened to you?"

"It was the night of the fire," he said. "I got a knock on the head and had concussion, the doc said. I still get real bad head-aches," he said in a bid for sympathy.

"But you've been working hard, according to Donnelly."

"Yeah, Donnelly's pleased. Say, Eve, that was a good piece you had in the paper about Dumlu Pinar. Halliday sent me a clip of it from one of the London dailies."

345

"Oh yes?"

"You had a world beat on that one, I guess."

"So Donnelly said."

He didn't know what to make of her, so quenched, so quiet, looking so like a sick cat. He said uncertainly:

"Looks like I've come back to Angora at the right time. I ran into Yusuv, the Foreign Minister, at Polatli last night, he was coming in by train, and he gave me a tip-off about big doings here today."

"Kemal Pasha's Message to the Assembly, yes, I know about that."

"I thought the news wasn't to be released until today!"

"Kemal Pasha was here himself last night."

Furious colour flamed in Jeff's tanned face. "You don't care what you say to me now, do you, Eve?"

"I don't, as a matter of fact. But Kemal came here to *talk* to me last night, and tell me that he had won his game of poker with the British. That was all."

"All!" said Jeff. "I had quite a talk with him myself, at Smyrna."

Evelyn had steeled herself to the cut and thrust of retort since Jeff came in. Now her strength seemed to fail her, and she leaned on the edge of the deal table, saying nothing.

"He told me he wanted to marry you. Is that right?"

"Yes. But—I'm not going to marry him, Jeff."

"My God! Was *that* what you talked about last night?"

"No. But I've written to him," she said almost inaudibly, "telling him why I know it wouldn't work."

"He was pretty damned sure of himself, those days in Smyrna," said Jeff with satisfaction. "I knew it wouldn't work out, either. . . . Maybe you were a little bit fonder of me than you knew, eh, baby?"

"Oh, Jeff, when will you ever be honest with yourself?" Evelyn said fiercely. "Can't you realise that you and I are finished? We were all washed up this day nine weeks ago, when you walked out of this house and left me on my own. You told Kemal at Smyrna you would let me divorce you if I wanted to, and for your own sake, for both our sakes, it's best we should be free. It doesn't make any difference that I can't marry Kemal, or that Leila's dead."

346

"You knew about that, did you?"

"*He* told me."

Jeff began to tell her the story then, with a wealth of emotional detail, self-chastisement and self-pity, and Evelyn, as she listened, felt as she had felt at Ushak, calloused and hardened by her experience of war. Leila was just one more innocent victim, among the thousands she had seen herself on the road to Smyrna, the thousands who would soon be taking the winter roads through Thrace. She tried to say sincerely:

"I'm very sorry, Jeff. She was very pretty, as I remember, and so young."

"Just eighteen."

"Did you want to marry her?"

Jeff remembered that he had tried to end the affair with Leila, that sending her to Greece was one way of making the break, but to say so, he felt, would be to betray his little maid of Athens, killed in that senseless brawl. He said,

"That's neither here nor there, because she's dead. What about—the Gazi? Think he's going to let you give him the gate and walk away?"

"He has his work, Jeff, and I'll have mine."

"What work?"

"Donnelly's asked me to go to Rome for three months, for the *Clarion*. And after that I'll establish residence at the ranch in Nevada—it's the easiest place in the world for our divorce."

It was only now that Jeff Barrett really took in the suitcase and the half-dismantled room.

"*Rome?*" he said, "for the *Clarion*?"

"I guess you're as surprised as I was," said Evelyn. "I haven't thought of anything but Turkey all summer long. But Donnelly thinks the Fascists mean bad trouble in Italy, and Mussolini's sure to try to take over Rome. So he wants a correspondent on the spot for the next few weeks."

"And he offers the spot to Evelyn Anderson? Well, congratulations, Eve!"

"Thanks."

"And you were really lighting out today?"

"Yes. I was trying to write to you, when you came in."

"But how are you going to go?"

"It's Saturday," she said. "The Osmanli Bank car goes down

347

to Ismid every Saturday; they said they'd make a place for me, any time."

"For God's sake, Eve," he said, "don't go off like that! Let me do something for you, *please!* I've got this car now, I'll drive you down to Ismid—on to Constant. if you like . . ." .

"You'll have to stay and cable today's story to Donnelly."

"Donnelly be damned." He knew she was bluffing; she didn't want "that gangster" to think she had left town with her husband. He said,

"Have you told Kemal about this Rome stunt?"

"I told him in my letter what I was going to do."

"Making sure that he'll come running after you, eh?"

"He's not the man to run after any woman, especially not now. He's brought his Revolution to victory, starting out from nothing; now he's got to found and guide the new Republic. He'll be . . . sorry, and . . . lonely for a while, but he'll have the thing he cares for most on earth to keep him from missing me. He'll have Turkey."

*   *   *

Jeff argued with his wife the whole way in to Angora. About the folly of having given Ayesha a whole month's rent by way of notice, of being about to take off "like a crazy woman" in the Osmanli Bank car, of expecting to find a compartment on the Orient Express without booking, until she silenced him with "Jeff! Can't you understand that if I don't go today, I'll never go at all?" Then he was struck with the white misery in her face beneath the black headscarf, and was moved to say,

"Are you sure you can go through with this, Eve? You look like hell!"

"I don't think I can go into the Assembly," she said faintly. "But I promised Kemal to be there. I shared the bad hour with him before Dumlu Pinar; I've a right to see him in his hour of triumph."

The whole of Angora, it seemed, was packed into the streets and open spaces round the little parliament building. The morning rain had laid the dust, and the sun was bright. It shone on the Crescent and the Star, as Jeff and Evelyn made their way through the crowd in the little public garden opposite the Assembly and saw the flag triumphant on the roof. They heard the cheering long before they saw the Conqueror; he came in an open car, slowly, with a cavalry detachment riding ahead and the Lazes in their black uniforms on either side. There was no need for a military band, or the clash of cymbals with which Angora had first greeted him only three years before; the roar of the crowd, the frenzy of their joy and pride in him rose up about Kemal like the music of the spheres.

"Looks like he finally made it," said Jeff reluctantly.

"What's that he's wearing?" said Evelyn. Her voice was hoarse.

"Must be the new war medal, I heard they meant to have one struck."

"But I can't *see* him!" she said desperately. The bodyguard stood back, the people swirled around Kemal at the gate of the Assembly.

"What are they hollering about?" said Jeff.

"They want him to go on to the Haji Bayram mosque, and he won't go."

Kemal appeared on one of the little balconies of the Assembly building. And now Evelyn could see him clearly: slim and straight, wearing on his breast the only decoration he would ever wear until his life ended: the medal of the War of Independence.

The deep voice rose above the silent crowd. It was so far across the street to the public garden that Evelyn had difficulty in following what Kemal said for a moment, and then she caught the familiar word "Mehmedjik" and said to Jeff:

"He is praising the Turkish soldier."

"Can you really understand what he's saying?"

"Oh, yes," she said, and there were tears in her eyes, "I've always understood him very well."

Slowly, and with emphasis upon one word, the future President of the Turkish Republic finished his brief speech.

"The world thinks this is the end," he said, "that . . . *we* . . . have reached our goal. But it is only after this that . . . *we* . . . shall begin to do something worth while. It is only now that . . . *our* . . . real work is beginning."

The cheers rang out again as he gravely saluted, turned on his heel, and went in to read his Message to the Assembly.

"Let's get out of here," said Jeff. "It'll take for ever to get up

349

to the Bank, if you really mean to go today. But Eve . . . listen, honey . . ."

He meant to say, please won't you give me one more chance. But he saw that she was not listening to him. She had glanced once at the Crescent and the Star, and turned away. He knew that he was nothing more to her now than a face in the crowd. For Jeff and Evelyn Barrett it was the end of an old story; for Kemal and his beloved country it was the beginning of a new day.

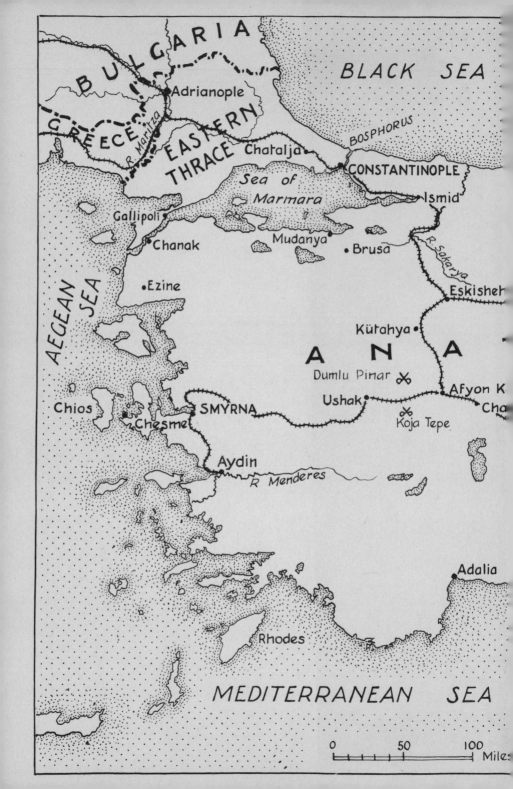